TIDES

OF

MUTINY

JIMMY PATTERSON BOOKS FOR YOUNG ADULT READERS

James Patterson Presents

The Maximum Ride Series by James Patterson

The Confessions Series by James Patterson

Confessions of a Murder Suspect
Confessions: The Private School Murders
Confessions: The Paris Mysteries
Confessions: The Murder of an Angel

The Witch & Wizard Series by James Patterson

Witch & Wizard
The Gift
The Fire
The Kiss
The Lost

Nonfiction by James Patterson

Med Head

Stand-Alone Novels by James Patterson

The Injustice
Crazy House
The Fall of Crazy House
Cradle and All
First Love
Homeroom Diaries

For exclusives, trailers, and other information, visit
jimmypatterson.org.

TIDES

OF

MUTINY

Rebecca Rode

JIMMY Patterson Books
Little, Brown and Company
NEW YORK BOSTON LONDON

JIMMY Patterson Books / Little, Brown and Company
Hachette Book Group
1290 Avenue of the Americas, New York, NY 10104
JimmyPatterson.org

First Edition: September 2021

JIMMY Patterson Books is an imprint of Little, Brown and Company, a division of Hachette Book Group, Inc. The Little, Brown name and logo are trademarks of Hachette Book Group, Inc. The JIMMY Patterson Books® name and logo are trademarks of JBP Business, LLC.

The publisher is not responsible for websites (or their content) that are not owned by the publisher.

Library of Congress Cataloging-in-Publication Data
Names: Rode, Rebecca, 1981– author.
Title: Tides of mutiny / Rebecca Rode.
Description: First edition. | New York : Jimmy Patterson Books/Little, Brown and Company, 2021. | Audience: Ages 12 & up. | Summary: "A sixteen-year-old girl hiding as a cabin boy must fight for her place in a world that executes female sailors, all while falling for a mysterious stowaway who could destroy everything"— Provided by publisher.
Identifiers: LCCN 2020050441 | ISBN 9780316705752 (hardcover) | ISBN 9780316705714 (ebook)
Subjects: CYAC: Seafaring life—Fiction. | Pirates—Fiction. | Secrets—Fiction. | Disguise—Fiction. | Princes—Fiction.
Classification: LCC PZ7.1.R639535 Ti 2021 | DDC [Fic]—dc23
LC record available at https://lccn.loc.gov/2020050441

ISBNs: 978-0-316-70575-2 (hardcover), 978-0-316-70571-4 (ebook)

Printed in the United States of America

LSC-C

Printing 1, 2021

For Lisa, who taught me that
there's more than one way
to change the world

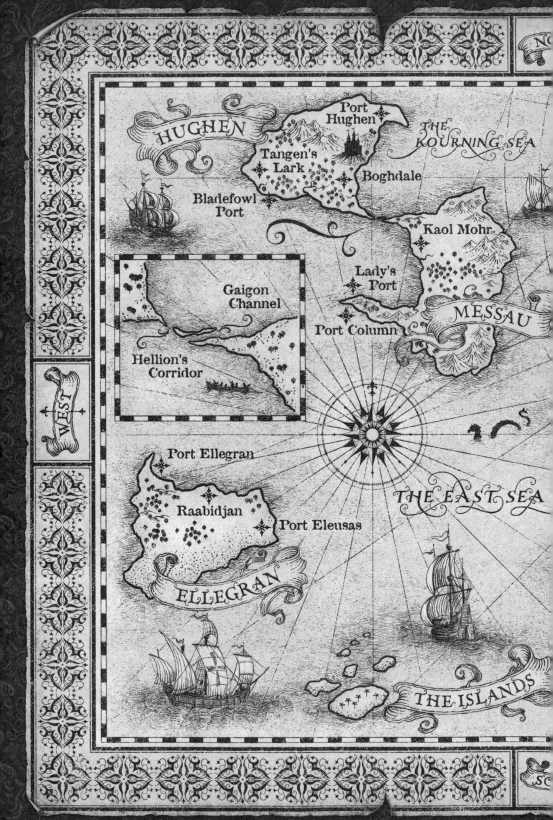

It was the boots that tipped me off.

There were other signs too—the cap pulled low over the young man's face, the hunched shoulders. Rather than watching the busy dockworkers around him, he stared resolutely at the mud near his feet. Even the too-bright and well-fitted shirt looked out of place despite the smear of dirt staining the front.

His shiny pointed boots, however, were completely impractical for a rainy day. Impractical for anything, really. Particularly taking a stroll about the harbor this early in the morning. This was no common sailor.

"Are you listening?" Father asked.

I snapped my gaze back to him and leaned against the ship's rail. "I'm always listening."

A heavy sigh meant that he thought otherwise. "I know you like to go ashore with the men, but it's too dangerous this time. Perhaps in a month or two when the festival is over."

And when King Eurion has better things to do than kill innocent girls, I wanted to add. But it would have been a waste of breath. Father never went back on his word once he'd declared it. Besides, I couldn't deny that the very air around Hughen's harbor had changed since I was here last. We'd had to pay extra for our usual berth. Raucous laughter had been replaced by quiet gossip exchanged among extra dockworkers. Most worrisome, though, was the increase in security. A patrol party passed by every ten minutes, its soldiers scanning faces in the crowd. It took everything I had not to adjust my disguise each time their gazes slid over me.

It didn't mean I had to like it.

"I know there are...things...you need in town," Father continued as a gust of wind swept his graying hair into his eyes. He brushed it aside with an impatient jerk. "Give your list to Dennis. He'll get them for you before the day's done."

I snorted at the thought of Father's crabby first officer selecting fabric for my chest bindings. "I've made the journey into town fifty times. Nobody ever pays me any heed."

"Then we've been lucky fifty times. I won't risk our luck running out on the fifty-first, not with the city on alert like this."

I was losing this battle terribly, but I refused to yield. "They're looking for women sailors, not a captain's boy."

He lifted one thick eyebrow. "They're searching for pretty faces, feminine features, and high voices—all three of which you possess. You'd see that if you used my looking glass on occasion."

I scowled. I'd perfected the art of hiding in plain sight—strutting about, training my voice to sound lower. Eating like the others. Nobody climbed the ratlines faster than I did, and I practiced with my axes nearly every day. I'd fooled hundreds of men over the years as crew members came and went. Yet none of that mattered to Father, the most paranoid man in the Four Lands.

He stood there watching me, his white shirt fastened right up to the collar as always, bright against skin weathered by long days at sea. A tiny shaving cut lay under his crooked chin. I'd lived on the *Majesty* for eleven years now, and I still didn't know what he looked like with a beard. Whether his day included meeting a client or sitting alone by the constant sea, every last hair would see the blade of his razor.

To my surprise, he placed his hands firmly on my shoulders. In an instant, the stern merchant ship captain was gone, replaced by my father. "Lane. I mean it. They've erected a new sign on the way into town, a big Jilly Black. Whether you agree about the danger or not, you'll remain inside my cabin or belowdecks until I return. Do you understand?"

My frown deepened. I'd been Lane Garrow since I was five year-days old, yet he still felt it necessary to lecture me. Did he truly think I could forget that the pompous king Eurion's palace loomed on the cliffs above us right now?

"I do understand the danger. Really."

It wasn't a promise exactly, but he finally nodded. "Good. I'll bring you back a crosuit. I'm dying for potatoes myself, ones that don't stink like Julian's armpits."

I fought a smile and lost. "Agreed."

Father gave my shoulders a squeeze. "I'll see you in a few hours. We'll dine like lords tonight." He stalked down the gangplank and past the odd stranger without giving him a glance. The boy still stood rooted in place, a stone in the river of workers, gazing at the *Majesty* behind me. He took in her grand masts and furrowed sails with the awe of a child. If he'd noticed the exchange with my father, he didn't seem to think much of it. Or he was better at pretending than I gave him credit for.

I examined him for a long moment. He was sixteen, possibly seventeen year-days. Medium-oak hair, skin untouched by the sun, slender build. I'd seen most of it before—boys leaving home for the first time, seeking work and adventure and escaping the demands of their parents. But something about this one felt...different.

Definitely the boots.

I waited till Father disappeared into the crowd before striding down the gangplank myself, set on driving the boy off. The *Majesty* took on sailors of all skill levels, but social levels were another matter entirely. He could take his pretty boots and pretty eyes to the *Mum's Commoner* across the harbor.

"Lane!" Barrie shouted, barreling up the gangplank to stop me halfway down. "Be Cap'n Garrow here? You won't be believing what I just heard."

At fourteen, my station partner, Barrie, was the youngest sailor on the ship. He just didn't know it, since I was supposed to be younger. His hammock was homespun rather than shop made, and he quietly sent most of his earnings home to his fourteen-member family in a distant farming town. He could wander Hughen alone without a second glance. Meanwhile, I had to hide like a scared child. Again.

"I can believe near anything." I kept one eye on the stranger.

"Not this," Barrie said, breathless with excitement. "That filthy pirate's been freed. Cap'n Belza."

Now I was the one gawking. Dread set me stiff as a board. "What?"

"It be true. Heard it in town. Two officials be talking about it, then I heard it again from a soldier. Messau's new ruler set him free for good. Raymus, I think?"

I tried to speak, but the words felt caught in my suddenly dry throat. "Rasmus," I managed. "He became khral of Messau when his father died last month. But Belza—are you certain?"

"Aye. Positive."

That *was* news. The last remaining member of Elena the Conqueror's pirate crew had rotted in a dungeon in Messau for the past decade. It had been incredibly difficult for the old khral to capture the pirate in the first place. Why would his son free the man?

"There be even more." Barrie leaned forward. His wide-set green eyes were a startling contrast to his black hair. It was a combination I wished the skies had bestowed upon me, instead of my rat-brown everything. "They say Cap'n Belza be asking around, looking for someone. Care to guess who?"

"King Eurion?" The Hughen king had been the one to deliver Belza into the original khral's hands. Both had been desperate to lock him away, declaring that he'd never see freedom again.

Barrie's eyes sparkled. "Our own Cap'n Garrow."

My stomach thudded.

"Captain Garrow," I repeated dully.

"Aye. Cap'n Belza—"

"Nay." I stopped him with a sharp look. "Just Belza. He's only captain if he has a ship, and he has no crew either." Nor would any self-respecting sailor join him. Not when the entire world knew of Belza and his brutal crimes.

"But that be it—the khral gave him a ship and crew. Now he's set out to find your father, Lane. He be looking for him now."

The fact that Belza was now a privateer on the new khral's errand was bad enough, but it barely registered. The second-most-deadly pirate in history sought *my father*. The paranoid man who charmed merchants and refused to carry a weapon and punished crew members who fought with one another. It couldn't possibly be the same Captain Garrow.

"Where did you hear this, Barrie?"

"Everywhere. The entire city be talking about it. Nobody knows why Belza be so insistent. Maybe Garrow and Belza were enemies. Now that Belza be free, he seeks revenge. Some even say—" He caught my expression and swallowed. "Never mind."

"What? You can tell me."

"You won't like it, I swear."

I paused, the dread sinking deeper into my gut. "Quit playing around and say it."

He lowered his voice, his eyes bright. "Some wonder if Cap'n Garrow be one of them. A pirate."

I snorted as the dread faded in a single, abrupt rush. *A pirate?* Certainly not." The very idea was ridiculous. Father's superstitious fears prevented him from even discussing pirates. If he knew that the history book hidden in my storage chest discussed the pirate captain Elena, he'd have burned it long ago.

Barrie looked grumpy at my dismissal. "But how do you know?"

"Because I know, all right?" I snapped. "Father is no more a pirate than you are, and I don't appreciate your implying otherwise."

He flinched.

Some of my anger drained away. Barrie received plenty of sharpness from the crew. He didn't need it from me too. "I only meant to say there are a dozen explanations for this. Belza could have the wrong name, or perhaps the wrong Garrow altogether. My father probably has family members all over Hughen." Except he never talked about them, let alone introduced us. He resented being asked about his past. I'd learned that lesson one rainy day at age eight.

It had been a simple question—"Why did you start sailing?"— and one many of the crew were happy to answer. Most sought adventure or dreamed of fighting pirates and traveling to distant lands. Others sought their fortune or escape from climbing debts. With a sly grin, one man had even admitted that he was simply avoiding his angry wife.

But Father's answer was a long, cold stare. It was the first and only time I'd ever wondered whether he would strike me.

"If I ever want to tell you of my past, Lane," he'd finally said, "I will bring up the subject. Otherwise, you will allow me my privacy. Understood?"

My childhood mind had invented all sorts of explanations for his reluctance. A father who'd beaten and driven him to the sea. Parents who'd died in a plague and left him to fend for himself. Perhaps he'd been raised by a set of cruel, wealthy grandparents who'd forced him to spend his days with tutors until he'd had enough and run away. None of my imaginings had ever involved piracy. Why would they? Father was the most honest person I knew—far more honest than I ever wanted to be.

Except there was one secret he would never reveal. Mine. And if he'd lied about that, what else had he lied about?

That dread was back, heavier than ever.

"He was never a pirate," I said again, less sure this time. "The rumor will die by this time tomorrow. My father is the most dependable merchant ship captain in Hughen, and everyone knows it. Especially the crew." Father respected his men and they trusted him. Surely his reputation would lift him above this silly rumor.

Barrie folded his arms. "Ignore it, then. We'll be completely unprepared when Belza be finding us. Which he will. Or you can be getting the truth of it from the cap'n so we can ready ourselves."

I flinched. He had a point. We couldn't escape Belza forever. But I couldn't exactly ask my father whether he'd served with one of the most deadly pirates in history. He'd either laugh or refuse to speak to me again. That meant I had to find my own answers—and I knew exactly where they lay.

Every bosun kept detailed records of his crew. If Father had been a pirate, his name would appear on the crew list preserved in town, carved into stone below the queen's statue. It was less than half an hour's walk from here. So long as I returned before Father, he would never know.

"Do me a favor," I told Barrie. "If anyone asks, I'm staying below-decks today. That's where you found me and that's where I stayed. Aye?"

"Aye."

He'd barely agreed before I plunged past him down the gang-plank and into the crowd. My feet moved of their own accord, but my mind ran miles ahead even as my heart lagged behind. This was more than disobedience. It felt like betrayal. Father was the only family I had. Frustrating as his fears were, they were rooted in love. Today I would repay him with the worst kind of doubt imaginable. But I had to prove his innocence.

More than that, I had to know the truth for myself.

It wasn't until I'd nearly left the docks that I remembered the strange boy. Did he have something to do with all this? Whirling about, I scanned the crowd once more. He was gone.

There are more important questions to be answered, I reminded myself. The seconds already slipped away too quickly.

The heaviness in my gut felt as thick as the crowd with each step toward town. But this would be nothing compared to the festival crowds in a few weeks. Those could suffocate a person, true as the morning sun. I could imagine it all. Blue ribbons strung through the streets, shop fronts packed with wine and expensive cheeses. There would be no geese or hens hanging from the butcher's cart here—Hughens were too superstitious—but the fish stands would be packed with fresh seafood. Drunken Messaun guests would stumble about until the sun made its appearance. Khral Rasmus's arrival would be celebrated with a parade through town ending at the palace. There, the two kings would renew their twenty-year treaty in front of a group of clapping lords and ladies.

Treaties, wars, politics—Father had kept us removed from all of it, and that policy had served us well for over a decade. The Hughen people could celebrate another twenty years of peace without me. This was my father's country, not mine. No country on the planet had claim on Lane Garrow. Especially one that would see me dead.

I walked quickly, sticking to the rails to avoid wagons and the occasional soldier. Only one thing felt exactly the same as before— the heavy, solid ground underfoot. Passengers complained about how our ship lurched and moved about with the sea, but to me, it was beautiful. A perfect balance between ship and water, neither servant nor master. If there was anything unnatural, it was trying to walk on land. Solid, unfeeling land.

At least Hughen's seasonal rain had cleared the air some. These docks still reeked of old fish and ill-drained refuse, but the blessed winds had swept most of the stench out to sea. Mud was a far cry better than stifling heat and the sweat collecting in the bindings that hid my criminal femininity.

I stepped around a pile of dung with bits of grass poking out like spiky green hair and continued on. They'd installed cobblestone since I was here last. Yet from the gaps along the edge marked by crude warning signs, I could see they weren't finished. So silly. What good were cobblestones to protect one's boots when horses did their business all over the place? I preferred dirt streets, even when it meant muddy winters. At least mud was honest.

There. A new sign stood at the footbridge leading toward town, larger and brighter than its predecessor. It boasted a figure wearing a black dress and holding an axe. A bloodred X had been painted over her. **NO PIRATES**, screamed bold lettering. The Jilly Black symbol. Like the old sign, it wore splatters of old spit along the bottom edge.

It was ironic—male pirates had terrorized the four brother nations for centuries, yet the universal symbol for pirate was a woman. Not just any woman, but the one who'd nearly accomplished the unthinkable. Captain Elena and her fearsome crew had defeated three of the Four Lands. She'd come closer to conquering the world than any man who'd ever tried.

Granted, she *had* nearly destroyed it in the attempt. And granted, her execution had spawned the King's Edict and complicated my life considerably. She'd scared the nations' leaders so badly, men cursed her name and spat at the thought of her. But there was one detail they'd gotten terribly wrong. Historians and witnesses all agreed that Elena had never worn a dress in her life.

I stared at the sign, imagining a crossed-out figure next to Elena. What would King Eurion do to my father if he really was a pirate? Did he face prison like Belza, or execution like the other members of Elena's crew? If this madness were indeed true, it would be just as important to protect my father's secret as my own. Nobody could know. As far as the world went, it wouldn't change a thing.

And yet it would change everything.

No matter how devastating the truth, I couldn't turn back now. I wouldn't be given this opportunity again. I pushed past the sign and strode on.

The walk into town required crossing three busy footbridges over unusually high water for this early in the season. I dodged between two carts and trotted across the street toward the fabric shop, only to find my path blocked by two well-dressed and incredibly slow women. A heavy lavender scent tainted the wind. The women swung their hips as they sauntered, looking much like fly-bitten mules. Did that actually attract men? I really had no idea.

Yet foolish as they looked, at least they didn't have to hide who they were.

I was about to walk past when I noticed a stringy-haired child trailing one of the women. Her once-yellow dress hung too short, exposing a pair of bare feet, dirty from the streets. An orphan. Rumors said many of Hughen's orphans had disappeared lately—kidnapped off the streets for military service, some believed, though I wasn't sure about that. Slavery was illegal here. More likely that the boys got picked up by sponsors wanting cheap labor. But the girls? Their options were begging or the brothel—both paths I'd narrowly avoided myself.

It wasn't her dress that tore at me, however. It was the girl's bewildered look, as if in disbelief that she was now utterly alone.

I'd felt that way once. The image emerged unbidden...reaching for the comfort of my mum's hand and watching her stalk away instead.

"Pardon, ma'am," the beggar said, ignoring me and addressing the taller woman wearing the blue gown. "Have you a coin to spare?"

The women's pasted-on smiles froze. Blue Dress lifted her nose, huffed, and backhanded the girl clean across the face. The child yelped and stumbled, hitting the ground hard.

I moved before I had time to think, blocking the woman's escape. "A simple *nay* would suffice, Your Ladyship."

The first woman just blinked, but the one next to her, in green, snickered. "Do not address us in such a manner, boy. Move aside

before I call the guards to remove you. I've no desire to touch...
that." She gestured to my clothes.

I folded my arms and waited.

"Oh, never mind." Blue Dress grabbed her companion's arm and
strode off into the road, shoving me against a shop window. A rider
jerked his bay gelding to a stop just in time, so close that the horse
could've sneezed in their faces. I wished he had. The rider watched
with gritted teeth as the ladies passed.

The orphan sat in stunned silence on the ground where she'd
landed. What faded yellow had remained of her dress was now a
uniform mud brown.

"Steer clear of lords and ladies," I hissed, hauling her to her feet
and digging my last two coins from my pocket. She snatched them
from my outstretched palm and scampered away without a word.
Her rudeness was a comfort. She'd learned a hard lesson today, but
she'd be all right.

The statue was only a few blocks away now. I picked up the pace
and had just turned the last corner when a long scream pierced the
air, pulling me to a sudden halt.

The distant sound of hooves on cobblestone echoed against
buildings from the direction of the docks. Travelers scrambled to
clear the road. Behind them, a team of white stallions clattered
toward us, hauling a tidy wagon filled with rigid soldiers. A single
woman sat at their center, bound in an intricate network of chains
save her hay-colored hair whipping in the wind.

"Three years since the last Jilly execution," someone muttered,
"and this'll be the second in a week."

Every muscle in my body went taut. I struggled to keep my face
impassive as I turned to the man, a baker, standing behind his cart.
"They're searching ships at port? For women?"

"Part of the king's cleansing. Random inspections from now till the festival." The baker grimaced, his lips covering a set of brown teeth.

I cleared my suddenly dry throat. "King Eurion's never done that before."

"Nay, but with the khral coming, s'pose he thought it best. The last prisoner kept yelling that she was a passenger, not a sailor, but they hanged her anyway. Must've got too hard to tell the difference." He shook his head. Whether for the poor woman or her excuse, I couldn't tell.

Horror held me rigidly in place. If I'd remained at the ship like Father had asked...

My heart drummed in my rib cage, so loudly I feared the man could hear it. It could have been me in that wagon. So close.

I straightened my vest and looked about, but the entire market's eyes were focused on the prisoner. The crowds parted slowly, forcing the wagon to a crawl. I could see the woman's terror-filled expression now. She skimmed faces and shouted again. This time I caught the word. *Marcu.* A southern name. Was Marcu a lover or a family member? Not that it mattered. Only the king could pardon her now, and that was as likely as a sea monster wearing a dress and dancing in the square.

The church bell began to toll. *Come witness a pirate's death.* It wasn't a request. The entire city was expected to attend.

A single thought pounded in my head like a hand drum. If they treated a suspected pirate like this, what would they do to a known one?

Somber mothers gathered their children. Men collected their purchases and trotted off, some looking eager. Those sitting behind carts full of wares only lowered their heads, silently tracing wards on their chests to shield them from dark spirits. It was good fortune to witness a criminal's execution—a person could send their troubles with the dead into the afterlife and come away cleansed.

But this wasn't a criminal. It was simply a woman who'd dared set foot on a ship. A decision that would cost her life.

My hands formed tight fists. Another hanging body that would haunt my dreams for months. Another innocent soul sent to join Elena in the afterlife, assumed a pirate simply because she lacked manly parts. Robbed of happiness and a future, and punished for violence she'd never dreamed of committing. She wouldn't even get a trial. Meanwhile, I'd set out to see if my father was guilty of the same crime.

Because if he bore pirate blood...so did I.

One thing was clear. Sprinting to the ship now would bring attention upon myself, and I didn't even know if it was safe there. Besides, the poor prisoner deserved at least one witness who cared. My errand could wait. I hoped.

I squared my shoulders, feeling hundreds of invisible eyes on me as the bindings beneath my shirt pulled tight. Then I followed the others.

It took only fifteen minutes for the entire town to pack themselves into the square, shoulder to shoulder. Hastily invented stories of the condemned woman's crimes whipped through the crowd. I placed myself on the group's edge, too far for the gossip to reach and hopefully too far to see well. I focused on the oversized woven hat of the plump woman blocking my view and tried to ignore the whispers filling the air like a brutal wind. The bindings beneath my shirt were damp enough for a good wringing.

A quick glance revealed that the nearest guard stood several horses' distance away. I felt his eyes sweep over me as he inspected the crowd. No reaction, but I tensed anyway. Beyond him, I could make out the gallows' highest timber. Several knotted ropes lay across it. Only one would be used today.

The gallows' placement was a chilling reminder of royal power. They'd built it upon the spot where King Eurion beheaded his wife's murderer, Elena the Conqueror. But that hadn't been enough for him. His infamous Edict had followed later that day. An Edict that would forever follow me like a thief in the shadows.

Today I felt the thief's hand on my shoulder.

I scanned the audience, but Father's three-cornered hat was nowhere to be seen. Engaged in business elsewhere, perhaps, and too busy to attend? Or did he have as much cause to hide as I did?

"They're unloading the Jilly," a man drawled from the rooftop above me. When I narrowed my eyes at him, he just grinned and tipped a bottle toward the gallows. He knew as well as I did that this woman was no Jilly, but now wasn't the time to correct him. Most of these observers would discuss the young woman's murder tonight along with other gossip like the upcoming festival and the palace's new cat, which was barely news at all, considering the royal family already owned fourteen.

Meanwhile, a new body would be rowed out to sea and dumped with the city's waste. A body that didn't look all that different from mine.

"They've put a sack over her head," the rooftop drunk continued, emboldened now. "The priest is exchanging words with the prisoner....Oh, he just turned his back on her! He's walking away. The Jilly'll die in her sins." He belted out a laugh. A few others joined him. I wanted to curl my fingers around their thoughtless throats, every last one.

The crowd quieted, brushing their trousers free of dirt or straightening their hats and placing a fist to their hearts in salute. Staccato hoofbeats from the front meant a carriage had arrived.

"Varnen is here," someone muttered.

My blood went cold. Varnen: the man who had betrayed Elena and turned her in. A strange concoction of emotion churned inside me—curiosity, respect. Disgust. People spat at an uttering of Elena's name, but from what I'd heard, Varnen wasn't much better. The king had rewarded the man's so-called loyalty by appointing him high advisor.

I rose onto my toes, a feat that only earned me a few worthless inches. I almost expected the man stepping down from the carriage to have three heads and scales, but he was very much human. He wore his gray beard to a sharp point and stood slightly shorter and stockier than his guards. If it weren't for the deep-blue uniform, he could have been one of Father's Hughen friends.

The thought was a bitter one. For all I knew, he was.

A single shout sounded across the square. A man in his early twenties threw himself into the crowd, waving his arms wildly. "Stop! Advisor, please!"

If word of the official's arrival had stirred interest, this new development arrested every pair of eyes. Townspeople stepped back to allow the man's approach, sending him nearly stumbling in his frantic haste. The surge allowed me to see clear to the gallows and its single prisoner, standing with her arms tied behind her and a cloth over her head. They'd already secured the rope around her neck. Even from where I stood, I could see her legs trembling.

"She's no Jilly, I swear!" the man continued, flinging himself at the advisor's feet on the platform. Guards yanked him back, but his shouts only grew louder. "That woman is my intended from KaBann, just arrived. Please, oh, powerful one. This is a terrible mistake."

Despite everything, a twinge of hope fluttered in my chest. Varnen could ignore the woman's story, but he couldn't dismiss the testimony of a man so easily. Not in front of a crowd like this.

"She has broken the King's Edict," Varnen said, far too calmly.

"Please, Advisor Varnen, give her a trial! I will assure the judge that I pushed her into taking passage on that ship. Or let me die in her place."

My hope drained away as I took in Varnen's disinterested expression. Marcu truly didn't understand. This wasn't just an execution—it was a demonstration. The nearby guard's eyes swept the crowd again. If I slouched any more, I'd be folded in half.

Calm down. Nobody sees a captain's boy.

A long silence hung over the square, like the wind holding its breath. It made Varnen's voice clearer than ever. "Then she fooled you too. You should thank me for saving you from such a woman. Now stand aside and witness justice done."

"This is not justice!" the man howled. "This is not right. How dare—"

I flinched as a guard's club sent him to the ground. Then it was quiet once again, save for the muffled sobs coming from the condemned woman. She and Marcu had begun their day focused on the altar. Hours later, everything would end at the gallows.

Love had no place in my future either, but what these two had made my chest hurt.

Ship or man, I reminded myself. *You can't have both.*

As it was, four men alive knew my secret. That meant four opportunities for betrayal, four people who saw me as vulnerable. Placing my life into yet a fifth person's hands would be terrifying enough. Handing over my heart as well, especially when any romance was doomed to end up just like this? Nay, never. Not in a thousand years.

If Elena's ship had always been enough for her, the *Majesty* would be enough for me.

"The Treaty Festival begins in a few weeks," Varnen called out. "No crime will be tolerated, especially not the treasonous crime of piracy. Women such as this nearly destroyed us once. We refuse to be tricked again. Long live our defender, our protector, our glorious king Eurion!"

The crowd raised a half-hearted shout, but most shifted in their boots. By Varnen's darkening expression, he noticed. He didn't spare the shuddering woman behind him a single glance. Justice indeed.

Varnen said something to a soldier, who saluted. A wave of quiet expectation swept over the audience. He'd given the order, then.

Movement to the left caught my eye as a young man pulled a cap lower over his face. His jaw clenched as he stared at the advisor, his shoulders taut. He had a stain on his shirt too, just like...

I cursed.

The boy from the docks turned to meet my gaze. Our eyes locked. Surprise flashed across his face—or was it confusion?—and he examined me, taking in my entire ensemble of ratty trousers and a worn vest. Then he grinned.

Panic shot through my chest like the ball of a cannon. I forced my hands into my pockets to keep them from shaking. First the docks, then here. I didn't believe in coincidences. He was following me—and there was only one reason he would do that.

I felt the boy's eyes still on me as I stepped backward, nearly tripping over someone's boot. I ignored the person's angry curse and headed for the back of the crowd. Something felt like it was closing around my throat.

It should have been you, whispers in the crowd said.

Next time.

Pirate.

The awful squeak of hinges tore through the square as the hatch beneath the woman's feet swung open.

My boots didn't stop moving until I'd reached the square, my lungs gasping for precious oxygen. I darted into an alley and hid in the shadows, straining for any sound of pursuit. But as the moments passed and my breathing slowed, I sat back with relief. If that boy intended to give chase, he would have found me by now. Even if he'd alerted a guard, what soldier would sprint after me when they could see a woman die instead?

I hadn't watched, but my mind provided the images far too readily—the victim convulsing, thrashing about, fighting to live with what instinctive strength remained. The image would reappear in my nightmares for weeks to come. Except her pale yellow dress would become my ratty pair of trousers and the delicate shoes a pair of dirty, too-tight boots.

That was way too close.

It was several minutes before the square filled with people again. Their conversations were somber, but the sound made me feel safer. Noise was natural. It was silence that was suspicious. The boy from the docks was nowhere to be seen. If I meant to complete my errand, now was the time.

I crept out of the alley and strode toward the statue of the dead queen. She stood too rigidly, looking down upon the square's inhabitants, every bit as proud and regal as I'd expect from royalty. It was this woman's death that had caused so much trouble. Why Elena had thought it necessary to murder Hughen's queen instead of its king was a mystery.

I let my fingers brush against the letters etched permanently into stone beneath the statue, the words forever branded into my mind.

Respecting my dear queen's memory and regarding the bloody mayhem Elena and her band of women pirates have left behind, I hereby decree that any woman found sailing upon our seas will be assumed Elena's spawn and executed.

—Noble King Eurion of Hughen (YBE 348)

The thing was, the Edict hadn't even brought peace like it was supposed to. Belza had launched a bitter campaign of revenge that would last ten years before his capture, taking the lives of hundreds more. Sailors suspected, betrayed, and even killed one another. And now innocent women passengers were being publicly murdered. If the Hughens would talk sense into their king rather than getting superstitious, maybe we could finally get somewhere with the whole world peace thing.

Father said not to hate King Eurion, that the man had announced the law in mourning. I snorted at the thought. Killing dozens of innocent women wouldn't bring back anybody.

To my right was another plaque, scroll shaped and nearly covered in smatters of old saliva. Elena's crew list. My heart hitched as I stepped closer, hesitated, and began to read. Each name was crossed out in a crude, almost angry way. It made them difficult to distinguish, but not impossible.

I read each name, paused, then scanned the whole list again. Only then did I let myself breathe deeply once again.

Father's name wasn't there.

A strange mix of relief and shame filled the space that worry had left behind. I'd jumped to a terrible conclusion rather than rely on what I knew about my own father. Rumors would come and go as they always did, but the *Majesty*'s first rule would always apply: loyalty. To the ship, to the crew, and to its captain. Surely that included my own flesh and blood.

If my father was a pirate, I would have known. It was that simple.

When time passed and the rumors evaporated like mist, Belza would still be just a man with a violent past. The Four Lands all despised him. If he lasted a month without a ball in his chest, I would be surprised. I examined the queen statue again, letting a familiar anger well up once more.

Belza hadn't killed anyone today, but King Eurion had. He was the one who stood in my way. *He* was my enemy. While that innocent woman hadn't survived, I would. I knew it sure as the ugly cobblestone and the waiting horses tied to shop fronts, heads lowered in lazy slumber. Not only would I survive, but I would command my father's ship someday, whether anyone liked it or not. As Lane, I was powerful—strong, safe, worthy of respect. Everything a captain should be.

The rain began again. I raised my face to welcome it as footsteps stopped behind me. I whirled to find Father standing there with a dark expression, his hat clutched in both hands. "You shouldn't have fled the execution like that, bringing attention upon yourself."

I frowned. That wasn't what I'd expected him to say. I considered telling him about the strange boy, then thought better of it. "I could have danced a jig and nobody would've noticed. Lands forbid they miss a second of someone's suffering."

"This isn't a joke," he snapped. "I should be angry at your blatant disobedience...but then, had you listened, it could be your body swinging back there."

That familiar tightening sensation returned, and I swallowed just to prove I could. "It wasn't."

"Because of a coincidence. We can't rely on coincidences, Lane. Things are changing here, getting more complicated. Nowhere is truly safe for you now." He shoved the hat back onto his head, seeming to gather himself. "There was a missive in the post today. From Nara."

I stiffened. *Nara.* The name felt wrong, like a word reflected backward in a mirror. She was "that woman" or "your mum," the tainted shadow of a life long past for both my father and me. He hadn't uttered her name in years.

"What did she want?"

"She's sent for you. Owns a manor in Ellegran now, said she'll set aside a room. Think of it. No more sharing a ship's cabin with your father, separated by a hanging sheet. Your own room."

My thoughts swirled until I felt unbalanced, like a giant crack had appeared in the deck and I was falling, falling, *falling*, trying to catch myself before I struck the water and never rose again. This couldn't be happening, not when the path I'd chosen depended so much on the *Majesty*. "My own room," I repeated flatly.

"All to yourself."

I gritted my teeth to gain a little control. "Why would I care about four walls and a floor? And you didn't tell me you've been speaking with that—that...*priss*. The woman left me on the docks for dead."

"She sends missives occasionally. It's only proper to answer. And she didn't leave you for dead—she trusted you to my care." His face twisted, like he was still trying to convince himself. There was a pain there I'd never seen before. For things done or left undone, I wasn't sure. "Now I'll be trusting you to hers."

I pushed back my rising panic and folded my arms. I knew what he wasn't saying. "This is about Belza, isn't it? You're afraid he'll find you, and you're panicking."

He blinked, but recovered quickly. "It's more than—"

"The inspectors aren't such a danger either," I plunged on. "If we avoided them today, we can avoid them again."

"You're sixteen now, Lane," he growled. "Only a year away from marriage age. We both knew this wouldn't last forever. You've a pretty face and a different shape even than last year. It won't be long before you start your womanly courses."

I kept my face blank. That particular surprise was three years old, long past. A dark day. I'd been vigilant with the laundry since then. But that wasn't even the hardest part of hiding who I was. I hunched my shoulders a little more, feeling the linen bindings under my shirt pinch tighter. "No matter."

"Aye? You look twelve, but even young lads grow up sometime. Where is the chest hair? Your voice change? The crew will notice things like you going to the bathhouse alone at port and sneaking your bucket around. I'm a fool. Should've listened to Dennis and sent you away years ago."

I blinked, his words sizzling into my soul like hot tar. This wasn't something that had just occurred to him. He'd thought this decision through, weighing each consequence and stacking them against me without my knowing. These were arguments he'd been collecting for a very long time. In my mind, it had always been Father and me against the world. The two of us, facing down inspectors and pirates and hard winters. As I watched for adventure on the horizon, had he been watching for Belza? As I dreamed of inheriting the ship, had he waited until the day he could finally be rid of me?

He'd even written my mum—that *woman*—and kept it from me. Somehow, that was the greatest betrayal of all.

"I'm no child," I said. "I know the dangers and I choose this anyway. All of it. The inspectors, suspicion. Belza."

"You know very little of it. 'Tis my responsibility to protect you, as your father."

"I'm not afraid. I refuse to let them beat me as they've obviously beaten you."

His eyes turned sharp as a pirate's blade. "And I refuse to see you on that platform with a noose around your neck. I'm protecting you from yourself as much as the world. Ellegran will be your home, and that's final."

I grimaced. The words hacked like a cutlass at my earlier resolve. The *Majesty* was home. My life there existed like the gulls overhead and the water below. It just was.

Father softened at my expression. "You'll have a better life in Ellegran than I could ever offer you anyway. With your mother's station, you could stop being Lane and become anyone you like. No more pretending, no more hiding. No more lies."

"*My* hiding? *My* pretending?" My voice was incredulous. I had spent my life hiding, perhaps, but never pretending. Lane *was* me. I

25

was meant to be a sailor, even if I had to wear boy's clothing to do it. Did he truly not see that? "Tell me what Belza wants from you so we can discuss lies in depth."

He flinched. My retort had found its mark. "I refuse to discuss either matter. You will return to the ship this instant."

I felt victory slipping away. "Father, I—I barely remember my life before. The *Majesty* is all I know. If you won't give me a choice, at least give me more time to prepare."

He watched me for a long moment. There was a heaviness in his eyes that scared me. "A choice, then. Pahn the hen farmer is looking for help. It isn't glamorous work, but it will provide what you need to survive. Or if you choose to return to the *Majesty*, know this—I will gauge your safety carefully on this voyage. If I feel your life is in danger, you won't question my decision to send you off. The *Majesty* sets sail at dawn." He opened his mouth as if to say more, then shut it again and stalked away.

I was left gaping after him. Sometime in the past hour, my life had taken a horrifying turn. He had to know I could never be happy raising livestock after the open sea. But when faced with being the daughter of some Ellegran lady, I wasn't sure which was worse.

A montage of experiences came to mind—canvas snapping in a taut northern wind, the slippery wetness of freshly scrubbed wood beneath my knees, the acidic heaviness of gunpowder in my nostrils after a long drill. Even the tiny slivers from mending line meant that I was *alive*, far more than the prettiest embroidery ever could. How could my own room in a quiet, lonely house ever compare?

The shock had fully drained away now, leaving behind a hard core of anger. What I wanted didn't matter. Not to Father, not to Eurion. It was about superstition, not logic. Never mind that I could tie a bowline knot faster than anyone else in the crew, one so tight the devil himself couldn't loose it. I was faster up the ratlines than anybody, and I knew the Gaigon Channel better than most sailors four times my age. I'd been born to sail, to command a crew. *Our* crew. I just had to find a solution that would calm Father's irrational fears.

I headed straight for the docks, adopting the wide-stepped swagger of a twelve-year-old boy, as always. It barely took a thought these days. A contingent of blue-clad soldiers marched by, likely returning to the palace from the gallows. They carried no body. The poor woman's corpse had likely been thrown into a wagon bound for the sea alongside those of the paupers whose families couldn't afford the burial fee.

My reflection in a shop window slid to an abrupt stop. A skinny figure with jaw-length hair pulled back into a tail stared back. Typical sailor. Sure, I was taller than most captain's boys—they usually rose to a midship position by thirteen—but nothing about me screamed *girl*. My bindings, stretched as they were, still kept all my curves flat. Nothing was amiss.

I took a deep breath and forced myself to look again.

And there it was. The trousers fit a bit more snugly than they should, the shirt too tight through the chest. A slender neck was barely visible under a dirty collar, and a sprinkling of freckles highlighted a hooked, very feminine nose. But above all, dark eyes glowered back at me with the wisdom of someone far older than the twelve years I pretended. Pain reflected back, the anger of a girl who'd spent her life reaching desperately for something the world had declared impossible.

I'd grown up around men. I spoke like them, walked like them. I knew how to swing my arms and stride around like the world was mine. I had the right clothes and the right words. Even the right build. But as long as men like King Eurion and Captain Belza pursued us, I would spend my life running. At some point I would have to turn and fight.

New clothes, I decided. A new shirt at the very least, and stronger bindings. Perhaps a hat. New trousers could come later. Once we put distance between the ship and Hughen, we could all relax again.

A sharp wind tore at my ponytail, grabbing a piece of dull brown hair and trying to send it eastward. The king and that horrid pirate could fall on their own swords. For once, I didn't hunch my shoulders as I headed for the docks.

I *would* command the *Majesty* someday. The world would just have to get used to the idea.

4

I was nearly to the ship when I spotted our gun master, Kempton, filling a tavern doorway. His white-blond hair was a tight knot at the back of his head, and his shirtsleeves were torn clean off as always. He insisted it was for convenience in battle. I knew better. Kemp wielded intimidation like a weapon, and he did it well. But as formidable as his stature appeared, it was the chilling gaze from his nearly clear Messaun eyes that made men's knees shake.

He muttered something to the handful of men surrounding him as I passed, his voice slurred. There was a smattering of uneasy laughter. Drunker than a rat in a barrel of ale. Last time he'd sounded like that, Father had been forced to pay half a month's wages to bail him out from the city dungeons. Yet somehow *I* was the one being kicked off the crew.

I was so distracted that I stumbled over a loose cobblestone in the road—only to smack hard into a man's chest. He grunted.

"My apol—" I began, but the words died in my throat. It was the boy in the expensive clothes with the dirt stain so close I could touch it with my nose.

Fear surged once again, and that familiar choking sensation

returned. It was too late to run. If he shouted, the guards would be upon us within seconds. Mustering every ounce of willpower I possessed, I folded my arms across my chest and returned his probing gaze with my best glare. *Nothing girl about this sailor,* my hard expression said. *Not an ounce of feminine weakness.*

His mouth—a perfectly shaped one—turned upward into a grin. "You were saying?" No accusations, no interrogating questions. He simply looked pleased.

I frowned. "No matter." I turned and stalked away.

He trotted up from behind and matched my stride, oblivious. "That was impressive."

I groaned inwardly. "Walking down the street isn't particularly impressive."

"Escaping the execution. Pretending to be sick was brilliant. Masterfully done."

I glanced at him again, but there was only amusement in his eyes. He hadn't given chase then, nor had he sent the guards after me. I'd run away like a fool and he'd been happy to watch me do it.

My gaze slid down to his boots again. No merchant could afford such expensive leather. The rich son of a lord, then. I shot him another scowl, which made him chuckle, then I sneaked a discreet look across the harbor to the *Majesty*. Her deck lay empty. No inspection teams, no soldiers.

"How fortunate that you were entertained," I said. "Now explain why you're following me about."

He hurried to match my pace. "Actually, I wondered if you'd help me secure passage." He spotted a contingent of guards at the other end of the dock and hunched his shoulders.

I eyed him. What kind of lordling feared royal soldiers? None I wanted to be involved with, that was certain. I began to jog. He did the same. My scowl deepened.

"You'll have to talk to the captain about that," I said.

"That's the traditional way to get passage, yes. But my situation is different. Could you just—" He grabbed at my arm, trying to pull me to a halt.

I whirled to face him, yanking my arm free. "Don't touch me, or you'll be taking a long swim. I say again, you're talking to the wrong person. Only the captain or an officer can grant you passage."

He dropped his hand. "Captain Garrow already refused me. He won't transport those running from the guards."

I raised an eyebrow. "Then we're done here."

"I'll pay well. It's extremely important. *Please*."

I sent him a flat look. Nobility were the cheapest people alive—they always undercut our usual fares. Lords and ladies considered their presence blessing enough for the merchants and captains serving them, as if being forced to bow and scrape was the purpose of a sailor's very existence. Only shadowy business would cause nobility to offer a huge sum for passage. Even so...

"We don't want your gold," I told him.

He blinked. "I'm short on other resources at the moment."

"Besides, we don't work with lords and ladies."

"Fortunately, I'm neither lord nor lady," the boy said with a half smile. "And I'd like to point out that I'm running *from* the king's guards, something nobility doesn't do. You need money, and I need passage. We can help each other."

I paused. "Why do you think we need money?"

He looked surprised. "Belza's interest in Captain Garrow has scared off all his usual customers. He's been asking merchants for loans all morning. I thought you knew."

So much for Father's reputation. The slightest doubt, and everyone he knew had abandoned him as though he were an injured gull. But I couldn't deny my interest in the stranger's offer. "You said you'd pay well?"

"Very." He looked over his shoulder at the guards again.

I hesitated. He was right that we needed to leave quickly, but this could all be an elaborate hoax. The boy was obviously upper class, no matter what he pretended. If he was lying about being from a lord's house, this conversation was already dangerous. Even as the fugitive son of a lord, he could have a personal relationship with King Eurion. Turning me in would be a simple task. But there was an edge of panic to his voice that couldn't be faked. Whatever he'd done, it was terrible enough to make him desperate. Desperation could be used.

If only he weren't so blasted nice to look at.

"Halt!" someone called behind us.

I flinched and turned slowly, my heart leaping to a gallop. But the guard stalked past me toward a wagon jostling by. The driver, a gray-haired man with a bulbous nose and hard eyes, yanked at the reins just as the guard jogged up and leaped onto the wagon bed. He began shoving around the man's load.

"What are you looking for?" the old driver growled. The guard shot him a scathing look, causing the driver to hunch his shoulders and turn back to his team.

A moment later, the guard jumped down and tossed a dismissive hand toward the driver, who snapped the reins. The guard strode in my direction with a scowl. I realized I was staring. I crossed my arms over my shirt and threw a glance toward the rail. The boy was gone.

"You," the guard said, stopping in front of me. "Have you seen a boy of seventeen, brown hair?" His breath stunk of old meat.

I couldn't speak. I just shook my head.

"Send for a guard if you see him." He was already walking away.

Air escaped me in a long, relieved breath. Two close calls in a single day. Our departure couldn't come soon enough.

"Thanks for covering for me," a voice said a second later.

I whirled to find the boy crouched behind a discarded coil of line. His too-perfect grin widened at my startled expression.

Why *had* I covered for him? I silently cursed his pretty face and resolved to be more careful. "I'm not doing it again, so you can be on your way."

He shot a glance at the disappearing guard. "Look, I'm desperate or I wouldn't be pursuing this. Here are the facts. One, there are no other ships going to Ellegran. Just yours. Two, I need to get there as quickly as possible."

"The *Mum's Commoner* over there is headed for the islands and balmy weather," I shot back. "I'm sure they'd stumble over themselves to serve a lordling throwing gold around."

"This isn't a vacation, and I already told you I'm not a lord. I need to get to Ellegran, and no, I'm not telling you why."

"And bring the guards down upon us for helping a fugitive? No thanks."

"I'll join the crew, then. I heard about the men you lost to these Belza rumors."

That made me pause. We'd lost men? I resented how much he knew that I didn't. "One sailor isn't worth the risk, especially one with no experience." His smooth hands and pale skin screamed *shoreman*.

He sighed, all good nature gone from his expression. "A bargain, then. Smuggle me aboard, and I won't tell anyone you're a girl."

My head snapped up. All sound on the docks went hollow, and the ground lurched beneath my feet. Had he just said...?

In a second, my knife was at his throat. My grip was wobbly, but I hoped the venom in my voice made up for that. "What did you just call me?"

The lordling looked exasperatingly unworried. "Now that I have your attention, let's go aboard and discuss this."

"I will *not* be threatened." My voice sounded choked.

"Relax. It wasn't a threat. Well, fine, it was a threat. But this position doesn't look good for either of us, so if you wouldn't mind..." He nodded toward the dock, where several workers had paused to watch. *Lands.* This was not a conversation I wanted remembered.

"Follow me," I growled, and stomped up the gangplank. He followed more gingerly.

I led the boy straight to the captain's quarters and shoved open the door, wincing as the inset glass rattled. The room was empty, the table clear of its usual maps and contracts, its two ornate chairs tucked neatly beneath. Father was likely still trying to secure that loan for supplies. I pulled the boy inside, letting the door close sharply behind him, and raised the knife toward him once more. "How did you know Captain Garrow is my father?"

"I didn't," he admitted, eyeing the blade. "I saw you both talking this morning. When he turned me down, I followed you into town. It wasn't long before I lost you in the crowd. But then at the execution, there you were." His mouth twisted. Whether his distaste was for the hanging or the woman who'd died, I couldn't be sure. "I realize what I'm asking might bring more trouble on you and the captain, but I promise to make it worth your while. I can tell you're a good person. You wouldn't have lied to that guard if you weren't."

I mentally kicked myself. "And you wouldn't have threatened to turn me in if you were."

"We need each other. That's all I'm saying. Show me where to hide, and you can keep your secret."

"And you'll do what, stay there for three weeks? You have no food, no water." No baggage either. His flight from the guards had been a sudden one. A curiosity I couldn't help crept up on me, but I refused to ask what he'd done to bring the entire city's guard down upon him. The less we knew about each other, the better.

"I'm certain you'll take good care of me. The crew doesn't know your secret, do they? Surely you want to keep it that way."

I almost dropped the knife that I'd forgotten I was holding. How *dare* he? If Father discovered my secret was out, I'd be off the ship the second we docked in Ellegran. "I'm no chambermaid. I take care of no one, and I refuse your bargain."

He looked genuinely surprised. "Pardon?"

"Hiding you is a terrible idea. You'd be discovered within a day. But since I obviously can't let you go either, you'll remain tied up until after we leave. Then I'll toss you over the rail and you can take your chances with the jardrakes." I paused. "Either that, or I can convince the bosun, Dennis, to let you sign on as an inexperienced recruit—which I may be willing to do for the right price." My voice was surprisingly calm for the turmoil I felt inside. I had the advantage here. I couldn't let it slide through my fingers.

He examined me for a long moment. I stared right back, trying to look like the kind of person who would follow through on such a threat. His gray eyes finally grew guarded. "How much?"

"Six hundred gold pieces."

It was an entire year's wages for the whole crew. An exorbitant amount, utterly unthinkable. I half expected him to throw a tantrum and stalk away.

To my surprise, he only frowned. "I'll give you four hundred."

Four hundred. How much did this boy carry? I cleared my throat to cover my surprise. "Six hundred. Feeding a crew for three weeks is expensive. If my father fails to secure his loan, your money will

35

ensure we can still leave. And if you want me to keep you a secret from my father, I'll have to invent some kind of cargo so he doesn't ask questions."

"Four fifty," he said. "You nearly bowled me over in the road and refused to apologize."

"And you chased me down. Quite rudely, in fact. Five hundred, final offer."

"Fine." He removed a bag from his pocket. Only the rich carried bags of coins around—it was too hard to disguise how much one had. The clever ones hid pouches throughout their layers of clothing. He plucked out a few coins before stuffing them into his pocket. Then he handed me the entire bag. "Deal. And call me Aden."

I hid a smile as I accepted it. Five hundred gold coins. I'd never seen such wealth in my life, let alone held it in my hands. I imagined myself sprinting toward town to buy ten shirts and another pair of boots. My axes could finally get the proper sharpening they needed. *Lands*, I could buy my own percentage of a ship if I wanted.

Aden's amused smile was back. I'd been grinning at the bag like a fool. He might be desperate, but he was still nobility. I had to be more careful.

I cleared my throat. "You'll sign the book as soon as the bosun returns." This solved several problems. These coins would buy our supplies and ensure we could leave tomorrow. The farther we got from Hughen, the safer Father would feel. The biggest problem now was keeping this stranger's secret so he would keep mine. This voyage had to go perfectly. I didn't like it at all, but the journey to Ellegran was only three weeks. I'd told far worse lies in my lifetime.

I gave my knife a last flick for good measure before shoving it back into its sheath, watching with satisfaction as Aden flinched and followed the blade with his eyes.

"As enjoyable as it is to stand here," Aden said, giving the cabin one last look, "perhaps we'd best get below."

An urge to snap at him overcame me, but I shook it off. If Father walked in and caught us here, there would be no bargain at all. I swung the door open. "Follow me. And be quick about it."

5

I showed Aden the cargo hold first, pointing out the empty holdings where barrels and crates were usually stacked. Then I showed him the gun deck, its heavy guns secured and gleaming. Our powder, all four barrels of it, was stored in a forward magazine for safety. I didn't point out the locked cabinet that stored our muskets and pistols. The lordling's money may have bought him passage, but it didn't buy my trust. Not even close.

I showed him the galley on the far end, where Paval was already at work preparing dinner for the returning men, then gestured to the crew's quarters behind the bulkhead. "This is where you'll sleep." There were usually sailors lying about, enjoying a few winks before their next watch. But today the crew was ashore, enjoying the leave they didn't know had been cut short.

"You never told me your name."

I hesitated, but he'd have discovered it soon enough. "Lane Garrow."

"Pleasure." His reply was suspiciously cheerful. Aden, if that was really his name, eyed the hammocks slung wherever there was space. "You fit how many men in here?"

"Sixty-five. They sign on for a year at a time. Some stay the full three they're allowed."

"Allowed?"

"My father likes to rotate his crew often. Keeps them from getting too comfortable. Except the officers." And Paval, of course. As my father's friend, he'd been here the longest. Dennis and Kempton followed at four and two years, respectively.

Aden nodded, but his lips twisted in distaste as he scanned the room. I frowned. It was cluttered, true, but the bulkheads and decks were scrubbed every single day. He wouldn't find a cleaner ship on the northern seas.

"Two watches of thirty-two men each," I said. "You'll be on the first watch under Dennis, so I can train you. The gun master and second officer, Kempton, oversees the other watch. You'll meet him later." Much later, if I had my way. Kemp wouldn't be sober till the moment we left, if then. "Now, let's fix your disguise."

He frowned at his clothes. "This will work fine."

I ignored his objection and strode to a crate in the far corner. The lid opened with a sharp whine. We had to close it tight because of the rats. They'd chew right through cloth if you let them. They'd eat anything when they got hungry enough. Kind of like people, but those stories weren't often told.

"What's in there?" he asked, eyeing the box warily.

"Clothes nobody else wanted. You won't convince the crew with that pretty shirt." Father would also remember the boy who'd asked for passage, new shirt or not. Thankfully I had an explanation prepared.

"You'll have to wear your own trousers, but they'll dirty up quick enough." I tossed a bundle of cloth to Aden. He caught it easily. "Nobody will know the difference unless they look close. And you'll want to mess up your hair a bit."

He lifted the old shirt to his face like it was a fish carcass and smelled it. Then he grimaced. I half hoped that a lordly tantrum would emerge, but he just shook his head and began unfastening his shirt.

My attention fixed on his fingers, glimpses of chest slowly exposing itself as he worked. I told myself I didn't care what a noble looked like underneath. It was curiosity, nothing more. Curiosity that made me feel strangely winded as he pulled the shirt off and tossed it to the deck.

Our gazes locked.

I managed to turn away, pretending to fumble through the storage chest again. Heat raged in my cheeks. I wasn't bothered by a little skin, but I didn't usually gawk either. Aden had no right to look so toned, especially when my plan involved breaking him a bit. Maybe sea life would suit him better than expected. Not that I cared about that.

I kept my back to him and said the first thing that sprang to mind. "You will also stop shaving."

"I thought this was a Hughen ship."

"Once you hit open sea, we follow a different law." Except for the whole girl-sailor thing, which apparently applied everywhere I wanted to be. I slammed the lid as the hinge shrieked in protest. "Out there, Hughens grow beards and even eat fowl." I turned around to see his reaction.

He froze, one arm extended in the shirtsleeve. "They do?"

Oh, torturing Aden was going to be glorious. "Aye. So will you, if you expect to fit in here."

He frowned, looking disturbed. I couldn't tell which bothered him more—eating fowl or not shaving. Hughens were so odd sometimes.

"Does it always smell like this?" he muttered. "I don't suppose there's a place for sleeping on deck."

"Contrary to what shoremen think, we don't halt every night for sleep. You'll have a full eight-hour watch every other night. You try to sleep up there and they'll kick you around like a yapping pup."

He sighed. "Let me try out a hammock, then."

I grinned again.

He threw his hands up in the air. "Oh no. Absolutely not. I refuse to sleep on the hard floor for three weeks."

"These are all claimed. Isn't my place to give a man's hammock away. Besides, by this time tomorrow, you'll be tired enough to sleep standing up."

He muttered a curse and dropped his hands, revealing that he'd only succeeded in fastening one of the clasps. "Why isn't this working?"

I cocked my head. "Don't tell me you've never fastened your own shirt before."

"Of course I have." He frowned. "These clasps are different. They keep slipping."

Different from what? I stepped closer and swiped his own shirt off the ground, examining it closely. "Buttons carved from *seashells*?" *Lands.* And he'd smeared dirt on it like the shirt meant nothing. I stroked the buttons with my fingers. "Do you still want this?"

"Keep it."

I wadded the fabric up and shoved it under my arm before he could change his mind. The buttons alone would be worth ten coppers at port. Aden's gold would buy the supplies we needed and purchase "cargo" for our journey, but I had my own expenses to worry about.

Aden was still standing there, fiddling with the clasps. He grunted in frustration. Even a child knew how to fasten his shirt. Were all rich boys so helpless?

I sighed, not moving to help him. This was a business arrangement and nothing more. If Aden expected me to cushion it for him, he was dead wrong. For the next three weeks, we were equals. If he stepped out of line, it was my right—no, *responsibility*—to remind him.

He finally got the second clasp fastened. With a triumphant grin, he moved on to the next. It would have been fine, except he'd used the wrong clasp. The shirt hung open at a strange angle, exposing his hardened chest.

This wouldn't do at all. I couldn't rightly spend all day seeing that and not stare, pampered rich boy or not.

With an exasperated sigh, I planted myself in front of him and began fixing the clasps, keeping my head down and pretending my face wasn't just inches away from his. Despite the old shirt, he smelled of oak moss and fresh rain. At least he wasn't doused in that nose-numbing, heavy cologne our wealthier passengers often wore around lady folk. I imagined this particular boy putting on nice clothes and cologne for my sake and swallowed hard.

"You'll practice tonight when the men are asleep," I told him, letting my messy hair fall into my eyes. Hopefully it would hide my flaming cheeks. "I'm not doing this for you again."

"Where do you sleep?" he asked. I caught a whiff of mint leaves on his breath.

"In the captain's quarters." That sounded odd even to my ears, so I plunged on. "He prefers to keep me close. In case he needs to send orders or anything."

I couldn't recall what a bed felt like. I was five when Mum had come to the docks and set me down in front of Father, saying she couldn't do it anymore.

Most of my memories of her were blurred, but that day sprang to mind with perfect clarity—her insistence that she wasn't meant for this life, that her dreams lay elsewhere. I'd reached for her then. She'd stared at my hands with a tight jaw before turning away.

I still remembered how her braid had shone like honey in the dying sunlight as she'd marched toward town. She never turned back to look at me. Not once. I'd looked at Father for reassurance, only to see my own pain reflected in his expression. Something inside him had cracked that day, something not even I could mend.

I thought of that terrible woman who'd struck the beggar earlier and grimaced. Sad as it was, Father should have known better than to fall in love with a lady of position.

"I saw you speaking with the captain alone earlier," Aden said, pulling me back to the present. "Does he not approve of your going ashore with the men?" He paused and shook his head. "Never mind. I know the answer to that."

I bristled. "Not that it's your business, but I come and go as I please. I join the crew ashore often. They're my family." It was mostly true. "Tell me why it has to be Ellegran."

"Because it does. Trust me on that." He lifted his chin to allow me better access to the last clasp.

The job wasn't done, but I let my hands drop and stepped backward, my face heating under his intense gaze. It looked better with the collar unfastened anyway. "You'll pass. At least until you open your mouth."

"What's wrong with how I speak?"

"You sound too stiff. Just...you know. Relax a little. Let your words slur together."

"Ligethis?"

"You seem drunk."

He smirked. "I thought most sailors *were* drunk. Isn't that why they sign on, for the spirit rations?"

I wanted to slap that sightly face of his. Of all the arrogant, ridiculous things to say. "The men are skilled and work hard. Their rations are a fitting reward for months at sea, and our ale's barely strong enough to get anyone drunk."

He held up his hands in surrender. "It was a joke. Forget I said anything."

The ceiling creaked. Someone had returned. I tensed as footsteps sounded on the stairs, then Barrie appeared in the doorway. He gave Aden a curious look, but to his credit, he didn't mention our earlier conversation and my mission ashore. "Captain's sent orders to gather the crew. I can't find Dryam. You seen him?"

"Probably visiting family. I think they live on the outskirts. Shouldn't be there much longer, though. He's always complaining about his gruff aunt."

"Ah, that's right." His eyes flicked to Aden, then he scampered away.

"So young," Aden muttered.

"Most start young. Barrie's a hard worker making an honest wage, and you won't speak badly of him."

He chuckled. "You imply my own wages are dishonest?"

"Tell me you actually worked for that bag of gold. Tell me you labored in the hot sun, drenching rain, and biting winds to earn your family's support."

"Oh? Tell me where you got those coins in your own pocket." He laughed at my glare and plunged on before I could reply. "You'd best make your preparations. The sooner we leave, the sooner we'll get to Ellegran." He headed for the stairs and gripped the rail, stepping up carefully like beginners always did.

I did have work to do, but it certainly wouldn't be on his order. I gritted my teeth, glaring at his backside. *Aye, lordling. And the sooner we get to Ellegran, the sooner we can leave you behind.*

Four hours later, I kicked a rock and glared at a wide office door. Decades of humidity had caused the wood to soften and curl at the corners, a stark contrast to the whitewashed sign with **CITY PLANNER** painted in bold black strokes. I considered testing the knob again but dismissed the thought. The door was just as locked as it had been an hour ago, and I didn't want a passerby to accuse me of trying to break in.

If the planner didn't return soon, though, my plan was doomed. I'd already approached my father's usual customers and gotten nothing but shoulders as cold as winter. Either Hughen had a sudden lack of desire to transport cargo, or the rumors of Belza really had spooked everyone.

"Of all days to feign ill and stay home," I snapped at the city planner sign.

"No feigning necessary," a voice muttered, and I jumped to find a stooped man with a narrow, pinched face climbing the steps toward me. His foot hovered with each step, as if making contact with the ground was painful. "Wish I could. King Eurion intends to work me till I'm a skeleton in the ground."

"Beg pardon, sir," I said. "I'm just in a hurry."

"Been forty years since I saw a sailor who wasn't. And that one was dead." He shoved the door open in a manner that made me wonder whether it really *had* been locked, then he stepped inside. A second's pause as I waited for him to invite me in, but it was clear the still-open door was all the invitation I'd get. When I followed, a heavy smell of mildew hung in the air. The lower decks of the *Majesty* after two months at sea smelled better. Oblivious, the old man plopped into a chair and busied himself with a stack of parchment on a table. City grid maps covered the walls in a haphazard manner, hanging askew and seeming long forgotten. This had to be the only man alive who owned more maps than Father.

He leaned back with a groan and looked me up and down. I hunched my shoulders out of instinct. If Aden had seen through my disguise, someone else could. Couldn't they? Too bad there wasn't time for another trip to the shops district. I had enough money now for a trunkful of trousers and bindings and anything else I needed.

Later, I promised myself, and straightened up. There would be plenty of time once I convinced Father I belonged. Besides, Aden had only discovered my secret by watching us argue at the harbor this morning. He must have overheard somehow.

I cleared my throat. "I—er, my captain heard that you have cargo bound for Ellegran. You're fortunate that we've just enough space left."

The man belted out a laugh. "Just enough space? You're clever, boy, but I know Garrow's ship is emptier than his pockets. Besides, I don't want my cargo stolen by no angry pirate, even if it is simply broken cobble from our streets. I've already signed with Captain Mass. He's far slower and has space only for the premium barrels, but at least they'll arrive."

It was the reaction I'd come to expect. Half the town was convinced we'd be attacked within the week, even though nobody actually knew where Belza was. But something between the old man's words stopped me. "What of the non-premium pieces, sir?"

The planner waved a dismissive hand. "Ellegran doesn't want those. Nobody does. Nothing but pebbles left over, utterly useless."

An idea struck me. "Are those in barrels?"

"Nearly all. King Eurion wanted them dumped into the ocean, but the port master threw a fit. Meanwhile, they're taking up valuable space out back."

I tried to hide my excitement. "And if we took them?"

There must have been something in my voice, because he clasped his hands and grew all businesslike once again. "Hughen doesn't pay for waste disposal. If Garrow wants barrels full a' pebbles, he'll have to buy them."

I thought fast. "We've no use for them. Just seeking to fill what's left of the cargo space. If you like storing barrels full of useless pebbles, why, then I don't see that there's anything left to discuss." I spun and walked briskly to the door.

"Wait."

When I turned back, the old man had stood. He looked about the room as if making sure we were alone, then sighed heavily. "You can't dispose of them in Hughen waters."

"Aye, sir. Of course."

"I can pay you five pieces per barrel. That's it."

I pretended to consider that. I'd planned to pay for cargo, but this was even better. "Done. Have your men deliver the barrels to the docks tonight."

I returned from town just after my father did. I didn't ask whether he'd gotten the loan. His scowl and the cage of fluttering hens in his arms were answer enough.

Still breathing hard—I'd run all the way from the city planner's office—I hurried up the gangplank after him. "We've cargo, Father. It will be delivered tonight."

His eyebrows shot upward at the news. "Did Dennis arrange this?"

"Nay, sir. I accepted the commission on your behalf. It's a... small shipment of bad copper shavings to be returned to Ellegran. We've already received payment." His eyes narrowed with each word, and I plunged on. "I spent some of it on corn and flour and that new line you wanted. If you wish it, we'll be ready to leave by morning tide."

"If *I* wish it." The words burst from tight lips. "How kind of you to give me permission, Lane Garrow."

I frowned at him. "You wanted to leave tomorrow. I made that possible."

"You were ordered to keep hidden. Instead, you wandered about the town so you'd be seen by hundreds of people, any of whom could have seen through your disguise and complicated our departure. Now everyone with half a wit will discern we're leaving tomorrow instead of next week." He sighed. "This pattern of disobedience is worsening by the day."

As are your lies, I wanted to shoot back. Surely he could be bothered to explain why a notorious pirate sought him, at the very least. Yet he hadn't said a word.

The caged hens fluttered again, sending white feathers into the breeze between us. He shoved the cage roughly into my arms. "You're certain the commission said Ellegran? Most copper mines are in Messau."

It was too late to change my story now. "I'm sure. There's a buyer waiting. I put the commission and payment in the chest." He hid his most valuable objects in a small chest in his cabin. The men were usually trustworthy, but they had their vices. Father didn't even know why I'd been avoiding Kempton for the past year. It had been the one secret I'd kept from him. Until now.

"Then we'll load the cargo under cover of darkness. Lands grant that Barrie can gather the crew in time." Father clenched his jaw. "You'll help secure the cargo in the hold tonight, but I don't want to see you again until then. This kind of behavior is exactly why it isn't safe for you here anymore."

A biting retort leaped to my tongue, but I kept my mouth firmly closed. I'd done more than sneak ashore today, but in the end, we would all get what we wanted.

By late evening when the cargo arrived, I had to admit that Aden was right. Nearly a dozen contracted sailors still hadn't returned and probably never would. Kemp was one of them, which was just fine with me. Those who arrived went to work loading the barrels, grumbling to one another in not-so-low voices about their leave being shortened. I obeyed my father's command, relieved to take the task of securing the barrels upon myself and careful to check each seal for signs of cracking. The last thing I needed was for Father to discover my deception before we'd even left. There would be time for explanations later—and I intended to hear the full story of Belza from my father's own lips.

By the dawn watch bell, my back felt like it was breaking into pieces. Even shorthanded, we'd accomplished in one night what normally took a loading crew two days. But we weren't finished yet. Every hand would be needed to get the ship out of port. Even Aden's, assuming he was still around. He'd disappeared before the night's work had begun. Probably sleeping somewhere. Or, if I was lucky, he'd lost his nerve and run.

I climbed the ladder and then the stairs, watching for my father.

He was nowhere in sight. I allowed myself a victorious smile as I emerged onto the deck, greeted by a brilliant pink sunrise. We had cargo, supplies, a destination, and nearly a year's salary hidden in the cabin. We'd be long gone before the pirate arrived. Now there was the not-so-simple matter of keeping Aden's secret from the crew.

Half the crew shoved past me to the stairs. There would be no true meal this morning. Port meals were always sparse anyway, but the men would fill their stomachs quickly before they were ordered aloft. I wouldn't be needed again until it came time to weigh anchor. I blinked away my exhaustion. Father had ordered me to stay out of sight until we left the harbor, and the nest was my favorite place to watch the shore shrink behind us.

I set my foot on the ratlines and scampered up, unable to hide the grin on my face. Soon we'd be free again—like a horse released to pasture—sails flapping, filling with ocean air. The gentle rocking and creaking as the ship cut through mighty ocean waves.

See, mapmakers put land as the center of their maps, like a picture surrounded by a frame of ocean. That was backward. Each sea had its own personality, something that made it different, whether it be temperature, color, salt, depth, or even roughness. The water supported the land. It was worthy of respect.

When I reached the nest, I gave the horizon another contented grin, grabbed the edge of the box, and leaped inside.

Someone was already there.

I twisted in midair, but it was too late. Aden released a heavy grunt as I fell on top of him, my elbow connecting with his gut. I was suddenly very aware of our bodies tangled together, legs and all.

"Thanks a lot," he muttered.

"Lands!" I peeled myself off and scrambled to my feet, feeling heat rush to my face all the way from my toes. "You aren't supposed to be here."

"And you are?" He sat up, rubbing his stomach with a grimace.

Of all the idiotic places for him to be. "You can't sleep up here," I snapped, looking over the edge to the deck below. A figure had just emerged from the cabin, scanning the docks. If Father looked up and saw me speaking with a strange boy...

Aden rose to his feet now, staring me down. "I'm not sleeping, and I don't have to defend my actions to you." The clasps on his shirt were half undone. He'd been practicing after all.

I told myself I didn't wish the morning light were brighter so I could see the chest beneath. It was harder than it should have been to tear my gaze away and peer down at Father again. He'd begun to pace in front of his cabin, still watching the dwindling crowd ashore. Waiting for crew members, or a pirate?

"You abandoned your work last night," I told Aden. "We don't take kindly to that."

His face was still shadowed, but I swear he was smiling. "Nah. I just wanted to see the view."

I scowled at his teasing. Worse, my stomach flip-flopped like a schoolgirl's. "Well, next time you decide to sprawl yourself out like that, give me some notice first. I won't try so hard not to step on you."

"And why are you here?" he asked, too casually. "I figured you'd be getting in some rest before we left. Or perhaps as my guardian, you grew worried about my disappearance and came to ensure my safety and comfort." There was that grin again.

I swore under my breath and sat myself down where he'd just been. I'd come to see the sunrise, and see it I would. "You should thank me for discovering you before someone heavier did."

He ignored my comment and plopped down across from me, next to my feet. "How do you get a ship this size out of port? Must be quite the undertaking."

I looked sharply at him, wondering at his change of subject. "It can be. Your harbor is positioned well, so trade winds and the tide should pull us out. If they fail, there's always kedging."

"That's where you take the boats out and pull the ship, right?"

"The *Majesty* weighs over a thousand tons. No rowboats are strong enough to pull her. Nay, they bring out an anchor attached to a line, then drop it. Here on the ship, we reel in the line to pull us free. Meanwhile, another boat goes out farther to do the same thing until the winds catch."

"Fascinating. I've always wondered about that." He settled himself with his ridiculous boots pointed skyward and turned toward the sunrise again.

The *boots*. I'd completely forgotten. "Remove your shoes."

"Pardon?"

"Just do it."

He stared at me for a moment, then slid off the first, revealing a brilliant white stocking. I tore the boot from his hands and launched it far over the rail.

"Wha—" he sputtered as the splash came, scrambling to the side and peering over as if he could call it back. "Why did you do that?"

"They're obviously expensive, so it's your secret or your boots." I motioned to the other one. "If getting to Ellegran is so important, it should be an easy choice." I shrugged. "Or I suppose you can take a little swim and think it over."

"You could have just explained the situation like a proper person," he growled, then slid his other boot off and gave it a toss. It seemed an eternity before the splash finally sounded.

"First lesson of the day," I said. "I'm not proper, and neither are you. You're a sailor now. You can keep the stockings, I suppose, since you'll wear holes in them soon enough. I bet somebody has an extra pair of boots to trade. Hope you saved a coin or two."

"How kind."

I expected him to descend the ratlines then, to put more distance between us. But instead, he turned to watch the lightening horizon. There was sadness in his gaze. He may have been on the run, but he didn't seem eager to leave.

"Will you ever come back?" I found myself asking.

"I hope so." His eyes met mine. "I wouldn't leave now, except... this is important."

"Oh." I wasn't sure what to say to that.

He examined my face before turning back to the sunrise. Part of me was cross that he'd presumed to take my favorite lookout spot. The other part was humiliated that a stranger could make me so rattled. My arm tingled a bit where our skin had met, and the closeness of his face, feeling his breath on my cheek as he exhaled—

I clenched my jaw. What was *wrong* with me?

An urgent shout sounded from the docks.

I leaped to my feet as Aden peered down. Far below, an unfamiliar figure pulled up on a horse and swung down from the saddle, waving a piece of parchment. I could barely make out his words. "Halt! Do not weigh anchor!" He wore a blue uniform with a brown cap.

My knuckles turned white as my fingers gripped the box's edge, tight and rigid so I couldn't be torn away. I stared at the figure, wishing him away, but he was very real.

Another inspection. This couldn't be happening. Not when we were so close.

I was trapped.

7

Aden was completely oblivious to my reaction. "Girard, the head inspector. I'd know that rat anywhere."

Breathing required a monumental effort. Had someone seen through my disguise and reported me? Perhaps the inspector wouldn't check up here, though that wasn't likely. Or if he examined the lower decks first, I could sneak off—but I would surely be spotted by the crew, who would wonder.

Aden's scowl faded. "You all right?"

Of course I wasn't. One man threatened to unravel my entire plan. Then Aden's words finally sank in. "The Inspector Girard who helped Varnen capture Elena the Conqueror?"

Aden snorted. "Don't call her that."

Anger flared in my chest. She'd almost united the four brother nations under the ancient Motherland flag before Varnen's trap had ensnared her for good, and that deserved some degree of respect. I clamped my mouth shut just in time. It was dangerous enough that I was speaking to a Hughen lord, much less one who knew my secret. I could give Aden no more excuses to remember me when this was all over. Besides, Elena had killed his king's first wife and nearly destroyed his country. I couldn't blame him for his feelings on the subject.

"We can't let Girard search the ship," Aden said.

I rounded on him. That inspector would haul me straight to the gallows, and all Aden cared about was getting to Ellegran on schedule? But something in his expression stopped me. It almost looked like…guilt.

"He's looking for you," I said, finally understanding. I couldn't hide the relief that flooded through me before a new wave of anger hit. "You knew they would come back, yet you didn't say a word."

"I suspected. I didn't know for certain." He avoided my gaze. "I'm sorry, Lane. I didn't even think about what this could mean for you. Don't worry—if they find us, I won't let them take you."

I imagined Aden revealing himself to defend me. Even if it worked, and if by some miracle the crew didn't discover my lies, Father would never allow me to stay on the *Majesty* after that.

Nay. Our bargain still applied, whether we liked it or not. They couldn't find Aden and they couldn't discover me, and that was that. "I'll fix this."

"No, you won't. I'm sure your father will sort it out."

It was exactly what Father would say, which ramped my stubbornness up a notch or two. I'd done enough hiding.

"Stay here," I muttered, planting my feet next to the edge.

"Wait!" Aden cried.

I leaped for the yard line. He cursed from behind me.

This route was faster and far more difficult than descending the ratlines. Father hated when I made the fifteen-foot jump, but he wasn't watching me now. And I didn't want to miss a single word of their conversation.

My landing was almost perfect. I slammed my weight down

onto the center of the yard, feeling it vibrate but not shift beneath my boots, and I caught the center line with both hands. It slid some, biting into my palms. Then I slid down, my feet taut against the rope to regulate my speed. I hit the deck sooner than expected and nearly sprawled onto the planks, but I managed to turn it into a stumble. I looked upward to see Aden openly gaping at me over the nest's side before pulling out of sight.

That's right, lordling. You don't belong here.

I strode to the mainmast and angled myself behind it, pretending to examine a splinter. The inspector stood just feet from the gang-plank as he argued with Father. Behind them, a wide-shouldered figure stalked up the gangway. Kemp was back. Twelve new recruits accompanied him, all with the same pale countenance and greasy blond hair, though they looked gangly compared to him. Kemp directed them to the stairs as if nothing were out of the ordinary.

I narrowed my eyes but didn't have time to think on it. The inspector shoved a piece of parchment at my father's chest.

"You may *respectfully disagree*, but I have my orders. By King Eurion's royal command, no ship is permitted to leave port."

"Till when?" Father wore his shiny land boots again. Either he'd been too frazzled to notice, or he hadn't yet removed them from yesterday.

"Maybe a day, maybe a week. My men are already on their way here. As with the other ships at port, we will conduct an inspection of your cargo and issue a certificate of clearance, but it won't be valid until the decree is lifted."

"And if we leave anyway?"

The man's eyes narrowed. "You will be considered a personal enemy of the king with a bounty on your head."

My father grunted, skimming over the orders in his hand. "What are they looking for? We run an honest trade on this ship."

"I'm not at liberty to say. Now, if you could gather your crew on deck, my team will arrive at any moment. We'll search the ship and interview the men one by one." The man examined the figures on deck, most of whom had emerged from the stairs out of curiosity more than a desire to help. He looked right past me.

I allowed myself a deep, relieved breath. Definitely Aden, then. Even if none of the other men had noticed Aden's presence, Dennis could provide an all-too-accurate description from my hurried introduction earlier. I couldn't give him the chance.

Father handed the parchment back. "I suppose we don't have much choice. Let me find you a seat. This will only take a moment."

"I'll stand, thank you. Just gather your crew and stay out of the way."

"Of course. As I said, we're loyal to the crown with nothing to—" Father choked as he caught my gaze. "Nothing to hide," he finished in a rush. Then he leveled his shoulders and strode toward me.

"He already saw me and didn't react at all," I whispered as he arrived. "That's not why he's here."

"Perhaps, perhaps not, and I'd rather not find out. That copper load, Lane. Did Dennis check the barrels before they were sealed?"

The guilt was a physical weight on my chest, but there was no alternative but to protect Aden yet again. I couldn't very well tell the truth now. Besides, I'd made a bargain. Captains often employed unusual solutions to difficult problems, so this was my first opportunity to act like one.

"Lane," my father said. "The load?"

My throat felt coated in mud, but my voice held. "They were filled with copper shavings, sure as anything. Checked them myself. Even swept a cudgel around inside to make sure nothing was hidden, just like you taught me."

"It's as I suspected, then. Someone doesn't want us to leave."

I paused, fighting back another surge of guilt. "Belza."

"That's my guess. Hughen inspectors have never accepted bribes before. I don't understand how this could happen."

No man was above bribery, but my father was too stubbornly attached to his country to admit it. Regardless, this was the perfect distraction. I adjusted my vest and gave Father a meaningful look. "Would you like me to call all hands *to the deck*, Captain?"

He pursed his lips. He'd caught my meaning. Father didn't want me in sight at all, much less involved. But staying would mean danger for all of us sooner or later. "Aye," he finally said. I didn't miss the warning in his gaze. *Be careful.*

I trotted to the bell and gave it three distinct taps followed by a longer one. It called all hands, but not to line up on deck. *Unfurl the sails*, the rhythm said. *Hurry aloft.*

And hurry they did. The inspector watched, bewildered, as the men charged up from belowdecks and leaped onto the ratlines. It would take them about four minutes to position themselves, then another five to get the canvas lowered and secured. Meanwhile, Father and I had to take care of the inspector before his team arrived.

I turned back to Girard, fixing an I'm-just-a-helpless-child expression on my face. It was a lesson I'd learned many times. Any mistake could be blamed on a captain's boy, warranted or not.

The inspector's face had turned a deep red. "Foolish boy! That wasn't my order." He whirled, his hand lifted to strike me.

Father barreled into the man, wrapping his arms around the inspector's waist like a determined wrestler. Girard sputtered as he stumbled backward, striking the rail as my father released him. The inspector flipped right over it with a yelp. The heavy splash came almost immediately.

I covered a gasp. A distinct curse shot from the crow's nest above. Some of the men had stopped climbing to gape. My father, the distinguished merchant captain, had waylaid one of the king's highest officials.

"Don't touch my son," Father snapped.

My mind moved slowly, refusing to process what I'd just seen. A few stragglers stood on the docks, watching the sputtering man in the water. They looked at one another. The shortest of the witnesses took off running for town. He'd gain a few coppers for his testimony, more than he'd earn loading cargo all morning.

Father, breathing hard, glared at the man in the water. When he finally turned, the movement was heavy and slow. "Lane, remove the dock line and tell the men to hurry."

I'd made him an outlaw. The man who'd once sung the Hughen royal anthem as a lullaby and spun golden tales of his homeland had just turned on his own people.

"May you...rot in prison...Garrow!" the inspector shrieked, still splashing about. I couldn't decide whether to be relieved or concerned that the man could swim. At least he wouldn't be climbing out of the harbor anytime soon. The nearest rope ladder was a twenty-minute swim away.

Dennis stumbled up from below, hair smashed like he'd been sleeping. "Stop standing about. We'd best get the ship free."

He pulled the gangway in himself while I loosened the fore line, then the aft. A shout sounded from above and a rush of wind tossed my hair aside. The sheets were down and would soon be secured.

I checked the tide. *Come on, winds. Bring us out.*

The men began to climb down, eyeing the inspector in the water with confusion. Dennis and I shared a concerned look. My father only had eyes for the sails. They hung there, empty and silent.

Then I heard it—dozens of hooves hitting cobblestone at a

furious pace. The inspection team had arrived. I squinted at the group, counting heads. Then I cursed. That was no inspection team. The witness hadn't gone to give testimony—he'd run to fetch the king's guards. An entire contingent galloped toward us now.

At their head was the high advisor himself, Lord Varnen.

Girard noticed Varnen at the same moment I did and began his shrieking again. Some of the crew lined the rail, looking uncomfortable as they awaited their next order.

"Well, well," Varnen called as he arrived and swung down from his gray stallion. "Attacking my head inspector, Garrow? I wouldn't have expected that even from you."

A crowd had begun to gather now, but I barely noticed as I stared at my father, suddenly seeing a stranger. What did Varnen mean by that? Could they possibly know each other?

My father's strong hands wrung the rail, his knuckles white. "Naught but a misunderstanding," he called back.

"Interesting." Varnen stood at the edge of the docks, close enough that I noted the thickness of his chin and a nose sharp as a rapier. The man who had casually executed an innocent woman just yesterday looked amused now. "Gangway stowed, sails released and being tied down. Is that a misunderstanding as well?"

"There has been some confusion. I assure you, my ship aligns itself completely with the king's will and law." Father leaned over, and I realized his next words were intended for me. "Get us away from this dock."

My mind whirling, I bolted for the bell. Two long rings, two short. The men responded and ran for the boats, although several hung back, watching the king's advisor uncertainly. I couldn't blame them. Those who stood against Varnen stood against the king.

"That's where the confusion lies, then, Captain. In the name of His Glorious King Eurion, no ship may leave until cleared. Call your crew back or risk being sunk here and now."

"Hughen law prohibits attacking a ship at port unless directly fired upon."

Varnen belted out a laugh. "The law serves me, not the other way around. You really think I'd let you sail away, just like that?"

"We've nothing to hide, Advisor. But then, you know that, don't you? I wonder what His Glorious King Eurion would say if he knew you'd aligned yourself with a pirate?"

An uneasy buzz shot through my body as chatter rose from the crowd of workers, several tracing shields on their chests to ward off Elena's spirit. Varnen's expression went so dark, I almost expected him to make an inhuman leap over two rails to strangle my father. Dennis had already positioned himself at one pulley, so I grabbed the other and began to turn the handle, avoiding his eyes. The first boat slowly lowered as the last man secured the anchor line. It descended in a jerky pattern before hitting the water.

"You're a foolish man, Garrow," Varnen said. Then he turned. "Bring the cannon."

I released a torrent of curses under my breath.

Father's face had drained of color, but his jaw was rigid. "The docks are full today. Surely you don't intend to risk lives over this."

"I fulfill my king's command." He nodded to his men, who began their preparations.

If we'd been hurrying before, now the men *moved*. The first boat was already away, the men throwing themselves into the oars. I recognized a couple of its occupants as Kemp's recruits. At least they were quick to help.

Hughen hadn't used its port cannon since the battle that gained it independence from Messau. It took ten guards to haul the cannon into position. By its length, it was meant for distance and power. My chest hurt at the sight of it. Varnen couldn't possibly want the son of a lord this badly. It had to be a bluff.

Or perhaps there was more going on here than I knew.

Dennis took his place at the helm now, absently rubbing the scar on his forehead, a stark white against his tanned skin. He wouldn't tell me where he'd gotten it, but Paval said it had something to do with pirates. "We won't be away for another ten minutes, Captain," Dennis said. "That cannon'll blow us to splinters by then. Maybe the docks as well."

Father nodded solemnly.

"Shall we order the men to stations?" the first officer pressed.

Father glanced at me. With a sinking stomach, I realized he couldn't back down now. Varnen would conduct an inspection so thorough, they were sure to discover me. "Nay. We'll follow this through."

Lands. What had I done?

"Men of the *Majesty*," Varnen shouted through cupped hands as his men positioned themselves behind the cannon. "If you abandon ship now, your lives will be spared and you'll be well compensated for your loyalty. You have ten seconds to comply."

A splash sounded in the harbor. Then a second, third. Fourth. The rest of the crew groaned but continued their work. One of the men at the anchor line pulley hesitated, eyeing the docks. The man beside him clapped him on the back. I could imagine the words being exchanged. *Captain will reward us handsomely. Keep to your work.*

I understood it now—Father's insistence on returning most of his wages to the crew. It was about loyalty. When trust couldn't be earned, it could sometimes be bought.

A *boom* exploded from the docks.

I flinched.

The ball smashed into the bow, beheading its naked wooden goddess.

There were shouts as the responsible party received a verbal lashing from Varnen. I let myself breathe once more, but we wouldn't get that lucky again.

A jerk, then a steady yank. The distant sound of cheering from the rowboats floated across the water.

We were moving.

The high advisor looked absolutely livid. There wasn't time to reload for another shot. "Guards, line up along the rail!"

A sudden jolt of fear held me in place as a dozen soldiers scrambled to obey, their muskets at the ready. Most of the crowd had cleared now, though it looked as if mayhem had unleashed itself on the docks. Entire crates were left abandoned in the road, some smashed, their contents covering the ground. Feathers floated in the air. A man lay on the ground, covering his ears and writhing as if in pain. He hadn't been able to escape the vicinity of the cannon in time.

I shot a withering look at the nest above. Lord or not, when this was all over, I'd lay into Aden until he wished for the safety of Varnen's clutches.

"Take cover!" Father shouted, yanking me into the cabin just in time. Dennis was only a hair's width behind.

"Now!" Varnen shouted.

This time, the explosion lasted a full five seconds. Pieces of the rail blasted clean off, balls whistling past the open door faster than I could see. There were no screams from injured men, no *thumps* of bodies hitting the ground. I hoped Barrie was safe belowdecks with what few crew members weren't in the rowboats.

"Reload!"

We'd cleared the docks now. Finally, the *Majesty* was moving on her own, headed for the bay. I caught the acidic scent of cannon smoke on the wind. *Just get us to the bay, and all will be right.* It had to be true.

The canvas around us expanded and snapped like giant pillows filling with glorious sea wind. Varnen and the docks began to shrink behind us at last. There was another volley of balls, none of which reached us, and a second explosion from the cannon. I nearly collapsed with relief as it landed with a splash in the harbor, falling short. Varnen's tiny figure flailed about, launching a tirade at anyone who stepped too close. Dennis clapped Father on the back with hearty congratulations.

But as the men cheered and began rowing back to the ship, an instinct I had learned to trust whispered that this battle was long from over.

It had just begun.

9

That evening, I slapped a wet rag into a pot and began scrubbing away the remnants of burned coffee. The pot was deep and my elbow kept knocking the side, sending pain jolting down my arm. Dennis's watch was just finishing their meal. I'd consumed mine quickly so I could help Paval clean up, telling myself it had nothing to do with the lordling still waiting in the nest. The one I didn't dare confront yet. Until I could trust myself not to wring his high-and-mighty throat, better to wait here and pretend everything was normal.

Except very little was normal today, and the men knew it. Dinner had been a tense combination of boasting about our port victory and sullen scowling at what might come next. The Hughen sailors sat staring at their tankards as if wishing their coffee would rise up and drown them. Their future was the least certain now that they'd rejected Varnen's offer of clemency. Our entire crew would be banned now, Hughen or not. They'd been cut off from their families in a single afternoon. All because of that stupid boy in the nest who couldn't button his own shirt.

I wrung out the rag and turned the pot to reach the other side.

My nerves felt tied in a series of bowline knots. The events of this afternoon could have gone so very differently. Men dying, the ship sinking. Father's body hanging from the gallows right alongside mine. I stoked the anger inside once again, but it felt hollow. It was easier to be angry at Aden than face my own part in all this. I'd risked everything for a bag of gold and a stranger. When Father discovered that that battle had been my fault...The guilt gripped my stomach tighter.

Maybe I didn't deserve to be captain of the *Majesty* after all.

Aden entered the room. There was only a flash of irritation as his eyes caught mine, but it fled quickly as he took in the remaining men. Most of his countrymen rose to leave, speaking to one another in soft tones. To my surprise, they barely gave him a glance. Aden didn't join them either. Instead, he grabbed a rag from my pile, headed for a table, and began to scrub it as Marley and Ross chatted over their empty bowls.

"Never thought I'd see the like," Marley said with a wide smile. "Captain standing there, daring the king's lackey to fire that giant gun."

"It's only funny because they missed," Ross muttered.

"Missed?" I snorted. "I suspect the goddess would think otherwise. If she still had her head, that is."

The men laughed, though Ross's scowl only deepened. The truth was, I owed Ross and every other member of the crew an apology. It was bad enough that Varnen had risked all our lives today. But hadn't Father done the same? He'd stood his ground to protect us both, no matter the cost. It was a side of him I'd never seen before and I still didn't quite understand why that was.

Was it possible that he'd made enemies of both Varnen *and* Belza? Varnen had never been a pirate, but he'd had suspicious dealings with them long ago. It was the reason he'd been positioned to betray Elena. And then there was Belza. How could one merchant ship captain stand against pirates *and* kings? What would such a stand cost us in the end?

I had to convince Father to tell me. I would go mad until I knew the truth.

Aden wiped a bit of food into a pile with his rag and looked around the room, as if unsure how to dispose of it. He finally swept the scraps into his hand and shoved them into his pocket. A chuckle rose within before I could stop it.

Marley downed what remained of his tankard and stood to leave. His bony elbow struck Barrie, who had just lifted a bowl to his lips. He looked down at his shirt and groaned.

Marley ignored the boy. "Oh, Lane! Heard you and Captain nearly lost your heads to musket fire while we were out in the boats. Wish I could've seen that."

I shrugged to downplay it, though a surge of excitement rose within me. Today's battle was the most adventure I'd seen since a pirate attack when I was eleven.

"You're mad," Ross said. "I saw the whole thing and it was terrifying."

Marley's grin only widened. "All the better. A man needs some entertainment now and again."

"Just wait till someone comes at you with a musket," Ross said. "You won't find it so entertaining then." He gave me an apologetic look. "Glad you're all right, Lane."

"It wasn't so frightening," I lied.

"I missed the entire thing," Barrie moaned, scrubbing at his shirt.

"Luck was with us all today, and that's what matters," Paval said, entering as Ross and Marley left. He limped to the stove in three massive strides. His long black hair hung free and straight as usual, though his shirt was tidy and tucked into his trousers. His shirtsleeves were rolled back, stark white against his deep brown skin. But it was his size most people noticed first. He had the frame of a warrior—thick arms, broad shoulders, a chest most men would kill for. He seemed to fill half the galley by himself, his head practically scraping the low ceiling.

Most found Paval an odd sight for a cook. Indeed, Aden stared as the man lifted the pot lid and sniffed the hot vapors rising from beneath. With a quick tug, Paval plucked a hair from his head and dropped it into the food. Then he gave it a long stir. Aden flinched.

I hid a smile. "You'll go bald soon if you keep doing that, Paval."

"Been doing it a long time," the large man boomed, "and I still got plenty up top. Besides, can't think of a better way to use the stuff than giving health to my friends."

One of the stranger KaBann beliefs, and definitely my favorite. "You know what the men think of that."

"Isn't a man on this ship who's died from illness since I took over the cooking. They can say what they like."

"And what of the lucky recipient?" Aden asked. "Does it mean something to get your little present?"

"It means you're my friend. Nothing less." He eyed the dirty water dripping from Aden's rag with amusement. "I'm Paval. Welcome."

"Aden, and thank you. You're a long way from home. KaBann?"

"Proud of it," Paval said with a pleased grin. "And by the accent, you're Hughen clean through and well educated."

Aden sent me a sheepish look. Blasted accent.

"Not many Hughen recruits this time," Barrie said through a mouthful of stew. "Most of them were Messauns. Can't be figuring why they stayed during the battle. Seems strange to me."

I'd forgotten Barrie was there. "Desperate for work, probably. I'm just glad you made it back to the ship before we left."

"Just wish we weren't missing a third of the crew," Barrie replied.

"Don't blame yourself for that," I said. Ten men hadn't returned to the ship and another four had jumped overboard at Varnen's offer. That meant we were shorter than we'd ever been. Dennis would be adjusting our schedules right now. As always, it would mean more work and less sleep—but at least we weren't rotting in the king's dungeons. Or worse.

Three bells sounded as Kemp's watch ended. Any moment now, two dozen men would arrive for their meal. Would any of them recognize Aden? Or would they look past him like the other Hughens had?

Barrie swallowed what remained of his bowl's contents in one massive gulp—his third helping, if I'd counted correctly—and rose. "Captain be having a meeting with the officers about what sparked the battle today. What do you think the reason be, Lane? Belza or the missing prince?"

Aden went still.

I choked and turned it into a cough. "Missing prince?"

"Aye. A soldier told me it's why they be searching ships. I don't think they meant to find that lady who got killed, but they sure seemed happy they did." He shrugged.

Prince. Son of the king.

Aden.

It had to be. Even now, Aden ducked his head and scrubbed the already-clean table with unusual vigor.

King Eurion's own son stood right in front of me—and he knew my secret.

10

That familiar tightening sensation returned, cutting off my air supply. I had an overwhelming urge to sprint for the stairs and let the cool sea air calm my galloping heart. But before I could, there was a heavy pounding on the steps, and Kemp appeared.

His favorite lackey, Digby, and the twelve new recruits filed in right behind him. They looked almost smug. Kemp took his usual place at the first table's head, his long legs sharply bent. His eyes swept around the room, missing nothing. I swallowed my panic and met his unflinching glare with one of my own, though it was surely unsteady.

Digby approached Paval with his and Kemp's mess bowls. The others lined up behind him. As second officer and gun master, Kempton always got his food first. And as Kemp's loyal pup, Digby got his second. My father and Dennis invited Kemp to take his meals with them in the captain's cabin. He always declined. He wanted the crew to see him in power, dominating the conversation as well as the watch he led.

Kemp swung his glare to Aden. "You look familiar. Who are you?"

My breath stilled.

Aden visibly tensed, but he recovered quickly. "New recruit. Not very experienced yet, I'm afraid. Lane's been kind enough to show me around."

"Lane barely knows the first thing." Kemp's mouth turned upward, but it wasn't a smile. "Ye'll join my watch. We'll have you seasoned as a man with five years before we reach Ellegran."

I squeezed the rag so tightly that filthy dishwater dripped onto my trousers. Kemp picked favorites, but they were usually Messauns with their stocky builds and foul manners. He'd seen something in Aden. *Likely the arrogance.*

Aden's reply was smooth. "Thank you, sir, but Dennis has already assigned me a place."

Kemp's jaw tightened, and the entire room went tense. Nobody turned Kemp down, especially an offer so rarely given. "You'd best learn fast and not slow us down. Even Lane occasionally has important duties."

"Of course."

"Ye'll call me *sir*."

"Yes, sir. Wouldn't dream of getting in the way."

"Wouldn't *dream* of it?" Digby barked a laugh, his spectacles slipping on his nose. "This here's a chicken lover, sure. Listen to him talk all formal."

"He'll be squirming tonight when Paval sets some broth in front of him," Kemp muttered, and they chuckled. The two were like schoolboys sometimes. Deadly ones. Kemp carried no less than two pistols on him—his right as an officer—and I knew Digby had a knife in his pocket. I gripped the half-cleaned pot in my lap, every muscle tense.

Aden's expression was unreadable. My father said it was unfair to tease a man for his beliefs, especially one who worked below you. Kemp and Digby didn't dare harass Paval and his KaBann beliefs, so they turned their disdain on Hughen sailors instead. The others were used to it. But Aden...still as he was, his shoulders were rigid. Defiant. Proud. A prince. Now that I knew, I couldn't believe the others didn't see it. It wouldn't be long before someone made the connection.

Unfortunately, Aden's silence only emboldened Digby. "Take young Barrie over there. He cried the first time he saw Paval snap a turkey's neck. Sobbed for half an hour. He turned right quick, though. Now he'd eat one whole if we let him." He chuckled. "They all come to their senses eventually."

Barrie flinched. The other Hughens in line scowled, but they didn't speak up. They knew the teasing would end. It always did.

Paval began tipping stew into Kemp's bowl. "Heard you met with the captain, Master Kempton." His voice was casual. I wanted to hug him for the change of subject.

"Aye," Kemp began. "Cap'n says the incident at the port this morning was for our good. Says the inspector warned him of disease, and we were restricted to the port till it passed. Since we had no signs of illness, he took it upon himself to get his men safely away."

It was quiet as the crew considered this explanation. Two of the men exchanged frowns. I wanted to groan. Father's lie didn't explain why Varnen had shouted offers of clemency to the crew as we pulled away, and it didn't address the rumors of Belza that the men had surely heard by now. And pretending to have done it for his men's sake...It felt like a blow to the gut.

Between the two of us, deception came far more easily to me. What was my life here but one massive lie? Nay, my father was the good one, the example. A man everyone trusted. I was the stain nobody saw.

But this...It was an absolute, unquestioning lie. A big one. My stomach twisted.

I could only hope that none of the crew had heard the missing-prince rumor. I resolved to ask Barrie to keep it a secret. In the meantime, I had some serious work to do. Aden stood too tall in Kemp's presence, almost oddly calm.

"Captain also said he's sending a missive of apology back to Hughen once we reach Ellegran," Kemp said. "He thinks to pardon us for his wrong."

"Do you believe it, sir?" Digby asked, holding Kemp's bowl firmly as Paval dumped a second spoonful of stew into it.

"Believe it?" Kemp boomed. "Ain't for me to say what's true. All I know is what I seen, and Captain's been acting strange. Tossin' that inspector overboard and defying Varnen, right there in front of everyone. And then he takes cannon fire without letting us return nothing. We had eight guns to their one, yet we sat there like kittens in a bag."

"A mite secretive too," Digby said, switching bowls. "Landing us for eight days' leave and then pulling us out after one, and so quiet about our cargo. Something isn't right."

The men's eyes slid to the ground in discomfort. Barrie took a sudden interest in his shirtsleeve, tugging at an invisible loose thread. Kemp's eyes flicked to me, then his voice lowered as if sharing a secret. "Makes you wonder what else Garrow's hiding."

The pot began to slip from my hands. I caught it just in time. The rag, however, lay in a puddle on the floor, utterly forgotten. If the room had been quiet before, now it was silent. The second officer had just slandered the captain. Blood rushed to my head, pounding in my ears as I glared at Kemp once more. His previous digs at my father had been jokes, small jibes that the men laughed away. But this wasn't something that could be dismissed.

If anyone else had said it, I would have defended my father and reported the gossip to him. But Kemp knew I could sooner swim the entire ocean than challenge him.

"It's fortunate that you boarded when you did, Master Kempton," Paval said coolly. "We nearly left without you and your new friends."

"Captain sent for more recruits. Many of the others refused to stay. Can't imagine why." He belted out another laugh, and the others reluctantly took it up. A few stared at their hands.

"Interesting that you recruited Messauns," Paval said. "Must've taken a lot of work to find experienced seamen from your own country residing in Hughen. Suppose that's why you were so late."

"The work wasn't in finding them, cook. It was convincing them to sail under the command of a coward."

I nearly choked. The room held its breath, like the moment between lightning and its resounding thunder.

Aden slammed his rag to the ground. "I'll not be standing by while you say such things, Gun Master. Take it back at once, or the captain will hear of your treachery."

I groaned inwardly.

There wasn't a sound in the room. Every eye was fixed on Kemp, who had gone too still. Then he unfolded his massive arms and stood, towering over Aden. A pinch of color formed in the large man's cheeks, just above his newly trimmed beard. Aden didn't flinch.

Paval paused before filling Digby's bowl, then turned slowly around, letting the contents of his wooden spoon drip on the floor. That said plenty about his state—he hated messes. "The boy's right.

We've endured your insults long enough. Tell your watch how much you respect the captain, or your stomachs will go empty tonight."

Kemp's voice was low and dangerous. "Talking ain't no threat to the captain. Nothin' in ship's law against a man's opinion."

"It's my galley. You'll take back your words or you'll regret you ever uttered them."

It was so quiet, I could hear the scuttling of roaches in the shadows. Seventeen pairs of eyes were on the second officer, who watched Paval with an expression that could cut steel. Digby gripped the two bowls, glancing between the men with his crooked spectacles. Barrie frowned.

It seemed like hours before Kemp finally spoke. "I recall any of my words proven to be untrue."

That wasn't an apology, but it was far more than I'd expected. Paval nodded and turned to Digby. "What have you to say?"

Digby chose his words carefully, eyeing Kemp. "I believe the captain is generally of sound reasoning."

Paval nodded. "No more nonsense. Nobody's more motivated to keep ship and crew safe than Captain Garrow. Give me that." He tore the second bowl from Digby, scooped some stew messily into it, and shoved it at Digby's chest. The Messaun barely caught it and glared back, his face scarlet.

Kemp simply watched Aden with narrowed eyes. I winced at the darkness that lay behind them. I'd seen that expression before.

"Come, new recruit. Our watch has already started." I grabbed Aden's shirt and yanked him after me as I stalked toward the stairs.

"You'd best tie up that mutt of yours, Lane," Kemp called as we passed. "I don't take well to unfounded accusations. They make me twice as angry."

I flinched and hurried away.

It wasn't until we'd reached the hold, dark and smelling of mold and rotting wood, that I released Aden. He tore away and smoothed his shirt as I whirled on him. "You lied to me."

His grin was tight. "What, no knife this time?"

"You're a prince. You didn't think that was important for me to know before I agreed to your little deal?"

"No, I didn't. You want to know why?" He took a step closer. "Because it doesn't matter whether I'm the son of a king or a servant or anyone else. I've paid for my right to be here."

"I thought you were a lord and charged you accordingly. You have no idea what you've done. If the king finds out—"

"You don't need to worry about that."

"Don't need to worry?" My tone was incredulous. "Do you realize what this looks like? They'll assume we kidnapped you. At best, we disregarded the king's order and aided your escape. Even if King Eurion doesn't sentence us all to the gallows, you've tarnished my father's reputation with his clients forever. We'll never be welcome in Hughen waters again, let alone to conduct business in port."

"You have to admit that he might have done that on his own," Aden said. "The whole Belza thing doesn't look good for him."

My mouth actually dropped. Of all the arrogant things to say. "Give me one reason I shouldn't march you up to my father right now."

He hesitated, looking torn. For a second, I thought I'd won, then he shook his head. "It's obvious you've worked hard to build trust with the crew. Your disguise is working, or at least they're willing to pretend along with you. But we made a bargain. You reveal my secret to the crew, and I reveal yours."

I watched him for a long moment. He met my gaze with a firm glare of his own. He wasn't lying.

I slumped against a crate, defeated. "You're lucky I don't have my knife."

He chuckled, then let his smile fade. "Look, I know I've made things harder for you. I'll make everything right eventually."

I snickered. Was it so simple for royalty to solve their problems? He had given me five hundred pieces with barely a thought. Aye, it was exactly that simple. "You'll make everything right this instant. You're going to tell me everything, starting with your purpose here. The truth."

I'd expected him to laugh and dismiss me yet again, but instead he sighed. "I know it's hard to trust me after what happened today. If it helps, I'm here for my family's sake."

"That's it?"

"It's all I dare say, yes."

"But your family doesn't know where you are."

"Not exactly, no."

I opened my mouth to retort, but he continued. "Look, you won't understand, and that's fine. But I'll do whatever it takes to protect them. I'm sure you feel the same about yours."

I should have been irritated at his implication. His willingness to do *anything* to protect his family meant risking a ship and crew he barely knew, and that didn't even touch on the risk I was taking. But all I could think about was the way Father had stood up to the inspector today. Maybe he and the prince weren't so different.

I halted that thought in its tracks. Father and Aden were as different as two men could possibly be.

"And if they send the Hughen navy to fetch you?" I asked.

"They won't."

"Oh? Did you have a chat with Varnen that I don't know about?"

Aden scowled. "He's dangerous, but he won't send any ships after us. He can't. Not without the king's order."

"And if the king orders it? He isn't likely to sit by and allow you to sail away."

"Trust me. He won't send any ships." There was an odd note to his voice. I'd hit a nerve.

I tucked the information away for later. "You speak of protecting family. Well, these men are mine. I won't have you risking their lives again. If it comes down to you or them, I'll choose them."

"Fair enough." He took another step closer. "Now it's my turn for questions. Tell me why I'm the one who defended your father against Kemp today while you just stood there."

Suddenly aware of how close we were in the dim light, I took a step back. "We aren't discussing me. Just ignore what Kemp says and keep your head down like we agreed. Remember how the crew isn't supposed to notice you?"

He was shaking his head again. "Blending in is one thing. But I refuse to cower to a Messaun who threatens the safety of a Hughen ship."

I groaned. "This is some kind of twisted political game to you."

"That man is dangerous."

Aden had no idea. "Kemp wasn't a threat to you until you challenged him. *Lands.* I can't believe you did that. And you both sleep in the crew's quarters. This isn't good."

His expression was incredulous. "It's not me I'm worried about. Don't you see what he's doing, telling secrets and starting rumors? I've seen it in court many times. Master Kempton is planting dissent. If you don't do something, those seeds will grow into mutiny."

His words were too familiar. They echoed those that ran through my head late at night, when the ship was quiet and my mental defenses had all but sunk into slumber.

"Let me worry about Kemp," I said firmly. "Focus on your own neck. If your secret is so precious, that should be enough to keep you busy. In the future, you will keep your mouth shut."

"Seems odd coming from you. You had no problem speaking your mind yesterday when you sent my boots to a watery grave."

I stabbed him in the chest with one finger. "I'll say what I like. But you're on your own if you go all princey on Kemp again. You don't want to bring his attention upon yourself."

Aden brushed my finger aside, watching me. I realized my hand was shaking, so I folded my arms firmly against my chest. Surely it was too dark for him to detect such things.

"There's something you aren't telling me," he said softly. Too softly. "Does he know about you?"

Blasted princeling. I kept my face smooth. Aden might have known who I truly was, but that didn't mean I had to reveal everything. Nobody but Kemp knew about the invisible chain binding my hands. I hadn't even told Paval, much less Father. The fact that Aden was the first to acknowledge its presence made me want to strangle him with it.

Aden had missed the point. Kemp was threatening, domineering at times, but he was also calculating. While the rest of the crew collected trinkets from ports we'd visited, Kemp collected secrets. And finally, just last year, he'd discovered mine.

I'd left my hammock in the crew's quarters one night and descended to this very hold, intending to wash myself while the men slept. The sloshing water bucket had covered the creaking of following footsteps on the ladder.

I'd washed myself quickly, leaving my bindings on. Satisfied, I dressed and gathered the lantern and bucket. That was when Kemp emerged from the shadows.

He hadn't touched me. At least, not with his hands. He'd sworn to keep my secret, but his eyes had betrayed something else. It wasn't until later that I realized his silence could only be bought with my own—and my entire salary of four silver pieces each month. It had later become six, then ten. By his *twice as angry* comment in the galley, I knew it had just doubled to twenty. My nerves were on edge.

I'd moved into my father's cabin the next day. Father hadn't required an explanation and I had given none.

Since then, I'd watched with gritted teeth as Kemp tore his enemies down from the inside, manipulating and blackmailing them until they transferred to other ships. One man, a particularly defiant Ellegran who'd dared threaten the gun master in a moment of rage, had disappeared during a storm.

Father blamed his loss on a large wave. The crew knew better.

Kemp's favorite currency was lies and his greatest weapon truth. If I told Father, Kemp would reveal my secret to the entire crew before turning us both over to the land officials—me for my lies and my father for protecting me. We'd both hang. I had no doubt that Kemp would take the ship after that.

Twenty silver pieces. A fortune for a captain's boy, yet I couldn't risk breaking our bargain. I shoved my hands into my empty pockets, wishing I could forget the first time I stole to meet my quota. It was a silver piece from Marley's discarded trousers as he slept. The guilt had kept me up the rest of that night. I'd chosen targets I didn't like much after that, though they were less trusting with their treasures. I'd never once rifled through Barrie's or Paval's belongings. They were off-limits. But now—twenty pieces. *Lands.* How was I supposed to meet that on a salary of four silver pieces a month?

There was only one solution: the chest under Father's bed, full of Aden's coins.

The thought made my stomach flop. I'd done plenty of things I wasn't proud of, but I would not steal from my father. Never that.

"Lane," Aden whispered. "You look pale. What's going on?"

I straightened, gathering what remained of my dignity. "Nothing you would understand."

"Oh?" A bitter chuckle. "Because I'm too lofty to have real problems, I suppose."

Because yours are solved with money. Mine worsened with each payment. My pride shriveled a bit each time I stole for that horrid man. Aden was right. Kemp was dangerous, and he obviously wanted to command the *Majesty*. But he hadn't made his move yet, which meant I had time to figure this out. I couldn't allow Aden to make himself a pawn. Not when my secret relied so heavily on his. If Aden fell, I'd fall with him.

"Kemp may seem like a simple Messaun soldier," I said, "but if you need to avoid anyone on this ship, it's the gun master. We're done here. Go help Paval in the galley. I'll ask Dennis to put you on lookout during tonight's watch, and then I'll see you on deck after morning watch, eight bells. Don't be late." I pushed off the crate and headed for the ladder.

"Late for what?"

Now it was my turn to grin. "Training. Time for you to become a sailor."

I woke with the sun. Like always, the first thing I saw was light stream-ing through the stained-glass window of the cabin door. It filtered into six different colors as it entered, grounding into colorful dust before ending abruptly at the deck. Funny how simple glass could alter light so dramatically, both igniting and destroying it at once.

Then I remembered. Ellegran. *Aden.* I wanted to pull the blanket over my head, but I was wide awake now.

The overstretched canvas of my hammock creaked as I swung my legs over. Thankfully, Father's snoring continued. The sheet sep-arating our living areas rippled quietly while I dressed. He'd offered once to build a proper wall, but the crew would wonder about that. They already thought it strange that I was here and not belowdecks with the others.

I pulled the sheet down and wrapped it around my arm, then stuffed it into the chest beneath my hammock, right on top of the coppers I'd stolen from Dryam's boots last night. As I reached in, my fingers brushed against my father's comb. I hadn't touched it in weeks. He'd carried it with him the day I was dumped off on him. Probably intended to give it to Nara.

Now it was decisively, unequivocally mine.

My hand hovered for a moment, then I closed my fingers around it and lifted it to the dim light. It was a cool metal, the spine full of sparkling, star-shaped jewels. A tiny inscription along the edge read *That We May Live Long Together.* The teeth were smooth and tapered to a point. Its maker had designed it for a lady with soft, long hair. It was completely impractical for someone like me. Ridiculous, really. But it was all I had.

I began running it through my messy brown hair. It caught before releasing the strand, pulling it straight. The next combful of hair was tougher. I had to start at the bottom and work my way up. It took several minutes of painful tugging to reach the point where I could comb my fingers through it unimpeded. My hair hung straight, though a bit greasy already. If only I'd had a proper bath in Hughen. Some ports even offered hair soaps made from flowers. I never used them, of course. Lye soap was far more practical.

I thought of the women I'd seen in the street, their skirts carefully pressed and hanging exactly right against their figures. The intricate braids winding about their heads must have taken several meticulous hours to create.

Father had only called Mum a lady, so I didn't know the specifics of her wealth. But that was how I imagined her—spending hours dressing each morning, ordering servants about, snapping at beggars in the street. Why Father would fall for such a woman, I couldn't say. But he had, and here I was.

She'd rejected all three of us, the family we could have been. If she hadn't, I'd look just like those ladies on the street instead of an oily-haired sailor in a soiled shirt and trousers that pulled tight in all the wrong places.

Everything about my life was wrong. A sea captain, a proper

lady, and a daughter dressed as a boy. Ours was a family fashioned as a joke.

I pulled my hair back into its tail like always, then tossed the comb into the box, wincing at the loud clattering that followed. Then I wrapped the axe scabbards around my waist and fastened the belt. I hadn't been able to practice since Aden's arrival, and my hands itched for a training session.

Before I closed the lid, I felt around for the bundle near the bottom. There, inside an old sock, was a pile of Aden's seashell buttons and the few gold coins I'd taken for myself. I counted them again. Kemp's next payment was due in just over a week. I didn't have half that. If I managed to stall Kemp, and Father sent me away, perhaps I could use the money to buy passage elsewhere. Maybe KaBann, the one place I'd never been. Paval said they appreciated women there, that they sailed with men as equals. The thought should have ignited excitement, but today there was only disappointment. Leaving my father would mean leaving behind the only family I had. It would make me like *her*.

"Send for my breakfast, Lane," Father croaked from across the room.

He lay in his berth, staring at the plank ceiling. The sound of heavy footsteps on the quarterdeck meant Kemp still had the watch. Dennis's turn would begin soon, as would my duties with Aden.

"Aye, sir." I secured the box's lid and slid my boots on.

"Oh, one more thing." He sat up now, rubbing his stubble thoughtfully. "That new boy. He approached me in Hughen, asking for passage to Ellegran. Did Dennis recruit him?"

"Aye," I said, keeping my tone casual. "We were short men, so Dennis forgave his inexperience."

"What did he call himself?"

"Aden. He didn't give a family name."

He frowned. "Hmm."

I hurried to change the subject. "Any sign of Hughen ships in pursuit?"

"Nay. Even Belza's gold wouldn't extend that far."

He still believed yesterday's events were the pirate's doing, then. I recalled his explanation to the officers yesterday and grimaced. The longer I waited to tell him about Aden, the worse his reaction would be. Especially now that the prince had made himself Kemp's latest target.

I wanted so badly to tell my father everything. But Aden's secret was hopelessly intertwined with mine now, and Kemp was a secret within a secret, clamped down and locked so deep I barely dared think it, let alone admit its truth aloud. It all felt like a storm gathering overhead—of which my father was completely oblivious.

"Don't worry yourself about pirates either," my father said, misinterpreting my silence. "Even if Belza's men did bribe the inspectors to detain us until his arrival, I didn't register Ellegran as our destination with the port officials. Nobody knows where we're headed. He'll wander the seas for weeks."

"Well done, sir." I forced a grin.

His smile looked just as strained. "Go on, then. You know my head won't clear till I've had my drink."

I hesitated. "We won't be returning to Hughen anytime soon, will we?"

He sighed. "Nay. And we'll have to be careful at all the other ports. Belza once had spies everywhere. I have to assume he'll do the same now."

"Wouldn't it be safer for us to go south, then? Visit KaBann and the southern nations? Just for a year or two, until the danger calms."

"Perhaps."

Hope replaced the worry inside. He hadn't mentioned leaving me in Ellegran. If there was the tiniest shred of doubt on his part, I'd have to cling to that. "Will you tell me how you know Captain Belza?"

The wall slammed down once again. "Not now. There's work to be done."

"Then tell me why you lied to the crew. It wasn't all about me, and you know it. Please."

His hard expression softened slightly. "I will never lie to you, Laney. But it doesn't mean I have to tell you everything either. This conversation can wait until the time is right."

I swallowed back the disappointment and stepped toward the door. "Aye, sir. I'll fetch your breakfast."

"Oh, and Lane—stay away from that boy Aden. There's something off with him. He isn't what he appears."

I turned, examining the man I'd worshipped my entire life. He kept his gaze fixed on the deck, his chin spotted with rare stubble and his eyes clouded. I'd seen this man face down pirates with the firmness of a king, yet news of Belza had shaken him in a way that tore at my insides. Why?

I knew what Aden was. It was my own father I questioned now, and a single thought gripped my throat so tightly, it refused release.

What else aren't you telling me, Father?

I swung the door open and stepped out into the light, leaving my question in the darkness where it belonged.

13

The galley was quiet as I retrieved Father's coffee. Paval worked in silence, his back to me. Soon the next watch would be in for their breakfast. But rather than hurrying up the stairs as I ought, I hesitated. Paval was the only man who knew Father as well as I did. He'd also kept my secret since the day I stepped aboard as a child. If anybody understood my frustrations, he would.

"Why won't Father tell me about his past?" I asked Paval.

He turned to examine me, pausing a beat too long. "What won't he tell you?"

"Take a guess."

A sigh. "Belza."

I slumped against the bulkhead. "I thought we had a good relationship, but lately he's acted so distant. Like I'm a child who can't be trusted."

"Well, are you?"

I scowled. "Of course not. I mean, aye, I can be trusted, but I'm no child." I thought of Dryam's coppers and shoved away the rising guilt. I could be trusted in some ways, perhaps, but not in others.

There was a hint of a smile on Paval's lips. "Your friend, the new recruit? Aden. He asked quite a few questions last night."

I groaned. Of course he had.

"It made me realize that there's a tale I never told you," Paval went on. "Perhaps you'd like to hear it now."

"About Belza?"

"About how your father won the *Majesty*."

I straightened so fast, I spilled coffee on my boots. The heat barely registered. "*Won?* He told me he bought her."

"Did he, or did you assume?"

That took some thinking. "I don't actually remember him saying it, but still." I gripped the flask tighter. "You aren't saying he stole her...?"

"Nay, course not. Everyone assumes, same as you, but nobody considers how a sailor was suddenly able to afford full share of a brig. It's quite the adventurous tale."

I let my shoulders relax. "Were you there?"

"Nay, but I've talked to men who were," Paval began in a pleased tone. He loved telling tales. "Garrow served as first officer on the *Majesty*. The captain had a few run-ins with the law that first year. When Garrow finally confronted him about his dishonesty, his captain threatened him and tried to blackmail him into silence."

"And?" I prompted.

Paval shrugged. "Garrow never liked being threatened. He challenged the captain to a Right of Steel duel, right there at sea."

I nodded. It was the seafaring version of a lord's duel. It ended when one man died. "Father won."

"Aye. His victory came with such a flourish, the entire crew sided with him. Garrow chose not to kill the captain, though he did leave the injured man in a rowboat to fend for himself. The captain was too humiliated to challenge his first officer's right to his own ship."

My heart soared. Father had done all that? It sounded almost mutinous. "Who was the captain?"

"I have my suspicions, but it's hard to say for sure. It's like I said. I wasn't there."

A sick feeling entered my stomach. My own suspicion was an uncomfortable one. But I didn't want to dwell on it. "Did you tell Aden this story?"

"Nay. Couldn't tell a stranger something I'd never told you." He winked. "Best get that food up to the captain before he gets grumpy."

He was right, but I felt as if the floor had dropped beneath my boots. First the Belza thing, then Varnen, and now this. "Why didn't Father tell me this story himself? I would have understood."

Paval looked about the room. Several sailors had arrived, but nobody lingered close enough to hear. "What do you think of your father, Lane? You know him better than most. Is he a good man?"

I thought of how Father quietly returned his wages to his crew, allowing them to send the precious money home to their families. He frequently paid for medicine for a sick crew member or gave a positive, encouraging word to those who struggled in their training. He'd taught me to treat the crew as family. "The very best," I said.

"What would you do if someone told you otherwise?"

"I would defend him, of course."

Paval nodded. "Perhaps that's what he needs from you right now. Trust him even when the rest of the world doesn't. Especially then. That's something few others can give." He leaned forward, lowering his voice to a whisper. "A word of advice. Good and bad aren't as clear as they want you to think. Most of us lie somewhere in between. Now get going before we both get an earful from the captain."

14

The watch bells rang just after I'd delivered my father's breakfast. Gentle sunlight glistened on puddles that'd collected on the deck during the night's rain. The watch hadn't gotten to sweeping the puddles off yet, and they didn't seem to notice them as they headed for the stairs with tired, glassy eyes.

Marley stood at the helm, steering the ship's massive wheel with one bony arm. He swayed like he needed an entire pot of coffee to himself. I knew a bit about navigation—every sailor knew the basics—but I wasn't allowed to take the helm. Father hadn't forgiven me for the East Sea incident, when I'd torn a sail by forcing the ship into the wind. Never mind that I repaired it myself.

A figure stood against the rail, staring at the coarse water as if deep in thought. Aden's curly hair was all tousled, his shirt open below the collar, and his stance almost relaxed. If it weren't for his pale skin and smooth hands, he would have easily passed for a sailor.

I was about to speak when he pulled a worn piece of parchment from his pocket. He opened it, holding the edges tight against the wind, and scanned its contents.

I cocked an eyebrow. Besides his ridiculous clothing and his gold, that parchment was likely the only thing Aden had brought with him. My feet inched closer almost of their own accord, angling myself behind him. I couldn't quite read it from this angle. Just a little farther—

My shadow fell across the parchment.

Aden folded it hastily and shoved it into his pocket, then turned toward me with a tired smile. "Morning."

"What's that?" I asked, trying to sound casual.

"Nothing pressing. Sleep well?"

I never slept well after stealing from the crew, even just a few coppers. I noted the bags under his eyes with satisfaction. He hadn't slept well either. "Shame that Kemp didn't put a knife in you during the night."

He chuckled. "I was surprised myself. I love sleeping on the hard wood floor with the rats. It's like a back massage all night long. So, what will it be today, the galley? I'm getting good at pot scrubbing. Or maybe sealing the ropes?"

"*Rigging* or *line*, not *ropes*," I mumbled. "And we only seal the lines at port. You don't want to climb them when they're covered with tar."

"I suppose that's true." He fell silent. My gaze dropped again to his chest where his shirt fell open. I'd have to convince him to keep it fastened, or he'd become a distraction I didn't need right now.

I turned to a coil, clearing my throat. "Lines and rigging basics first. Now, we mostly use the same two knots over and over, but they aren't hard to learn. The hard part is getting them tight enough that they'll hold yet release when you pull them right."

He hefted the coil. "It's heavier than it looks."

I grabbed the rod we used for practice and showed him a square knot, which he learned quickly. The lansing knot was harder, and it took him several tries to get it right. I stood back to let him practice. He kept trying to use his arm strength. It wasn't until I showed him how to use his weight that the knot was pulled decently tight.

"So, Lane," he said as he tried again. "Tell me how you pass the time off watch. Do you have a favorite book?" He wrapped the last end around itself and tucked it in, then stood back to admire his work.

I snickered, stepping over to his knot. I gave it a sharp tug, and it pulled apart in one swift movement, recoiling onto the deck. "Again."

"It's what we do in cities, Lane. Make conversation. Learn about each other and ask questions." He hesitated a moment before taking the line.

I felt heat where his fingers brushed mine. "Then choose a different question."

His eyes widened a bit. "Oh. I assumed you—I mean, I've heard a lot of sailors can't—"

"I read." Few sailors could. Most were here because of their lack of education, and I'd quickly realized that reading wasn't a popular subject among the crew. I hid the scholar part of me like I hid the girl I truly was.

My father owned six actual leather-bound books, and I'd read each one many times. At night, of course, when nobody but Father could see. They were about wind currents, trade, and vessel construction mostly. He didn't know I'd stolen his copy of *A Maritime History of the World*. I hoped he never found out. Father hated Elena the Conqueror as much as any other Hughen did. He flatly refused to discuss her. I'd never questioned why until lately.

Aden smirked. "How am I supposed to make small talk if you don't cooperate?"

"Why talk small when there are so many big things to discuss?"

He sighed, then eyed the line like it was a snake before trying again. After a couple of attempts where he looped the wrong end, I realized talking helped him focus. I finally gave in. "How many books do you own?"

Aden paused. "I—uh, own quite a few. Well, my father does." He tugged on the end and handed it to me.

I pulled. Tighter, but not quite there. "And you've read them all?"

"The library is huge. I've only read a small percentage of them. Now I feel like a fool for bringing it up in the first place."

"What are they about?"

"History and politics, mostly. My favorite is the Pyrian farmer legend. Do you know it?"

"Nay."

He seemed surprised. "Well, it was hundreds of years ago. The farmer's kingdom was attacked, and he rushed to the palace, only to find the king's daughter being held captive. He freed her and persuaded the other farmers to fight. They won the kingdom back. He married the princess, and they crowned him king. That was the beginning of the Parrish Empire."

"Sounds like a hundred other tales." I shrugged. "Now, if a peasant girl rescued a captive prince? *That's* interesting."

He set the rope down on his lap and turned to look at me thoughtfully. Our eyes locked like two ships engaged in battle. At first I didn't dare pull my gaze away, and then I realized I didn't want to. I hadn't noticed how thick his eyelashes were before, nor how perfectly his cheeks met his jawline.

"A peasant girl," he said softly. "That's a tale you don't often hear."

Someone laughed across the deck, making me jump. Then the moment was gone.

"Try again," I snapped, irritated that I'd briefly lost my wits.

Aden grinned and slid his hand back to the rope. Then he jerked it away and stared at his palm. I caught a glimpse of blood.

"Careful," I said. "Rough line'll give you slivers right easy. Here, let me." I grabbed his hand to examine the wound. I pinched the sliver between my fingers. Not the biggest I'd seen, but pretty deep. I kept my nails short, so it took several tries before it finally came out. Then I hesitated. There was something odd about his palm. An indentation. I brushed my fingers against it, then recoiled when I realized what it was.

"Thanks," he said, and yanked his hand away. He wore a strange expression on his face.

"You handle a blade."

A pause. "Of course. Why is that surprising?"

I shrugged, unsure why it bothered me. "Seems odd when you have thousands of soldiers to fight for you."

"As do our enemies. Sometimes a nation's peace comes down to its leaders' strength in battle. I've been training since I was two." He nodded to the axes at my waist. "How about you? I'm guessing those aren't exactly decorative."

I gave my axes a pat. "Sharp as a needle, both."

"Interesting choice of weapon for a captain's boy. I thought axes were..."

"A pirate weapon?"

"Illegal. Hughen blacksmiths don't make them these days. Haven't since Elena's beheading, when her axe was destroyed."

"We aren't in Hughen anymore."

"No," he muttered, rubbing absently at his stubble-lined chin. "We aren't."

I stood back, a new realization dawning. "You've never left your country before."

He frowned and pretended to examine the knot in his hand.

Lands. What kind of ruler never left his home? "How are you supposed to guide a country when you can't compare it to the outside world?"

"I'm not supposed to lead anything," he said quickly. "That's up to my older brother, Mael. My role is to protect the king, the crown prince, and our country. None of that has ever required traveling elsewhere."

"Until now. Does Mael have something to do with this important quest of yours?"

He sighed, long and slow. "Look, I shouldn't have even told you that much. I know what you're trying to do, but there's too much at risk to continue this discussion."

"Risk?" I blurted. "You know nothing of risk. Wherever you're going, whatever it is that's so urgent for you, you risk nothing. Gold will buy you protection and silence and anything else you want. We're the ones who nearly lost the ship and our livelihood on that dock."

"I'm not taking a vacation here," he snapped. "This is bigger than me or your precious ship."

Several men looked over from their work. I forced my shoulders to relax and lowered my voice. "I don't care who you are, Aden. This *precious ship* is all that stands between you and miles of seawater. Insult it again, and you'll find yourself swimming with jardrakes, wishing the pirates would save you."

He watched me for a long moment. When he finally spoke, it was in a whisper. "I know you resent me, and I understand. But my situation here is precarious enough. We can't be seen arguing for three straight weeks. Can't we agree to *pretend* to get along?"

"I thought I was doing that quite well." I slapped the line onto the rail and threw together a hasty knot. It was perfect.

He gave a heavy sigh. "I'm not just protecting myself here, all right? I just want this voyage to go smoothly." He set himself to untying what I'd done. It took him a satisfyingly long time to loosen.

Pretend to get along. I'd been pretending for over a decade. It had always been me and my father against the world—protecting each other, protecting the ship that had become our lives. With one secret, I'd allowed Aden to yank us apart. "If you're so innocent and noble, why are you asking Paval questions about my father's past?"

He pursed his lips. "I'm no spy, if that's what you're implying. I was just curious."

"Then stop being curious. I know what you hope to find, and my father is *not* a bloody pirate."

"Maybe not now, but he could have been once."

I thought about what Paval had said, and frowned. "Stop trying to find trouble where there isn't any. There are no pirates here, nor will there be. Belza will have a knife in his back before the month is out. We're too far north for island pirates, and Elena the Conqueror and her crew are long dead."

His gaze leveled on me. "The way you talk about Elena the *Pirate*, I wouldn't be surprised if you'd stolen a ship or two yourself."

I dropped the line, gaping at him in disbelief. Had he just accused me of being a Jilly?

Of course he had. He was Eurion's son, no matter how friendly he sometimes acted. Even Father could see it. I'd been a fool to let my guard down so easily when I knew better.

"I'm sorry," he said quickly. "I shouldn't have said that."

"You know nothing of me or my family, so don't pretend you do." My voice was ice-cold.

"Fair enough." He shook his head and returned to his work, fighting a smile.

"What?"

"At least I know how you really feel about Elena. You had me worried."

My father emerged from his cabin just then, cutting off my angry reply. He scanned the men's work and frowned at the puddles that hadn't been swept yet. I turned away, telling myself that my warming cheeks had nothing to do with Aden and everything to do with Father catching us together.

Aden may have known nothing about my family, but thanks to Father, I didn't know all that much either.

Aden finished the knot and stood back for inspection. But there was a shadow across his face as well, and he wouldn't look me in the eye. Good. Better for us both to know our places.

I nodded. "Now release it and start again."

I swung my axe at half speed, arcing at shoulder level. The freshly polished blade gleamed in the afternoon sunlight. I rounded my shoulder to avoid an invisible strike and brought the second axe up to cover my head. A sharp exhale, then a quick slash downward followed by a spin at full speed. I finished with a slow, controlled bow toward the sea.

Barrie clapped. "Well done."

I could have fallen on my face, and Barrie would have said the exact same thing. I grinned anyway and wiped the sweaty axe handles on my shirt. This was normally where Paval stepped in to give me pointers, but he had declined to come. Aden hadn't shown either, though I wasn't sure what I would have done if he had. Was it possible to ignore the piercing eyes of a prince while wielding a pirate weapon with any degree of skill? He already suspected Father, and he'd made it clear that suspicion extended to me.

Even without Aden, my forms had felt choppy and unfocused today. It wasn't fair how the presence of a single person could shift everything in my world out of place. In quiet moments between watches, when I usually felt relaxed, I now found myself tense and alert, expecting a familiar pair of shoulders and that irritating smile to appear at any moment. Worse was the mixture of relief and disappointment that followed when he didn't.

Aden was probably helping in the galley again, hounding Paval with his questions. I mentally chided myself for not warning Paval about him yesterday. He needed to know that Aden wasn't what he seemed.

I snorted at that. The problem was, Aden was exactly what he seemed.

"Done already?" Barrie asked, sounding disappointed.

"Too hot," I lied.

Barrie eyed my axes hungrily. "Last time, you said you'd be thinking about teaching me. We have a few minutes before watch."

I'd completely forgotten. The thought of someone else touching my axes gave my stomach an odd little flip, just as it always did. I hesitated. "Barrie..."

He scowled and shook his head. "Don't be worrying about it. Aden said he'd teach me a card game anyway." He stalked toward the stairs, his shoulders slumped.

With a heavy sigh, I watched him go. Barrie had no knife, couldn't swing a blade without dropping it, and shot a musket about as well as a blind squirrel. Maybe he would take to axes like he had nothing else. But that meant sharing them during a battle, which I most certainly couldn't do. I wasn't sure I could hand them over even now. My axes felt like... an extension of myself. Loaning them out wasn't as casual a thing as Barrie supposed. Not when I kept every piece of myself hidden tight, guarded with a rigid hand.

An idea struck. I couldn't use Aden's seashell buttons for Kemp's payment, but I could trade them in Ellegran. Surely the market would have a suitable pair of axes for Barrie.

Smiling, I wrapped the blades, slipped into the cabin, and stowed them carefully in the storage chest. As I moved to close the lid, I caught sight of the history book resting on top of the pile and paused. The next watch would begin soon, which meant I should scrounge for what remained of the midday meal. But I found myself picking up the book and flipping to a familiar page. The story of Elena's death had become legend, a tale of warning for rebellious children. The last page held a sketch I'd spent long hours studying.

The Hughen king—Aden's father—stood with his fist pumped to the sky in victory. The pirate Elena's body lay at his feet. It wasn't true to life, as she'd been beheaded, after all, and her head was clearly attached here. I liked to think the illustrator had done it out of respect for the woman who'd almost succeeded in uniting the Four Lands.

"Elena the Pirate, indeed," I muttered. Aden's title made her sound like every other greedy thief who sailed the seas. But *Elena the Conqueror* described her as exactly what she was: a revolutionary with a plan. A woman who meant to tear the world apart and put it back together her own way. What had ignited that desire in her so long ago? What had driven her to win or die trying?

Had she begun her career by stealing coins from her crew members' boots?

Disturbed by the thought, I stroked the illustration with my thumb. It smeared the ink ever so slightly, smudging Elena's features to a smoky gray. Had she truly been as evil as Hughens believed, or had she simply meant to improve the world? Maybe Paval was right, and she lived somewhere in between.

I turned my attention to the king standing above her. It was his imposing stance, fist to the sky, that captured my interest. Like he meant to draw the attention of the gods themselves in challenge. That part seemed accurate enough.

I examined his face, looking for Aden in his features, but saw no distinct similarities. The artist had given the man a prominent nose and powerful build, but that was common in illustrations. For all I knew, the artist had only imagined what the dreadful scene had looked like. Even more unfortunate, there were no likenesses of any other crew members in the background. Not that I could have distinguished a younger version of Father from the others anyway.

His name wasn't on the list, I stubbornly told myself. Paval was right that I knew my father better than anyone, but I resented his implication that there was more to the story. If Father was a pirate, I would have seen it in his eyes long ago. Despite that, a single thought doubled back, no matter how I resisted it.

Had Father's name been absent because he wasn't a pirate...or because he hadn't been caught?

The next few days passed quickly. Dennis had a man in the nest both day and night despite seeing no sign of ships, Hughen or pirate. The fact that Aden was right about Varnen both relieved and irritated me, and having my favorite spot taken made me itch for solitude. When I offered to take a watch up there, Dennis only scowled and said to worry about my own duties.

And worry I did. Aden's skills were improving, but it was obvious by the Messauns' glares that he was the object of conversation. An invisible line had been drawn—Kemp's men on one side, Hughens and Ellegrans on the other. The gathering storm felt like a constant buzz in my veins.

On the afternoon of day six, I decided to check on Aden. I found the prince sitting next to Barrie in the galley, playing cards with five others. Barrie looked up and grinned. "Join us. We're playing oh-tag-four."

I hid my irritation. Popular with the nobles, oh-tag-four was a bluffing game. The key was to look impassive while sweeping the table of their winnings. But instead of gold, the piles in front of the crew were trinkets—old watches, hand-painted cards from the isles, even a vest.

Aden's offering included three coppers and a razor. He smiled. "Sure, Lane. Do you have something to trade?"

You, I wanted to say. *I'll happily give you away.* He could be so infuriating. A noble's game? It was like he *wanted* to be discovered.

"Nay," I finally said. "But I'll watch." I situated myself at the empty table behind them and folded my arms.

Aden shrugged and turned back to the game. "Now deal."

Barrie shuffled the deck and passed out six cards each. To my surprise, two Messauns also took cards, watching Barrie's hands carefully. They wanted him to cheat so they could take his pile— a pair of new stockings and a still-usable bootlace he'd bought in Hughen.

Barrie turned over two cards, and the game began. Everyone waited for the first to make his move. The men would bluff about what they had, each bluff higher than the last. When someone lied, they could be called out. But if the caller was wrong, the victor gained his entire offering stack.

"Three sixes," Aden said.

It was a safe bluff. Sixes were easy to get, and he wasn't likely to be called out this early. The Messauns frowned but continued to wait.

"Sevens," Julian said just as Barrie said, "Eights."

My mind wandered as the game continued. I didn't know I'd

been staring at Aden until he met my gaze and smiled. My spine snapped straight and I returned his grin with a scowl.

His shoulders shook from silent laughter. Then he turned back to the cards for his turn. "Elevens."

"I call."

It was Jamus who had said it, a muscular Messaun with a beard that probably hid half his meals from the past week. He held his cards close and stared Aden down, obviously expecting a fight.

Aden's grin didn't fade as he placed his cards on the table. Three elevens. The other men groaned as he swept the winnings into his pile.

"Again," Jamus snapped, and Barrie dealt another hand.

Aden's smile pulled the men in too easily, I decided as the game began. Most respected him enough to withhold their usual teasing when he refused fowl at mealtimes. Paval had even begun making him a separate hen-free meal, something none of the other Hughens received. I hoped Paval spat in it for extra health.

But I knew the real person behind the smile, and I would not be fooled. Not by a smile or anything else.

"Three twelves," Jamus said.

Barrie lifted an eyebrow. "I call."

I frowned. Barrie wanted desperately to be seen as an equal, but this wasn't the time to take risks.

"Very well," the Messaun said, and placed his cards down for everyone to see. There, at the top, were three twelves.

Barrie's shoulders slumped, but Aden was calm. "Worst sleeve trick I've ever seen. If you need stockings that badly, I know where you can find a pair. Can't guarantee they aren't infested, though." He picked up the set of twelves. Each card had a different design on its back from the others.

The Messaun slammed his hands onto the table, making the cards shake. "This deck isn't a full one, Hughen. We've pieced it together."

It was a lie, and everyone in the room knew it. Aden seemed ready to throw his cards and lunge at the man. I gave him a warning look. To his credit, his jaw snapped shut, and they simply glared at each other over the table.

"Be careful, chicken lover," the Messaun growled as his friend rose to stand beside him.

"Or what, you'll steal my stockings too?"

The other spoke now. "Filthy Hughen. Kemp'll make sure you get what's coming, and plenty of it."

Aden bared his teeth. "I've had worse threats from a dying mule."

I rose to my feet, but Barrie beat me to it. He inserted himself between the men and shoved the stockings at the Messaun's chest. "Here. Take them." Then he shot Aden a look.

Aden took the hint. He shook his head and stomped toward the stairs. I watched him go, my mind numbed by the fact that Aden, a Hughen *prince*, had just defended my friend—a young sailor he barely knew.

I rose to follow. Despite the Messauns' eyes burning into my back, I wore a smile of my own.

After the dim lighting below, the bright sun made me squint. A few men at work paused to watch me cross the deck. Only when we'd reached the bow near the decapitated wooden goddess did Aden turn to face me. "What?" he snapped.

"*Oh-tag-four?* Very subtle."

"It was Barrie's idea. He wanted me to teach him." He sighed heavily, looking upward as if pleading to the sky for assistance. "Things get heated during cards sometimes. It was a harmless game."

"Why do you hate Messauns so much?"

He looked surprised. "I don't."

"Your actions just now prove otherwise."

"It's not where they're from, all right? It's what they represent."

"Which is?"

He turned away. "Forget it."

Odd. Hughens had always hated Messauns, but this felt like something more. "Look," I said, more quietly this time. "Not all Messauns are like that, and not all Hughens are good people either. Every man on this ship is needed and therefore deserves respect. You'll just have to figure out how to live with them. Meanwhile, those men aren't the only ones watching you. You're getting sloppy. The crew listen to your choice of words, catch the sharpness of your language and the way you move." And some would pass the information along to Kemp. "You can't afford to be relaxed in your disguise, not even for cards." Not even for Barrie, who looked at Aden like a smitten pup these days.

A thought occurred to me then. What if Kemp's men had been looking for clues in Aden's game? Maybe Kempton suspected Aden wasn't who he claimed. He *had* said he looked familiar.

Aden's smile returned. "The way I move? How is that, exactly?"

Heat rushed to my cheeks. "You know. Just—everyone has their own way." I couldn't very well say that he moved with a smooth precision and confidence that captured attention. "And don't upset yourself when they cheat. They all do it, even the Hughens. That's the fun of playing cards, not getting caught."

His grin faded. "Then what's the point of rules?"

"If you want rules, go ashore. There's only one law here—ship first, self second. It's not something I would expect a royal to understand."

I thought he'd argue, but he was quiet for a long moment. He clasped one arm with his other hand, staring at the broken figurehead. I settled next to him, surprised at his silence yet content to wait.

"You have a point," Aden finally muttered. "We've been going about this wrong. The accent practice and deck training are helpful, but my disguise won't be convincing until I understand how these men think. I need to know what their lives are like. *That's* what I need you to teach me."

"You want to learn about…common life?"

"Yes." He turned back to me. "Not only for this voyage, but to take back with me. I may never get to travel like this again."

I kept my gaze fixed on the goddess. "That is disturbing."

"What?"

"It's just that…Has it really never occurred to you before? To speak with common folk and ask questions and see what their lives are like? I don't see how you can lead a people you don't know at all."

An invisible wall slammed down between us, his eyes growing hard. "I've told you before, I won't lead anyone. But commoners can raise complaints anytime they like. All they need is a noble sponsor who will represent them in court."

"And the majority are turned away. What of them? Those with desperate needs—starving children, sick parents. The people who can't work any longer or never could. The only commoners you've bothered to know are those the nobility wish you to see." My fingers were clenched around the rail, white at the knuckles. I peeled them off and met his gaze with a fierceness that surprised even me. "You scorn Messauns like Kemp, call them conniving and prideful, yet your own government models theirs. The system of representation your king boasts about, Meldon's Legislative Parallel? It has only hurt your country. It's added distance between you and the people you govern and shielded you from real life.

"Do you even see the orphans living in the street, fighting for scraps? Do you bother to act when good families lose their homes after a poor harvest? Did your father give a moment's thought that the women he sent to the gallows last week could be proven innocent at a trial? Don't act like a benevolent god simply because you've descended to show interest in us. This is something you should have done long ago."

His mouth hung slightly open, his gray eyes wide. "I...Meldon's Parallel has brought more wealth to the country than the previous system ever did."

"Don't ask your tutors. Don't ask lordlings who use sweet words at court. Ask real workers what happened to their livelihoods when that law took effect. I think you'll be surprised at their answers."

His jaw clenched. "Lane Garrow, expert on foreign policy and political history."

I bit back another retort I'd regret. I meant every word, but this was the *prince*. Making him angry wouldn't remove the Edict. It would just get me thrown into the dungeon when we arrived in Ellegran. Or sent directly to the gallows. "Sorry."

He sighed. "No. You aren't sorry, and you shouldn't be. That is precisely what I asked for. I just wasn't expecting it to come in such a forceful manner or from such an unusual source." He gave a lopsided grin. "Next time you lecture me about politics, let's find a more private location. The men are too interested in this conversation."

I looked past his shoulder at the men who'd inched closer during my tirade. They weren't close enough to hear, but word would rapidly spread that I'd been yelling at Aden. "No more gambling," I shouted, hoping it would satisfy their curiosity. "Not until you have respect for our rules."

He flinched. "I suppose I deserved that."

"Aye. You did."

Aden chuckled and joined me at the rail, looking down upon the poor goddess figurine leading our charge. She'd be repaired eventually, but it wasn't worth the carpenter's attention right now. He was busy enough trying to keep his patch in place from the cannon blast.

"Who is she?" he asked softly.

"The night goddess Medachumen." Father said it honored the religion of the Motherland, when the Founder had sent her children to inhabit the continents hundreds of years before. Few even remembered what the religion was called. "I'll teach you, but when we're alone. At night, off watch."

He nodded. "Where?"

"In the hold. It's dark, but we won't be overheard." Or discovered, if my luck held. I'd have to think of a good excuse, should anyone find us alone.

"Tonight, then?"

I was about to agree when I heard the call from the nest above. "Ships ahoy!"

Ships? Occasionally, two ships sailed together for protection. But that was more common in the islands, where small bands of pirates roamed.

Father barreled out of his cabin and onto the quarterdeck to meet Dennis, who had already lifted the glass to his eye.

"Stay here," I said. "Please."

Aden nodded, already squinting at the horizon.

Father barely registered my arrival. He watched Dennis with an impatient frown. "How many?"

"Four, sir. I can't make out their banners yet."

"A convoy. This far north?"

Dennis nearly dropped the glass, then raised it again. "It can't be."

"What, man?"

"A b-black flag with a red blade in the center. That's...Belza's."

I sucked in a quick breath as the two men stared at each other. Not one, but four ships. How could Belza have gathered such a following already? And how could he possibly have found us so quickly?

Father tore the glass from Dennis's hands and squinted into it. "Impossible. Belza's on his way to Hughen from the east."

"Perhaps we were wrong about his whereabouts," Dennis said.

Father growled under his breath. "They must be imitators. Belza wouldn't dare raise his old pirate banner as a privateer. He'd be arrested again within the week."

"Why would a convoy pretend to be pirates?" I asked. "And if they're pirates, why pretend to be Belza's?"

"Scare tactic, I'd guess. When he discovers they're using his name, he'll hunt them down to the last man." He didn't sound convinced.

Dennis scowled as he took the glass back. "Imitators or not, four ships block the channel, and they've likely spotted us. We'd best turn around. We'll sail north and hire a ship in Messau to deliver the copper instead. Or take the longer route south around the continent."

"That will add six additional weeks," Father said, looking at me now.

I tried unsuccessfully to tamp down my irritation. Father had allowed fear to guide him at the port, and we'd all suffered for it. I refused to be the cause of such a decision again, especially when we were already low on men and provisions. But my father had a Hughen prince on board and didn't even know it. Did Aden have something to do with those ships?

I considered telling Father about Aden. A captain deserved to know who served on his ship, didn't he? It would lessen the burden of lies that I carried. It was the responsible thing for a captain's boy to do, much less a daughter.

Then I remembered everything Father refused to tell me, and I clamped my mouth stubbornly closed.

"Sir. There are figures running about, clearing the decks. They've been ordered to give chase." There was an edge of panic in Dennis's voice. "If we veer hard north straightaway, they won't catch us. I'll issue the order immediately."

Father still watched me, his frown deepening. "There's no guarantee we can outrun them that way. Our destination is Ellegran, and no pretenders are going to stop us. We'll thread the Needle and come out on the other side. They won't dare follow, and we'll be two days ahead."

My chest felt tight. "You said it was unsafe. The last time—"

"Unsafe but not impossible. The Needle should be passable this time of year. Aye, 'tis the best heading."

"Captain," Dennis moaned. "You can't be serious."

"You heard me." He raised his voice. "Marley, head six degrees east. Dennis will assist you with the map."

"Aye, sir," Marley said, gripping the wheel with tight knuckles. He hadn't missed a word either.

This wasn't about the copper. Father intended to dump me off in Ellegran before fleeing south until the pirate threat disappeared. But that could be years from now. Decades, perhaps.

Father brought the glass to his eye once again before returning it to Dennis. His shoulders were high and rigid, his mouth tight. I felt light-headed. Four pirate ships. If he truly saw the Needle as our best option for survival, he knew exactly who those ships belonged to—and they were no impostors.

Kemp trotted up to the quarterdeck. "What news have ye, Cap'n?"

"Gather the men, Gun Master. We're steering into Hellion's Corridor."

Kemp's smile froze. "Not the Needle, sir?"

"Aye."

Kemp tore the glass from Dennis's hands and extended it toward the ships in the distance. When he finally pulled away, there was an odd expression on his face. "Captain, I don't think—"

Father whirled on him. "Gather the men. Now."

The two glared at each other so intensely, I feared the air between them would catch aflame. It was Kemp who finally stepped back, muttering to himself. He shoved the glass into Father's hands and stomped down the steps.

I dragged my feet back to the bow, where Aden still waited. He looked as grim as I felt. Every man on deck had seen the worry on the captain's face. When they discovered where he intended to take us, that concern would multiply considerably.

My voice was numb. "We won't be meeting tonight. Father is taking us through the Needle."

Aden's eyes widened. "Then it's true. Captain Garrow *has* done it before. That's how he crosses the sea so fast."

"He once worked as a pilot on Two Light Island," I explained. "Ships paid him well to navigate them through. But then the storms worsened, and now nobody else dares attempt it." I didn't mention that my father hadn't done it in three years himself. Our last crossing had been barely successful, and that was in the calm waters of summer.

That wasn't all that bothered me. Kemp's reaction to those ships had been odd. Not like he'd expected them, exactly, but he certainly wasn't happy about fleeing.

Aden nodded. "I'm looking forward to seeing the captain guide us through. We'll meet tomorrow night, then. After our watch ends at the first bell."

"First bell," I agreed, although my mind was a thousand miles away.

16

The Needle was exactly how it sounded: a narrow, rocky channel in which visibility was always poor. Its riverlike current barely fit a single ship across in some places. Even now, as I squinted at the high cliff walls in the distance, I could see the remains of decades-old shipwrecks floating out to sea. Hellion's Corridor. The shortcut ships entered but rarely exited intact.

My father had addressed the crew this morning to explain where we were going and assure them he'd pilot the ship himself. He knew where the rocks lay, he'd said, and they needn't worry except about their work. He'd finished his speech with a dire order of quick obedience. Anyone who didn't set themselves immediately to his orders would receive a lashing once we were through. I'd doubted that particular warning would help, but the men seemed almost comforted by it. As if a lashing was the worst they could experience this day.

The clouds grew dark and thick above us as the Needle entrance grew larger in the distance. Rain pelted and then assaulted our exposed faces. The wind was relentless. I pulled my coat tighter and watched the men work, aware of Aden's presence beside me. He wore a coat I didn't recognize. I didn't ask who he'd bought it from.

My father paced the quarterdeck above, giving Marley an occasional order and glancing worriedly behind us. The pirates had guessed our plan and increased their speed, determined to catch us before the cliffs. We'd only have one chance to make it into the channel, so Father would take over the wheel as we approached the entrance. It wouldn't be long now.

Aden leaned over, looking somber. "I'm not watching the men work for an hour. There must be something I can do to help."

He'd echoed my thoughts precisely. Half the crew were already aloft, positioning themselves along the yard lines for both masts and preparing to secure the shrouds. "You won't be climbing in this weather. Dennis approves your training before he'll send you aloft. Up there, one mistake can endanger the entire ship."

He frowned. "What about you?"

Father had forbidden my going up the moment dark clouds closed in above us. I hid my irritation, shielding my eyes from the rain. Climbing the ratlines when they were swaying like that, with the canvas flapping by your head, threatening to flick you off like a fly...most men would be relieved to keep both feet on deck.

But I wasn't most men, and it looked positively exhilarating.

A cry rose from the quarterdeck above. Marley stood gripping the wheel with one hand, pulling the other away from his forehead. A trickle of blood wriggled its way down his cheek and under his jaw. There was tapping from behind me and a yelp from above. It wasn't until I looked down that I realized what was happening.

Frozen rain, the size of marbles.

I shielded my eyes and dared a glance upward. Millions of white balls plummeted from the sky. They began to fill the deck—billions of sharp ice pebbles. They grew larger even as I watched. The men aloft paused in their climbs to shield their chests against bad fortune.

Marley's voice was shaky. "The spirits defend this place. They won't let us through without a fight."

"Then fight we shall," Father said, making his way over. The sound of ice hitting the deck made his next words difficult to hear. "I'll take over. Get shelter...Clean that wound."

The navigator didn't argue. Still holding his forehead, he stepped carefully toward the stairs, avoiding the icy marbles rolling about his feet.

The men preparing to climb pulled their coats over their heads, glaring at the rigging before them. None dared wear a hat in this wind.

Another wet gust slammed into us. I hurried under the ledge jutting out above the cabin doors and plastered myself against them for protection. Aden followed. Balls of ice pelted the deck in a continuous round of clattering. An occasional cry sounded from above. If it was this bad on deck...

Aden cursed. "They're completely exposed up there."

Dennis shouted from the quarterdeck above. I strained to hear past the pounding of ice. "Timing is critical, Captain. We'll barely have enough time to furl sail before we get dashed upon the rocks at the opening. Even if we make it in unscathed, visibility will be extremely poor. How can you navigate currents you can't see?"

"Position men at the bow and shout directions back to me," Father called. "We'll get her to the other side."

"Sir, we can still turn around. It isn't worth risking more lives!"

"And fall to pirates? Nay. We'll make it through because we must. Tell the men to stay alert and listen for orders."

A pause. "Aye, sir."

I shifted in my boots, for once agreeing with Dennis. Pirates could be defeated. Plunging between two narrow cliffs was suicide.

One rogue wave shoving us off course, and the ship would be driftwood.

Another gust tore a sail somewhere overhead. I cringed at the sound and looked up, but I couldn't tell where the rip was. It stopped, then started again, longer. A bad one. The sheets flapped now, like they were about to tear right off their yards. Even if we made it through the entrance untouched, we'd get nowhere without our sails intact.

Father realized it too. "Furl the fore and mainsails! Harbor furlough, nice and tight. Quickly. Then get the men down from there!"

Dennis hurried to relay the order. This was one he agreed with.

The men moved to obey. All except Barrie, perched at the foresail. He clung to his line like a rider on a bucking stallion.

I groaned.

Aden held a hand up to shield his eyes. "What's wrong with him?"

"It happens sometimes. He just freezes up." It was understandable. Being aloft in storms like this made even grown men wet themselves.

"But they can fulfill the order without him, right?" The wind whipped Aden's words away almost immediately.

I shook my head, dread seizing my thoughts. "Takes at least twelve men at each yard in good weather. In a storm like this…"

He nodded, understanding what I hadn't said.

Come on, Barrie.

Barrie's foot slipped and his leg went clean through the ratlines. He struggled to find his grip again. The other men waited at the yard, but Barrie wasn't even halfway when a huge gust of wind nearly picked him right up. He yelped as he thrust his arms through, holding himself there against the wind, shaking like a boy facing death. The rest of the crew shouted to him, but he didn't respond.

"He's not going to make it," Aden said.

I turned and lifted onto my toes, straining to see my father on the quarterdeck behind us. He was completely focused on the helm, fighting to keep the rudder straight. He'd ordered lashes for disobedience—a sentence I'd thankfully managed to avoid to this point in my life. But I couldn't very well stand here while the wind drove the *Majesty* headlong into a cliff either. No reasonable sailor would.

Ship before self.

The frozen rain only intensified by the minute. I willed the numb cold from my fingers, hunching my shoulders. Then I stepped out into the onslaught and raced for the ratlines, dodging rolling pieces of ice underfoot.

"Somebody help," Barrie cried from above, his voice weak.

The wet lines creaked under my weight. I focused on grabbing hold of one before releasing the other, balancing my weight carefully. Another gust of wind sent me nearly sideways, but I paused, clinging tightly with my head ducked. It barely helped. Ice pelted my back, arms, my frozen fingers. I'd have a hundred bruises tomorrow. The ship groaned like a downed animal.

An eternity later, I reached Barrie. Blood dripped down his forehead as he watched me approach. There was a wild look in his eyes. "I can't be g-going up there."

"Go join Aden on deck. I'll take it from here."

Barrie looked down. "But he be climbing."

I followed his gaze and cursed. Aden was only a minute behind me. What did the princeling think this was, some kind of child's adventure? Men died in storms like this.

"He's coming for you," I told Barrie, not caring whether it was true. "Climb down to meet him. I'll take your place on the yard."

He nodded so vigorously, his damp black hair flopped into his eyes.

Dennis shouted something from below. I couldn't make it out. Gritting my teeth, I ducked my head against the ice and set myself to climbing once again.

I scrambled over the top, the lines beneath my fingers soggy and cold. The others noticed my arrival and eased down the yard farther, allowing me the position next to the mast. Now the slow, tedious work of pulling and folding the canvas began. Ice slammed into my head, my face. I sent thoughts of pain elsewhere and focused on my work. Reach, fold. Reach, fold. My arms trembled from the exertion—the mainmast was far heavier than the fore. I lay with my stomach across the yard, allowing it to take my weight, but the foot line bearing us all up swung in the wind.

"Hurry!" Dennis called from below.

I dared a peek at the Needle and gave a start. It was nearly upon us. My mind registered that the icy rain had begun to ebb.

The foot line beneath my boots jerked again, vibrating oddly. I paused in my work and looked down just in time to see it unraveling.

"Hold to the yard!" I shrieked to the others, and threw myself across the sturdy wooden bough.

The foot line snapped.

Dryam yelped beside me. Thankfully, he'd thrown a leg over the yard at my warning and now gripped it tightly with both arms. A scream pierced the wind. I looked over just in time to see a sailor named Errick flailing, his legs up over his head as he tumbled toward the water. My exclamation hadn't carried to him. A wave swallowed him up as though it were a massive whale.

"No!" Dryam howled. "Man overboard!"

Horror grasped my mind as I stared at the water. A somber

silence settled over those now wrapped around the yard for their very lives. Shouts echoed from below as sailors rushed to the rails, looking for any sign their comrade had survived the one-hundred-twenty-foot fall. The man nearest to Errick's position, Lyman, was weeping.

There was nothing to be done, I realized with a sinking heart. Even if we turned sharply and missed the Needle's entrance, the wind would ram us against the cliff walls and finish us off before we could turn completely around. It was likely to happen anyway, given the speed we approached the entrance with now. We'd be dashed upon the rocks sure as the angry waves, unless Father prevailed upon the rudder.

I traced the sign of life on my chest, fixing Errick's face in my mind. Mourning would have to come later.

Three sharp bells followed by a long one. *Come down and brace for impact.* The mainsail was a loss, and there was no time to string a new foot line so we could finish our work.

I scrambled on my stomach toward the mast. The others pushed along on their bellies after me, watching the canvas snapping below them with an experienced wariness. Our falls would end at the deck, not the sea. Infinitely worse.

What remained of the foot line whipped at me as I lowered myself down the mast rungs. I swept it aside only to pause, breath catching. It hadn't simply unraveled. The end was too clean to be explained by wind or the onslaught of frozen rain.

Someone had sliced it with a blade.

"Get moving!" Dryam hissed from above me. I lowered myself down to the ratlines secured to the ship's side, the implications of this revelation whipping my mind about like the freed mainsail over-head. Someone had intended for the foot line to break. If I hadn't looked over when I did...I closed my eyes against the image of all twelve sailors plunging to their deaths. *Our* deaths.

I'd been the last to make that climb. That meant one of two things—either another man at the yard had done it, risking his own life in the process, or someone had sliced it earlier and it hadn't torn till now. But why? What would the deaths of a dozen sailors accomplish?

The shouts from below intensified as the ship listed portside, then starboard again. The tearing sail held too much wind. It was taking us off course. I didn't dare gauge our distance from the entrance now. It was obvious we had seconds left, and I still hovered fifty feet above the deck, clinging to the mast with all my strength.

"Hurry!" Dennis screamed.

Aden appeared at my feet. "Too late!" he shouted. "Hold on."

I weaved my arms through the ratlines to secure myself. Dryam cursed and did the same.

The ship lurched hard.

My fingers burned as the lines slid through my hands. Then there was just air. I grabbed for the ratlines, reaching, flailing. I hit them again, lower, and bounced off once more. The rope netting directed me toward the waves now. My stomach flew up into the sky and I couldn't breathe, couldn't grab anything, couldn't scream, couldn't...stop...

Something grabbed my arm. Pain wrenched through my shoulder a second later, and I gasped. Aden grunted heavily. Then an arm snaked out around my waist and *yanked*, shoving me against the ratlines again. I grabbed the rope beneath my fingers and pried my eyes open to find Aden's face inches from mine.

"Thank the spirits," he gasped, rain dripping down his hair and into his eyes. His hand was still around my waist.

A terrible screeching of wood and rock filled the air, far louder than the wind's cruel bellow. The hull. Father had almost succeeded in taking us in; we'd hit at an angle and the battle between ship's hull and rocky walls had commenced. I'd fallen and...Aden had caught me before I hit the waves.

I stared at him, speechless, willing my brain to form a complete sentence. *Thank you. Remove your hands. I'll take it from here, thanks.* Anything at all.

Instead, the world had frozen in that moment, our faces inches apart, my lungs suspended in time, and a strange rawness in his expression. He looked exposed, uncertain, the prince stripped clean away until he was simply a boy.

"Ow," I finally managed, then flinched. Of all the stupid things to escape my mouth.

His guard went up again, and he gave a tight smile. "Let's get you down from here."

My brain finally responded to commands, allowing me to wiggle free of his embrace and wince at the deep pain in my shoulder. I scrambled down, grateful that the hull's inhuman shrieking had ended, bowing to the sound of wind whistling violently through the cliffs on either side.

My head spun, thoughts jumbling into a concoction that closely resembled Paval's stew. I still felt the grip of Aden's fingers around my waist—how *dare* he—and this was no time for distractions. The rocky walls had slowed us nearly to a halt, but we were finally inside the Needle's cliffs.

We'd made it.

No cheer rose from the men, no pats on the back. Instead, they stood transfixed, watching the waves behind us.

"Check for hull damage belowdecks," Dennis snapped at the

gawking men at the rail. This wasn't over. If we'd sprung a leak, we'd be the Needle's latest shipwreck.

"Lane!" Barrie said, hurrying up to me. "That was quite the tumble. If Aden hadn't gone back for you—"

"So lucky," I said dryly, rolling my shoulder to test it. I didn't need a description of the corpse I'd nearly become. And my father would have seen the entire thing from the helm, reinforcing his belief that I needed protecting. Not to mention that odd exchange between Aden and me that most of the crew would have seen. My secrets felt like lines being yanked from my fingers.

Barrie rushed on, oblivious. "I told Aden to stay and brace for impact, but he refused. Said he couldn't stand by and watch you die."

That was the part that bothered me—he could have. Nobody would have judged Aden for obeying orders and holding his position. In fact, my death would have removed the only other sailor who knew what he was. I looked up at the ratlines, measuring the distance by sight. He'd climbed faster than should have been possible.

Focus. I'd sort out Aden later. We had a saboteur aboard, someone who didn't want us to reach our destination.

I marched up the quarterdeck steps to confront Father, who struggled with the wheel. "That was far too close, Captain," Dennis was muttering.

"Beg pardon, sir," I said, "but there's something you should know."

"Not now, Lane," Father snapped.

"We've lost a sailor, Captain," Kemp said from behind me. "An honorable commander would do everythin' in his power to save the poor man."

Father grunted. "What would you have us do, Master Kempton? Toss you overboard to fetch him?"

Kemp continued, raising his voice still louder. He meant for the entire crew to hear this conversation. "Wasn't just Errick, sir. Ye just risked all our lives, every man. And for what? A few harmless ships in the distance?"

"You know full well what those ships intended, Gun Master," Father muttered through clenched teeth. "Lower your voice now, and stop questioning my orders."

"We've a right to question our lives being tossed to the wind. Literally, in this case. We'd have preferred fightin' those so-called pirates. We've plenty of guns and the courage to use 'em, yet ye ignored our advice and did as ye pleased."

The crew gathering at the quarterdeck steps had gone quiet. Hushed whispers peppered the group. I found Aden's eyes in the crowd. We'd both underestimated Kemp's determination. Not only was the gun master trying to undermine his captain, but Kemp had just played a very dangerous hand. That meant he had confidence that a good percentage of the crew would back him if things went sour.

Dennis placed himself between Kemp and the captain. "You are out of line, sir. Let's take this discussion to the captain's cabin and discuss it like gentlemen, or I'll escort you to the brig."

A man clattered up the steps from below. "Only a small leak starboard fore. The carpenter is already on it, sir!"

I released a long breath, wishing the news were more comforting. The *Majesty* had survived, but our crew was breaking open at the seams—and it was Kemp who held the pry bar.

"If you refuse to explain yer actions, Captain, at least address the fact that three sailors disregarded orders this day. Including your own son."

"Father," I jumped in. "That foot line didn't break by itself. Someone—"

He spun on me. "Get off my quarterdeck!"

I took a step backward. "But—"

"Go," Father hissed, looking crazed with his windblown hair. "This instant, Lane. I'll deal with you later."

My body was too numb for anger as I descended the steps. The men made way for me, and I plunged into the crowd, fighting the flush in my cheeks. Several pairs of eyes were on me, watching, evaluating. If they hadn't already connected my position aloft to Errick's death, Kemp's accusations certainly would. I wanted to light into every one of the fools with fierce words and angry fists.

Kemp positively shouted now, his voice carrying easily to the deck. "Young Barrie sits by instead of following orders, your boy disobeys to take his place, and the chicken lover ignores orders to save him. I expect you'll be ordering a triple lashing before this is over. Or do you mean to go back on your own orders, sir? I suppose Master Errick's death means nothing at all to such a lofty captain."

"This is hardly the time to discuss it."

"The men have concerns and won't be put off any longer, Captain. We'll have your judgment on this before we reach the Needle's end."

The crew gaped up at the gun master. He'd just issued the captain an order. My cheeks were aflame now, but it wasn't from humiliation. The man knew my father would never order me whipped. It would reveal us both.

"Aden acted well, and Lane's disobedience will be dealt with privately. However, young Barrie let his fear endanger the entire crew in a critical moment. He will face punishment." Father's voice seemed barely controlled as he turned back to his second officer. "Now, if you say a single word more, Gun Master, you will join Master Errick. Understood?"

Barrie went pale as Kemp looked over the crew, the corners of his mouth turned upward at their stunned reactions. He'd forced the captain's hand and, in doing so, had torn at the fabric of the ship even more. No captain could legally send a member of his crew to death, especially not an officer. For a moment, I saw my father as they did—not a strong, capable sailor, but a tyrant who cared little for the lives of his crew. A dictator ruled by emotion and fear.

A pirate.

A chill settled over my numb heart. Kemp hadn't changed how the men saw the captain. Father had done that himself.

Satisfied, Kemp barked an order for his men to sweep up the scattered bits of ice, then turned back to his post as if nothing had happened. Dennis, looking disturbed, sent a few men aloft to fetch the torn mainsail for mending. The crew shuffled slowly back to their work. Several muttered Errick's name followed by hurried prayers. They all avoided my gaze. Father had protected me yet again, but it had come at a cost.

I sent a silent prayer of my own to follow Errick into the afterlife, then hurried to join the rest of the crew, ignoring Aden's accusing glare. If Father was determined to fuel a mutiny and ignore the facts, he was welcome to it. Meanwhile, I was certain that foot line had been Kemp's doing. I had to figure out how to stop him before we ran out of time.

Something told me we had very little left.

Three hours later, cliff walls still extended high above us, their peaks jagged against the darkening sky. Broken rock cradled the ship on both sides. I knew the remains of a hundred rockslides lay buried beneath us. The entire channel seemed asleep compared to the disaster we'd just faced on the open sea.

I stood at the rail, letting my sore arm rest upon it. The surgeon had advised a sling and rest for my shoulder, but I'd refused both. A sling would mean a visual reminder of my ordeal to Father, and nothing short of a direct order would make me miss a Needle crossing. Perhaps not even that.

Aden joined me, nodding to the bag sitting at my feet. "What's this?"

"A pilot trick Father taught me." Long ago, when life had been simple and I'd known exactly who my father was. We felt like strangers now.

Aden eyed the bag. "I don't see how mud will help."

"Watch." I lifted it and scooped up a handful of the goopy black mess. Then I tossed it toward the water and hefted the gaslight lantern high overhead so he could see.

As the mud hit, a thousand tiny specks broke free and zoomed back toward the sky. But the animals had already seen them. Several of them burst from the water, jaws extended, their black teeth glistening in the night. Then their jaws slammed closed over the insects and they plunged into the water.

Aden gaped. "Jardrakes."

"Aye. They follow us. If I dumped this whole bag, you'd see the school of them. Some are longer than three men head to toe. When you get enough of those monsters swimming beside the ship, they'll push us along and cushion the hull from the sharpest rocks."

"Instead of avoiding them, you use them," he muttered. "Brilliant." Even the shadows couldn't hide his exhaustion. Aden's hair was plastered to his head, still damp from the relentless drizzle. A tiny red cut was visible midway down his nose. A raindrop perched on one of his eyelashes as he watched the water, and I was overcome with an urge to brush it away. The feel of his hands earlier still filled me with a strange sensation.

And his expression. There was nothing casual about it. It was one I'd seen between couples, a wordless one that meant entire paragraphs.

Once we emerged from this terrible channel, we'd be two days closer to Ellegran and leaving Aden behind. I'd never see him again.

"Can I try?" he asked.

I held the bag for him. He reached in and scooped some mud out, grimacing at the texture. Then he leaned over the rail and tipped his palm.

The insects, already invigorated at my earlier touch, escaped more quickly this time. But the jardrakes were ready. They devoured the black cloud with snapping jaws before slipping back into the dark water.

"The insects don't have a chance, do they?" Aden said, wiping his hands together to clear the remaining dirt. "Seems like nothing would against those things."

"No. Whatever they want, they get." I felt a swell of uneasiness. People said similar things about Captain Belza. We'd managed to avoid those four pirate ships, but we still didn't know whether they were truly Belza's. Hopefully we'd never find out.

"That was certainly exhilarating," Aden said, turning to lean against the rail. "The storm, the pirates, the ice, and now this. I see why you love it. Definitely more exciting than court life." A shadow crossed his face.

"Aden...," I began, unsure what I meant to say.

He waited, watching me in the shadows. Half his face was illuminated by gaslight, and I resisted the urge to move the lantern to better examine how his shirt pulled tight around the shoulders. Surely he had a dozen ladies after him now that he was of marriageable age. Strange that he'd left it all behind to board a ship and flee across the ocean. Maybe that was the question I couldn't ask: *Why?*

He yanked his gaze back to the water. The moment had passed. "I'm glad you're fine," he said. "You had us—had *me* worried." He glanced down at the deck. A hundred tiny indentations from the ice were visible where the light touched. I brushed my arm, a series of purple bruises dotting my skin like giant freckles. It was nothing compared to poor Errick's plight.

I wished I could be glad of my survival. But Barrie would be punished for nothing more than fear, Kemp was growing bolder, and Father was too angry to listen to me. I'd heard hushed conversations between several sailors today already. Dennis and Father weren't the only ones who'd seen Belza's banner. The longer my father kept Belza's sworn revenge a secret, the less the crew would trust him.

And then there was Aden. The thought of being in a boy's arms, even if he'd only caught me, sprang a strangely pleasant shiver. Even now, despite the cliff walls around us and the black fins flapping about in the water, my awareness was captured by his presence. I felt his nearness like a thousand tingles, felt his breath like a shift in the wind. If he touched me again, my skin would ignite.

Maybe it was time to lie down after all.

He still waited for a response. I forced a smile. "Father always said I was stubborn. Guess he was right."

"I knew as much when I met you." Aden's tone was low and husky, like he struggled with his own voice. A full two feet lay between us, and yet I couldn't tear my eyes away from him. There was just something too captivating about the way his sleeves clung to his arms.

"Thank you for...helping." I couldn't find the right words. *Thanks for watching out for Barrie, for catching me. For taking a risk I never expected you to take.*

"I was relieved to be of help." There was an emotion in his eyes I couldn't place, lighting something inside that I'd never felt before. Like the shock of rough fabric rubbing against itself or sudden light in a dark room. It danced on the edge of pleasure and pain.

I took a shuddering breath. "We'll reach the end of the Needle soon. Father wanted the mainsail mended, if possible. I should help."

"Lane, I..." He tore away, shaking his head as if censuring himself. It broke whatever spell he'd cast on me, and I melted against the rail to put space between us.

"Ocean in sight!" The call came from aloft. "Not ten minutes ahead."

The rest of the crew cheered, exhaustion heavy in their voices. They couldn't wait to get belowdecks and shed their wet clothing.

Then Kemp's watch would take over as we emerged into open sea and prepared for Errick's memorial service.

I shoved the mud bag at Aden and headed for the cabin, fighting the flush that spread through me like a virus. I no longer knew who my own father was, but I knew exactly who I had to be—and that was a captain's boy. Not a waist-swinging lady in eight layers of skirts.

Somehow it was getting harder to remember that.

I yanked the door open and practically leaped inside to the safety of the captain's cabin. Shoving the door closed, I tried to calm my ragged breathing. What had just happened?

It didn't matter what I longed to say. No words could change what was.

I wrenched my heart into submission, scolding it until I felt the softness fade. I was the daughter of a sea captain, not a courtier. I would never be the type of girl Aden wanted. Keeping our secrets until he was safe in Ellegran was what mattered right now.

When my breathing finally slowed, I pulled my shoulders back and lifted my chin as Lane always did. Then I headed for bed.

18

Morning dawned a muddy gray.

The channel had deposited us into the sea mostly unscathed. The sails had been hastily, if temporarily, repaired. The rudder was damaged but seemed to function adequately. Yet another issue for the carpenter to address, but at least it was a small one. The real problem was Barrie.

I hadn't been awake ten minutes before the call came to witness punishment. It seemed my father wanted to get the lashing over with before the men took their breakfast and prepared for Errick's memorial service. I wasn't hungry at all.

The crew lined up along the rails. Dennis stood at the mainmast with Barrie. Kemp's men bunched around them, all looking smug. They knew the crew disapproved of the captain's decision. Even now I heard whispers as the stragglers made their way to the group.

My father remained in our cabin. He would emerge once everyone had gathered. He'd need every ounce of authority today, even if it was simply appearances.

"You mustn't judge your father too harshly for this," Paval said, taking a place at my side. His black hair hung in a tidy braid down one massive shoulder. "I know how you care for Barrie. We both do."

I glanced at the stairs—no Aden yet, not that I was looking—and forced a noncommittal shrug. If yesterday's encounter hadn't revealed Kemp's intentions to my father, nothing would.

"I know why he's doing this," I said. "But he could have assigned Barrie scrubbing or galley duties instead." The cat-o'-nine-tails broke men's minds as quickly as it did their backs, leaving behind night terrors and darting eyes that lasted long after their scars had healed. I'd seen it happen before.

Barrie fidgeted as he waited next to Dennis, bare from the trousers up. His face was as slashed from yesterday's ice as any man's.

"Captain Garrow is beholden to the safety of ship and crew," Paval said. "Better for him to show a firm hand than a weak one. Especially now." He frowned and glanced at Kemp, who was chuckling at something Digby had said. Kemp caught my gaze and motioned with his fingers—a slight movement, undetectable to anyone else. *Two.*

I frowned. Two days until my silence payment was due. I was still considerably short. Kemp never accepted anything but coin for his payments, so the seashell buttons would do me no good. If I delivered only part of the sum, would that negate our bargain altogether?

My father emerged from the cabin, and everyone went quiet.

"Captain on deck," Dennis called. "We will now witness punishment for disobedience."

Barrie visibly stiffened as he turned toward Dennis, who picked up the knotted cat and wrung it with rigid hands. It was the shorter one, at least, with rope tails sixteen inches long instead of thirty and no bone entwined. A compromise on my father's part.

Barrie straightened. "If you please, sir, be using the man's instrument."

Dennis's eyebrows shot up, but he recovered quickly. "Captain ordered the lesser sentence. Gun Master, string him up." Kemp stepped forward eagerly.

Barrie stood his ground, a stubborn tilt to his chin. "But—"

"If he desires the greater punishment, that is his choice," Father said.

I wanted to pluck his words from the air and shove them back down his throat. Barrie worked alongside the men, but he was still a boy—a boy who'd made a tiny mistake. This wasn't fair, and Father had to know it.

Dennis only hesitated a moment. "Aye, sir." He retrieved the larger cat from his bag as Kemp positioned Barrie at the mast. With a jerk, the boy's wrists were yanked high above his head. His back was smooth and tanned. The flawless skin of a child.

My father stood on the quarterdeck, looming over us like a king overseeing his obedient servants. He'd stood right there, just like that, years before.

I was eleven. Two dozen boats full of islander pirates had flanked us on either side in the fog-filled night. It was clear from the jeering men that we were outnumbered three to one. Worse, they carried weapons that flung fire onto our deck. Pirates we could fight. Fire, on the other hand, was a sailor's greatest fear.

Any reasonable captain would have surrendered the ship, hoping the gesture would save himself and his crew from certain death. But Father had given a soul-stirring speech instead. He'd called for courage and skill from his men. He'd reminded them of their families and the people waiting for them to return. He'd looked every man in the eye like he knew what they were capable of and expected precisely that. There were no lies, no false promises of glory. Just a captain asking his sailors to fight with everything inside of them.

And they'd done it. With Captain Garrow at the helm, we'd destroyed half the boats and sent the pirates swimming with the jardrakes without losing a single man. The story of our impossible victory had since become legend.

As I'd watched Father speak that night, his eyes narrowed and the men watching him in awe, something stirred within me. I'd experienced the deepest, most gut-wrenching hunger I'd ever known. I knew then what I wanted.

I would be captain of the *Majesty* or nothing at all.

Now, years later, my father looked different. He wore the same coat and boots, though his hair was littered with gray. But the determination in his stature, his gaze, his clenched fists was a more disturbing variety. He refused to meet my gaze. Clearly, that noble captain from long ago was gone. The thought cracked something at my core, something I hadn't realized was there. Because if Father was a liar, what did that make me?

I knew the answer to that. I was the sea's greatest hypocrite, for I judged my father for being exactly what I was.

Aden was the last to emerge from below, staring at the ground with a tight jaw. He appeared as miserable as Father. Maybe my ship wasn't as different from Aden's twisted kingdom as I wanted to think. The thought made me shift in my boots.

Now Dennis was ready. This cat hung longer than the other, and I spied the bits of bone woven into its knots. The rope was scrubbed after each use, but the ends were stained a dark red regardless. Several of the men flinched at the sight. How many times had Father covered for my own indiscretions, things that should have earned me stripes of my own?

"This sailor was ordered to furl sail," Dennis called out. "He allowed his fear to overcome him instead, costing us precious time and putting others at risk. Captain has executed his right to punishment. Fifteen lashes." He eyed Father. "Let it be a lesson, particularly in a storm, when every second means life or death."

Normally, sailors called out *Hear, hear* or *Aye* at this point. But today there was nothing but the creaking of the *Majesty*, her sad mourning for what was about to happen. Most faces were long and somber, but others looked flushed. A tiny triumphant smirk crossed Kemp's face.

"When you're ready, Dennis," Father said. His voice was familiar and confident, everything a captain's voice should be.

"Ready yourself, Barrie," Dennis said with a touch of pity. He'd rolled his sleeves back for this. At least Dennis was accurate. There wouldn't be any wasted blows.

Dennis swept the cat back. The whip whistled through the air, then sliced into Barrie's skin. He gasped, arching his back, teeth gritted and eyes narrowed to slits. That crack inside I'd felt earlier began to widen.

"One," my father said.

The whip sailed again and landed true. Barrie jerked. His jaw was clenched so tightly, I marveled that he could breathe at all.

"Two."

Another crack. Kemp's mouth twitched.

"Three."

Someone muttered a curse and was quickly shushed. Digby looked triumphant, as did several of Kemp's comrades. An urge to tear the cat from Dennis's hands and erase that smug smile nearly overcame me. Instead, I clasped my hands together and rooted my gaze on Barrie, wishing I could lend him strength.

"Four. Five. Six." My father's voice was growing strained.

Barrie's legs trembled so badly, I wondered how he remained on his feet. As his head arched with every blow, a wrenching cry tearing from his lips as new slashes appeared in his bloody back, I felt a piece of myself die.

"Nine. Ten."

Barrie hung by his wrists, his trembling legs a useless heap beneath him. My father's counting had quickened, and I realized that Dennis had increased his speed to match. Barrie's back was a mass of bloody flesh now. My heart felt suspended in the air each time the whip flew backward, preparing for another strike.

"Eleven."

Finally, Barrie raised his head and released a long, animal-like wail toward the skies. A deep chuckle emerged from Kemp, one he didn't attempt to hide. Those behind him giggled like obedient children.

"Halt," Father said, the sound barely squeaking past his clenched teeth. He stretched a hand to stop Dennis. The first officer straightened, looking relieved. The cat swung in his hand, flinging drops of blood onto the deck. Barrie's blood.

"Please," my friend whimpered. The rope binding his wrists was all that kept him upright. He was utterly defeated, body and soul. I'd seen older men lose consciousness before now.

But it wasn't Barrie my father watched. It was Kempton. The two men locked gazes, their hatred searing across empty space until there was no doubt where either of them stood. The father I knew would never have a boy whipped to the sound of men's laughter. By the expression on his face, Father was considering placing his own stripes on Kemp's back. I would have happily strung the gun master up myself.

"The boy's sentence has been served," Father announced, to my relief. "Cut him down and assist him belowdecks."

"But, Captain," Kemp said. "He has four stripes left."

My father whirled on the man so suddenly that Kemp stumbled backward and grabbed at the pistols on his belt. I'd never seen the captain so enraged. Not in battle, not ever. There was an alarming wildness to his eyes.

"Don't cross me again, gun master," Father hissed in a deadly tone. "Or I swear I will gut you here and now." He looked about at the men, who'd begun to murmur. "Well? Cut the boy down and see to his wounds."

Dennis repeated the order this time, but it was unnecessary. A few of the men jumped forward to help like eager mutts. Others hung back, uncertain of what had just occurred. Digby and Kemp exchanged a long look as the men gathered Barrie into gentle arms. The surgeon had several hours of work ahead of him. The wounds would need cleaning and bandaging, and Barrie would have to be watched carefully tonight. I'd already volunteered.

Barrie had been spared a little pain, and my father had shown mercy. So why did I feel so sick inside?

I released a shuddering breath and found my father's gaze again across the deck. Some of the wildness had left his eyes, but there remained a fierceness that whispered I'd missed something important here.

Perhaps my secret wasn't the only one he'd protected today.

My nerves felt as frayed as the edges of a storm-worn sheet. Paval wanted me to believe the best of my father, to trust him. But my silence this morning had cost Barrie dearly. Who would suffer next while Father and I hid in the shadows of our secrets? How long could I pretend that my father was precisely who he said he was—yet did I dare confront him again if it meant risking banishment?

That moment hadn't arrived, not with Barrie's punishment and Errick's memorial service today. But I was tired of waiting for answers that might never come.

It was time to find out the truth about Father's past for myself.

That evening, when Father retired to the quarterdeck to speak with Marley about our heading, I left my corner of the cabin and retrieved Father's secret chest. It opened silently. The bag of gold coins still lay tucked inside, though it appeared smaller than I remembered. I hefted it in one hand and realized why—it was about half the weight it had been before. What could Father possibly have spent that much coin on while at sea? Or had he hidden it elsewhere for safekeeping?

Disturbed, I returned the coin bag to its corner and dug through the rest of the contents. Maps, a watch, a few pieces of KaBann silver. Nothing that proved a history of piracy. A few pieces of folded parchment at the very bottom. I shot a glance at the closed door, feeling the seconds tick by, and decided to take the chance.

The first was a missive addressed to Father. I didn't have to read far to know who had written it. I grabbed the other letters and scanned through them, anger rising with each word. The woman who'd given birth to me clearly had no regard left for her former husband. Each missive felt more urgent than the last, more demanding. She wanted me returned to her as if I were some valuable foal Father had stolen from its rightful owner. As if she hadn't flung me aside like a worthless piece of rubbish.

A single sentence on the last page caught my eye.

> *You hide our daughter away, but I would present her to the world. I resent that you've taught her to be ashamed. She deserves to walk with her head high, to take pride in who she is just as I do—not spend her life cowering in the shadows, defeated and guilty. Give her the opportunity to choose for herself.*

The last line reminded me too much of my own words to Father, that last day in Hughen. That realization bothered me just as much as this woman's disparaging tone with a man she'd once claimed to love. But they were both just as wrong as ever. I wanted the opportunity to be what neither of them wanted—a sailor. A captain. *Free*.

With a sigh, I folded the missives carefully and returned them to their place. Nothing here proved that Father was a pirate. A mixture of emotions battled inside. Disappointment. Relief. Frustration. A heavy guilt that I'd sought answers this way. Anger that he'd forced me to this in the first place.

Trust him even when the rest of the world doesn't, Paval had said.

If anyone deserved to know who Father was, surely I did. But he hadn't left any answers here in the cabin. Father was too smart for that. He probably suspected I would dig through his belongings for clues. He hadn't trusted me before, so why would he change his mind now?

I stared at the chest's contents a moment longer, letting the hurt sink deeply into my heart. Then I grabbed the money pouch, dumped a few coins into my hand, and stuffed them into my pocket.

Trust went both ways, and I had a debt to pay.

19

I stood in the hold at midnight, waiting for Aden to arrive. The watch had just changed and our group was asleep, Dennis and my father included. Darkness filled the hold, save for the gas lamp in my hand. A candle would have been better as even this felt too bright, but open flame was strictly prohibited belowdecks. Although I'd spoken with Aden down here once before, this time my skin felt abuzz. The very air encircling me seemed to whisper that this meeting was the biggest risk I'd taken yet.

It's just training. Nothing has changed.

That felt like another lie.

Aden stomped down the ladder, obviously unfamiliar with stealth. But my irritation fizzled when he approached, casting shadows in the low light. His shirt was streaked with black. He'd spent the watch cleaning out the guns under Kemp's direction. By the look on his face, it hadn't gone well.

"I don't know why your father likes that conniving son of a—er, Kempton." He scowled.

I couldn't hide a chuckle. "Too highborn to curse now? Maybe we'd best start your lessons there."

His frown faded. "My mother often says I swear like a seaman.

She'd be horrified to see me now." He shrugged. "No, it's because I respect your father's judgment. He must see some speck of competence in the gun master, or he'd have sent him off long ago."

It wasn't Kemp's skill that had gotten him the post. It was more that he commanded the respect of the crew—respect tinged with a bit of fear. A balance that had worked well for the past two years. In fact, Barrie's lashing had been the first in months. The men were usually quick to obey and skilled at their work, two attributes that meant good leadership, as my father often said. But Father didn't know what Kemp did to his enemies, and I didn't dare utter the words. Not now, with Kemp watching for the slightest excuse to expose me and take the ship. I decided not to tell Aden that we'd already cleaned the guns last week.

The thought fled as Aden watched me, shadows from my gas lamp bouncing across his face. That expression was back, the raw one from earlier. He watched me as if nothing else in the room existed—not the barrels of stones and bags of rice behind him, nor the scampering of tiny rat paws hiding from the light.

Even now, after a day's worth of distance, I was painfully aware of *him*. He'd drawn closer now, and I had to look up to meet his gaze. His frown was gone, replaced by a wistfulness. Like he waged a battle in the silence of his own soul. I wanted to lift my hand and caress his face to assure him that he wasn't alone.

Panic slapped my mind in a wave of wakefulness. I yanked my gaze away. This boy seemed honorable enough, but he also had the power to destroy me.

"You mentioned your family," I managed, then cleared my throat. "Do you think your mother worries about you?"

"I shouldn't have said that. Sometimes you just bring things out of me." He smiled grimly.

I frowned.

"It's not that I don't want to tell you more. I do. But the less you know about this, the better it will be for you if—" He paused, choosing his words carefully. "If something happens."

"Like what?"

"Don't concern yourself. We're two days ahead of schedule now, thanks to your father. I'll be gone very soon, and then everything will go back to normal for you."

Right. I couldn't remember what normal was anymore. Even if I managed to secure a future on the *Majesty* after our arrival, something would be missing. Something I couldn't admit had ever existed in the first place. Something very, very dangerous.

"So," he said, rubbing his hands together. "You're the teacher. Where do we start?"

I'd planned a lesson that would force more details from him. I hoped he wouldn't see through it. "Music. It's a big part of life on a ship."

He lifted an eyebrow. "You're singing me a song?"

That was laughable. I could sooner hold a handful of water than a tune. "Hardly. The men would suspect something if you suddenly knew all their songs. But you should know some, especially island tunes. They're known for their music. Have you ever played the carrigan?"

He stared at me blankly. "Does it have strings and a bow? If it's similar to the viola, I can probably play it."

Far from it—carrigans were dried reeds fashioned into rough flutes. He really hadn't traveled much. "The viola?"

"Most people choose the violin or the cello. I thought the poor, ignored viola could use a voice. Besides, it's deeper and feels more... mournful somehow." He actually flushed.

It was so endearing, so unexpected, that I had to will myself not to stare. "It would be better to pretend you don't play anything, then. But try to participate in their music. Learn the songs."

"I will. But first, you handled today's ... situation ... very well. I feel terrible for Barrie. I hope he heals quickly."

I grimaced. I'd checked on Barrie on my way down here, and I'd heard quiet sobs in the darkness. The boy wouldn't sleep well for weeks. "It's the way of things. Most men have cat scars on their backs." Not me, of course. Yet another injustice.

"It's all gotten so complicated. This voyage was supposed to be quick and uneventful." He released a long breath. "I shouldn't have brought this up. Let's talk about something else."

I folded my arms. "Well, we've discussed your clothing and your gambling issues already, as well as your interesting musical talent. Perhaps it's time to discuss your obvious arrogance."

"One of my finer qualities." He grinned. "You're terrible at small talk, you know that?"

"I had a poor teacher."

Aden made a kind of gurgling noise that turned into a cough. It sounded like a sorry attempt at covering a laugh. He sat himself down on a pile of bags and patted the spot beside him. "Tell you what. Let's discuss you for once."

I sat, putting a full bag between us. "That's not why we're here."

"Actually, these lessons were intended to teach me about sailors in general. That includes you. Being an only child must be nice. Nobody to compete with, no expectations or roles to fill."

I didn't bother to hide my laugh this time. I had more expectations than anyone. Men and boys weren't expected to be anyone but themselves.

"I'm serious. This life of yours is so unique and carefree. And your father is proud of you."

"Why do you say that?"

"I see it when he looks at you."

I blinked. Father was a kind and responsible captain, but he rarely acted like a father with me. And I'd certainly never seen him look proud of the things I did.

"*A Maritime History of the World*," I said.

"I don't follow."

"My favorite book. You told me yours, but I didn't tell you mine. I've read it over thirty times."

"A scholar," Aden murmured. "Interesting."

"The best captains are scholars." It came out before I could stop it.

There was a moment of silence. When he finally spoke, there was awe in his voice. "You want to be a captain. Sail your own ship and lead a crew."

It sounded foolish when he said it aloud, but I kept my gaze steady. My father would retire in the next twenty years. It made sense that his son would inherit the vessel.

Aden nodded. There was no doubt in his eyes, just acceptance.

"I want to discover islands that have never been charted," I said, watching him closely for a reaction. "To meet the cultures I've read about, and study history. I've heard that they eat insects in Honnicker. Don't even cook them—they just pick 'em up and shove them in their mouths. It sounds revolting, but I want to try it. I want to try everything." The truth of it burned in my chest. I'd never admitted this to myself before, much less said it aloud. "But it's not likely to happen." At least, not while King Eurion had a vendetta against everything I was. And here I sat, baring my soul to one of the last people I should be speaking with.

It was just so easy to be myself with him, utterly and completely. I didn't even feel that way about Father these days.

"I can feel how badly you want it. I hope it happens for you." His face was infuriatingly blank. I couldn't read a thing.

"It's just a dream. I need to make other plans—preferably far from Hughen, because we won't be returning there anytime soon."

"You don't mean that," Aden said. "You aren't the type to accept things as they stand."

That had me speechless. "What?"

His wry smile returned. "I know more about people than you think, Lane, and I know determination when I see it. If you wish to be captain, you won't be swayed until it happens. Nothing else will ever be enough for you. And I admire that, especially in someone who didn't have that attitude drilled into them from birth by expensive tutors."

He'd moved closer at some point, and now we sat right next to each other. We didn't touch, but I could feel his warmth extending across the space between us. If I leaned over just an inch...

Nay. I was tired of all this—the lies, the pain. The pretending. The doors slammed in my face, jeering that everything I wanted was beyond my reach.

"Drilled into them from birth," I repeated bitterly. "Because I'm so lowborn, I shouldn't have dreams at all."

"No, because you dare to dream and it's refreshing."

I didn't have a retort for that. We sat watching each other for a long moment. Then he raised his hand, slowly lifting it to my face. His fingers hovered there for a moment, just inches from my skin. He brushed aside a lock of hair that had fallen into my eyes.

His touch sent a shiver down to my boots. My mind screamed at me to run from this, to hide. That a world lay between us, and that was how it had to remain.

His hand dropped, and he rose to his feet. "I, uh, should probably get some sleep. I'll see you tomorrow."

He fled before I could gather enough air to reply. His footsteps pounded up the ladder, much faster than they'd been coming down.

I stood, my legs still shaking, the skin on my face burning where he'd touched it. My body felt exhilarated, like I stood in the nest without a harness during a violent storm. I'd never felt so utterly and viciously alive.

Was it possible to live both dream and nightmare at the same time?

I was about to leave when I noticed something white and flat on the bag where Aden had sat. A fold of parchment. It must have fallen from his pocket.

I picked it up with trembling hands. The creases were yellowed and the edges bent, which meant Aden had carried this around for some time. The parchment felt smooth, soft, not coarse like my father's books. I cupped it in my hands like gold. Dread and excitement pulsed through my body, and my head felt light.

Footsteps on the ladder. Aden had realized the parchment was missing. There would be no time to read it.

I slipped it into my pocket, smoothed my hair, and turned toward Aden.

But it wasn't him. Dennis stood there, bleary-eyed and somber, the scar on his forehead a dark slash in the shadows. "There you are. Your father's looking for you."

My heart dropped to my feet. Had he discovered our plan to meet at night? But why send Dennis to fetch me when we could discuss his concerns in private? Surely he trusted me that much.

"Aye," I mumbled, and began to step around him. But he moved to block my way.

"Lane," he whispered. "A serious charge has been made. You'll want to distance yourself from all this."

A chill swept over me. "From what? What are you talking about?"

He paused. "Aden has been accused of sabotage."

20

A heavy tension hung in the air as I climbed to deck two. A crowd had gathered around the guns—mostly Kemp's watch, although a few of ours stood sleepily at the bulkhead opening. The usual snoring from the crew's quarters had ceased. The entire deck was silent, gripped in a tension I felt as keenly as the dread in my chest. Aden and Kemp stood next to the ladder, glaring at each other. Aden's face was flushed in the deep shadows of gaslight.

I caught a glimpse of Barrie near the back, pale as death. He held his blanket like a shield against the world.

"Lie to me again," Kemp growled, "and I'll give you a punishment that makes young Barrie's ordeal look like mum's kisses."

"I won't admit guilt for a crime I never committed. Sir." Aden stood with fists clenched, as if ready to defend himself with more than words if necessary. My father stood near the steps, his shirt untucked and half-fastened. Even in the low light, he looked exhausted. We'd survived one problem only to encounter another.

"What happened?" I asked Dennis, who'd come up behind me.

But it was Kemp who answered. "The bloody whelp doused our gunpowder."

A stir went through the crowd. My skin prickled. Dousing gun-powder with water, rendering it unusable, was a dirty pirate trick.

"How much?" my father asked.

"Three barrels, but only because I caught him before he moved to the last."

Dread settled in my bones.

"You saw him do it, then?" my father asked.

That gave Kempton pause. "Didn't actually see it, though I heard him moving round in here. I came down to investigate and found the boy trying to sneak away, his shirt streaked in powder."

Aden's eyes narrowed. "That's because I cleaned your guns earlier, sir, and you know it."

"Do I? Surely I'd remember such a task."

Aden ground his teeth. My stomach sank. Kemp's order had been about more than torture. He'd been setting Aden up. One thing was clear—Aden had been with me, and those minutes since our parting hadn't been enough to commit a crime like this. But only he and I knew that, and it wasn't something I dared reveal. If the crew discovered Aden and I had been hiding in the hold alone together so late—well, it wouldn't take long before the men recalled how often we worked side by side and began to wonder why. That would lead to questions I didn't want them to consider. Neither of us would escape *that* train of thought unscathed.

I met Aden's eyes. There was a weight to his gaze that meant he was thinking the same thing.

I pushed past the crowd to the barrels. I could smell the gritty acid even before I saw it—three barrels with the lids removed, dark puddles of water near their bases. I took a handful of powder off the top. It was heavy and moist. I didn't have to plunge my hand deeper to know the bottom of the barrel was completely immersed.

Our nearly empty rain coffer stood in its usual place to the side, though it was crooked as if hurriedly replaced. The water in the barrel was still cold. The deed had been done recently. Very recently.

That left us with only one barrel of usable gunpowder. We'd been essentially disarmed in a single night. And with our rain coffer emptied, we were dangerously low on drinking water. We'd have to ration or halt in Messau to replenish our stores.

My father turned to Aden. "What have you to say, boy?"

Aden didn't hesitate. "I was restless from the events of the day, Captain, so I read for a while before retiring. Nothing seemed out of the ordinary. I'm a poor witness, sir, but most definitely not the guilty party. I didn't even know water could destroy gunpowder."

"Liar," Kemp hissed.

Aden whirled on the larger man. "What motive would I have, Gun Master? I want to survive as much as any man here."

"Enough!" My father shoved his way past the watching men and examined the barrels, his face drawn in anger. The shadows carved at his face in a disconcerting way. "This is an abomination."

"Indeed, sir," Dennis muttered. "A well-placed blow, it is. We have a saboteur on board. If we run across more pirates—" He cut off abruptly, meeting Father's pointed glare.

I raised an eyebrow. My father had obviously forbidden Dennis to speak of Belza and his pirates. That was the closest Dennis had ever come to insubordination. Except he was wrong about one thing. Being caught defenseless would be far worse than a blow. It would mean the annihilation of the entire crew.

"Pardon my boldness, Cap'n," Kemp said, "but it had to be the boy. The guilty party was obviously interrupted, as the last barrel was left untouched. Besides myself, young Aden is the only person who's come through here recently. He even admitted he hasn't seen anyone else."

Kemp's argument was a sound one. If I hadn't been with Aden just moments ago, I would have assumed him guilty as well. Except he wasn't. That left Kemp. Injuring the ship hurt him as well as the rest of us. Why take such a huge risk simply to get back at Aden? Or did this fall into his plan somehow?

The thought was unsettling. The pieces were all there—his meeting in Hughen, his countrymen recruits, the sliced rope, and his outburst at the Needle. *Mutiny.* It was the only logical conclusion. I just didn't understand how all the elements fit together.

"Do you have any witnesses to confirm your testimony?" Father asked Aden.

I tensed. I was the only witness.

Once more, there was no hesitation in Aden's reply. "None, unfortunately. I was alone until meeting Master Kempton."

A treasonous relief swept over me, followed by disgust in myself. I'd hidden behind my wall of secrets while Barrie was punished. Could I do it again while Aden was punished to protect me?

"You said you were reading," Dennis said. "Where?"

"The cargo hold." Aden pointedly avoided looking my direction. "I borrowed a book on naval history earlier. I wanted to finish it before we arrived, and gaslight was too bright for the sleeping men."

I felt Dennis's gaze. My cheeks grew warm. Dennis would eventually tell my father where he'd found me. But there was a larger issue at hand. If Aden wasn't convincing enough, he'd be strung up and whipped. It wouldn't be fifteen lashes either—it'd be the full thirty. And once that was done, Aden would spend the rest of the voyage in bonds. I could only imagine the king's reaction when he heard about *that.*

It felt as though a leash of lies extended between Aden and me. His fate was now bound to mine.

"Gun Master," my father said. "What witnesses have you?"

"Several, Cap'n. They'll affirm my presence on deck until I found the boy. And I've no doubt several heard what happened after that." He looked smug. Kemp knew few dared speak against him, even if they suspected his lies. Barrie stood huddled in his corner, staring at the barrels of destroyed powder.

"If you'll forgive me, Captain Garrow," Aden said, "there's a discrepancy in the gun master's story. It can't be as he says."

Kemp began to sputter, but my father raised a hand to silence him. "Explain."

"Master Kempton said he heard noises and came down to investigate, finding me alone and then seeing the sabotage. But when I climbed up from the hold, he stood by the ladder. He couldn't have seen the damage from there, especially in the darkness. I believe he already knew it was there and waited for someone to blame it on."

"You dare accuse me of sabotaging my own ship?" Kemp snapped.

"I accuse you of attempting to frame me for your treachery."

"You bird-loving weasel." Kemp's voice lowered to a deadly pitch. "You issue a challenge."

"I speak the truth as I see it."

The room was silent and still except for the flickering of the lantern. Even my father stood there, rigid, as if uncertain what to say. Kemp's face turned a deep purple, and for a moment, I thought he was suffocating. Then he whirled to face my father. "I demand Right of Steel. I'll be having nothing less."

Right of Steel.

The other men stared at Kemp in disbelief. Dennis opened his mouth to protest, then he seemed to think better of it and clamped his mouth shut again.

"The boy rendered us incapable of defending ourselves, then

challenged me in front of the crew." Kemp's voice was barely controlled. "I'm within my rights, and I'll not be talked out of this."

There was a long pause as the gathered men waited for my father to speak. He examined Aden for a moment, and I knew a silent exchange was taking place between them.

"In all my years at sea," Father finally said, "I've only experienced one duel. It was a bloody affair that still haunts my dreams. There will be no duel, but a trial."

A stir went through the group. A captain was the ultimate authority in matters of discord and ship law. But a Right of Steel duel was a matter of a sailor's honor. It went beyond his jurisdiction.

"Captain, sir," Digby said. The man actually grinned. "In cases where we've two men who accuse each other and no witnesses, Right of Steel is the appropriate course. I'm sure the first officer will confirm it. Right, Master Dennis?"

"Don't you dictate to me the rules of my ship, sailor," my father snapped.

"Captain," Dennis said apologetically. "He's right. We haven't time for an investigation nor a trial. The men will duel upon our arrival anyway. May as well hold it here, where the crew can witness and the officers can ensure proper rules are followed."

Kempton's eyes shone now. He looked almost giddy, like this had gone better than planned.

Some of the pieces clicked into place, and I finally saw the truth of it. Kemp suspected Aden wasn't the sailor he claimed. Even if Aden managed to survive, which wasn't likely, the men would see his skill with the blade and accuse my father of deceiving them as Kemp had always implied. More than the powder had been destroyed tonight. I wanted to slink into the shadows and melt between the deck planks.

Instead, I straightened. "This is wrong. We should set to draining the powder and putting the ship in order, not watching a fight."

"You aren't entitled to an opinion, captain's boy," Kemp said. He'd given *boy* the slightest of emphasis. A warning.

I nearly snapped back anyway, but Aden gave a tiny shake of his head. My defense of him wouldn't do any good now that a direct challenge had been issued. This wasn't about who was guilty. This was about who was the stronger man.

My father watched Aden now, seeing him as if for the first time. His expression was dark. "Do you accept the terms, sailor?"

"If a duel will prove my loyalty to this ship and its crew, I accept."

Whispers floated from the crew's quarters. Father examined me, with a heaviness to his stature that seemed to come from his very soul. There were questions in his eyes. He knew I had something to do with this, but he'd never draw the crew's attention to me so long as danger lurked. I shrank under his gaze.

"The duel will commence at dawn," he finally said. "I want all hands on deck to witness. Dennis, make sure both men are watched closely until then. And have the others clean up this mess. We must salvage what we can."

21

Dennis's idea of having the two men watched involved Kempton returning to his hammock and Aden being banished from the crew's quarters. Before Dennis left to take his post above, he leaned over my shoulder. "I'm sending men down to drain the powder. Have Paval take the boy into steerage. Make sure he gets some sleep."

Then Aden and I were alone. The gaslight lantern still sat where I'd left it. I grabbed the handle and started toward the galley. Paval's quarters lay just beyond. "This way to steerage," I said. "You'll be able to sleep there."

"I can't sleep anywhere." But he followed anyway.

When we reached Paval's door, Aden stopped me. "Don't wake him yet." He slid to the floor and sat himself against the bulkhead, one knee bent to the ceiling.

I sank down beside him, careful to give him plenty of space. Even here, the awareness of him scrambled my mind until I couldn't think straight. Aden was being far too calm about this. Surely King Eurion would be furious if Aden died tomorrow. None of us would escape the noose.

"At least we know one thing," Aden said. "Kemp believes this duel will get him closer to command. There's no question of that now."

The duel itself, he'd said. Not Aden's death. Never that. He hadn't acknowledged what I already knew—that he couldn't beat Kempton. His training was casual, using thin foils and padding for protection. Aden's confidence was admirable, but Kemp was a brutal and effective soldier.

I couldn't discuss Kemp's motives right now. I felt my heart flip in my chest, hyperaware of how straight Aden's posture was against the wood, how far his legs extended before us, and how he fidgeted with his hands like a distracted scholar.

"Tell them who you are," I blurted out.

"Who?"

"My father. Dennis. Barrie. I don't really care."

"And ignite Kemp's mutiny? The men will never believe Garrow didn't know about me. It would only prove Kemp's point that the men can't trust their captain. I never meant to cause harm to your ship." His tone was sad. "Besides, knowing why I'm here would endanger everyone, especially you. I'm not willing to take that risk."

I thought of Aden's parchment in my pocket and shifted uncomfortably. "But you'll risk your own life in a bloody duel instead? I don't see how you can accomplish anything dead."

"Who said anything about dying? I've fought men bigger than Kempton before and won."

A cold shiver wriggled down my body. "You've fought nobles, Aden. Never a soldier. And never for your life."

"I'll do fine."

"You won't," I hissed, then lowered my voice again. "Look. The men will discover your identity anyway, from the second you begin to fight. Noble duels are more flashy, more drawn out and entertaining. Ours are over in seconds. If you're certain you want to do this, show Kemp that you won't be used. Disguise your skill but defeat him quickly. Be deadly and accurate."

He chuckled. "Remind me never to cross you."

"Don't you get it? Kempton knows we're lying about who you are. He'll draw out the fight to expose you, but in the end, he intends to kill you."

He sobered. "I know."

There was a long moment of silence. Our shoulders touched now, though I wasn't sure who had closed the distance. I was painfully aware of every breath he drew, the way he held the air as if considering it, then released it into the world. Every muscle in my body was taut, humming with something alive and very much awake.

"I appreciate the advice, Lane. You've risked a lot for me on this voyage, and you've kept your word even though you didn't understand why. I'll make sure you don't regret it." His grin was so open, so positively unguarded, that it stole my breath.

Lands. How was I supposed to reply to that?

Silence fell upon us once again. I filled the emptiness with another selfish, utterly impossible dream deep within my consciousness where Aden would never find it. I let myself believe that Aden could remain as crew on the *Majesty*. We could explore the world together, far from the Edict and the noose and everything that awaited us in Ellegran. We'd live out my dream together—me as captain, him as first officer. Or perhaps more. I let myself imagine what it would feel like in his warm, strong arms. It would be us against the world.

Then reality burned its way in, leaving nothing behind but smoke. Eleven years of lies, and I'd never longed so desperately to throw it all away. I wanted to rip the rotting lies free and fling them into the ocean to drown. I wanted to demand the truth and tear down the walls between us.

I wanted to touch him, to *be* touched as who I truly was.

I wanted *him*.

This is what you signed up for, I reminded myself. *You chose the life of a seaman over that of a lady. You can't have both.*

But I wanted both. More than that.

I wanted a world where I could *be* both.

"Thank you," I finally whispered. "For not saying anything, I mean."

Aden turned, looking down upon me with warm eyes. They had a million levels of depth to them, like a stormy gray sea, capturing me. "Of course. It's what we princes do." There was a hint of bitterness to his tone.

A very real pain stabbed through my chest, and I knew I couldn't stay here any longer. It was tearing me apart, piece by lying piece. My father had been foolish enough to fall for someone high above his station. I wouldn't make the same mistake.

"I'm going to tell my father," I said firmly. "He'll know what to do." I moved to rise.

"No, you won't. We had a bargain, Lane. Nobody can know."

"Tell them who I am, then, because I'm not letting you die."

His hand covered mine. "Wait."

His hand.

It gripped mine with a strength that left me weak. If Aden's closeness had made me dizzy earlier, his touch left me drunk now. I couldn't rise if I'd wanted to. The cold from before was completely forgotten as his heat transferred to me, zinging through my body in a most pleasant way.

Then I met his gaze...and all was lost. He looked at me with a fierceness I'd never seen.

I watched the emotions warring in his expression. He seemed like a man tortured, searching for words that refused to come. Through it all, the weight of his hand on mine made words utterly impossible.

We stared at each other for a long moment. The creaking ship, the acidic smell of wet gunpowder, the snores of sleeping men—it was a distant history. Aden was here, now. Soon even this moment would be a memory.

"I wish I could tell you everything," he said softly. "But for now, please trust that I know what I'm doing. I swear it will all make sense eventually."

"But a duel? You can't help your family at all if you lose. It's too risky."

"Maybe, but I know the risk. It's mine to take, and I accept what comes of it."

His words brought me back to the Hughen square, next to the dead queen's statue, where I'd begged Father to let me stay on the *Majesty*. Where he'd refused to let me make my own choices for my future. Aden was right. I couldn't demand my own freedom while taking away his.

"Fine." My tongue felt like a piece of lumber. "I won't tell Father."

He looked at me in wonder. "You meant it, didn't you? You really would throw your safety away to save my life."

I shrugged, but only because I couldn't speak. A reflection of the lantern's light danced in his eyes as they searched mine. I felt suspended as if caught in rigging high above the ship.

His hand squeezed mine. It sent a shock of warmth up my arm. "Thank you. It's nice talking to someone I can trust." A bitter chuckle. "I haven't had that in a really long time."

A muffled sound from the other side of Paval's door brought me back to the ground. I cleared my throat and yanked my hand away. Rising to my feet felt like swimming through mud.

"Come on," I told him, turning away. "I'll ask Paval to take you in for the night."

As I made my way back to Father's cabin, I shoved my hands deep into my pockets. Aden's parchment still waited.

I had no gas lamp, but there would be one on deck. I wouldn't even have to get very close in order to make out the parchment's words. I could read it right now and Aden wouldn't know a thing about it.

A few days ago, I wouldn't have hesitated. That parchment most certainly explained why he was here, or he wouldn't have gone to such lengths to hide it from me. The *Majesty* was my home, not his, and I wouldn't have questioned my right to assess the danger Aden brought.

But something stopped me now. Aden had seen through my disguise in an instant. He'd endured my suspicion and scorn and expressed interest in who I was anyway. And now he knew my driving desire to become captain when nobody else did. Somehow, I'd grown to trust a prince of Hughen more than my own father. And somehow, that prince trusted me—a sailor girl who'd swindled and teased him and harbored a ridiculous dream that contradicted everything his kingdom stood for. I didn't want to lose that.

I couldn't bring myself to open that parchment. Not when its contents could shatter the brittle happiness that had settled around my heart.

I'll read it after the duel, I reasoned. When Aden was safe and the danger of mutiny was over.

It wasn't until I'd gone to bed and lain in the darkness for hours that I dared admit the truth. Respect for Aden hadn't kept me from reading that parchment. I'd been hunted by soldiers, chased by pirates, and shot at by Hughen guards. But none of that compared with the feeling of Aden's hand on mine.

It was the deepest, most terrifying fear I had ever known.

22

Father called all hands once the horizon released the sun into the sky. He'd already been up for hours. By the shadows under his eyes, he'd slept as poorly as I had.

In fact, the only person who appeared rested was Kempton. He emerged wearing his Messaun uniform, of all things, green with a trim sharpness to the edges. And tassels on the sleeves, of course. I'd never understand Messaun fashion. Kempton had eaten cold pork for breakfast, washing it down with a double dose of coffee chased by rum. His favorite pre-battle ritual.

Aden hadn't eaten anything. He stood with his back to the rail, clenching and unclenching his fists as the shadows began to flee. The sleeves of his borrowed shirt were rolled up, his collar open. The sun had touched him in a favorable way, giving his face a warm flush, and his chin displayed a bit of dark stubble. Sea life suited him after all. I tore my gaze away after a moment so the others wouldn't notice my gawking.

The last men arrived. When this duel was finished, the watches would switch, and all would resume as normal. Except that there would also be a body to deal with.

"Take your weapon of choice," Dennis called out.

It was a formality. Kempton had already chosen his usual cutlass, curved on one end and nearly as tall as a man stood. Aden had passed over the thin rapier, thankfully, and chosen a broadsword instead. It wasn't practical for naval combat—broadswords were meant for a level battlefield or a dueling court, not a bucking ship. The only comfort was how easily he gripped it, the copper hilt resting lightly in his right hand.

At Dennis's command, Kemp and Aden held up their weapons for all to see. Neither weapon appeared to have been tampered with. It was time to begin.

Dennis's eyes flicked to me, then back to my father. "They're yours, Captain."

My father nodded. "In accordance with ship law, these two sailors defend their innocence in the matter of sabotage. Winner is the last man standing. Are you ready?"

"Ready," Aden said, and he seemed it. He stood with a look of intense concentration, switching the weapon's copper hilt from right to left hand. Then he settled into reverse dueling stance. It was the stance of a soldier, intended for speed and agility.

If Aden was the fox, Kemp was the hunter. He stood squarely in front of Aden, cutlass raised at shoulder height as if he was determined to hack right through him the moment the duel began. Kemp's eyes were tiny slits in a grizzly, gnarled face, but I knew he was sizing up his opponent. The man had a head for combat in all its forms. It was another reason my father had appointed him gun master.

"Ready, Cap'n," the large man said coolly.

A trickle of sweat traveled down my chest, suddenly making my bindings unbearably itchy.

"Then . . . begin!"

I expected Kemp to lunge first, but something about Aden's

demeanor must have made him pause. Kemp lowered his sword slightly, calculating, then took a step forward. Aden moved backward at the same moment. As Kemp advanced, Aden retreated. It was a slow, agonizing dance of wits.

A second later, Kemp's eye twitched, and he lunged, cutlass swinging downward toward Aden's neck.

But Aden was ready. Rather than stepping back, he circled around the side and blocked Kemp's sword with his own. The sharp slam of metal on metal reverberated, causing the watching men to cheer.

Kemp pulled back, and Aden took his stance again, calm as ever. There was something new in his expression. He'd seen something in Kemp's attack, and he was forming a plan.

Kemp lunged again, this time swinging his sword overhead in a high arc, as if he meant to slice Aden down the middle. But Aden was too quick, moving aside and allowing Kemp's momentum to send the man stumbling to his knees. Enraged, Kempton leaped to his feet, charging with murder in his eyes.

Aden blocked the first blow, though it clearly threw him off-balance. He managed to regain his stance just as Kemp launched into one heavy strike after another. Aden stood several inches shorter, and Kemp's attacks carried the strength of two men. Steel clashed, echoing sharply against the hard deck. It seemed it was all Aden could do to block the blows aimed at his head. He still held the sword in his left hand.

He was disguising his skill, I realized, even though it made him weaker. Just as I'd asked him to do. A wave of frustration swept over me. Much as I wanted to respect his decision, this felt incredibly foolish. I imagined myself shouting out who he was and watching Kemp drop his sword, stepping back in horror. Could I truly stand here and say nothing while the gun master shoved his blade through Aden's chest?

"C'mon, Kemp," Dryam shouted through his beard. "Show 'im what we do to those who mess with our defenses."

Aden tripped and fell under another heavy blow, sending a wave of men stumbling out of the way. He swung his weapon at Kemp's waist, forcing him back, and climbed to his feet, breathing hard. Then he snapped into soldier's stance again.

Kemp snorted at the sight. "You'd have me believe you're military trained?"

"Believe what you like," Aden said. "Unfortunately, your own style can't easily be described, Master Kempton. The best description is that of a lovesick gorilla."

There was a collective gasp. Even my father gaped now, his eyes clamped on Aden as if seeing him in a new light. The crew's whispering began in earnest. If Aden had a death wish, insulting his opponent was the fastest way to fulfill it. My heart hammered so hard, I was beginning to see odd flashes of light.

Kemp reddened. "Served in the navy for sixteen years. I been fighting since before you were born!"

"Fighting what?" Aden shot back. "Bulbous manatees?"

"I'll ram my sword down yer lying throat."

"That would require aim. Something you haven't figured out yet in all these years, it seems."

Kemp's sword shot out in an arc, faster than I thought the man could move. It would have sliced right through Aden's stomach if he hadn't been ready. His sword met the threat with a clang. Now it was a real battle.

Both men lunged, parried, retreated, and met the attack clash for clash. Their swords whipped faster than my eyes could follow. They didn't talk now—the fight took every ounce of their focus and energy.

The crew's chatter quieted as well. Their gun master had just met his match, and they knew this would change everything. Digby's smile was tight. The other Messauns watched with dark expressions. I was completely mesmerized. Aden hadn't exaggerated his skill at all.

Kemp grunted and growled as he fought, while Aden wore a quiet intensity. Aden was faster, but it was clear Kempton was stronger. The larger man focused on Aden's weak side, hammering in until Aden was nearly backed against the rail.

Then Aden made a mistake.

Kemp had struck at his stomach several times in a row and then switched to the head, but Aden didn't anticipate the change. His sword lowered, he watched the blow come and leaped sideways just in time, sending Kemp stumbling forward.

But the bigger man redirected his blow in midflight. The thick sword arched toward Aden's spine.

It would have severed it, except Aden was already parrying with his own blow, knocking Kemp's sword aside. Then Aden elbowed the gun master in the nose.

Kemp grunted, dropping his sword as the ship swelled above a large wave. The cutlass hit the deck and slid down the stairs, bouncing down its steps with a series of metallic clangs. The larger man barely had time to register the loss of his weapon before Aden tossed his blade aside and leaped onto him, knocking the larger man flat on his back. Then Aden was pummeling him with his fists.

I smiled weakly. Only a soldier would resort to a fistfight. Aden was embracing his disguise to protect our secrets. And in doing so, he denied a part of himself to protect me. The strange warmth from last night returned, filling my body with a nervous, excited energy.

Something stirred deep inside me, a feeling that awakened only when Aden was nearby. Something I'd been denying almost with a sense of desperation. And I knew it then, positively and entirely.

I was falling for a boy I barely knew and could never have.

Kempton immediately bucked his body upward, forcing Aden to catch himself with both hands. Then the blow came. Kempton slammed a fist into Aden's temple, throwing him rolling across the deck and into the crowd.

The crew stumbled backward, leaving Aden sprawled on the deck. He stared at the sky for a long moment, holding his head with both hands like it was splitting apart. One eye had already begun to swell up.

"I've had better fights with my own sister," Kempton said, climbing to his feet. I noted with satisfaction that his nose looked like it had been smashed, and blood trickled down into his teeth.

Still breathing hard, Aden's wits finally returned, and his eyes cleared. Then his gaze settled on me.

And stayed there.

A spark of hope ignited deep inside, reminding me of that devastating dream of having him sail at my side. What if he also harbored feelings . . . for *me*?

A silent exchange took place between us—Aden gathering the strength to win, me urging him on with everything I had. His jaw clenched in determination.

Kemp withdrew a knife from his pocket and began to advance on Aden. I gasped.

Aden took in the threat and scanned the deck for his broadsword. It lay clear across the deck, behind Kempton. He'd never make it.

"The captain didn't approve the use of knives," Aden said, struggling to his feet. "You can't change the rules of combat."

Kemp grinned. "Rules of combat? What will you expect next, a break for tea?" The Messauns behind him chuckled.

"If there are no boundaries, there is no true victory," Aden said.

"It'll be true enough when I stab ye through, little whelp," Kemp said, and leaped for Aden's chest.

Aden dove.

Kemp bellowed as his blow missed, but Aden was already scrambling past the gun master toward the sword. He grabbed the hilt and swung it just as Kemp arrived, letting it stop at the larger man's throat.

"Drop the knife."

Kemp's eyes flew wide. He stared down his nose at the weapon, then back at Aden. His grip on the knife only tightened.

Aden refused to budge. His swollen eye was turning an ugly purple. *"Drop it."*

Kemp raised his clenched jaw, exposing his throat as if daring Aden to slice it clean through.

The deck was quiet as the two men glowered at each other. The blade in Aden's hand quivered, placing the slightest of pressure on Kemp's throat. One swell of the ship, and the gun master was done for. I found myself holding my breath, afraid to move a single inch.

"Captain," Aden called out. "I request that you call the duel."

Father looked dumbfounded. He cleared his throat. "I fear there's no clear winner yet."

"In announcing the rules, you said the winner to be the last man standing, not the man who lives. This ship needs its gun master, and Master Kempton is a good one. Declare me winner and allow this duel to end peaceably so we can continue our voyage."

Kemp's wide eyes flicked sideways. A thin red line appeared on his neck where Aden's blade rested.

"Is that acceptable to you, Master Kempton?" Father asked. "Or do you prefer a quick end?"

Kemp waited far longer than he should have to respond, but finally his lips moved. "'Tis."

I stood there in shock. The crew began to applaud as Aden stepped back. Well, half of them anyway. The Messauns were dead silent.

Aden grinned and pumped his fist to the sky in victory.

Kemp lifted a hand to his throat. There was no relief in his expression. Just hatred. Raging, barely controlled hatred.

"You have received Right of Steel and acknowledged your loss, Master Kempton," my father said. "I declare Aden the winner and a sailor of equal standing under my protection. If something should harm him, blame will fall immediately on you. Do you understand?"

Kemp's reply was once again slow in coming. "Aye."

"Then let us return to work. This ordeal has already cost us precious time, and Dennis still has an investigation to conduct. Kempton, assign a guard to watch the gun deck until our arrival, day and night."

Kemp spoke through his teeth. "Aye, sir."

"Return to stations," Dennis called out. The men began to shuffle away, muttering to one another in low voices.

I barely noticed. All I saw was Aden, his fist raised to the sky. His stance was identical to that sketch of King Eurion. The man who wanted me and every other woman sailor dead. *His father.*

Or had I forgotten that?

I strode quickly toward the stairs, my feet moving automatically despite the numbness in my mind. The crew members had divided into camps—those muttering about the captain's unfairness and those slapping Aden on the back for his victory. Nobody seemed to care about the captain's boy hurrying toward the solitude of the hold, a piece of folded parchment clutched in both hands.

I paused at the bottom of the ladder and angled the parchment to the light, ignoring how my fingers shook as I unfolded it.

To King LeZar, Monarch and Leader of our Brother Nation Ellegran:

I've sent this missive with Cedrick in the most urgent manner, as I've just received intelligence that Khral Rasmus means to assassinate me at the Treaty Renewal Feast.

I've taken precautions to ensure that does not occur. However, I request the immediate arrival of your fleet to prevent Khral Rasmus and his military from taking further action. I believe our two navies will dissuade him from doing anything foolish. We both know that if he is to succeed, his conquest will not end at my kingdom. He will not rest until the entire world flies a Messaun banner, Ellegran included.

I need not remind you of the numerous occasions on which I have employed my navy to assist you in the past. I declare your debts to have been paid in full once this threat is dealt with. Until then, please keep my son safe until I send word that all is well.

Yours,
King Eurion of Hughen

The missive fell from my hands. It fluttered to the floor and slid into the shadows beneath the ladder. I stared at it for a long moment, frozen in place. There wasn't enough air in the entire room. It may as well have been filled with water, and I was slowly drowning. This was so much worse than I'd thought. No wonder Aden had been kind to me. It was a wonder he'd been able to hide his guilt at all. I wasn't helping a runaway prince.

I had placed the *Majesty* squarely into the middle of a war.

23

I should have been exhausted after that night's watch, but sleep eluded me once again. I lay in my hammock for an hour before giving up. I sneaked out to the sound of my father's snoring and, wincing at the deep ache in my shoulder, climbed up the ratlines. They were heavy from the evening's rain.

Barrie had the nest watch. By his pained, bleary-eyed expression, I could see he needed a break, so I offered to take his place. He accepted with a tired nod. His movements were careful and stiff as he climbed down. I doubted he'd slept much the past two days either.

I'd forgotten my coat, but I wasn't about to go back for it despite the night's chill. I curled up against the wall to guard myself from the wind. The wood was still slightly damp from the storm, and the cold seeped through my clothing. It fit my mood.

The still blackness of the night sky felt familiar. No matter what poor decisions we made, at least the ocean was always the same. Dependable. Storms came through now and again, but it always returned to this state eventually. This was home. But the sameness failed to calm me tonight.

Aden was a true royal, and I should never have assumed differently. He'd used me as surely as any servant, manipulated me into delivering ship and crew. Listened to my fears and then used them against me. I'd happily walked into it all. Fallen for him, even.

Not Aden. *Cedrick.* He'd even lied about his bloody name.

I sighed and tightened my arms around my knees. Aye, the sea was constant, but my thoughts were stormier than ever. The girl I kept locked away had crept from her hiding place and taken flight, dreaming like she'd never dreamed before about a boy she barely knew. For a brief, impossible moment, I'd allowed her to hope. Then a missive had torn that hope to ribbons.

Aden—Cedrick—was simply obeying his father, ever the dutiful son and errand boy. The very thought that we could leave his kingdom behind and sail off together was laughable.

The lines slapped against the wood. Someone was climbing. I knew without looking that it was Aden.

His arm appeared first, then his leg as he pulled himself over. The hard landing made him grimace. His eye and part of his cheek were a deep purple, evident even in this light. I could practically see Kemp's knuckle marks.

"Hard to see the ropes in the dark," he panted. "Er, lines. I keep forgetting."

I turned away, irritated at my traitorous heart, which had begun to pound. Even the wet wood seemed to warm at his approach. The world might arrange itself to please him, but he didn't control me.

"I've been looking for you," he said. "You disappeared after the duel. Are you all right?"

I kept my voice flat. "You fought well. Congratulations on your victory."

He snorted. "What victory? Kempton is furious, and his men

have been glaring at me all day. It's a good thing we only have about a week left." He paused. "Did something happen?"

"I'm glad," I said, ignoring the question once more. "You even managed to defeat Kemp without revealing yourself. You must be very proud."

"Lane." Aden took my arm and pulled me around to look at him. His face was drawn in concern. "I'm not a complete fool. Please. Tell me what's wrong."

I yanked my arm free and turned away, setting my gaze rigidly on the night sky.

He went quiet. "You know why I'm here."

I didn't answer.

"You found the missive, then. Do you still have it?"

I nodded but didn't offer to return it yet. Did Aden truly not see that he'd branded us forever? Trade ships remained strictly neutral, avoiding political entanglements to protect business and crew both. My father's stand in the harbor had been bad enough. He'd be horrified to hear that we were now wanted in both Hughen *and* Messau— Hughen because he'd broken the law in leaving, and Messau because he was helping a Hughen prince fetch an army against the khral, however unknowingly.

A part of me wanted to wake my father, wave the king's order in his face, and beg for mercy. He'd know what to do. But that would also involve admitting my part in it, and I couldn't bear to see his expression when he discovered I'd plunged us headlong into a war.

I missed being able to talk freely with Father about things like this. Well, not precisely like *this*. I missed talking about insignificant matters with the crew and discoveries I'd made and jokes I felt were worthy of sharing. But this was no joke, and there were lives at stake. I'd been too self-absorbed to see that. Too withdrawn into myself, worrying about what people saw when they looked at me. Concerned about Kemp's mysteries and Aden's secrets, and whether this was my last voyage on the *Majesty*.

The lies had become such a part of myself, I couldn't discern what was real and what wasn't. What had I become?

Aden sagged against the box. "Look, my father ordered me not to show it to anyone, and...no, you deserve better than that. I risked your life and didn't allow you to choose otherwise. It was wrong of me."

The frustrating thing was, I still couldn't tell the crew. If they discovered Aden was a prince on a secret mission to save a doomed kingdom, Kemp's mutiny would spring without question. Most of the men resented nobility as much as I did, let alone royalty. Half would be livid at the captain's deception and the other half would try to use Aden as some kind of prize. Maybe even ransom. He wouldn't be safe and neither would my father. Nor I, for that matter. But that didn't take away the pain.

"I know you're angry, and I understand," he said softly. "But I need that missive back."

"First you'll answer my questions."

He gave me a long look. "That depends on the questions."

"Tell me why he sent you instead of a messenger. And why a merchant ship when he has an entire navy fleet at his bidding?"

"That's complicated." The air left him in a long sigh. "My father's high advisor, Lord Varnen, initiated a secret alliance with Khral Rasmus. Or perhaps it was the other way around. We aren't sure. My father was too trusting from the start and allowed Varnen to oversee the king's guard and his military generals. By the time my father discovered the plot to assassinate him at the Treaty Renewal Feast, the betrayal was too deep to determine where it began."

I nodded, though it still didn't quite make sense. Hughen had gained its independence from Messau shortly after Elena's death. If Messau wanted to end the twenty-year treaty, why not simply refuse to renew it?

"They intended to murder him in public," I said. "Seems unwise with so many witnesses."

"Varnen drew up the guest list himself. The 'witnesses' would be plants, paid to lie about my father attacking Rasmus first. There was no time to root Varnen's spies out of the military without signaling that the king knew their plan. So Father sent my mother and sisters to visit family and wrote this missive."

"He didn't trust any of his men, so he sent you. His own son."

Aden's—*Cedrick's*—voice was slightly bitter. "The son he could spare, that is."

Now I remembered. "Your mother is the king's second wife," I said. "Because Elena murdered the first when Mael was a child. Why did you tell me to call you Aden?"

"My father named me Cedrick after a distant grandfather. My mother has always called me Aden. I prefer it."

The missive's sharp folded edges dug into my waist. "What is your father doing in the meantime?"

"Pretending nothing is amiss. He knows he'll be safe enough if Rasmus and Varnen intend to wait until the feast. As the second son, few will have noticed I'm gone." There was that bitterness again. "My father's life depends on what you choose to do with this information, Lane. If you can keep it a secret until we arrive, King LeZar just might have enough time to gather his forces and return before the celebration begins."

I grimaced. King Eurion's life was in *my* hands? It was the last thing Aden wanted to tell me right now, I was certain. And even if we arrived as scheduled, it would be difficult for the Ellegran king to send his navy in time. But I didn't want to quell Aden's hope, so I let it lie. "Your father didn't send Varnen after us at the docks. The advisor sent himself."

"Father and I feigned an argument before I left," he said. "He planned to say that I ran away in anger. I suspect Varnen wasn't convinced. And then that port incident...If you hadn't agreed to help, this mission would have failed before it began."

"How certain was your father of this threat?" I asked, feeling a mite dizzy.

"He didn't make these decisions lightly. He wouldn't have thrown away two decades of peace with Messau without evidence, not when peace came at such a high cost. He's also a proud man who hates asking for help. If he sent me away, he must have seen no other recourse."

His last words were strained. Now it was him who stared at the sky.

I moved to sit closer to him, knowing his pain too well. It was the sorrow of a child trying to accomplish the impossible to please a parent. "You worry for your family."

"I warned my father that my mother and sisters weren't hidden well enough. He said he would keep them on the move, but I doubt he'll find anywhere secure in Hughen. Varnen's spies are everywhere." A brief pause. "Mael was left completely exposed as well. My father couldn't increase the number of guards without Varnen getting suspicious."

"Why not bring your family aboard with you?"

"My father's own law. No Hughen merchant ship would agree to take women as passengers. Even if one had, sailors aren't exactly..." He trailed off. "One never knows what the crew will be like."

I couldn't deny that. Our crew was more refined than most, but nobody could order away a sailor's superstition. Father had a sound mind, and even he would have balked at the thought of bringing a queen and her children on board. The crew would have stomped off and refused to return at all.

"It was harder than I thought it would be," he said softly. "The stories, the disguises, the lies. It wears on a man's soul after a while. But I have to admit that the hardest part was lying to you."

Warmth surged inside me at that. At least I hadn't imagined the connection between us, however inappropriate it was.

"Listen," he continued, leaning down until his voice was almost a whisper. I felt his breath on my lips. "It's impressive how long you've managed to fool the men, but you aren't any safer here than I am. Rasmus has agents in Ellegran, men who will kill me on sight." He paused, looking at me with the same intensity I'd seen in him during the duel. "Lane, we need each other."

I snorted. "You don't need me."

His expression was raw again, uncertain. "I know this will sound strange to you, but something else happened that first day we met." He chuckled. I sat up straighter at the hesitance in his voice. "There I stood in my ridiculous muddy shirt, and you in your ill-fitting men's clothes, and you stared back at me, and I just...felt something. Like you could help me win this."

His words only deepened the numbness in my mind. A prince saw me as a sign. An abnormality that marked his path, nothing more. A talisman for a noble knight to retrieve and use along his journey.

Two facts remained. First, Aden had used me, lied to me, and taken advantage of my friendship for his own ends. I couldn't trust him. Second, he served his father. That would forever place us on opposite sides. I would never risk myself to save a tyrant who wanted me dead, no matter how addictive his son's smile was.

"You don't even know who I am," I said. "Do you want my axes, or me? Do you want a servant or a companion? A hunting hound, perhaps?"

He pulled back. "I didn't mean it like that."

"I don't care what people see when they look at me. I'm not leaving this ship. Not for you, not for anyone. And I'm definitely not being forced off by a twisted Edict from a man who would send his son into danger to save his own head." I turned back to the edge, looking out over the black sea.

"Lane." Aden's voice was rough now. He slid his hand down the inside of my arm, toward my hand. His finger brushed my palm, hesitantly. When I didn't pull away, he enclosed my hand in his. "That came out wrong. I do need you—as you are, no deceptions or lies. I'm asking you not as a prince, but as a man. Would you consider leaving with me when we reach Ellegran?"

His hand was warm. New calluses had formed on his palms, but his nails were trimmed, and his skin was still soft as a royal's. It was the exact opposite of my hands, which had seen storms and harsh winters abroad. I'd given myself slivers mending lines and sliced my fingers too many times to count. He was probably wincing inside at the roughness of my hand beneath his.

If signs existed, that was mine. It was as if the stars had shouted that we didn't belong together, that we fit like a dove and a stone. Aden had been made to explore the world in a way I never could. I could be thrown and soar with him for a moment, but the ground would always claim me in the end.

I tore free, then retrieved the missive and shoved it into his hands. "I can't help you save your father. I'm sorry."

In daylight, I would have attempted the fifteen-foot leap and slid down to the deck. But it was too dark for that. I'd have to put distance between us the slow way. I swung my leg over the side and began to descend the ratlines.

"Can't, or won't?"

I paused. "A little of both."

"Then if you hadn't read that missive first, you would have come."

"You have the watch." I set my feet on the next set of rungs.

"At least tell me why."

My insides were cracking down the middle, but I managed a casual shrug. "It's simple, really. You're a prince."

"And you're a sailor girl. I don't see why that decides anything."

My lips refused to form words. I just shook my head. He hadn't been abandoned as a child by a mother of station, nor had he seen a father's suffering over their shattered marriage. He couldn't understand.

"You'll never forgive me, then," he spat. "No matter how I try to help, ultimately, it's what I am that matters."

"That's right."

He gave a sad smile. "I never thought I'd hear that from you."

My heart threatened to wrench apart. I still felt that draw toward him, and the girl deep inside screamed at me to climb back up, to throw myself into his arms and tell him I'd changed my mind. But my legs had better sense, and I found myself descending once again.

It wasn't till I reached the deck that I looked up. His dark form stood motionless overhead, watching me over the edge of the box. He hadn't moved.

I hurried into my father's cabin and closed the door softly behind me before sinking shakily to the hard deck floor.

24

I lay on my hammock the next morning, one leg hanging off. I let it swing lazily back and forth, to and fro. One side and then the other. Two opposites, forever apart.

My fingers stroked the calluses on my palm. The warmth of Aden's touch had long since faded, but his hurt expression remained stubbornly rooted in my thoughts.

I never thought I'd hear that from you.

I'd made the right decision. I had. Aden was generous and thoughtful, but he was still a prince who saw me—us—as objects to be used. If I'd agreed to help him again, he'd return to his life of fancy clothes and court banquets before I could blink and abandon me just like everyone else had.

My mum wormed her way into my thoughts again. Her honey-brown hair, falling in soft waves over her shoulders, was what mine would look like someday.

Which meant I would never, ever stop cutting it.

There was a squeak across the room, then a heavy *thump* as Father slid out of his berth. His familiar step sounded, heading in my direction. I kept still, hoping he'd assume I was asleep.

The sheet parted and his face appeared. "You awake, Lane?"

"Aye," I sighed.

He stepped inside and let the sheet fall behind him. "Doesn't look like you slept much."

I didn't answer. What snatches of sleep I'd managed to get were flooded with dreams of Aden taking my hand, pulling me back into the nest with him, holding my face in his gentle hands, and leaning forward—

My traitorous cheeks were warm again. I flung the dream aside and tried to focus on my father. There was more silver in his hair these days. He looked older today than he ever had.

"There's something I need to discuss with you, Lane. Something we've needed to talk about for a long time."

I went still. Was he about to tell me his pirate history?

"I said I would be making a decision about your safety. I worried that the pirates were the bigger threat, but now I fear something far more dangerous. Something I didn't realize was a problem until that duel." He paused. "Your mum would've been better at this."

I realized where this was going. Ellegran. *Mum.* He'd made his decision.

Dread settled in my gut.

"You have to actually *raise* a child before you can be good at it," I said with more confidence than I felt. "Dropping her at the docks doesn't count."

His eyes were distant. He hadn't even heard me. "She wanted a baby, you know."

"What?"

"'Twas me who balked when she said you'd be coming. But that all changed when I first held you. Visited you several times between trips while you were growing. She was so proud to show you off, dressing you up and waving from the docks."

I gaped at him. The woman he'd just described couldn't possibly have written those missives I'd found in his belongings. "That's not the way I remember it."

Father leaned against the wall with a weary groan. "Aye. That's because she changed. Nara was always a restless woman. Her heart must have wandered until…well, she decided we were a mistake, you and I both."

I set my jaw, locking my emotions up tight. "She did us a favor, then. Don't know how you could have loved someone like that in the first place. That's not what love's supposed to be."

"Oh, you know all about love now?" He chuckled. It had a bitter edge to it. "I saw how you looked at Aden during the duel. This fascination you have with him isn't love, Lane. Love is thinking about someone all day and dreaming about them at night, missing them so much it scrapes your insides. Feeling like a whole person when you're together, like you can leap over the ocean and then some. Them looking at you like you're the best thing that ever graced the globe, making you want to be exactly that. Love is somebody you never knew you were missing until the day you meet."

Something happened that first day we met, Aden had said. *I just…felt something.*

Something inside me twisted, an ache that shouldn't have been there. I shifted uncomfortably, pulling my knees tighter against my cursed chest. The bindings were painful these days, and my trousers weren't fitting the way they should. My body was bursting out of my clothes like the hurt betraying my heart. Whatever love my parents once had was gone now. It had been gone for over a decade. All except the trickle I saw in my father now, the whisper of an affection hidden deep as the ocean floor.

"I don't regret your mum. I truly don't. Everybody deserves love, even if it won't last. Even wanderers like you and me. Perhaps especially us." He reached out and mussed my hair like I was a child. "Besides, I got you out of the deal."

"She was a lady and you were an inexperienced merchant captain. It should never have happened in the first place."

"These feelings hit stronger than you think. One day you're going about your business, the next you're staring at a woman like a sailor who's seen his first lichen whale, glorious as the ocean itself. It can't be helped. One day it will happen to you. All I ask is that you learn from my mistake. Make sure it happens with someone free to give you their entire heart. That boy Aden is most definitely not for you, and he can't be trusted with your secrets." He leaned forward. "Let's agree that soon after you settle down in Ellegran, you'll find a nice lord and forget about all of this."

After I settle . . . "You don't mean that."

"Aye. 'Tis the right thing. You'll be going ashore to live with your mum and have a safe, normal life."

My face burned hot. "How could you still not know me at all? I don't want to marry. I want to fight pirates and have adventures and speak every language there is." My voice grew louder, but I didn't care who overheard. "I don't want to stitch pretty flowers. I want to repair giant sails to be filled with the sea wind. I don't want to wake to the same home, the same life, every day. I know the risk of staying, and I accept it. The Edict isn't what stands in my way. It's you."

I expected him to snap back at me and issue immediate punishment. But the expression on his face was even worse, as if I'd stabbed him in the gut.

A sailor whistled outside, a happy tune that sliced through the tension hanging heavy around us. Father glared at nothing for a long moment. I didn't feel any better for my words, but I refused to take them back. I meant them all.

"I raised you to love all the same things I do," he finally said, "and I can't blame you for it. You may be right about the life of a lady. I can't rightly say. But at least you'll be safe in Ellegran."

"The Nara you loved doesn't exist anymore. There's no future there for either of us. Don't do this." My voice betrayed an edge of panic as I pictured watching the *Majesty* sail away without me, my father along with it. It would be like separating a piece of myself.

"There's no future for you here either, I'm afraid. Nara was my anchor and my north for a long time. I'd be pleased if you became much like her."

I gritted my teeth, knowing that beneath his stern expression was stubbornness matched only by my own. The man's ears had to be plugged with seaweed. "If she's what it means to be a woman, I'll be precisely the opposite."

Father sighed and tried again. "I nearly lost you once."

I stared at him, speechless. If he'd looked like an old man before, he looked ancient now. His very flesh seemed to sag. He'd borne this weight for a very long time.

"You were seven," he whispered. "A crew member had suspicions about you. Instead of coming to me like the others had, he took shore leave in Hughen and went straight to the king's guards."

Like the others had. "You mean...more than one knew?"

"Over a dozen suspected, all told. They left soon afterward. Didn't want to be implicated if you were discovered." He shook his head. "Usually a little gold was enough to seal their tongues, but I suppose this man thought the king's offering would be greater. He was right."

I recalled how light that bag of gold had been in his secret chest. Horror gripped me until I could barely breathe. "You don't give the men your share to be kind. It's a bribe."

"Most were smart enough to keep quiet. I figured paying the entire crew well would dissuade any bad ideas in the future. When I heard the inspectors were on their way, I sent you off with Paval to order supplies in Boghdale. They arrested me instead and searched the ship."

I remembered now. Father had disappeared for an entire week. Dennis had told me he was away conducting business, but everyone was tense and tight-lipped about the whole affair. Then Father had returned, and we'd left within the day.

"What happened?" I asked softly.

"The hen farmer, Pahn, visited me in the dungeon and offered me a bargain. If I sold him the *Majesty*, he would use a portion of it to bribe the guards. I agreed. They dropped the charges and released me the next day. It took me six years to buy my ship back. It's... expensive to halt tongues once they've started wagging."

"That's why you limit the crew to three years of service. So they won't suspect my age."

Father nodded, his eyes guarded.

Most of the crew had become family, but there was the occasional sailor who stopped talking when he spotted me nearby, or excluded me while playing cards, or hurried off the ship at leave so I couldn't join him. I'd assumed they thought me likely to carry their gossip back to the captain. Apparently, it was far worse than that.

Some of the men even made the double cross sign on their chests while boarding. Had they been warding off Elena's spirit... or my own?

All the hiding, the acting, even the lies. Thinking it meant something had been the biggest lie of all.

"Kemp knows too," I said carefully.

"Aye, unfortunately."

I openly gaped now. "He *told* you?"

"He wanted a position, not gold." Father shifted his feet. A strange mixture of shame and anger crossed his face. I saw it now, the weariness in his very soul. He'd been the best father he could, but the lies had him bound and gagged.

It wears on a man's soul, Aden had said. He was exactly right. I barely knew where Lane ended and Laney began. Did my father struggle with his own sense of identity? He loved his ship and crew, but how many secret conversations had he endured where money had exchanged hands? How many filthy men had discussed me in the darkness of the galley, whispering about the captain's daughter, who paraded around like a fool? How many threats had my father taken from Kemp over the years? The full magnitude of my impossible dream hit me then. I hadn't seen any of it—the suspicious crew, the gold. I'd dreamed of standing on that quarterdeck like Father did, delivering a soul-stirring speech that would lead us all to victory. But a captain needed a crew. It was clear now that no crew I'd ever known would serve under a woman. Even Elena's crew had mostly been women. Now I saw why.

I could tell him about the cut foot line right now. I imagined Father stomping down to the crew's quarters to confront the gun master himself, perhaps even with pistol drawn. He kept his weapon in the lockbox, loaded and ready. But a hard realization made me pause. Did I truly believe one confrontation would be the end of it, that Kemp was unarmed and unprepared? He'd whispered his lies in too many ears. Father's authority was an unraveling line, slow and inevitable. My telling Father now would mean taking a knife to what remained. It would only bring Kemp's mutiny upon us faster.

Deep down, something revolted at my silence. Was it Father's power I protected now, or my own secret?

"I stole coins from the chest to pay Kemp," I murmured. The rest came out in a rush. "From the crew too. He said he would tell them about me, and I knew that would cause an uprising, and if they arrested me at port, they'd also arrest you for harboring me, and I... I couldn't let that happen."

"I suspected as much."

A huge weight in my chest lightened. "You did?"

"Aye. Dennis wanted to have you disciplined, but I assumed you needed more wages for your...girl things." He pressed his lips together. "No matter. When we arrive in Ellegran, you'll be safely with your mum, Master Kempton will lose his hold on us both, and I can deal with the pirate threat without worrying for you."

I flinched. "I don't want to go."

Father watched the emotions playing out in my expression. "I'll miss you, my Laney, but it's what my duty as your father demands. Your protection should have always come first. Now, I hear embroidery is a skilled art. Perhaps you can stitch me a landscape of the sea, full of beautiful Hughen blues and greens."

I felt a door close on my soul. My time on the *Majesty* was truly finished.

There was only numbness. Aden the kind prince didn't exist, nor did the untouchable captain I'd known my father to be. Not even the captain's boy I'd tried so hard to become. Everything I'd believed felt insubstantial, like a heavy ocean mist. The only thing that was real for me was a woman I could barely remember in a land far away.

The businesslike captain was back. "I'm reassigning Aden to help Paval in the galley. You will return to your regular duties until then. A little distance will do you both good."

I couldn't muster the strength to protest. There was little I could do now—I wasn't being sent away because my disguise had failed or I wasn't brave or skilled. Our protections had simply run out, and captains often made hard decisions.

"Are you a pirate, Father?" I asked softly.

His expression fell, as if I'd placed a wagon's load onto his shoulders. His gaze swept the maps littering the table, the trunks containing his belongings, the large window illuminating the room. He was no longer the stern ship's captain, but a man in pain.

"People can change the world in all kinds of ways, my Laney. Sometimes we choose the wrong ones."

There it was.

The news should have rocked me, but I just felt limp. Defeated. Now that I had the answer I'd so desperately craved, I felt as if my entire life had been laid bare, exposed under a harsh sun. I'd chased the answers so doggedly, I hadn't considered how it would feel to receive a confirmation of what I already knew deep inside.

"Why did you keep this from me?" I whispered, not bothering to hide the tone of betrayal in my voice. "I would have understood. We could have faced it together. You're my *family*."

My father actually flinched, still staring at the floor. I hadn't realized how much his admission would cost him. He'd aged years in the past ten minutes.

"Safety concerns, at first," he admitted. "You were young. You already bore a secret no child should have to bear. I couldn't place another on your shoulders, especially one so dangerous to us both. Ours is a world that refuses to spare anyone with pirate blood, young or not." His gaze slid to the axes at my belt. "But later, a different concern arose."

I gripped the handle of one of my axes and stared at him, a terrible realization descending like the darkness of night. "You thought I wanted to be a pirate."

"Your obsession with Elena. That book you keep hidden and the way you fight with those axes Paval gave you." There was a hard glint in his eyes. "Elena was a seasoned warrior, perhaps the best the world has ever seen. Even her path ended at death. I swore I would keep my secret until I knew you wouldn't follow that same path."

Every word felt like a slap to the face. He may as well have said it—he didn't trust me. After eleven years together, my own father thought me a child, pushed about by the tides of an unpredictable sea.

He placed a calloused hand on my arm and squeezed it. "I've a lot to be sorry for, but I protected you the best I could. Your mother changed who I was, and then you changed the man I wanted to be. I wish—I wish you could stay." He paused, swallowing hard. "Take a minute. I'll get my own coffee." He shoved the door open, and the sounds of singing sailors grew louder before cutting off at the sight of their captain. The door slammed behind him.

"Aye, sir," I whispered into the silence.

25

I sat on a stool in the galley that afternoon, slowly stirring the broth in my bowl. It had long since gone cold. The galley conversation was the same as always, involving conquests with enemies and women and everything in between. Most of these sailors had covered the same topics long before I'd set foot on the *Majesty*, and they would continue to do the same long after I was gone.

Did pirates also discuss such things? Did they lead the same lives as sailors, different only in their purpose? I wanted it to be so, if only to reconcile the two warring images of Father in my mind. My peaceful father, a pirate. My mind still rejected the idea, no matter how deeply I knew it was true.

"Tell that war story again," Barrie said to Aden. "The one about the two giants? I don't think Marley has heard it yet." Barrie sat too rigid, obviously in pain, although he could tolerate a shirt now. Dots of blood stained the back where the occasional scab had broken open. He looked at Aden as if he was . . . well, a prince.

Marley muttered into his ale in response, but his eyes were as bright as the other men's. Every sailor loved yarns of battles won, of good triumphing over evil. Did pirates consider themselves the good or the evil? Had Garrow the pirate thought himself a murderer, or had he even cared?

Aden pressed his lips together, scowling at his food. "Maybe tonight, after watch."

As Barrie grumbled, I examined the prince. Kemp and his fellow countrymen had glared at him as they grabbed their food and retreated to the crew's quarters to eat. Kemp was planning something, and he was being far from subtle about it.

The Hughens and Ellegrans, however, had suddenly accepted Aden as one of their own, questioning him about his military service and the challengers he'd defeated. He gave minimal answers and turned the conversation to safer topics, but the men always guided it back. This mysterious boy, skilled with a weapon yet unscarred, had managed to command their respect.

I'd been so concerned about Aden fitting in with the crew that I hadn't thought about what it would all mean—that a lying prince was welcome where I could never be.

I realized I was staring at Aden and turned back to my bowl. In just over a week, Aden would leave for his quest and Father would send me away forever. Once I sold Aden's buttons, I'd have just enough for passage somewhere. But where?

The opposite direction of Aden, I thought wryly. *Wherever that may be.* He had ignored me since our discussion in the nest. He was probably probing the men, looking for another loyal companion to accompany him on his mission. Aden could never desire me as a man desired a woman. He wanted a friend, and he'd find plenty of those willing to accompany him. And as for the other thing... well, he'd find plenty of eligible ladies willing to serve him in that way too.

The thought made me grimace. I stood to scrape my bowl clean and headed for the stairs. I needed a moment alone. A lifetime, if possible.

The captain's cabin was empty. I knelt beside my chest and lifted the lid, catching sight of my scabbard and axes tucked away near the top. After Father's words, I hadn't been able to put them on this morning. I couldn't even remember when I'd last practiced.

I found the book next to my stash of gold pieces. I tucked it under my shirt, then closed the lid and hurried outside to the steps. I managed to sneak down to the hold and settled back against a pile of bags filled with cornmeal.

I found what I was looking for quickly. In this image of Elena, she was very much alive, her long hair swept back into a tail, vest unadorned and trousers stained. Unlike the illustration of her death, this was a commissioned portrait. She held her axe in one hand and formed a fist with the other, looking off to the side with a scowl. Witnesses said she rarely smiled. In this case, at least, I understood why. Standing still in such a manner must have grated on a woman with so much business to attend to. When there was a wide world out there for the taking, what did a portrait matter?

I took a long, deep breath. Maybe Father was right about my obsession with Elena. But admiring her didn't mean I wanted to become a filthy pirate. If Father didn't know me well enough for that, maybe it was better that he send me away.

Something creaked, and my heart leaped into action as boots appeared on the ladder. I shut the book and tucked it behind me. But it was just Paval, his long dark hair swinging with each step.

I mentally kicked myself. No matter how I hid it, the girl part of me burst out when I least wanted her to. Aden wasn't coming, and that was fine by me.

"You need help cleaning up?" I asked.

"Nay. Aden'll take care of it."

I caught the scent of coffee as Paval crossed the room and sat himself down next to me. The bag looked smashed beneath his weight. "I came to speak to you. You're looking right sad these days."

"I can't imagine why. Maybe the fact that my father has lied to me my entire life, and he's forcing me off the ship when we arrive so I don't get killed by an old pirate enemy bent on revenge?"

He only nodded. "He finally told you about his past. Good for him. Going to live with your mum, then? I figured it would be time soon."

I groaned and put my face in my hands. "Don't tell me you agree with him."

"Of course. Your safety matters more than anything else."

I slumped. Paval had kept my secret for years, but he was also a friend. A mentor. He'd taught me axe fighting against Father's wishes and told me stories I should have heard much earlier. I'd assumed he would be on my side. "How could you keep quiet about Father being a pirate? If anyone had the right to know, it was me. I'm his daughter. All this time, I thought I was..."

"Fooling everyone?"

"A competent sailor. A person with a place in the world. A good child."

He raised a thick black eyebrow. "You're still all those things, pirate blood or not. Nothing has changed except how you see yourself."

"Right."

"Nay, really. You're more aware of the world as it is, perhaps, but you're the same person. And a right good one, I'd say. But you're wrong about one thing. Your father isn't a pirate. He *was* a pirate. People are allowed to change."

"Not according to the law. King Eurion would have us both executed in an eyeblink."

"King Eurion dictates what's right for his country, not what's right for the world. There's a lot to see beyond Hughen. I've met plenty of people, and I say you and your father are among the best. It's why I've stayed so long. Your mum'll be pleased to see how you've turned out."

I flinched. "I've no desire to please her."

"She isn't as bad as you think. A little stubborn, maybe, but quite beautiful."

I hesitated, resenting the curiosity rising up inside. "Did you know her well?"

"Of course. Took dinner at their home a few times. A bit fancy for me, I'll admit, but a far cry better'n ship biscuits and watery coffee." He held up his hand. "I wasn't the cook then, you'll remember. My biscuits and coffee are much better."

"What was she like? Were you there that day, when she brought me to the dock? Did she say why...?"

He shook his head. "Nay. I was on shore leave. When I returned, there you were. Captain was right proud to have you. Still is, I expect."

If only that were true. He was abandoning me as surely as Nara had. I wouldn't stand for it this time. "What is KaBann like? You said women sail there often."

"Aye," he said, though his tone was reluctant. "They do. Women captains, even."

"Like Elena."

"Like her. But your obsession with her, Lane—it isn't healthy and it isn't right. She wasn't *kumba-tah*. Pirates rarely are. Your father is an exception."

196

Kumba-tah. KaBann for *beautiful person*. It referred to the soul, if I remembered correctly. We didn't meet many KaBann, so I hadn't made much effort to study their language.

"There are bad folks everywhere," I said. "I'm not afraid."

"You could find a place as a sailor there, that be sure. But I don't think you'd want one. The politics are...Well, I left for a reason."

I frowned. "Why *did* you leave?"

He looked back at the ladder, fingers fidgeting with his shirt sleeve. "We all make ripples in the world, Lane. Some ripples die off, while others turn into waves that topple cities. I got myself caught up in one of the latter."

"I don't understand."

He'd torn a thread free and was now playing with it. "When King Eurion released the Edict, KaBann went rat-raging mad. Overnight, half their industry was gone. While the rest of the world quietly disposed of their women sailors, the southern countries revolted. Women slit the throats of their sleeping comrades until they'd taken over entire ships. Shop owners who refused their business were poisoned. Some burned homes to the ground. Everything women lost here, they seized in my homeland. And then some, I suppose."

I couldn't blame them, although I couldn't imagine killing the sailors I worked with simply because they were men. "But that doesn't explain why..." I trailed off, the answer hitting me like a slap. "You were a captain."

"Aye. Garrow agreed to take me in. The danger's long past, I think, but the pay's better here anyway." He shrugged. "Don't know what it's like now. Wouldn't risk it, if I were you."

I wanted to shake my head in wonder. Even Paval wasn't who I'd believed him to be. Was no one on this ship as they appeared?

"Sounds like the perfect place for a woman sailor, actually, but I'm sorry you lost your home."

"See that? You, Lane—you are *kumba-tah*. You have a good heart. You're more concerned about who a person is than what society says they are."

I swallowed hard. It did little to ease the tightness in my throat. Paval saw a version of Lane that didn't exist. A version that was far better than the real thing.

He patted my back—it nearly threw me off the bag altogether—and stood. "You can always go south if Ellegran life doesn't suit you. Give your mum a chance first."

"Paval?" Aden ducked down the ladder, caught sight of me, and immediately glanced away. "Ah. Sorry, but Captain Garrow requested ale, and I can't find where it's stored."

A flush rose to my cheeks. Whether from embarrassment or anger, I couldn't tell. For once, I was glad of the darkness surrounding us.

"That's 'cause I have to hide it," Paval grumbled, giving me an apologetic smile before heading for Aden. "I'll fetch the ale. When the galley's scrubbed spotless, you're relieved for a spell."

"It's finished." He paused. "I'll have a word with Lane first, if you don't mind."

Paval looked at me. "Lane?"

"It's fine. Let him come." The heat in my cheeks intensified. Definitely anger. I had done nothing wrong in rejecting Aden. If he had a problem with that, I would make my intentions clear once and for all.

"Very well." The large man pushed past Aden and pulled himself up the ladder with a series of tired grunts.

Aden stood hesitantly, staring at his boots, until Paval was gone. The stubble on his chin looked even darker today. "I'm not rehashing our previous conversation, so you can relax."

I took in his rigid shoulders and darting gaze. "I'd say you're the one who needs to relax."

He chuckled, but his flashing eyes buried the mirth. "You never stop giving orders, do you?"

"And you keep ignoring them."

Now he looked directly at me. "I always valued your advice. That's why I wanted you with me in Ellegran, because you've proven yourself capable."

I rose from the bags and hugged the book against my chest. "I've no desire to become some kind of royal servant, thank you. Now tell me your question so you can get back to kissing Barrie's boots."

"Barrie's boots? *Servant?*" A shadow passed over his face, and he looked genuinely baffled. "Lane, I never wanted—you really thought I was asking you to come because I needed a servant?"

I couldn't put into words what I'd thought. Aden was a hopeless dream like my wish to become captain—yet another unattainable aspect of my life. I raised my chin and stalked past him toward the ladder.

"Wait." He grabbed my arm.

I yanked away. "Don't touch me."

"I'm sorry." He raised his hands in surrender. "You're right. It's just that I need the missive back."

I blinked in confusion. "What?"

"The missive. You returned it, but it was gone when I woke this morning. I thought maybe you'd taken it again."

I felt my eyes widen and saw my reaction mirrored on his face.

He took a step back. "You don't have it. I looked everywhere. That means—"

"Someone else took it." I swore under my breath. If Kemp had gotten his hands on that missive...

The bells above began to sound.

I frowned. It couldn't be the hour yet—it wasn't even half past. I counted them slowly.

"What is it?" Aden asked, watching my face carefully.

"A musket drill," I said.

"Now?"

It *was* odd. My father only called for drills when the winds died and we had little else to do. But now felt like a strange time for it, especially considering how low we were on gunpowder. Had something happened? Had more pirates been sighted?

Aden must have been thinking the same thing, because there was alarm in his expression as we stared at each other. Then we sprinted for the ladder.

26

Neither Dennis nor Father was in sight when I reached the deck. No ships or storms on the horizon. I immediately knew something was wrong.

Only Kemp's watch was there, standing in neat rows, muskets hefted and aimed straight at us.

Muttering every curse word that sprang to mind, I sent Kemp a murderous glare. This was it. He was making his move. Why hadn't I forced Father to stop him?

Kemp greeted us with a triumphant smile. "To yer stations, nice and slow."

Paval burst from the cabin door like a dark, angry hound. Despite his limp, the large man looked downright dangerous. "What is this? None but officers are allowed weapons without the captain's order."

"A musket drill?" my father thundered, emerging right behind Paval. "I didn't order such a thing, Gun Master, and you know it."

"Gathers the crew right quick," Kemp said. "They're nearly all here."

He was right. Dennis's watch still streamed up the steps with their bags of powder, although they were missing their muskets.

They looked confused. It took me a moment to realize Kempton had armed his own men and locked up the rest of the pistols and muskets. I should have considered that possibility long before now.

Except Kemp wasn't the only one with a key to the gun cabinet. Dennis had the other—and he wasn't here yet. If I could sneak away and warn him...

I stepped closer to the stairs.

Kemp's men aimed their weapons at the others, who were just beginning to understand their situation. They raised their arms and shuffled over to where Aden and I stood, watching the captain in bewilderment. Barrie was one of the last. He looked at me questioningly, but I just shook my head. While Kemp's men busied themselves getting everyone situated, I took two more steps.

Kempton began. "As it be my duty to protect this crew—"

"Nay, it's *my* duty," my father snapped, "and any man who does not lower his musket this moment will receive the lashing of his life."

"A tired threat and one that the men'll disregard for reasons I'm about to share," Kemp said. "Now, I called ye all together for a frank discussion. Many of you have heard about Belza's sworn revenge. He intends to kill us all and steal the ship for himself."

I flinched. There it was.

"I've received word that pirates have blockaded the Ellegran harbor," Kemp went on. "They lie in wait for us. Garrow sails us right into Cap'n Belza's hands."

"Ridiculous," Paval said. "You couldn't possibly know such a thing."

"We communicated with a passing vessel in the night," Digby said with a pleased grin. "Seven ships, all flying Belza's banner. Said we'd best replace the captain with someone with more wits if we wanted to live. I call for a strip of position immediately."

I growled under my breath. Kemp's lies were so blatant, so obviously untrue. But his plan was brilliant. Only he, Dennis, and my father could interpret mirror messages. If he had indeed communicated with another ship while the rest of us slept, nobody could tell what the message truly said. And no sailor would dare question a warning of pirates, especially so soon after Captain Belza's release. No doubt Kemp had reinforced or even passed the rumors along with the help of his *friends*. I was halfway to the stairs now. Not a single pair of eyes looked my direction. Just a little closer, and I'd make a run for it.

"Seems like a drastic move for one man's word," someone said. "We'll need more evidence than a passing ship's opinion."

"It's more of a warning than most ships get," another man muttered. "I say we turn round and head back. If the captain won't change course, we replace him."

A third man cleared his throat. "You're talking mutiny. We'll be hanged."

"It's *pirates*, you fool. I'd rather take my chances at trial than accept death at a filthy pirate's hand."

"Assuming there *are* pirates." A cough. "All due respect, Gun Master."

It went quiet. Nearly half the crew was armed and the other half unconvinced, shuffling their feet. Kemp frowned. My heart leaped. Despite bringing more Messauns on board, the crew was still loyal to their captain. Maybe we could win this after all.

Kemp gave a tight smile. "Of course. Were that the only issue, I would understand yer hesitation. But unfortunately, I've also found evidence of dishonorable conduct on the part of our captain." He lifted a piece of parchment high over his head. It flapped in the sea wind, but he didn't release it.

Aden's jaw clenched.

"It's a missive from the Hughen king himself, ordering a spy to deliver a message to King LeZar. The spy? Young Aden."

The men turned to stare at Aden, but he simply looked puzzled. I felt the same. Why hadn't Kempton announced Aden was Prince Cedrick? It would only strengthen his case. Father cocked an eyebrow at me.

"But that ain't the worst of it, I'm afraid," Kemp continued. "The document requires that the boy not only deliver a message, but stab King LeZar in the heart afterward."

I openly gaped now, the stairs forgotten. A couple of men crossed their chests, muttering prayers for their king's protection. I'd expected Kemp to accuse my father of hiding a royal, perhaps point out the danger he'd placed us in regarding the war. But lying about Aden being an assassin? What would that accomplish?

Aden snorted. "Rubbish."

Kemp ignored him. "Odd things have been happening since he boarded. The doused gunpowder, lies spread among the men about a military career he's surely too young for. Then an experienced sailor falls mysteriously to his death. And now I've discovered the captain's precious cargo, the load he insists on risking our lives to deliver, are simple stones worth barely fifteen coppers."

My lies were boulders now, burying me until I could hardly breathe.

"Assassin?" Father broke in. "Stones? Enough of these lies, Master Kempton. You'll not be turning the crew against me today. Our cargo is copper shavings bound for Ellegran, and I know nothing about any murderer. If our saboteur is at work again, we'll address the issue here and now. The only man being stripped of his position today is you."

"Then why did we fight our way out of port, sir?" Digby asked. "I'd surely like an explanation."

My father's face turned dark, but it was Aden who spoke. "If that missive names me a killer, it's a forgery. I'm just a messenger, and Captain Garrow is still the honest man you've always known him to be. Any untruths and misconduct occurred on my part, not his. Put me in chains if you must, and let us be on our way."

My last meal threatened to make an appearance. Aden's assassin mission was the perfect story, I now realized. It would reinforce Messaun prejudice, anger the Ellegrans, and plant doubt into the minds of the Hughens. Even those most loyal to my father would hesitate to stand against Kempton now. Any one accusation couldn't stand, but all of them together...

Dryam noted my position and placed himself between me and the stairs, lifting his weapon in warning.

I cursed and glanced at the steps once more. Maybe Dennis was unlocking the case right now, gathering what remained of the weapons. Once armed, we could contain Kemp's little mutiny within minutes.

"This is all nonsense," my father said. "Any secrets I've kept have been for the protection of my men and nothing more."

"Their protection, Captain? Or yours?" Dennis said, emerging from the cabin. "They know that Captain Belza wants your head, but that's only half of the truth. Surely you'll tell them the rest."

My heart sank to my boots.

Dennis joined Kemp at the mainmast. His hair was pulled back into a tidy tail, making the ugly scar on his forehead more visible. As my father went sickly pale, Dennis turned to address us. "The khral didn't commission Belza as a privateer. He appointed him an admiral. He leads not a band of ragged sailors, but a fleet of military vessels. It's entirely possible that those pirates we escaped were indeed Belza's, just as that embargo awaiting us is as well. Belza likely studied our usual routes, guessed where we'd be, and sent his ships to intercept us. But then, we've had this conversation before, haven't we, Captain? You refused to listen, as always."

Devastation haunted my father's face. "Dennis, don't do this."

The first officer wasn't done. "I told you when Belza was released that he would come for you, yet you ignored my warning. I told you the men deserved to know the risk, but you hid that too. I'm tired of bearing the brunt of your lies and your secrets." He turned to Kemp. "I'm relieved to be done with him, Master Kempton. If you take the position of captain, I'd be honored if you'd allow me the post of first officer."

Digby scowled. He'd obviously been promised the position.

But Kemp looked as if Dennis had handed him a fleet of his own. He clapped Dennis on the shoulder. "Pleased to accept, Master Dennis."

"How dare you," I snapped.

Kemp lifted an eyebrow and turned toward our group. "Pardon?"

I pushed past the others, ignoring Aden's tug on my sleeve, and planted myself next to my father. Then I turned so the entire deck could hear me. "This isn't simply disagreeing with your superior, men. This is mutiny, even thievery, because it's my father's ship you're trying to steal. You have no idea the kinds of sacrifices he's made for you."

"Lane, that's enough." My father's face was red, and his eyes darted about. He wouldn't fight this.

It made me even angrier. "You'll hang for this, Master Kempton. I'll see that you do."

"Interesting that ye'd mention hanging, boy." Kemp looked positively delighted. "Or maybe not such a boy after all."

I felt eyes grazing my body, taking in every inch of me. There was a low murmur across the group. I stood my ground.

"Gun Master," Aden said, stepping in front of me. "I'm the one you take issue with. I'm sure the captain will address the crew's concerns in a respectable manner."

Kemp ignored him and turned to my father, who looked positively ashen now. "Let us discuss Lane, shall we? Another lie on the captain's part. How many of you has he paid for yer silence? How many of you thought yourselves mad at the strange behavior of our 'youngest' crew member? I say this is the most dangerous lie of all, for if a girl were discovered on our ship, we'd all be in danger." Quick as a cat, Kemp whipped back and threw a massive punch to my father's face.

My father fell to the deck with a strangled gasp.

I yelped, but Aden was there, holding me back. If only I hadn't hidden my axes away. The thought nearly made me bolt for the cabin to retrieve them. Aden sensed my thoughts and gripped my arm more firmly. Fighting wouldn't solve anything, not with those muskets pointed at us.

"Time to know where you stand," Kemp called out. "If you care for yer lives, you'll come stand with me. Those who remain portside will be imprisoned with our fallen captain."

The Ellegrans moved first. The Hughens followed more slowly, most staring at Aden in disgust. Nobody seemed to recognize him as a prince, which wasn't surprising, considering their station. Barrie was one of the last to go. He shot a glare at me like I'd betrayed him. In a way, I had. If there was anyone I should have told, it was Barrie. He would have taken it better than most.

The crew stared at their feet, unwilling to meet the eyes of the captain they now betrayed. Paval, wearing a deep frown, leaned over to clap my father on the shoulder. I saw his lips move just barely, then he shuffled over with the others. My father swayed as he stood, fighting off the dizziness Kemp's strike had bestowed.

"Master Dennis," Kemp began. "See these men and the girl to the brig. Then meet me in my cabin. We have a change in course to discuss."

27

The *Majesty* was a merchant ship, built to carry cargo and adapted for battle at sea. She had never carried prisoners before, so her brig was a barred crate large enough to house ten hogs or, in this case, a defeated captain and two sailors. We sat waist to waist, shoulder to shoulder, with the crate's roof just inches above Aden's head.

Four Messauns served as our guards. They held muskets loosely in their arms, sometimes pacing next to the ladder, often standing above us like executioners. It was almost laughable, really. We couldn't even lie down cooped up like this, much less attack anyone.

Father, sitting to my left, still looked pale from Aden's admission of his identity an hour before. There had been no lecture today. Not a good sign.

"I still don't understand," Aden whispered from my other side. "Why would Kempton hide who I am?"

"It's simple, Your Highness," Father growled under his breath so the guards wouldn't hear. "The only thing Kemp fears now is mutiny. If his men knew there was a royal aboard, there would be chaos. Our countrymen would demand to have you returned to Hughen immediately, something Kemp doesn't want. The inspectors would question his position and the ship's ownership. The Messauns, on the other hand, would sell you off to the highest bidder and split the winnings. If Kemp wants control over the ship's finances, he'll have to keep your identity a secret. I just wish he hadn't exposed Laney."

I knew why he had. Kemp wanted me defenseless. Even now, I caught knowing grins directed at me from the guards. They'd been ordered to keep their distance, but for how long? As Lane I was safe. As Laney, I was completely exposed. If only I had my axes. When I got my hands on them again, the blades would see their first taste of blood.

"Kemp is lying and hiding things from his men," I muttered. "Just as he accused you of doing."

Father's jaw tightened. "He'll suffer for it, live in fear of losing his position or being discovered for a fraud. He'll be tossing in my berth right now, dreaming of shadow assassins in the night. I don't understand why he kept *me* alive."

"He fears the pirates," Aden broke in. "If they do find us, he intends to use you to bargain for the ship." There was sorrow in his eyes. He felt responsible for our situation, but I knew the pain was greater than he let on. Not only would he fail to reach Ellegran, but he would soon become a political prisoner. He'd spend weeks locked behind bars while his father was slaughtered.

It was quiet for a long moment, the guards' laughter the only sound. They surrounded a barrel, playing a game of cards by gaslight. They sat on the same bags Aden and I had used when he'd brushed my hair aside, as if about to—

I swallowed, wishing for water. Kemp had ordered us fed once a day like the hogs our crate usually sheltered. Our meal wouldn't come until morning. My stomach rumbled at the thought.

"I'd like to know our new course," my father said with a frown.

"Kemp can't return through the Needle. If he follows our original course through the bay, those four ships will spot us immediately. The only other route to the Kourning Sea is around the Messaun cliffs, and that would take an extra six weeks. We've only enough water for a day more, maybe two." He sighed. "Surely Dennis will talk some sense into him. I never thought..." He trailed off.

"Shut yer mouths and go to sleep," a guard snapped, hefting the musket off his belt. One of Kemp's new recruits. "Or don't. I'm happy to bash yer teeth in." He smiled at me, his rows of crooked teeth gleaming yellow in the shadows. Right. Like that wet smile and pair of disgusting eyes would help me sleep.

Aden sat forward, leaning in my direction as if to place himself between me and the guard. I felt my father stiffen.

The man finally turned away. The three of us sagged against the bars once more. The ship listed starboard. Rough water.

There was a long silence during which the guards began to sag in their chairs, shooting us glares in the shadows. Minutes later, the snoring began. I relaxed, noting that Aden's eyes were closed as well. But then my father shifted, and I saw that his eyes were still open. The chilled deck had to be uncomfortable for a captain used to cushioned chairs and a wooden berth.

"Will you tell me about Belza?" I whispered, so quietly I could barely hear my own voice.

He turned back to face me. I grimaced, suddenly wishing I hadn't asked. Despair. Hopelessness. Sorrow. Sometime in the past few hours, my father had given up.

His eyes flicked to the sleeping Aden. Father's shoulders were slumped, his voice full of defeat. "We were...boys together. Belza wasn't always as he is now. He told everyone he met that he would command a ship someday. Even though I was older, we both knew

I'd serve under him. He had this hunger, this drive that I couldn't match. I was content with a quieter life."

I nodded. I'd been right about Belza, then. "But you had a disagreement that ended in a duel."

"You've talked to Paval. Aye, Belza saw a different future for us than I did, and he was angry that I wanted out. It killed me to injure him." There was no triumph in his voice. Just regret. "I dressed his wound myself and packed his rowboat with enough provisions to last two weeks, but I didn't know for sure that he'd survived until word of pirates reached me a year later."

"He swore to kill you and take his ship back. But he never found you in all those years?"

My father snorted quietly. "Not for lack of trying. It was rough work, certainly, trying to stay ahead of him. It only got harder when I took on a new crew and married your mum. I think he fancied her."

I shook my head, trying to consolidate this new information with my memories. Captain Belza knew *both* of my parents. Now that I'd had a taste of the answers I craved, it was nowhere near enough. "But where were you raised? Why haven't I met your family? When did you first sign on with a crew?"

Father shook his head. "I've said enough for now. I have questions of my own. Did you know who Aden was when you smuggled him aboard?"

I hesitated. "Not till the second day. I thought him a runaway lord at first." It was a weak excuse, and by the hurt in Father's expression, we both knew it.

His voice was tight when he finally spoke. "He blackmailed you."

I raised an eyebrow.

"Don't look so surprised. I like to think you would have told me, otherwise."

I doubted that. Aden was an excuse for my behavior, but he certainly wasn't the cause. I'd chosen to keep my secrets just as Father had chosen to keep his. I'd intended to hurt him like he'd hurt me—and we'd lost the ship because of it. The realization only drove the guilt deeper.

"He did threaten to tell the crew about me," I admitted, examining Aden now. His breathing was slow and deep, his body completely still in slumber. I could have watched him for hours. As it was, I tore my eyes away, my cheeks heating. "But I don't think he would have. His bargain was nothing more than desperation. I knew that almost from the beginning. Then I didn't want to tell you because you'd send me away, and I...I'll do anything to stay on the *Majesty*, Father. Anything."

He searched my face. "And I would do anything to protect you. Lands grant that it doesn't come to that."

We fell silent for a long moment, considering where this voyage had taken us. A prince's bargain and a pirate's threat. Would we still be here without one or the other? Had my deal with Aden doomed the *Majesty*, or would it save us in the end? Would Lane Garrow die or triumph at last? I looked at my pirate father and clenched my jaw.

Garrows didn't run. We fought—and we would protect each other.

"There's another reason I didn't tell you," I finally admitted. "I was angry about Belza. That you would keep secrets from me."

There was a heavy sigh. "I feared that would be the case. I assumed I had time, that there would be other voyages, other quiet moments to explain. That was perhaps my greatest mistake of all."

"We do have time. I swear it."

It was as if he hadn't heard me. "There's so much I should have taught you. I wanted you to learn how to conduct yourself in the world, how to be confident and safe as a captain's boy. I neglected to teach you about surviving in the world as who you truly are. For that I'm sorry."

"Maybe this *is* who I am. Maybe I want to be Lane Garrow forever."

"Lane Garrow doesn't exist. He's a disguise, Laney. A lie. Don't let them convince you that only boys are capable of big dreams."

"I have plans, Father. Things that Laney could never accomplish. When this is over, I'm not going back to Nara." He opened his mouth to interject, but I plunged on. "We're going to win the ship back from Kemp, turn it around, and take Aden to Ellegran in time to save his kingdom. King Eurion will be so grateful for our help, he'll insist that I stay aboard. Nobody will blink an eye when you make me captain of the *Majesty* after you retire." I grinned. "Just think of it—your own room in a nice, quiet house, with walls instead of a hanging sheet..."

He snorted as if covering a laugh. The smile faded too soon. "If only the world were so simple."

"You said you chose the wrong way to change the world. Maybe this is the right way."

He stared down at me for a long moment. "When did you grow up, my little Laney?"

"When that filthy pirate threatened my father."

I expected to see pride in his eyes. But as the shadows shifted, there was only guilt. He glanced at Aden. "There's one thing more, but it isn't safe to discuss here."

I shoved away the disappointment. "Then we'll discuss it when this is all over. No more secrets, no more lies. Aye?"

A slow, tight smile appeared. "Aye."

I awoke to find my head resting on Aden's shoulder.

I stiffened and pulled slowly away, hoping he hadn't noticed. But when I turned back, I found him looking down at me with a sad smile.

"Sorry," I muttered, grateful to see that my father was snoring at my other side. He lay pressed against the wall of our cage, curled up on the cold ground.

"It's probably good that you sleep in your father's cabin," Aden said softly. "When that sarcastic tongue is at rest, you're positively striking."

Nobody had ever called me striking before. I felt a warmth in my chest and resented it immediately. I'd grown too comfortable with Aden. *Cedrick.* I couldn't let his sweet words reach my heart. Once we took the ship back and delivered him to Ellegran, we'd be strangers once more. His princely shoulder would belong to some girl in a puffy dress with long, carefully tended hair. Her hands would be smooth and smell of soft lavender.

"You're less a gentleman every day," I said. "This ship has ruined you forever."

He grinned ruefully. "Life at sea suits me far better than life in court ever did."

"I doubt that."

"Truly. This voyage has been incredibly refreshing. I've been told what to do my entire life—who to talk to, what to say. Even what to wear and how to eat. This has been the most freedom I've ever had."

Freedom. Two weeks ago, that was precisely how I'd seen sea life. But something about his words stung me. I'd also been told who to talk to and what to say. And I was even more restricted in what to wear and how to eat. We were both prisoners in opposite worlds.

A piece of hair stabbed at my eye, and I swept it aside with numb fingers. If we were to survive this, I would need every ounce of strength in the next two days. I had chosen this life—fought for it, again and again. And I wouldn't stop fighting until the noose tightened around my neck for good. Maybe not even then.

The guards had been changed in the night. Only two now. They sat with their backs to the opposite bulkhead, whispering in the dim morning light. Two was better than four. If we proved to be no threat, perhaps Kemp would make it one. Three of us against one guard—now that had possibilities.

"You're unlike any girl I've ever known," Aden said, still watching me. "I just want you to know that, in case I don't get the chance to tell you again."

I forced a smile. "You mean other girls don't carry axes and climb rigging during storms? For shame."

Aden just chuckled. "My family and my home are in danger. Yet all I can think about is this girl who wants to become a sea captain."

Heat crept up my neck. I was glad my father slept. "Aden..."

"Don't say it. I know I've made a big enough mess already. But I need you to promise me two things. If we escape this, and I leave you behind, swear that you'll be safe here. I won't go otherwise."

I stared at him in wonder. He met my eyes with an openness that made my stomach flutter oddly. There was nothing but concern there. He truly meant his words. I just nodded, my throat tightening.

"Good. And the other thing... When everything is resolved and you return to Hughen, I—I'm wondering if you would consider—"

He cut off as steps sounded on the ladder. The guards leaped to their feet, trying to appear alert. It was only a scowling Barrie carrying a tray full of plates—the captain's tray, ironically. Three forks were stacked to the side. Our morning meal. They hadn't even allowed Paval to carry it in.

"No forks," the guard barked as Barrie approached. He removed the forks, then handed the tray to the first guard, who inspected it carefully. Then Barrie turned and trotted back up the ladder. He didn't even give us a second look. It stung, but I was also grateful he couldn't see my flame-red cheeks.

"It's clean," the guard said to the other. He unlocked the cage to place the tray at our feet while the other stood over him with his pistol raised. As they locked us away and returned to their game once more, my father roused. Aden and I separated as much as was possible and pretended all was normal. My stomach felt weightless, almost disconnected. I'd been starving until about two minutes ago.

I knew exactly what Aden had been about to ask. Lands grant that he never voiced the words.

The plates contained only cold biscuits and boiled potatoes, and there was no coffee, but Aden dug in as if he hadn't eaten in days. I detected a bit of pinkness to his ears. Or maybe it was only the light.

I'd just handed my father his plate when Aden groaned. "The hair thing. I like Paval, but sometimes it's just too much." He grimaced as he pulled a black hair from the potato mash and dropped it to the ground.

I mixed my food around until I identified another hair. He usually placed a single strand into the entire pot. One per person? That felt significant somehow.

"He's trying to give us strength," my father said. "Dear Paval. A knife or weapon would have been more helpful."

I grinned, remembering what Paval had said about the hair meaning friendship. "He's reminding us that he's on our side."

Aden swallowed and reached for more. "A nice thought, but it doesn't exactly help us."

I sat back thoughtfully. I imagined Paval preparing our meals, knowing the guards would search the food for weapons. But hair? They wouldn't touch that. "Aye, it does. It's a message."

"I'm not sure I want to know," Aden said.

Father and I exchanged a look. For the first time, a glimmer of hope appeared in his eyes.

A slow smile crept across my face. "Paval means to break us out of here. We just have to be ready."

28

At six bells, the watch changed again, and our plates were taken away. One of the new guards was Digby. By the flush on his face and his deep frown, he was still upset about Dennis's appointment.

I dozed here and there as light from above pooled at the bottom of the ladder. It wasn't possible to get more sleep than that—the rats and insects had grown more active now that we'd taken meals down here, and occasionally one of us would yelp as something scampered across our legs.

Our prison was well placed. There were no coils of harmless line within reach, let alone blunt objects that could serve as weapons. A simple shift in position brought the guards' sharp eyes upon us. By afternoon watch, I thought boredom would steal my wits altogether.

I drummed my fingers against my thigh, trying to work some warmth and feeling into my hands. The cage's ceiling was too low to stand, even if the guards had allowed it, and my back ached from the poor posture. My thoughts ran on a continuous loop. Kemp's course had to be for a nearby port. Our water storage would be dwindling by now. That meant we were headed for Messau, his homeland and the land of Aden's enemies. If we could escape our guards while the other men were ashore...

That brought me right back to examining the room around us, wishing weapons had somehow appeared in the past three minutes. What if I was wrong about Paval, and we were truly on our own? I glanced at Digby, who watched me with dark eyes, then shifted again.

"Lane," my father whispered. "I want you to do something for me. If you manage to escape, take one of the boats."

I gave him a flat look. "I'm not leaving you behind. Either of you."

He grunted but went silent.

"I don't—" Aden began, then paused at the sound of heavy boots pounding above us. Was that shouting on deck?

The guards went rigid, pistols raised, and their eyes trained on the ladder. There was a heavy *thump* overhead. A body.

I rose to my knees.

Boots appeared on the rungs and descended quickly. Digby rushed the intruder just as a blast sounded. It flung him several feet backward into the other guard, who yelped as they landed in a tumble together. Then he shoved Digby's still form aside and struggled to his feet as a second blast came. This time he slammed into the bulkhead, slid to the ground, and lay motionless.

Paval stood at the bottom of the ladder, a smoking pistol in each hand. He shoved them into his belt and glared at the bodies. I swallowed back my surprise, ignoring the lurch of nausea in my stomach. Two shots, two deaths. Our cook was as good a marksman as our gun master.

"Thank you, my friend," Father said. "Lane knew you'd bring us to safety."

Paval's mouth tightened as he retrieved the key from Digby's belt and attacked the crate's padlock. Paval's hair was messier today, and there was a chilling solemnity to his eyes. "There's no safety to be found on deck, I'm afraid. Only way I made it past Kemp's guards was the pirates."

I stiffened. The room had gone still.

"Pirates," Aden repeated, dazed.

The word slipped through my own mind, refusing to take hold. *Pirates.*

"Whole fleet of them, not four miles behind us. Belza's banner."

Another *thump* sounded, and I realized the shouts above hadn't ended. If anything, they were multiplying.

"Kemp wasn't lying." My father's voice was dull, his face draining of color.

Paval shook his head. "Appears not."

Aden cursed. I was too stunned to join him.

Father's eyes were wild now. "Skies above. If Belza's on one of those ships, we're all dead men."

Paval swung the door open and pulled Father to his feet, looking somber. "They already sent us a message. Said Belza was aboard and we'd best surrender now."

My stomach turned again. I tasted bile. This could *not* be happening. Not now.

"They're closing in fast," Paval continued. "Kemp decided to negotiate and ordered the white banner raised, but half the crew disagreed and engaged his men, arguing that our only defense is a quick getaway. They're fighting over control of the helm now."

At least some of the men had any sense. "We don't have time to argue about this," I said. "We need Father commanding the ship."

"Tell those men that," Paval said.

A gunshot sounded, followed by a massive crash that made the deck vibrate, like the ship was being dismantled piece by piece.

"Captain," Paval said. "If you desire to retake the ship, I'll charge out there with you carrying any weapon I can find. But even if we win the battle…" He didn't have to say it. Fighting would take too long.

My father grunted, obviously feeling the full weight of dozens of lives. "The alternative is worse, my friend. Surrender would doom us all. We'll take the ship back and try to run. If we must, we'll fight the pirates until our remaining powder is gone." He paused. "Or we'll turn me over to Belza and hope it buys you time to escape."

My spine snapped straight.

Paval shook his head. "It wouldn't work, Captain. No prisoners, no survivors, remember? He'll never let the ship and crew go free, no matter how badly he wants you."

"Nevertheless, I won't rule it out." Father turned to me. "Lane, you'll stay—"

But I was already moving. I swept up the pistol by Digby's hand, avoiding the body's empty gaze behind his broken spectacles, and bolted for the ladder.

"Lane!" my father hissed. Aden muttered something as he hurried to follow.

The deck was utter chaos. Either the crew had full access to the pistols and muskets now, or the Messauns' own weapons had been turned against them. Men fired at one another, occasionally hitting their targets. Others had tossed their smoking weapons aside and now attacked with blades. At least four men wrestled in a pile near the quarterdeck's steps, their forms barely visible through the musket smoke filling the air. Men who'd gotten drunk together now hacked at one another with enraged yells. Bodies already littered the deck.

I recognized all of them.

My morning meal came up so quickly, I barely had time to run to the rail. I heaved over and over, grateful I hadn't eaten much in the past two days.

Warm tears slid down my cheeks. I wanted to scream until I had no breath left—at the men because they'd allowed Kemp to turn them so decidedly against one another, and at myself because I'd asked for this. I wanted adventure. On the pages of my book, mutiny and battle at sea had sounded so exciting. But each of these bodies, broken and bloody and still, was a man who should have lived decades longer. It was secrets and lies that had killed them. All of us had taken part in it.

Even Father hadn't been able to save them.

Pirates.

I jerked my head around and squinted behind us. A dark gray mass was visible on the horizon. It was so large, I would have assumed it an island. Every one of those ships had enough guns to send us to the ocean floor.

Paval shoved past me, his knife in one hand and the cat in the other. He'd grabbed it on the way up. With a shout, Paval sliced the whip through the air. It landed upon one of Kemp's men. He screamed and stumbled backward, clutching his face as his companions scattered. Paval was clearing the way to the captain's cabin. That had to be where Kemp hid like the coward he was.

I charged behind Paval, dodging a flying cutlass, then lifted my pistol to clear a Messaun sailor who aimed his musket at my friend. The blast shocked me with its power as it always did, bucking upward in my hand. But the sailor took the worst of it, the shot hitting him dead in the chest. He flew right through the cabin doors, bursting them open as the stained-glass windows shattered around him.

I slid to a halt, breathing hard. *Julian.* I'd eaten with him just the day before.

Inside, Kemp rose from his perch beside my father's storage chest—the decoy, not the smaller box hidden in the mattress. By the flush in his face, he hadn't found the gold yet. Perhaps he intended to bribe the men into submission. A half-eaten plate of fine food sat on the map table in the room's center.

"Ah, Lane the girl. Kind of you to pay a visit." Kemp gripped the cutlass at his belt.

"Lane!" Aden shouted from behind me.

I whirled to find a man barreling down on me, a blade raised above his head. I tossed my now-useless pistol aside and dove for the corner just as he swung his weapon through the air. Broken glass crunched under my shoulder as I rolled. I landed and brushed the glass aside, scrambling for my storage chest.

My pursuer slowed, staring at the door as Aden stalked in. He carried a bloody sword and wore a look of exhilaration and rock-hard anger. He lowered into dueling stance, chest heaving. "Me first, friend."

"Save yer fancy swordplay for the pirates, princeling," Kemp said, his cutlass drawn. "You'll need it."

I heaved the chest's lid open and flipped through the contents with a curse. Kempton had gone through my belongings too. A stab of fear shot through me at the thought of losing my axes. Then I saw them near the bottom. I hefted them, letting the familiarity of their weight settle in my hands.

Aden still stood there, waiting for the sailor to engage. Instead, the man grinned and whipped out a musket.

I leaped, one axe slashing through the air. The sailor turned as I hefted the blade downward. There was a sickening *crunch*. It had caught his arm just below the shoulder. He shrieked and pulled free, but his arm hung now, useless, the musket forgotten on the ground. He stumbled out the doors.

Aden scooped up the fallen weapon and faced Kemp. I stepped to his side, axes raised.

"Nay." My father stood in the doorway, broken colored glass littering the deck by his boots. "Master Kempton is mine to challenge." His mouth was pressed in a firm line, a long axe held easily in one hand. He looked...powerful. Far different from the broken man of a few hours ago.

Kemp smirked. "It's Cap'n, actually. Or did yer stay belowdecks scramble yer wits?"

"A Right of Steel duel, then," my father said. "Winner commands ship and crew."

A duel. I swallowed what felt like a stone lodged in my throat. Aden could defeat Kemp again. He was quick and skilled. But Father...I'd never actually seen him fight. And that axe—he held it as if he knew how to use it.

I wasn't the only one caught between two worlds, two identities. This wasn't Garrow the merchant ship captain. This was Garrow the pirate.

Kemp smiled. "Agreed."

Father didn't wait. He raised the two-sided blade high over his head and charged.

Kemp looked taken aback, but he managed to raise his cutlass just in time. The two weapons smashed into each other with a brutal metallic *clang.* Before the vibration had stopped, my father had withdrawn his weapon and advanced from another angle. Kemp met it with a grunt, still looking bewildered. He'd likely never confronted an axe-wielding opponent in his years as a Messaun soldier. Axes were considered a pirate weapon, after all.

Kemp tried to swing the cutlass over his head toward my father's neck, only to slam into the axe's handle once again. He switched to the side with the same result, then tried a backhand approach, exposing his other side. My father took the opportunity to get a good slice into his back, though it was too shallow to hit spine. Kemp howled and they parted, resting for a second. Kemp's back was sticky with dark blood.

The shouts outside were growing quiet. I heard footsteps as men crept up to the smashed door to watch the fight. There was no need to explain—they knew the significance of what was happening. Their fate was being decided by two fighting men in the captain's cabin.

I couldn't tear my eyes away from my father. He'd grumbled about my axes and refused to help me practice. I'd always assumed he disapproved of pirate weapons. But here he fought, a bold and angry sailor wielding an axe like it was part of him, bent on victory. A man with nothing to hide and nothing left to lose.

"He's almost fearsome," Aden whispered next to me.

I couldn't answer. I saw beyond Father's enraged expression, his lip curled back in a vicious growl. *Fearsome* didn't quite describe it. He was glorious.

"We waste time, Kempton," my father said, gasping for breath as they pulled apart once more. "The pirates will catch us before this is through."

The large man's face was pink with exertion. "Aye, that's the idea. We'll soon be rid of ye, and the ship will be mine."

"If you think Belza will bargain, you've the brains of a half-dead gull. It isn't too late to do the right thing. Help me save the crew."

Kemp blinked rapidly, the color in his face deepening. He answered with an angry yell and a series of blows toward the head. My father stumbled backward, startled by the onslaught, and struggled to find his balance as he blocked blow after blow. If only we had a shield. Even Elena the Conqueror had used a shield—

Kemp's blade sank into my father's arm.

My father yelped and dropped his weapon.

I gaped at his arm, hanging weakly, the sleeve filling with blood, and then my father's axe at his feet. My boots felt tarred to the planks.

Kemp yanked his blade free. "I don't take yer orders anymore, *Cap'n*. None of us will." He lifted the cutlass once more, preparing for the final thrust.

The room had gone quiet. Too quiet.

Do something, my mind screamed. *Do it now!*

His cutlass swung downward.

Then I was there, my axes raised in a perfect X block and my knees bent in the defensive stance I'd practiced a hundred times.

The cutlass slammed into my crossed axe handles, the force of it nearly breaking my block and making my legs buckle. I pried my eyes open and found myself staring at a heavy blade, just inches from my face. Beyond it, Kemp's expression was dumbstruck. He'd beaten me down with cruel words for so long, he hadn't actually expected me to defend my father now.

It had taken years, but I'd finally done it.

"Wait!" Dennis pushed past us, leaping over broken glass to place himself between Kemp and me. "Don't kill them yet. Belza will want them alive. He's nearly here!"

The words seemed to shake Kemp back to the present. Breathing hard, he lowered his weapon and glanced toward the watching faces in the doorway. Their eyes dropped. If some had fought on my father's side, it was clear the captain's defeat had drained the fight from them. That, or they knew it was pointless to run now.

"Line up the prisoners," Kemp ordered. "Any who resisted. And raise that white banner again. Then we wait."

29

It took nine men to strip us of weapons and drive us to the main-mast. Father lifted his head high in front of me, ignoring the pistol at his back, though he did cradle his injured arm. Barrie walked at my side, a pistol held loosely in his hand. He seemed too distracted to be taking orders from Kemp. He stared at the sky, shoulders slumped, an occasional shudder racking his body. Not a drop of blood marred the clothes his mother had made for him. He'd likely hidden himself while the men fought. The fact that he'd emerged at all meant he was resigned to whatever fate awaited us.

The guards lined us up. Aden stood on my right and Father to my left, his sleeve soaked in red. His eyes were full of pain but sharp, darting from Kemp's men to his own to the ships closing in behind. At one point his eyes found me. I detected a hint of pride there.

As Barrie turned to join the others, my father leaned toward him. "Barrie, go stock a boat. When I distract them, take Lane and Aden and row away with everything you've got."

Barrie blinked out of his trance and turned to look at the boats, considering the words. Paval, on Aden's other side, nodded thoughtfully.

I shook my head. "We'll wait until the pirates attack. Then we can slip away unnoticed." I looked at Paval. "All of us."

"Seven ships, Lane," Paval said. "They'd be on us in seconds. If you intend to run for it, it's got to be now."

Aden swore.

I turned to find sailors leaping into the rowboats. Kemp shouted at them, but they'd already begun to lower themselves down. Our guards were half what they'd been a moment ago, but the boats were no longer an option.

Rumbling sounded in the distance. A collective gasp rose from Kemp's men. Barrie tightened his grip on the pistol. I didn't realize what had happened until I heard the splash. Belza was already firing upon us. The ball had fallen short, but it sent a strong message.

The men raising the white banner hurried to finish securing it. The pulleys squeaked as they raised it high above the deck. It snapped like parchment in the wind. Beyond, a dozen men rowed away in our boats. The rest, white faced and visibly trembling, obeyed Kemp's commands to furl sail and drop anchor. It was the naval equivalent of tossing aside our weapons and lifting our arms to the sky. There was little hope in their faces. Every second made my heart pound harder.

Cheering carried over the wind. The pirates already celebrated their victory. It wouldn't be long before the advance ship cut us off from retreat.

"Lane," Aden whispered. "We'll have to swim for it. Is there a way to climb aboard one of their ships without being seen?"

"Not without hooks." The island pirates that had attacked us years back used smaller ones, climbing in the shadows with remarkable speed. "I suppose we could hide under the netting at the bow, but only one of us would fit. And my father can't swim in his condition."

Aden pressed his lips together. "Lane, Kemp will never let him escape. But we can. We just have to act before the pirates arrive."

"I won't leave my father behind," I snapped. I wasn't my mother, nor would I ever be.

Pirates jeered as they circled our stationary ship. One, two, three vessels—all with their hatches open and guns ready. Hundreds, maybe thousands of men watched us from the rails. It wasn't worth trying to count. Anything more than two dozen meant we were outnumbered anyway.

Then the rowboats appeared, filled to the brim with armed men. They crossed the water between us quickly. Kempton placed himself at the rail, adjusting my father's best three-pointed hat. His pocket bulged. He'd found Aden's gold.

The pirates began to board.

At first, they looked much like we did, except perhaps more coarse and worn. There was greed in their smiles as they pushed one another aside in their haste to reach us. Their eyes swept the group, taking us all in with confidence, weapons raised. I felt like a tied calf watching the approach of a butcher. Until recently, I couldn't have imagined Father among these men. But today I could almost see it, his strong form striding alongside them, a giant axe gripped in one hand. His familiar voice shouting orders that would chill the spine. His shout of victory when they'd felled yet another crew.

A part of me, something hidden deep inside, stirred at the thought. I could almost see myself with them, lifting my axes to any who opposed me.

I took a shuddering breath. The threat had obviously rattled something free in my mind. Paval was wrong. Some things had no in-between, and pirates were one of them. I had no intention of letting them take my father *or* our ship.

Kemp had ordered us stripped of weapons, but there hadn't been time to bind our hands. And our guards were distracted. I scanned the deck and spotted my axes piled near the shattered remnants of the cabin door.

Barrie, standing on my father's other side, kept his hands raised as a pirate fumbled around at his pockets. His pistol was gone.

Then a hush stilled the air. The only sound was the flapping of our traitorous white banner.

Captain Belza had stepped onto the deck.

Rumors about Belza's size weren't exaggerated. If anything, they were insufficient. He stood a full head taller than Paval and wider than two men, though his skin was as pale as Paval's was dark. His blond beard hung low and tied neatly in two braids. His shirt lay open to expose identically thick, light hair on his chest.

What chilled me, though, were his eyes. They were as light as Kemp's except clearer, and they pierced through the smoke like a sword, sweeping over each of us in turn. The longest cutlass I'd ever seen hung at his belt along with a collection of pistols. This man had been born for battle.

"Honors from a fellow Messaun," Kemp said, coming forward with his hand outstretched. "Welcome aboard the *Majesty*, Cap'n. I've captured the ship for you as agreed. If you'll proceed to my cabin, we can make the exchange—"

Belza swiped a pistol from his belt and pulled the trigger. There was an explosion of sound. Kemp jerked, then toppled over. He lay on his back, gray smoke rising from his chest, wearing a permanent expression of shock.

I covered a gasp. Dennis snapped to attention so quickly, I wondered if he'd strained something. My father just shook his head.

Kemp had made a fatal mistake in trusting pirates. They dealt in deceit. They would never share when they could simply take.

Belza handed his pistol to a man at his side, who quickly went to work reloading it. Then Belza shoved his hand into Kemp's pocket and yanked out the bag of gold. "Perfect."

Kemp's men swayed, stricken at the sight of their fallen leader. Barrie trembled violently.

The pirate captain pocketed the bag, taking in the state of the deck and the pile of bodies. Then he approached the line of prisoners with searching eyes. His strides were firm and sure, the steps of a man accustomed to winning.

To my surprise, Aden moved to cut him off. "Captain Belza."

The larger man's throat gurgled in an odd way. A delighted cry of surprise, perhaps. "Young Prince Cedrick. Now this is unexpected."

I stared at Aden. What was he *doing*? Was this a distraction so my father and I could escape? I glanced to the pirates on either side, weapons trained on us. Running now would be unwise. My fingers itched for my axes.

"I was a child when we last met," Aden said. "You were bound for prison."

"How delightful to have the situation reversed, young prince."

The captain motioned for the men to surround Aden. They shoved me aside and hurried to bind him. My chest felt tied in a bowline knot. Panic raced through my veins. I'd insisted on escaping with my father, but I hadn't considered that Belza would want Aden just as much.

He had known Belza would recognize him, yet he'd stayed with me instead of escaping.

You're unlike any girl I've ever known. I just want you to know that, in case I don't get the chance to tell you again.

Aden ignored the men holding him in place. "I heard you're a Messaun admiral now. Interesting that you're attacking Hughen merchant ships in peacetime."

"Peacetime," Belza repeated. "Young prince, this is far from peacetime, and you know it."

"Perhaps you'd content yourself with a royal prisoner instead. There will always be other opportunities to chase old enemies."

"Perhaps. But why capture one whale when you can have two?"

Aden barely had time to turn before a pirate rammed the butt of a musket into his head. I cried out as the prince dropped where he stood, collapsing to the deck.

As the men scooped him up by the arms and dragged him toward the rail, his head slumped forward, and Belza came over to examine me. I straightened, hoping my bindings still held. I didn't dare fold my arms to hide the shape of my chest, not now when any movement could provoke an attack.

"You look familiar."

It wasn't what I'd expected him to say just now, and I couldn't decipher his meaning. Not while Aden was being dragged away. I watched the men toss him into their boat, flinching at their roughness. *Lands.* Belza had won more than a ship today. He now had a very valuable captive. One I hadn't thought to protect.

"Tell me where you're taking him," I snapped.

Belza's men paused in their work and turned, watching me with dark expressions. The captain raised an eyebrow. This was not a man accustomed to demands.

My father stepped forward, shoving me behind him. "You've done well for yourself, Belza."

The pirate's frown vanished. "There you are. I assumed you'd be the first body stacked in that pile over there, Naamon. Seems your crew didn't take well to the threat."

"They found being rid of me more difficult than expected." His voice hitched on the last word, the only indication of his pain.

The pirate noticed it too, because he smirked at the injured arm. "How thoughtful of you to survive so I could be the one to kill you."

"Captain," a scout said from the stairs. "There be a leak on the gun deck, crudely repaired, and their powder is unusable, sir. The cargo's stones piled heavy in barrels. Barely any drinking water left. Lost their minds, I say."

Belza glowered at my father. "I always said you'd make a terrible captain."

"The *Majesty* has another fifty years left in her," my father said. A trickle of sweat dripped down his jaw. "As do the men, if you'll spare them."

"Spare them?" The pirate got right up in my father's face. "You know that's not how we do things, Naamon."

"Then make an exception for my crew. As for the *Majesty*, she is mine, legally bound."

"We have our own laws, most of which you broke the day you stole my ship." Belza raised his voice. "That's right, Master Garrow's crew. Your beloved captain was a pirate. Has he not told you? A shame, really, that he should have wasted his life pretending to be something he was not."

Our crew gazed upon my father now. Their expressions ranged from surprise to utter disgust. I hoped that when they looked at him, they only saw themselves and the atrocities they'd committed. More interesting, however, was how Belza's crew suddenly looked at Father. There was a collective expression that could only be described with one word: *respect*.

Men had lost their lives trying to steal women or jewelry or even food from Belza. My father had stolen his ship. And while Belza had rotted in prison, my father had escaped the law altogether. As fearsome as Belza was, my father was the ultimate pirate.

It was then that I realized something. My fascination with Elena and Belza and everything pirate—it wasn't rebellion. It was my heritage.

"I've made mistakes," my father said. "Terrible ones. But my life now is far better than the one you chose."

"An estranged love?" Belza asked. "The loss of a ship and a crew who turned on you at a moment's notice? Your career will end where mine began, Naamon. You always thought yourself better than I."

"We both had the opportunity to choose who we would become. I chose to change. It's not too late for anyone. *Anyone*." Father eyed what remained of our crew. The men ducked their heads.

"Fine words, though bloated as a king's belly."

"If you're determined to kill me, let us duel. Winner gets ship and crew once again."

Belza eyed Father's arm and grinned. "I already have both. Why challenge you now? Nay, your demise will be as cowardly as how you spent your life. 'Tis more fitting that you perish with the worthless ship you stole and the crew you couldn't save." He turned away.

A pistol appeared in my father's hand. Barrie's pistol.

He aimed at the captain's back before the pirates could cry out a warning.

And fired.

30

Belza roared. The shot had caught him in the wrong side of his chest, and too high besides.

My father stumbled, grunting at the effort of lifting his injured arm. The pirate guards closed in on him, but they were an eternity too late. Belza whirled, his face contorted in rage. Then he gave his shoulders a shake and stalked over to where my father stood, hunched over. Belza drew the massive cutlass from his belt as he walked. Father straightened to meet him.

I grabbed for my axes. They weren't there.

Belza stopped before Father. The two men stared at each other, their eyes full of hatred. The deck fell silent as both crews watched. My lungs ached, but I didn't dare draw breath. Two pirates and one ship, same as before.

Something stirred deep inside me. What I witnessed now would change history. Would Belza change his mind and challenge Father to a duel? Would he—

Belza plunged the blade through my father's chest in one swift movement.

A scream tore from my very soul.

I couldn't stop it, couldn't hear anything else.

My father sank to his knees, then fell to the ground.

The pirates around me faded. All that registered was that blade extending from the rib cage—vibrating slightly, ending at a large curved handle. Father's expression, frozen in shock. Someone's gasping breaths in the distance. Maybe mine.

Belza yanked his sword free. "Down the ship." Then he stalked away as several pirates moved to follow. They were an insignificant blur in the background.

I fell to the deck beside my father. His chest shuddered, and his eyes stared at the sky in horror. He coughed. The spaces between his teeth were red.

Something warm and sticky clung to my leg. Blood was pooling beneath him. His blood. His life, draining away like rainwater. The red blossoming on his chest was a harsh brushstroke against his once-white shirt.

He shuddered again, his face twisting in a kind of pain I'd never seen. It was that sight—the utter agony he wore so blatantly, so honestly—that made me turn away, my eyes squeezed shut against the truth. A single word stabbed through my mind sure as a dagger, and I struggled to fight it off.

Death.

I couldn't think. I couldn't acknowledge, couldn't even dream that this could happen. If he would just get better—if he would just *live*—I would do anything. I'd be the perfect son he'd always insisted on. I would even meet my mum, just to see what she was like. I wanted him to be the one to introduce us. If it made my father happy, I would do it.

For a single moment in time, we'd be a family.

A family. The very idea was like grasping at air. No matter how far I reached or how strong my grip, the air dissipated between my fingers. Nay. This man *was* my family. He'd fought for me, let himself be cornered and manipulated and stabbed and...and...

I hadn't seen it. He had tried so hard to protect me, and I'd fought him every step of the way.

"My Laney." His voice was little more than a whisper.

I opened my eyes. They were blurry and warm. "I'm here." *I've always been here. I never would have left you.*

"There were so many lies. You still don't know the truth...."

"Father, please don't fret yourself."

His hand fumbled until he found mine. His grip was a tight one, as if I tethered him to life. "The ship, my position. I'd have given it all up if—if it meant your happiness."

"Neither of us would have stood for that." My voice broke, scattered like a thousand insects before the wind. I steeled my nerves and focused on here, now. "I was always content to stay with you."

I meant the words, but they didn't feel complete. It wasn't just that I wanted to stay with him. I wanted to *be* him—to experience adventure yet choose peace, to be adept at lying but prefer the truth. To be seen as what I was and not what some distant king decided I was allowed to be. To be called by the name my father had given me and a title he willingly bestowed. *Captain Laney Garrow,* daughter of the great pirate captain Naamon Garrow and defender of the innocent.

But it all felt so foolish now. None of that would have meant anything without my father here to see it. Nothing would ever mean anything again.

Another hacking cough left him drained. His next words were even weaker. "I told you to hide, to run, to keep quiet. To—to be what I wanted, then what the world wanted. But a life of lies is a terrible way to live." He grunted softly, his face contorting in pain. "Go now. Stop pretending and be the strong woman you are."

The woman I was? I hadn't the slightest guess what that meant, other than a prisoner condemned to die at the hands of pirates.

"*Go*," my father said. It was barely a burst of air from his bloody lips.

I threw myself around him instead. Warm blood seeped into my shirt, but I barely noticed. There were only his familiar arms, though limp, and the usual tooth-powder scent of his breath. His normally clean-shaven face held a bit of stubble today from our hours in the brig. It felt like his own rebellion.

He turned his head to rest it against mine, and I let myself *feel* him—to register the musky scent of his shirt that I knew so well, the brush of his eyelashes against my cheek when he blinked, how his shoulder held firm against my embrace. He placed his hand against my back and patted it.

In a second, I was taken back to those desperate moments after a nightmare, an injury, an unkind word. Those hundreds of moments he had offered me, moments like this that I'd brushed aside long ago. *Weakness*, I'd thought. *Girly foolishness*. I'd never considered that it would be those moments I clung to now.

His hand went heavy against my back. His shoulder sank into the deck, and his rough chin fell away.

The life left him in one last rattling breath against my ear, long and slow. It extended to the horizon and beyond, past a thousand painted sunsets.

He was still.

I must have pulled away, warm and sticky blood coating my shirt. I must have heard Paval's last desperate order to fight. And the crew must have responded, because the silence filled with the shouts of men fighting for their lives, rushing the remaining pirates and swiping weapons off the ground. Somewhere it registered that my father was right, that they *had* changed in the end, and that Captain Belza was preparing to row away with Aden's slumped, unconscious form at his feet.

But none of that mattered now. What mattered was how my father's eyes stared unseeing at the sky, as if a curtain had been drawn between us. Even in death, my father had defied Belza. He would never see the demise of his ship and crew.

I pressed his eyes closed and crossed his arms over his chest as a sailor deserved. He had no hammock, and I had no time to stitch one closed around him anyway, let alone give him the service he deserved. I hoped he would forgive me. There was so much to ask his pardon for, so much that I hadn't said. I couldn't have voiced it all if I'd had a hundred years.

"Thank you," I whispered. The words felt strangled in my throat. He didn't answer.

He would never answer again.

Go.

I tore away, scrambling for my storage chest in the cabin. It still lay open. I fumbled through the contents, still uncertain what I searched for. The only thing of worth was the comb. I stuffed it into my pocket and felt along the bottom of the chest. The knot lay near the back corner. I lifted the false bottom and went still. The seashell buttons were still there, but so was a small coin sack.

Father. He'd hidden them here for me. There had to be at least ten gold coins inside, enough for several nights' lodging and food. The warmth in my eyes turned hot, the grief so heavy now I felt I would collapse beneath its weight. Instead, I blinked back the hot tears, scooped the buttons into the bag with shaking fingers, and tied it to my belt. Then I gave the room one last glance.

Go.

I rose, scooped up my axes near the broken door, and sprinted after Belza.

31

The pirate captain sat tall in his rowboat as his men lowered it to the waves, a king surrounded by chaos. Men fought on deck with pistols, muskets, swords, even knives. Paval's cat cracked over a pirate near the bowsprit, the inhuman shriek that followed evidence of a direct hit. Even more bodies were strewn about. One had a scar across his forehead. Dennis.

I launched myself toward the rail, but Belza was beyond my reach. I swore. A few seconds earlier and I could have caught him. My death would have *meant* something.

"May your life be short, Captain Belza!" I shouted.

The man looked up in surprise, then amusement.

My yell brought the attention of two other pirates to me. They downed a man—Marley by the sight of his bony arms—and approached, taking in my bloodied shirt and full pockets with cutlasses raised.

I lifted my axes just as the first man arrived. His blow came hard and fast, sending the handles vibrating under my hands. I grunted from the force of it, but my block didn't break.

I want to fight pirates. One of the things I'd told my father a lifetime ago. I wanted to recall the words, to scream into the sky that I hadn't meant it. I just wanted him back.

Another strike, another block. It was just as I'd practiced, except today my opponent wasn't Paval delivering a series of careful blows. This was a *pirate*, a man who had made murdering and stealing his life's work. And I stood in his way.

Unfortunately for him, he was also in mine.

As he lifted his sword for another strike, I threw one axe upward to intercept it while the other axe swiped at his chest. He leaped backward to avoid it and redirected his sword, coming at my side. It was a move I'd seen Kemp attempt with Aden, and it would have worked, had I only one weapon. I threw an axe sideways, slamming the blade aside as my other arm crossed my body in one massive strike.

It nearly decapitated the man. There was a sickening *crunch* as my axe slid through flesh. He didn't scream—simply dropped his cutlass and sank with a dumbfounded expression. I didn't have time to gape. The next pirate was only a step behind him, followed closely by another.

My grief gave way to anger like I'd never felt before. It wasn't enough that Belza had taken my father from me. He wanted everything.

My arms trembled, but not from fear. It was absolute and utter *rage*.

I met the first pirate with a yell and an axe to his thigh. As he yelped, I spun and struck the second in the head with the flat part of my blade. His sword nearly skewered me as I pulled free for another strike. I twisted to the side and sank into soldier stance.

The first, now boasting an axe-sized hole in his leg, limped away. He wasn't fast enough. Paval reached him then, the cat swinging over his head. I didn't watch the blow, but I heard the cry that followed.

The man I'd hit in the head stood firm. His filthy lips turned into a greedy smile as he looked me over, his gaze hovering on my shirt. "Land of the bloody sun. A wom—"

My axe smashed into his face, the other following it with a brutal strike to the throat. His words gurgled as he slid to his knees, still clutching his sword. I placed my foot on his stomach and kicked him over like a tree. Hot tears cut into my cheeks. I wiped them on my bloody sleeve and looked across the water at the rowboat that carried Aden's slumped body.

Belza still watched me. The amusement in his expression was gone.

"They're preparing to fire!" a sailor screamed.

Go.

The ten remaining men—crew and pirates both—cried out, some diving off the deck while others shouted at their peers across the water, demanding another boat so they could return. That ship across the way, a third taller than our own, had to be where they were taking Aden now. Belza's black-and-red banner flew from the mainmast. I wanted to rip it to shreds, set it aflame, and ram it down Belza's murdering throat.

A series of explosions at the stern sent the *Majesty* rocking underfoot. I stumbled but managed to stay on my feet. Heavy smoke filled the air until I coughed. Screaming and more splashes of diving men. If there was a fate sailors feared more than any other, it was death by flames.

I hurried to the mainmast to gather the others, only to be met with the silence of bodies. Only I remained. Had Paval left without me? Where was Barrie?

More explosions portside. The ship listed sideways. This time, she stayed there. We were taking on water. I blinked against the smoke obscuring the air, giving the deck one last look—the rail where Aden had practiced his knots, the quarterdeck where my father had stood during Barrie's punishment. The rigging overhead where I'd spent so many hours. The cabin. A body with his arms folded respectfully across his chest.

I caught sight of another body against the mainmast and sucked in a painful breath. Long black hair. Broad shoulders. Paval's half-lidded eyes stared at nothing. It had taken three shots to down him.

It felt as though someone had squeezed the very air from my lungs.

Another explosion.

This time, the world went white. There was no sound. Just a high-pitched ringing.

I flew through the air, slow as a feather. Tiny bits of wood pelted my head, my eyes, my lungs. I couldn't breathe. Smoke had replaced the ocean air. I strained for the slightest part of it, just a small lung-ful, but it eluded me. A flash of white canvas.

And then the cold hit.

Or rather, I hit it. My body plunged into the chilled green waves—down, down. Still farther. I opened my eyes and was rewarded with the instant sting of salt. There was nothing to see but tiny white bubbles and shards of wood. Then a floating body.

I rolled, trying to get my bearings. I kicked in what I thought was an upward direction, my lungs screaming for relief. My heart pounded until I thought it would burst from my chest.

I reached the surface and gasped, sucking in air. I let myself focus on the act of living—breathing, in and out, refusing to choke on the salty waves threatening to drag me under. Then I allowed myself a look at the ship I called home.

She listed even more now, nearly flat. There had to be several holes in her to fill so quickly. The *Majesty* was following her captain into death.

My earlier rage began to cool into ice-hard determination. I would survive this. I could fight at least as hard as my father had. Perhaps this lie, the impossible belief that I could live, would keep me afloat until I found a way to make it true.

Another blast, followed by two more. One cracked into the mainmast, which lurched but held. Another ship circled after the first, preparing for another round.

A new sound cracked through the wind. Gunfire. The pirates were *shooting at the swimmers*.

Go.

I took a deep breath and dove underwater once more. The noises of battle took on an otherworldly sound. Beneath the water's surface, I could almost believe it was a dream.

I'd already begun to shiver. I wouldn't last long in water this cold. What was it Father had said—a man could survive for twenty minutes? Or was it thirty?

Just survive. I could worry about everything else later.

More gunshots. They still watched the surface above.

I kicked hard and kept my arms moving. It was difficult to do both with the axes at my belt restricting my movement. I didn't care. The axes stayed. The want of air was gripping my mind, begging, screaming there was nothing more important than surfacing right this moment. I struggled to keep focused and ignore the pain in my chest and ears. The deeper I plunged, the worse it would get. A distant flutter in the water chilled my blood even more. A jardrake slithered past. More wouldn't be far behind.

The pirate ship before me still loomed far in the distance when there was a mighty groan from behind, like an injured animal giving up the ghost.

My lungs heaved desperately. My time was up.

It seemed like forever before I reached the surface. I broke through with a desperate gasp, gulping precious air. I had nearly made it. The tallest ship loomed far overhead. The men cheered, obviously fixed upon the *Majesty*'s remains, or they would have seen me easily. Rows of cannon head still stuck out, ready for another round. There was no sign of Aden.

I dove underwater again and swam to the bow. To my relief, I was met only by empty waves on the other side. I hadn't been seen. A goddess figurine extended from the bow. Below it hung a network of netting. It was often used for fishing and sometimes bathing while on a long voyage. More importantly, it lay empty and out of sight. But how to get up there?

I flattened myself against the ship's hull, shivering violently. So cold. My mind felt as numb as my fingers. I needed something long and thin to throw upward, like a line. My shirt would work, although I couldn't very well go naked. But what lay underneath...

I tore my bindings free and wrapped them together in some semblance of a rope. The roughness of the knot would have made a rigger recoil, but with my trembling hands it was the best I could do. Then I gathered myself for one great leap, throwing the makeshift line upward. It didn't catch.

Another try, then another, to no avail. My legs were growing numb and uncoordinated. Another ship was bound to circle us soon. I would not be defeated by a few feet of ocean air. I had to get up there *now*.

I growled and fell back against the water. A new wave lifted me gently upward. *Stop fighting and work with me*, it seemed to say.

Another great swell came. This time, I timed my leap at its height. It gave me an extra two feet.

It was enough. The cloth caught, wrapping around just as I descended. I grabbed at it with my other hand. The wave descended without me, leaving me dangling in the netting. It had worked.

I swung my bare feet upward—I'd lost my boots in the swim—and plunged my limp legs through the ropes the way I'd done as a child so many times. Then I hung there, gasping for breath and shaking from the cold.

I'd escaped without being seen. If I didn't freeze to death first, I wouldn't be discovered for a few hours yet. And if I did—well, at least it would be a death I had chosen for myself.

The cheering above grew louder. I dared a look at the *Majesty* to find . . . nothing. Only wreckage and broken wood shards, and the sea would destroy those soon enough. The ship, my father, Paval, Barrie—it was as if they'd never existed at all.

I collapsed into the ropes and let the brittle wind carry me away.

32

The world faded in and out. There were only the ocean waves and their cold blasts of sea spray. The shivering stopped and began again. Water dried from my clothes, leaving the salt behind until my skin itched. The waves grew in size, causing the ship to climb high and then descend quickly, drenching me in cold water with each plunge into the waves. Somewhere in my numb and half-conscious mind, I wondered why the sea I loved had betrayed me.

The men above shouted and sang and laughed, their voices slurred and carefree. At one point, a gruff voice stabbed through my dreams, demanding silence so the captain could sleep. The other ships sailed along behind us. If they pulled ahead, they'd see me.

I almost didn't care if they did.

The minutes turned into hours as I hung there. My body still functioned, as my lungs drew breath and my heart pumped blood through my cold fingers. But I felt like just that—a functioning husk, the soul long gone. My thoughts weren't really there. They lay with a corpse at the bottom of the ocean.

As the day faded to darkness and then to light again, I clung to memories of my father. They came in flashes of color and light. His smile, rare but worth all the more for it. The shiny land boots he cared for in his meticulous way. His silly Hughen lullabies.

Were the Hughens right, and a glorious bird had taken him to the Land of Souls? I had already dismissed the Messauns' beliefs as false. They refused to discuss death, saying anyone who succumbed must deserve it. And the KaBann believed the dead joined a massive army in the afterlife, fighting to save the living from demons.

That was the interpretation I liked most. I could see my father as a mighty general, swinging his pirate axe with his fiercest yell.

Only Aden and I had survived, and I wasn't even sure of that. They could be planning to kill Aden and deliver his body to King Eurion as a warning. Or perhaps Aden was fine, and the corpse found at voyage's end would be my own, frozen and tangled in the netting at the bowsprit.

My stomach rumbled, sending another round of pain through my body. It seemed decades since I'd last eaten. In the brig, next to my father. I'd handed him his plate and we'd discussed Paval's hair…oh, *lands*. It felt so real. *They* felt so real. It was this new reality that felt like the dream.

It was nearly evening again when the call came from above. "Land ho!"

I jerked and instantly regretted it. My binding harness still held, but the constant weight had rolled it until it bit into my armpits and my upper back. I'd have dark welts by now.

Land ho. My mind fought against the deep fog that had settled in my thoughts. I'd assumed Belza would order his fleet back to Hughen so he could sell Aden to Rasmus. But we couldn't have arrived yet. Hughen was nearly two weeks away. It had only been a day since the pirates had attacked. Hadn't it? A wave of dizziness hit, distracting me from the pain in my stomach and the chill in my bones. Maybe two days, then.

It wasn't until we got closer, men scrambling on deck behind me, that I recognized the outline of the coast ahead and groaned.

Messau.

Port Column had a shallow harbor, so the pirates dropped anchor in the bay. Only two ships had escorted Belza's this far. They clustered closely as the rowboats were lowered. Six boats, all full of men.

I plastered myself to the bow, hardly daring to breathe. If the men looked over, they'd see my shadow. I could only hope it looked like no more than that.

As they began rowing away, I sneaked a quick peek. I perked up at a man with brown, wavy hair near the front of the nearest boat, but his beard was too thick to be Aden's. I scanned the faces once more. They were too far to tell. *Please let him be alive.*

A figure loomed over the rest at the center of the loose formation. That had to be Belza. What was his purpose here? The boats gave me no answers.

I sagged against the netting as the boats grew smaller in the distance. All I knew was that I couldn't stay here. The only thing standing between me and discovery was an overly curious fishing boat or patrolling vessel.

I reached upward and began to tug at the knot holding me fast. It had gone tight from the weight, and with my frozen fingers it took far longer to untie than it should have, but it finally slipped open. I tried not to yelp as I tumbled into the gentle waves below.

Bursting free, I took in a long breath of the evening air. A bit of cloth bobbed away on the water's surface. The bindings.

Stop pretending and be the strong woman you are, Father had said.

My route had never been one of comfort, so what did safety matter? The pirates had left my soul shredded and bleeding. Nobody would believe I was an innocent captain's boy now, bindings or no bindings. Lane had spent life hiding and fearing death. The waves had taken that person along with everything else. But Laney emerged from them a survivor, brave and determined. It was Laney I needed now.

Even if that version of myself had been stripped of everything she owned except trousers, a pair of axes, a bag of coins, and the memory of a prince's hand warming hers.

I let the bindings float away.

Belza's plan was a mystery, but it changed nothing. I couldn't leave until Aden was safe. Not because he was a prince, but because I was a Garrow. I had faced down pirates and even death itself and survived. If rescuing Aden meant defying my father's murderer, I would happily oblige.

Is that truly why you want to save him? a little voice whispered.

I silenced it immediately. My decision was born of duty and loyalty. Never mind how Aden's gaze captured me and his touch lit me aflame. I wasn't one of those silly girls back in Hughen. I'd just survived an attack by Captain Belza. Surely I could see Aden one more time and leave with my heart intact.

I turned my back on the floating cloth. Then I started for shore.

An hour later, I pulled myself out of the waves and into the cold evening wind. It was rocky here, and the stones cut into my bare, frozen feet. With a grimace and a curse, I stepped carefully up to the walk and stood there, shaking from exhaustion and the cold.

The weight of my axes was a comforting one, though they'd need a good scrubbing after all that salt water. I felt around my belt and was relieved to find the bag of gold intact as well. I could buy a few nights' lodging in town while I decided my next course.

Except the town lights seemed miles away, and my legs trembled under my weight like they would give way any second.

A voice called from the rocks. "It's a bit late in the season for a swim."

I jumped at the sound. My legs chose that moment to give way beneath me, and I found myself heaped upon the walk. The sky was sideways. Perhaps I was weaker than I'd thought.

A figure arose from the rocks and stood over me. A woman with pale skin and a dozen blond braids. She was carrying...a bucket?

She saw me staring and held the bucket tight against her stomach, as if afraid I'd steal it. "Oarvigs. Ye can only find them at night. Takes hours to shell them, but it's worth the work. Ye a stowaway?"

"I, uh..." It came out a moan.

"Ye shouldn't be swimming here. The Peak is safer." She stopped and cursed.

I followed her gaze to my shirt. It hung open, two of the top clasps broken. I'd torn it sliding my bindings free. There could be no doubt of my sex now.

I shoved myself upward, intending to stand. But my shaky arms wouldn't hold my weight, and once again I lay on the ground, looking up at a dark sky. No stars tonight. Just a woman holding a bucket. *Oarvigs?*

"Show me the road to town," I tried to say. But another groan was all I could manage.

"Yer a mess," the woman said somewhere far away, and then everything faded.

33

I awoke to the sound of a fire crackling nearby.

Fire.

I sat bolt upright, breathing fast. The surface beneath me felt too hard and flat to be my hammock. The tiny room around me was hidden in shadow except for the bright stone fireplace. A bundle of blankets lay in the corner. I couldn't tell if there was someone in it or not. The floor didn't sway, which meant this was no ship.

Confusion held my mind in its grip, and I wanted to lie down again until my surroundings made sense. I lifted the rough blanket only to find myself wearing an unfamiliar shirt with my old trousers.

"Yer shirt's ruined." The woman from earlier approached. Her braids had been replaced by a series of long, tight waves cascading halfway down her back. In this light, her pale eyes were unsettling. She tossed a bundle of cloth into the corner with the rest and stood above me, her tone bordering on accusing. "That one's mine. People are in and out of here all hours picking up their laundry, and I couldn't have ye wearing what ye had on."

I looked out the window. Still dark. My skin itched with the memory of salt, and there was a soreness in my arms that should have meant something...

Then it all came back.

The pirates. Our ship. Paval, Barrie, and Aden.

Father.

The pain hit with such force, it left me gasping. Everything I loved had been torn from me, and for the first time in my life, I felt completely and utterly alone.

The woman turned away, muttering under her breath.

I remembered now. I'd collapsed at this woman's feet. Thank the stars it wasn't a man who'd seen me so broken.

I pulled my feet out from beneath the blanket and tested my weight. My legs held. I struggled to stand, swiping the axe belt off the floor next to my makeshift bed. Then I froze. The bag wasn't there. I plunged my hand into my pockets, but they were empty. The comb was gone too.

Across the room, the woman folded a pair of trousers. She set them on a table and reached for the next. Had her skirt looked so new when she'd found me? And that shirt—it was too bright, too fancy to belong to a laundry woman.

"Give them back," I snapped. "The comb *and* the coin sack."

She snorted, her back still turned. "What comb? And I'd remember if ye had money, believe me."

I stalked toward her and shoved her aside. She stepped back in surprise as I scooped up an armful of her clean laundry and headed for the fire.

It only took her a moment to see my purpose. She threw herself in front of the fireplace, arms outstretched. "Wait!"

"I've heard clothing burns quickly," I said. "Let's experiment, shall we? Or you can return my belongings to me right now."

She frowned. "Ye didn't have any money when I dragged ye here. The waves must have taken it."

"You're lying." The coins had been tied to my belt when I fell. It was one of the few things I remembered. "Go fetch them, or your customers get a pile of ashes."

She straightened, keeping her arms wide in case I made another move toward the fire. "I didn't have to help ye."

Infuriating woman. "I didn't ask for your help, but I would have paid you for it anyway. Tell me what's left."

"Only the comb." She tore it out of her apron pocket and shoved it toward me. "Worthless. The market wouldn't take it, said the jewels were fake. Poor imitation too."

I dropped the laundry to the dirt floor and took the comb back. She immediately went to work retrieving the pile of cloth and glowering at me. She needed to rewash it now, but she was lucky to have it intact at all.

"Your market is open at night?" I asked, processing her words. She'd managed to sell Aden's seashell buttons and spend all my gold in a single night. If I weren't so angry, I'd be impressed.

"'Twas this afternoon, while ye were asleep. Didn't think ye'd wake at all, to be honest. Spent the night before tipping soup into yer sorry mouth until you gagged. I'll be right happy for my bed back." She glared at me again and dumped the armful of laundry into the corner.

I groaned. I'd wasted an entire day, and now I had no money. "Are the pirates still here?"

She frowned. "Admiral Belza's ships loaded up with supplies and left this morning. Bound for Hughen, they say."

Some of the strength left me, and I felt myself swaying again. That was it, then. Aden was gone. I imagined him locked up in a real brig, possibly injured or beaten, believing he'd failed in his mission to save his family. All because he'd bargained his future on the wrong ship and crew. Did he regret meeting me at all?

A million questions and no answers. I'd go mad if I thought on this any longer.

The aproned woman set herself to examining the now-dirtied clothing. "Yer a...friend...of Admiral Belza?"

I snorted. "Far from it."

"An enemy, then. Sworn to take Belza's head and avenge some lover." She chuckled softly. "I've heard that story for years. Funny thing—nobody ever succeeds."

He'd taken far worse than that from me, and I *would* have revenge. The hunger for retaliation was a dim fire in my chest. I slid the comb into my pocket. Now I had nothing of worth to trade and no boots, not to mention no way to escape from here. "I have to get to Hughen. Are there any other ships in the harbor?"

She yanked a shirt from the pile. "I've a mind not to say, after ye've treated me in such a deplorable manner. Saved yer life, I did, and ye stomp around threatening to burn things."

"I didn't have to *threaten*," I said with a pointed look. "Answer me and I'll leave you in peace."

She scowled at the laundry. "None in the harbor, but there's a ship in the bay near Lady's Port. Looked to be Ellegran built, although I spotted a few women in the bunch. Must be KaBann." Her mouth twisted in distaste.

Eurion's Edict was law here in Messau as well. How a KaBann crew had docked so publicly without repercussions, I had no idea. I tucked the information away. "Do you know where they're headed and where they hail from?"

"What am I, some kind of informant?"

"I want to leave as much as you want me gone."

She paused at that. "Heard they intended for Hughen but got turned away. That's all I know. Ye'll find out more in town if it's that important."

"How far is that?"

She glanced away from my bare feet. "Eight miles. If ye left now ye'd reach it round sunrise."

Her boots were new too, I realized. They squeaked when she moved, which meant new leather. At least she hadn't spent the money all on liquor.

"I'll take those boots," I said. "And some food for the road." The woman's build looked more slender and slightly shorter than mine, but it was close enough. "Actually, give me your blouse and skirt too. Everything you're wearing now. Then I'll consider us even."

Her eyes flashed. "Enemy of a pirate, eh?"

I ignored her jab. "I'll take what's mine or I'll take what's yours, but I'd best be holding what I need in one minute."

The woman growled but obeyed. She scurried about her home, gathering food into a bag. Bits of green cheese, a crust of old bread, even what looked like a slimy marinated tomato. Then she retreated to another corner to change. She managed a fitful stomp as she shoved the pile into my hands.

I smirked and donned the clothes, tossing my old ones onto her bed. The blouse fit fine, but the skirt pulled too tight around my thighs. I tugged at it to no avail. These pockets would never hold all I needed them to hold. Besides, my belt and scabbards looked ridiculous.

Finally, I slipped my trousers back on and tossed her the skirt. Blending in would be difficult anyway with my short hair. Let them wonder about the girl who wore men's trousers and had axes at her belt.

The woman pinched the skirt between two fingers, eyeing it in distaste. "Ye never told me yer name."

"Laney Garrow." Two words that hadn't left my mouth in eleven years. The significance of the moment felt both sweet and bitter, like old candy. I slid the boots on and gave them a shake. They were a bit large, but a far cry better than going barefoot.

"May Belza find ye, Laney Garrow." The woman stood there, stone-faced. She hadn't offered her own name. She probably would have lied if I'd asked. She lived behind a wall of half-truths and uncertainty. It was a life I knew too well.

I gave her a nod as I stalked outside.

The moon lit the road as if directing my path. Gathering resolve around my heart like a shield, I headed for the distant lights of town.

34

My boots slipped on the sandy road as dawn began to drive away the shadows. I'd walked for hours, yet the city still remained far in the distance. Structures dotted the road, their fronts half-covered in sand blown in from the coast. Even now I felt it, the fierce winds determined to rip my breath away. What Hughen had in rain, it seemed Messau had in wind.

Another gale hit, threatening to lift me off my feet. I wrapped my arms around myself for warmth. There were no trees or mountains to offer shelter. No wonder Khral Rasmus wanted Hughen back. This land was a dead thing, a country that stretched a dozen miles before the next hill. I'd have given anything for Hughen cobblestone about now.

A market wagon appeared in the distance. A man with a large girth held the reins, swaying as if drunk. Armed guards perched in the wagon bed behind him, facing a crowd of about twenty people shuffling along behind. As I drew closer, I realized they were secured to the cart. If they tripped, the mule-drawn wagon would simply drag them along.

Slaves. Messaun ports were full of them, whipped like mutts

when they stumbled or failed to move quickly enough. The slavers were one reason I always stayed aboard when we docked in Messau, though my disguise had given me some degree of assurance. Orphan boys could serve as apprentices and were therefore more worthy of protection. Few noticed when orphan girls disappeared. In the city's eyes, it only meant fewer beggars lining the streets.

I squinted to better see the group of enslaved people. My suspicions were confirmed. Children.

They varied in size, the youngest a girl of perhaps five years. She stumbled after the rest, struggling to find her footing in the rocks. Only a few wore shoes. My breath hitched as I detected streaks of blood in the graveled road.

As I approached, the small girl turned as if startled by my footsteps. There were bruises along her face, neck, even the collarbone beneath her torn dress. Her haunted eyes darted to me under choppy brown hair, her face splotchy with sunburn. Five year-days old. The same age I'd been when my own world had shifted forever.

The guard lifted his whip as a warning and snapped at her, but she watched me a second longer. Then, as if deciding I was neither threat nor hero, she turned back to the cart and let it jerk her along.

Brown hair. Deeply tanned skin. One thing was clear—this was no child of Messau. The girl was clearly Hughen.

King Eurion had publicly denounced the rumors of enslaved Hughens appearing on Messaun front lines of late, but now I wondered. Could the khral be kidnapping Hughen's most vulnerable citizens to build his forces quickly? When would King Eurion see the truth and take action?

A sickening realization made me stop in my tracks. If the king died, this was what Khral Rasmus had in mind for Hughen. It was exactly what Aden had been fighting against. And I'd been too caught up in my own problems to care.

I tried to recall what the history book said, wishing I'd been able to salvage it. Hughen suffered decades of starvation and slavery under Messaun rule—until Elena defeated Messau and took control. Finally freed from their captors, Hughen had gathered its military and fought back, defeating Elena and striking at Messau, which struggled to regain its footing. Within weeks, King Eurion declared independence and drew up the treaty that had kept Hughen safe for twenty years. It would've kept them safe for another twenty had the former khral lived to renew it.

I hadn't required Aden's missive to know the new khral, Rasmus, had a chilling reputation. I had a feeling his betrayal of King Eurion at the Treaty Festival would be just the beginning of a bloody reign—one designed to make Hughen suffer. To make King Eurion and his family suffer.

A hitch of panic drove me on. I sent the little girl one last look. I couldn't help her, not with armed guards eyeing me from the wagon. But I could help Aden, and he could convince his father to help people like her. As much as I hated King Eurion, he was a hundred times better than Khral Rasmus. I just had to reach Hughen before the exchange happened.

Before they killed Aden too.

I would fight for him, for that little girl. For every sailor who'd hung from the gallows, and for Father and Paval and Barrie. I would not let evil men like Belza and Rasmus succeed.

They would know my name before this was over.

My lungs felt raw in this dry wind, but I increased my stride and let my too-large boots eat up the distance between me and town.

I reached the town before the sun peeked over its rooftops, trying to ignore the blisters forming on my heels. I passed through the stone gate and followed the line of wagons toward the market.

It looked similar to the market squares I'd visited in Hughen, though a far cry dirtier. The biggest difference was the people. They kept their eyes downcast like the girl had, barely giving one another a glance rather than engaging in lazy conversation. No lords and ladies walked about on these streets. They must have ridden in carriages, beyond the city's grime. Or perhaps there just weren't many at all.

The smell of freshly baked bread and sausage permeated the air. My stomach growled as a city guard trotted past on his chestnut gelding. A few minutes later, a second rode past, followed by a contingent of soldiers on foot. I plastered myself against a wall and kept my head low, but I felt their curious gazes as they marched by. I gave a shiver as the last one passed.

A man with a flat tasseled hat walked by. He looked harmless enough, and I was running out of time. "Excuse me," I said. "Where is Lady's Port?"

His eyes ran down my body and stopped at my trousers. He gave a smirk and walked away, shaking his head.

Right. People saw me as a girl now.

A quick stop at a baker's stand and I had my directions, though the woman's eyes bored into my back as I left. She wasn't the only one staring. I gripped one of my axe handles and returned their scowls with my own. My trousers set me apart like a flame in shadows. I began to jog.

The roads grew narrower and traffic thinned. Soon I was alone in the quiet streets, my footsteps echoing harshly against the tall buildings looming over me. Each stood right up against the other with no space between them, most three stories high with faded paint and centuries of history. Despite its sandy streets, Messau's capital city made Hughen look like an infant just finding its legs.

A rotten fish smell grew stronger as I reached the edge of town. A right turn, then another, and I was there.

The port was smaller than Hughen's, with one hangar and a single dry dock for ship repairs. The laundry woman had been correct. The waiting ship was of Ellegran make. The only odd part was the figurehead at the bow. Instead of the usual big-busted, unclothed goddess, the figure was a bare-chested man with a scarf wrapped about his throat and trailing behind him. The sight was so bizarre, I gaped for a moment. Definitely KaBann.

Paval's warnings about KaBann politics brought a tumble of nerves to my stomach once more, but I had little choice. Now that I was Laney, no ship would transport me to Hughen as a passenger.

I had to try anyway. Nay, I had to succeed. Aden had nobody else to count on.

I remembered the city planner and his barrels of stones. *Everyone wants something.* I just had to discover what this particular captain needed most. Blowing out a breath that lifted my hair, I strode onto the docks and sauntered to the gangplank.

The man waiting there wore a copper necklace above his bright white tunic, his chest exposed to reveal a fistful of dark hair. His gut hung over his belt, and what hair remained on his head looked matted, but I could tell by the way he stood that he knew his way around a blade. He smirked as I approached. "We've enough hands, lass. Those axes for sale?"

I gripped the handle to my right. "Nay, and I don't want work. I need passage."

"Passage? To KaBann?" He snorted. "That would cost you indeed."

Disappointment hung heavy in my chest. "You're going to KaBann?"

"Aye, soon as the captain arrives. Sure you don't want to sell those axes? I been looking for a good fighting pair."

"They're not for sale, and I don't intend to travel to KaBann." Someday perhaps, but not yet. "I need to get to Hughen immediately. Please tell me where I can find your captain."

"My darling." The man placed a fist to his heart and gave a slight bow. I blinked before realizing he addressed someone behind me.

"Hughen?" The tall woman made a *tsk-tsk* sound. Her bright clothing contrasted starkly with her skin tone—dark skin, the same tone as Paval's, which wrenched my heart a bit. She wore an identical copper necklace to the bosun's, and her tunic dropped nearly as low, revealing more cleavage than I'd ever boast in my life. "I'm afraid that's impossible, dear. Hughen's new embargo has southern merchants quite upset. Thankfully, I managed to sell most of my cargo in town, but you can bet I won't be returning next year. If you'll excuse me." She slipped past, her movements as graceful as a dancer's, and picked her way up the gangplank.

I blinked, watching her go. The khral's navy blocked ships from reaching Hughen. Surely King Eurion wouldn't have stood for that. It wasn't a good sign. I rubbed my temples, feeling another headache forming.

"Thank you, Captain," the bosun called behind him. His eyes were mirthful as he studied me. "You've been dismissed. Unless you've other business, you'll have to find another ship headed north. Though that isn't likely."

I slid to the ground and leaned against the post, knees bent to the sky. He was right. Even if I found a ship bound for Hughen, what did I have to offer? A pair of ill-fitting boots and a sad tale of woe? There wasn't time to work and earn passage fare. I could leave right now and still be too late to save Aden.

"You look a little rough there, lass," the bosun said, looking down on me.

I snorted. "That's what a mutiny, pirates, and near drowning will do to you."

"Pirates?" the captain repeated, turning about at the rail above. "You said pirates attacked your ship?"

"Aye. Captain Belza himself."

The man scowled. "You're mistaken, lass. If it were Belza, you wouldn't be alive."

"I stowed away undiscovered. You probably saw his ships in the harbor yesterday." He'd likely spent every coin of Father's gold by now.

The bosun looked shaken. A look passed between him and the captain. "Belza didn't come into town," she said, "but I recognized his men in the market. If they're bound for Hughen, best travel the opposite direction as fast as you can. Belza doesn't like survivors."

"They took a prisoner. A valuable one." That sparked an idea, and I straightened. "There will be a reward for his rescue, the likes of which will set me up for life. I hoped to share some of it with those who helped me, but it seems you're bent on going south, so I'll look elsewhere." I shrugged and pushed to my feet.

The captain chuckled. "You're a clever one, but my ship doesn't operate on promises. Especially when pirates are involved. Unless you've enough gold to run half a kingdom, our conversation is finished."

I cursed that laundry woman and pulled Mum's comb from my pocket. "This is the only item of value I have."

The bosun swept it from my hand and hurried up the gangplank, passing it to the captain. She examined the comb in the sunlight, her eyes widening. "*That We May Live Long Together.* An intriguing inscription. I haven't seen one of these in ages." She held it for the man's inspection.

"It's fake," he grumbled. "Even I can tell as much."

"It's not about the jewels. Where did you get this, girl?"

I blinked, trying to hide my surprise. "It was a gift for my mother, but she rejected it. Now it's mine. Grant me passage to Hughen, and I may consider parting with it."

She cradled the comb in both hands and fixed her sharp gaze on me, looking alarmingly like a chef considering how to butcher that evening's dinner. "A gift, you say. Interesting."

"It's the truth." I held her gaze calmly despite the urge to squirm. I'd met many sea captains before, but none had looked at me like this. I ran through my options once more and came up with nothing. This woman was it.

The captain shoved the comb into her bosun's hands and folded her arms. "The voyage will be dangerous. I want seventy percent of the reward money as well as your dedicated service with the crew. Everyone contributes on my ship."

Relief hit so strongly, my knees nearly gave way. "I'm a sailor. I'm not afraid of a little work. Can you really get us past that embargo?"

The captain grinned. It was more the baring of teeth than anything. "We're KaBann. We've been slipping past northern ships for decades. Do you agree to the terms or not?"

If King Eurion truly offered a reward for his son's safe return, I'd give her 100 percent and the clothing off my back. But something felt off about all this. She'd agreed too quickly. There had to be something the captain wasn't saying, some other reason she'd agreed to this wild journey.

"Very well," I said carefully. "Aren't you afraid of Captain Belza, though? You only saw two of his ships. He has an entire fleet of Messaun navy vessels at his command."

The captain rolled her eyes. "Belza is an impostor, a whiny child. He'll be dealt with eventually. I'm Captain Dayorn. My first officer, Plete." Then she gestured to the vessel behind her. "And that is the *Bram's Uncle*. Welcome aboard."

35

The *Bram's Uncle* was smaller than the *Majesty* and much older, but *he*—as the crew called the ship—had been built for long-distance travel. The hull had been reinforced with tin rather than extra layers of timber. It gave the lower decks a heavy, metallic smell.

It was strange sailing aboard a KaBann vessel. It felt familiar in some regards yet wildly different in others. The vessel rode the waves in a more sluggish way, as if the sea itself resisted our presence. The sails were triangular, the rigging inefficient, and the workers more relaxed. Even the officers seemed less involved in daily matters. Disagreements were resolved with fists belowdecks. I hadn't realized how orderly the *Majesty* truly was.

I'd also forgotten how much the KaBann loved their tobacco. Paval hadn't used it, but he'd referred to it often in stories. Now I saw why. Ship's girls and boys as young as eleven chewed it, spitting the dregs with precision. The oldest sailor was a sixty-year-old man with only three teeth left. It didn't bother him, though. He just slopped the mess around in his mouth, walking about with a dirty shirt and a strange gurgle. My father would never have stood for it.

I threw myself into my duties, thinking it would help distract me from the darkness that lingered at the edge of my memories. I volunteered for every single night watch, working myself into an exhaustion so deep that I collapsed into a dreamless sleep afterward. Even then, I awoke screaming. By the third day, I barely allowed myself to sleep at all.

On the evening of day four, we spotted the Needle cliffs.

We wouldn't pass through now, of course. Our voyage followed the safer, longer route around to the northeast. I doubted Captain Dayorn had even considered it. But the sight of those cliffs drew me to the rail and held me in place.

Things had been so different when I'd passed through last. My once-complicated life was now utterly simple. There were no worries of mutiny, no pirates chasing us. My deepest concerns no longer included Barrie's punishment or my lies about a certain passenger or stealing from the crew for Kemp's payments, nor my father's trade and reputation. I would never dream of inheriting my father's ship again. It was only me now. My world involved work, a meal here and there, and perhaps a little sleep.

I would have given the world itself to have all those worries back again.

The girl who'd passed through the Needle before had big, impossible dreams. The girl who approached it now was little more than a hollow, beaten stranger. Not a daughter, but an orphan. Not a sailor, but a survivor. And now I worked on a KaBann ship with a respectful crew and a woman captain who accepted me as exactly who I was, trousers and all. It should have been a dream come true.

Instead, it felt like a nightmare.

The work was the same. The crew were friendly, though blunt and pointed in their questions. I found myself at the rail often, the only place I could count on solitude. Although today I wouldn't even get that. A bearded man lay curled up in sleep right there on deck, his body flopping back and forth with the rocking of the ship. Yet another difference in discipline between the two ships. If it weren't for the color in the man's face, I would have assumed him dead.

A body lying still on the deck, his eyes closed...

My chest lurched and I tore my gaze away.

"Knew I'd find you here," Captain Dayorn said. She wore a simple robe today. Well, simple except for the elaborate grouping of red and pink jewels at her belt. She filled the empty space beside me and placed her elbows on the rail, mirroring my stance. "Plete is concerned about how much time you've been spending alone. Thought I'd check in on you."

"I'm fine."

She nodded but didn't leave. For several minutes, we watched the ocean together. The cliffs were still a tiny lump in the distance. There were endless miles of deep, cold seawater between us.

She tried again. "If you're searching for Captain Belza, put your mind to rest. We're a full two days behind him."

Captain Dayorn didn't understand. It wasn't the cliffs nor Belza I watched for now. It was a distant ship with two masts, eight guns, and a polished rail. It was a KaBann cook with a ready smile, offering me watered-down coffee. It was a boy with new scars on his back and deep questions, and an old hammock that creaked and swayed when the waves got rough.

Above all, I searched for a familiar figure on the quarterdeck. He wore a face I knew better than my own, every line purchased from decades under an unpredictable sky, hard on the surface yet gentle as a smile when he approved. I searched for another decade or more of quiet nighttime talks in his cabin and stories of my childhood and that one last secret that he'd never been able to tell.

Something told me I'd never stop looking.

"It was a massacre, wasn't it?" the captain asked.

"I'd rather not discuss it, if you don't mind." I focused on a knot in the wooden rail. It had splintered terribly. Father would have had this ship back in its former glory within a day or two.

"You've honored their memories well with your sorrow this past week. But I'm sure they would also want you to find happiness."

I ducked my head. Here I was, living my life's dream in a very real way. Here I had no secrets. I could be exactly who I was meant to be—a woman sailor, a full and unapologetic embrace of sea life. Yet it felt empty now, a mindless list of tasks to be performed on a rigid schedule.

Sailing was supposed to fill my heart, not drain it.

The scruffy sailor nearby coughed and then pushed himself up, swaying like a drunken man. I'd forgotten he was even there. I watched the man shuffle away until he was out of earshot.

"An uncle," she said with an apologetic look. "Northerners leave their families behind, but the KaBann bring them along. Sometimes it's too hard to say goodbye."

I didn't answer.

"I don't enjoy traveling to Hughen," she continued, as if nothing were wrong. "Not that I fear their ridiculous Edict, of course, but they're so uptight. King Eurion is insufferable these days, arresting his own people and executing innocents. A prideful man leading a prideful people. A few more years and they'll be as bad as the Messauns."

Weeks ago, I would have agreed with her. But now I knew better. Despite my father's piracy adventures, he'd been pure Hughen. And Aden was far from the stiff princeling I'd once considered him. He was tender, gentle. Thoughtful and determined. Everything the Hughens had once been. Perhaps he would do exactly what he meant to do and defeat Rasmus after all. Then the kingdom would go back to normal, bestowing freedom to everyone.

Except innocent sailors.

Was that what held me back? Was my hatred of Eurion so deep that I would let Aden fail? The thought was disturbing.

"My crew tell me you're a hard worker who knows her task well," the captain said.

"I've sailed since age five."

"Have you, now." That thoughtful tone was back. "Your father was Naamon Garrow, wasn't he? I didn't know he had a daughter."

"I disguised myself as his son for protection."

The woman nodded. "You should hide that comb of yours when we reach Hughen. Show it to no one."

I looked at her in surprise. "I thought you wanted it." Plete had returned it to me, but I assumed it was for safekeeping.

She actually cringed. "No, no. I never want to see it again. Bad fortune. You haven't shown it to the crew, have you?"

Bad fortune? I shoved my hand into my pocket, letting my fingers close around the comb's sharp teeth. "Nay. Only you and Plete have seen it."

"Good. Keep it well hidden."

I stared at her. "This comb changed your mind about helping me. Why?"

"Let's just say an old debt is being repaid, one I've long desired to make right." There was pain in her eyes now, something familiar that tugged at my insides.

The firm set of her mouth indicated she wouldn't be elaborating, and I didn't push further. Likely it meant she'd known my father and only wanted to help. A captain's creed, perhaps, a loyalty stronger than one's fear of bad fortune when faced with an orphan girl and her worthless comb.

She cleared her throat, and the stern captain was back. "Now, keep to your work. Once the king's reward for this 'valuable prisoner' has been bestowed, you will leave the political nonsense behind and join us on our voyage to KaBann. With your experience, you'll make captain by twenty. It's a good thing I found you, child. Your skill would have been utterly wasted in the north." Her tone left no room for argument.

Captain. I had a family out there, a country. A culture that wanted me for who I was and the skills I offered. I could earn my own ship. The possibilities went so far beyond my dreams that I could barely breathe. This woman had just uncovered my place in the world and adorned it with gold and sunshine. Then why did her offer feel so empty?

I knew the truth. It was because, bindings or not, I was still pretending.

Aden needed me. He always had, now more than ever. And I was beginning to wonder if I needed him too. But he wasn't mine, nor could he ever be. The girl he married would have proper breeding and manners. She wouldn't wear men's clothes, and she certainly wouldn't carry axes.

Aden's path had been chosen before his birth. Mine had taken a sharp turn at age five.

The memories were little more than glimpses: Mum's strained smile, her distant expression when I played. How her voice wobbled when she sang to me at bedtime. She'd always smelled of salt and warm bread. They were moments I'd entombed deep in my mind, all except the one that had refused to leave—the moment she'd walked away from me on that dock.

I'd already been rejected once by someone I loved. The wound she'd created that day was a jagged, painful scar on my heart. Now Father was gone too. If Aden sent me away, I wasn't sure I would ever recover.

I don't regret your mum. I truly don't. Everybody deserves love, even if it won't last.

I leaned forward. Several miles away, dark cliffs stood tall against the blue sky. A harsh black scar revealed where we'd emerged from the channel. It was where I'd fed jardrakes with Aden and dreaded Barrie's whipping, where I'd seen my father's weaknesses exposed and wished he could be a better man. It was where I'd denied what I wanted most—freedom, respect. Family.

My throat tightened. That was it. The ocean had been the same for thousands, maybe millions, of years. The sun had risen and set for many pairs of eyes just like mine. There would always be lightning storms, huge waves, the Needle, exotic ports, and jardrakes. It wasn't the sea itself, but the people I enjoyed it with that gave sailing its flavor. It was the connections between us, the bonds of loyalty and family and friendship.

If I abandoned Aden and left for KaBann, I'd be embracing a lie for the rest of my life. A lie that King Eurion and Captain Belza had beaten me. A lie that my career mattered more than helping that poor little girl in Messau and the murdered sailors in Hughen. A lie that my past never happened, my father never existed, and I could forget Aden forever.

You are kumba-tah, Paval had said. *You have a good heart. You're more concerned about who a person is than what society says they are.*

Paval's easy smile returned to my mind with such force, I couldn't swallow. I hadn't been able to bid him farewell, and I'd never get the chance to tell him he was right. The KaBann were so focused on King Eurion's shortcomings, they couldn't see the truth about Hughen. At the very least, it was a kingdom of good people trying to climb out of poverty. A land that produced people like my father and Aden. A nation that deserved protection from a man such as Rasmus. And if one man could destroy a country, surely one woman could protect it.

A gull soared high above us, barely giving us a glance. It didn't care which waters belonged to whom. Borders were invisible things drawn up by humans. I saw in that moment what the Hughens meant when they said birds were sacred. It was freedom that they worshipped. It encompassed everything that Aden was.

Perhaps I was half-pirate, but there was a second part—and that part said I was done hiding.

"Thank you for your kindness," I said. "But I'll be staying in Hughen. There's something I have to do."

36

A week later, we arrived in Hughen after midnight. We'd slipped past five Messaun ships and were detained by the sixth, which demanded to know our business. When the captain declared we'd been invited, the ship had allowed us to pass without another word. I didn't ask her what our invitation was supposedly for. I didn't really want to know the answer.

We avoided the docks altogether and dropped anchor in a bay miles from town. Tiny lights moved about on the coastline. The sight made my heart skip. If Messaun ships patrolled Hughen's perimeter, those lights on the coastline weren't likely to be friendly.

Captain Dayorn was the first to climb into the rowboat. Six others took the oars, including her first officer, Plete. Apparently he was also her husband. I'd asked the captain whether the marriage had taken place before his appointment or after, but she'd just smirked.

I bade the crew on deck farewell. Then I climbed into the boat, fighting a surge of nervousness and clutching the comb deep in my pocket. I'd managed to hide it the entire journey, pondering Captain Dayorn's strange warning until my brain hurt.

A silent crew lowered us to the waves. Then we were off.

Besides the tiny lights, the distant coast seemed quiet and unthreatening from here. I wasn't sure whether it offered me a gentle welcome or lured its prey into the open jaws of danger.

Captain Dayorn sat tall, her posture nearly perfect as the six crew members threw themselves into the oars. They watched me with blatant interest as they worked. I wasn't sure how much they knew. Admittedly, I wasn't sure how much Captain Dayorn knew, or even cared. She didn't seem concerned with northern politics. If I told her outright that I was in love with a Hughen prince, the woman would likely roll her eyes and change the subject.

I cleared my throat and turned to the first officer, who rowed across from me. "How long have you served the captain?"

"Twelve years," Plete said, not sounding winded at all. "And your next question—we've been married for ten. Known each other since childhood. I followed her to the navy when we were nine years old. Knew if I didn't, she'd see me for the gangly, sea-fearing lad I really was."

I gave the man a sideways look. "Does it bother you, serving under your wife?"

He threw back his head and laughed. It was so Paval-like that my lungs constricted. "Northerners. Doesn't matter what a person is if they can do the work. Believe me, Captain Dayorn is as good a commander as any that's sailed the world." He threw his wife a fond look.

She didn't speak, though her lips turned upward a bit. Then she squinted toward shore. "There are a lot of them tonight. At least forty on the coast alone."

"Definitely not Hughen, then," Plete muttered. "They don't have those kinds of numbers."

The captain shook her head. "Not all of them are Messaun. See how some of the lights are more orange than white? Those are true flame. Ellegrans refuse to use gaslight."

Why would Ellegrans be patrolling with Messauns? I swallowed, feeling sick. I could do without the reminders of what awaited.

It began to rain. Not the light, comfortable kind, but the sudden type that pelted the skin. One second it was still, the next it poured.

"We'll never sneak you to shore without being seen," the captain said, seemingly unaffected. "When I give the order, you will slip into the waves and swim toward the north shore. I will hold their attention as long as I can."

"I appreciate it." I paused. "Before I go...You mentioned an old debt once. What was that for?"

The smile in her eyes disappeared. "Your father was a good man. He got me out of a difficult situation once. It's a pleasure to do the same for his daughter. Not that I'm passing up the reward money, mind you. The crew still need to be paid."

I grinned. "Of course."

The captain dug under the bench and pulled out some cloth. "It's almost time. Place your boots in this bag and pull them along behind you. You'll need them ashore." She paused. "Are you certain you want to do...whatever it is you plan to do here? It isn't too late to accept my offer. The Council back home would be thrilled to meet you."

Plete jerked, then looked at his wife in irritation. Whatever this Council was, he didn't approve of her mentioning it.

I hesitated, still gripping my boots. "Is that a group of nobles?"

"Not at all. The Council is a group of powerful individuals who wish to make a difference in the world. I can't give you an official invitation without their consent, but given your heritage, that won't be difficult to secure."

My heritage as a captain's daughter, or a pirate's offspring? I wasn't sure what she knew. "What kind of difference in the world?"

The captain leaned forward. "The Four Lands will feel the Council's hand very soon. Our next meeting is just two months away. Think of it. You would never fear for your life in northern waters again. You'd be respected, even worshipped. No disguise necessary."

A suspicion tickled my mind. "Are some of these 'powerful individuals' pirates, by chance?"

Plete shot his wife a warning look. She ignored it, sitting back on the bench to examine me. "Perhaps," she finally said. "One never knows."

One always knows a pirate, I wanted to shoot back. It was a lie. Designed to fool me, or disguise the truth from the crew rowing around us?

At least Captain Dayorn had answered one question. Now I knew how she sailed and docked where she pleased. Such power. Such a *reputation*. A deep hunger began to stir inside. I considered her offer for the briefest of moments before Aden's memory pulled me back.

"I do intend to change the world," I told her. "But I'll do it my own way."

Plete's shoulders relaxed.

A tiny downward tug of the captain's lips was the only indication of her disappointment. "Very well. We'll sail around to Kalina, then. Send word when you've seized payment, and I'll return. May you have success, Laney Garrow." She brushed two fingers against her chest. A KaBann sign of honor.

"Thank you, Captain. I'll be ready," I said firmly, stowing my boots. Then I dove into the next wave. The chill was a punch to the gut. I came up sputtering.

The crew copied the captain's action before throwing themselves behind the oars once more.

The swim was much farther than it had appeared. It seemed an endless struggle against cold waves before my feet touched rock. I barely felt it for the numbness that had taken hold. After the events of the past few weeks, I wondered if I'd ever be warm and dry again.

I let the waves deposit me on the rocks, ignoring a sharp pain in my leg from a stone beneath the surface, then picked my way carefully out of the water. No soldiers in sight. Hopefully that meant Captain Dayorn's distraction had worked.

I sat on the gravel, resting and folding myself against the cold wind. My body shook so violently, I doubted I could even speak. Now that I'd reached land, it was impossible to ignore the rain beating down from the black sky. I had to find shelter or I'd die where I lay.

I pulled on my boots, then followed an overgrown trail leading into the woods, stepping over fallen trees and through brush until I wished I was back in the cold waves. A long thirty minutes later, the trail ended in front of a watch house. Or what had once been a watch house anyway. The front door hung on its hinges and the windows hadn't seen glass in decades.

It wasn't much of a shelter, but it was better than the trees. I pushed the wet hair away from my eyes and stepped through the doorway. The floor creaked underfoot, and I moved slowly and deliberately around the soft spots in the wood.

Any furniture had long since been taken. The ceiling appeared rotted, and the attic above had to be in worse condition. I imagined it all caving in on my head and grimaced.

A dark mound sat in the corner. It set my heart stumbling until I realized it was only a pile of crates. A folded blanket sat on top. My chilled, exhausted body screamed for rest at the sight of it.

I stripped down to my underwear, laying my clothing and boots out to dry, then dried my axes with the blanket. Finally, I curled up to sleep.

The nightmares claimed me immediately.

I awoke to a gray sky directly overhead, visible through the broken roof. I threw my not-quite-dry clothing back on, nibbled on a bit of old jerky I'd found in a bundle on the crate, and started for town. If there was one thing Hughens excelled at, it was gossip. A single sighting of Belza's ships, and the entire city would know about it by now. I could only hope that someone knew where Belza was staying. Aden had to be with him. The pirate captain wouldn't let such a valuable prisoner out of his sight.

It took forty minutes to reach town and another twenty to find the market. I was early. Most of the bleary-eyed workers were still unloading their wagons, their carts set up but empty. I glimpsed a woman setting out a table of weapons—an entire line of exotic knives, several cudgels, and even a broadsword. The woman unwrapped a tight bundle, and I found myself inching closer to investigate. An axe pair with short wooden handles and curved blades. Practice axes.

The perfect size for Barrie.

My throat squeezed tight. I choked back the tears, resisting the sudden and overpowering urge to curl into myself and sob. There was only one way to help Barrie now, and that was to avenge him— him and every other person I'd lost.

"You going to stand there all day? I have a wagon to unload."

I turned to find a man glaring at me, clutching a basket of bread loaves. My breath hitched. It was the same man I'd spoken with on the day of that innocent woman's hanging. His eyes widened in recognition, his gaze sliding down my clothing. Without my bindings, it was all too clear what I was.

He swore under his breath. His teeth were as brown as I remembered. "You one of those pirates who blew in and paraded about town like they owned it?"

I finally found my voice. "Nay, but I'm searching for them. Do you know where they went?"

He belched and turned to call over his shoulder. "Hey, Izza. Come on over here. Some girl wants to know about the pirates."

Too alarmed at the volume of his voice to shush him, I looked about as more eyes turned to me. They took in my old shirt, my trousers still itchy with salt water, and my ocean-ratted hair. Everything about me screamed *sailor*. I expected them to run off any second to fetch the soldiers, but none moved. Instead, a boy set down the crate he'd been holding and came over to join us.

I blinked. It wasn't a boy. It was the beggar I'd defended from those ladies weeks ago. A pair of overalls had replaced her tattered dress, and she'd chopped her hair, but I recognized her round cheeks and piercing eyes.

She grinned at the sight of me. "I knew you were a girl. Copied your disguise, I did."

The baker chuckled. "My wife took her in to help me. Can't walk so well these days." He pointed to a bandaged foot. Bloodstains covered the wrappings. "Izza, she wants to know where the pirates are staying. You hear anything new?"

The girl's mouth rounded into an O. "You don't want to go there today."

"I'm not afraid of Belza," I said.

Her gaze settled on my axes, and she shrugged. "Follow this

road till the end, then turn left and take it six blocks down. Green warehouse down by the end. Try the back window."

The baker tossed me a crosuit, then leaned in to whisper. "Don't tell anyone, all right? I'd lose my business. It's been hard enough since the Messauns came."

I assumed he meant the free food, but then I realized his warning was for the girl. A girl apprentice wasn't illegal, but it was certainly frowned upon. Yet another wrong that needed righting. If I ever saw Aden again, we were in for a nice, long conversation about his country's injustices.

"Of course," I said, smiling at the girl. "My thanks to you both."

37

The green paint had faded, and the structure looked more like an inn than a warehouse, although there was no hanging sign and the windows had all been boarded up, save for one on the upper floor. A pole extended from the roof's peak. My father had told me once that those poles were hoists, acting like pulleys to help citizens lift heavy furniture to the third floor. The building jutted right up against its neighbor, which was covered in scaffolding.

More importantly, the building had a deliberately careless appearance, as if its owner valued privacy over business. Or maybe privacy *was* his business.

Four men stood across the street, talking in hushed tones. Only a sharp eye would notice how they angled themselves so they could watch the building. Their hands hovered above the weapons at their sides. One man watched me approach and nudged his neighbor.

I lowered my head and hurried past, then circled around the corner to the rear of the building. The alley was empty. And as I'd hoped, the building had a kitchen entrance.

The initial twinge of excitement faded as I reached the door. I hadn't expected the series of rusted locks around its frame. They held firm. The window was boarded up too. I growled in frustration. No wonder the guards hadn't taken the time to watch this entrance.

Then I noticed it—a notch in the board, like the corner had been cut out.

I placed my fingers inside and pulled. One of the boards had a coarse hinge attached to it, allowing it to swing aside with a soft *squeak*. The glass was long gone. Someone had rigged a hidden opening. A small one, given its width. Street children were more clever than people realized.

"Thank you, Izza," I muttered.

I listened at the window. Silence. If the pirates were inside, they weren't in the kitchen. I scrambled onto the ledge and slid through, then swung the board back into place. It immediately cut off the sunlight.

My eyes adjusted quickly. An old stove boasting an impressive array of spiderwebs stood in the corner, next to a woven chair with a burn mark in its seat. A dusty broom sat propped in one corner.

Voices floated down from above. There was an angry shout, and the ceiling overhead squeaked and clattered. A wrestling match upstairs, perhaps. But there was something alarming about the sounds, like they were closer than they should have been. I inspected the ceiling and found an opening where the stove's pipe had once been fitted to an upstairs bedroom stove. The patch of ceiling was boarded closed, but one of the boards hung by a single nail.

I stepped onto the stove and balanced myself on the burner. My head was only inches from the ceiling now, and the sound of the men fighting was clear. They grunted and grappled until one man yelped. Then a third voice snapped, "Oh, come on. Surely we can be respectable about this."

"You'll not...be getting...my weapon," a strained voice said. But the fighting abruptly halted. I couldn't see who had won. Through the small opening, all I could see was a wall covered in yellowing flowered paper.

"We'll continue with your permission, then, Sire," the third man said.

"Proceed."

Sire? Alarm lurched through me, and I nearly toppled off the stove. Khral Rasmus was *here*? But his voice was wrong. It sounded far too old, almost tired. Not at all like the monarch son I'd imagined.

"As I was saying, the boy is a perfect hand. If Rasmus fails, Hughen will pay any ransom to get the prince back. And if Hughen falls, Rasmus will be just as desperate to silence him. Imagine the power you will hold."

My breath caught in my throat, and I resisted the sudden urge to cough it free. I knew that voice. Captain Belza. He was here too, not four feet above where I perched. I gripped my axe handles and listened, every muscle in my body tense.

"The khral is a fool," the second voice said, still out of breath. "Executing the boy would only spur his people to action. The royal children are well loved. Wouldn't you say so, Your Highness?"

"That isn't your problem." Belza again. "All you need worry about is staying silent until this is over. You'll hold power over Hughen and Messau for the first time in a decade. Surely that's worth a little gold."

"Your price is too high."

"Not for an Ellegran king. I know of your investments in the islands. This will yield more benefit than empty land ever will."

An Ellegran king...

The older man was Mortrein LeZar, the very ally Aden had been sent to beg for help. We'd raced across the ocean to take Aden to him, yet he was *here*. Why would he be in the center of the Hughen capital? And why in a run-down building conversing with Captain Belza, of all people? I remembered those Ellegran guards on the shore last night and adjusted my grip on the axes. Something was very wrong.

"I need no power over Rasmus," LeZar said. His voice wobbled with the effort. The man was older than I'd thought. "Our agreement is enough. Ellegran will retain its freedom and emerge from the war unscathed."

Belza growled. "Freedom from Messau, perhaps. But war comes in many forms. I can see to it your country never finds peace again."

There was another scuffle. The king's guards seemed to be having a rough day.

"My navy has sixty ships, all hardened from decades at war," the Ellegran king snapped over the noise. "We can easily overcome your fleet of unskilled thieves."

Belza snorted. "The world closes in, yet you keep your eyes shut. The riots, the burnings, the border disputes. Your own people turn against you. Ellegran falls apart and you know it. It's time to claim your position and secure your nation's future."

There was a long silence. Then the king spoke, his voice strained. "Your price is still too high. I see no advantage to taking the boy, even if you truly have him."

"He's in the other room." I detected a smile in Belza's voice. "My men will escort you to see for yourself."

"No." LeZar's reply was too quick. "No, I don't want to see him. I don't want to be here. I don't—" He paused, then his voice grew quieter, like he was turning away. "I should not have come. You and Rasmus may keep my armies for now as agreed. I'm leaving."

My knuckles on the axe handle were turning white. I'd called

Kempton a coward, but at least he'd fought for his own interests. I wouldn't trust this man to drive a wagon, let alone rule a kingdom. Aden had more courage than a thousand LeZars.

I forced myself to take a deep breath and consider the facts. Aden and his family had been double-crossed. Not only had LeZar agreed not to interfere with Rasmus's brutal takeover—which meant the slaughter of a friend who trusted him—but he'd also committed his own troops to the bloody cause. He was no better than Belza.

"You had your chance, LeZar," Belza said, his voice cold. "I will not forget this day."

"Do not speak to me in such a manner, pirate," the older man shot back. "Powerful you may be, but a king you are not."

"A king rules a spot of land. I rule the sea. I'll have you remember it when your ships disappear and your country falls to starvation."

Heavy footsteps fell overhead. They faded, then grew louder behind me. They were descending the stairs on their way out. Those guards outside had to be LeZar's. I wished the man would fall and smash his face in.

Belza waited until the door slammed. Then he spoke again, his voice dangerous. "Bring the boy to me."

My heart hammered until I was sure it would tear free of my rib cage.

"Sir." Someone ran off, then several men returned a moment later. Their strides were uneven, as if struggling with their prisoner. I followed the sound with my eyes. They'd come from a room near the front of the building. Probably the third floor, since I hadn't heard footsteps above the next room.

"I'm disappointed, little princeling," Belza said in a low voice. I squinted through the crack, but there was only a shadow on the wall. A hulking, wide-shouldered shadow.

Someone groaned. I straightened, my heart leaping into a furious gallop.

Aden.

There was nothing but planks between us now. Well, besides a conniving pirate and his men. I still didn't know how many there were.

"Poor boy. Nobody wants you, I'm afraid. Your father sent you away. The Ellegrans rejected you. Seems I'll be delivering you to Rasmus after all."

Aden's reply was drowned out by the sound of a fist finding its mark. Then a body hit the floor. I covered a gasp.

"Take him back," Belza snapped.

I strained to see Aden, but he wasn't visible through the crack. By the sound, he pushed to his feet and stumbled out under his own power, still surrounded by guards. Their footsteps headed for the stairs before fading out. Definitely the third floor.

I'd never make it up two flights of stairs unseen. That meant I'd have to get to him from the outside.

Moving quietly, I lowered myself from the stove and slipped out the window.

I strode back toward the street, keeping my eyes down. The four guards were gone. I examined the building's front with a casual eye. The pirates had chosen their location well. There was no trim that could be climbed, the front door was easily defensible, and the windows were all shuttered. Only one window remained open to the sunlight.

It was on the third floor.

38

For the first time in weeks, I hesitated. This wasn't like breaking a criminal out of a half-staffed prison cell. These were pirates, and I knew better than anyone what they were capable of. If Captain Belza recognized me as a survivor, he'd plunge his cutlass through my gut himself. It should have sent a wave of fear through me. Instead, my eyes narrowed.

He'd plunge his cutlass through me...*if* my axe blades didn't get to him first.

I glanced around. The street was still. Then I strode to the next building, its scaffolding squeaking in the breeze. It looked sturdy enough. Grasping the lowest rail, I swung my legs upward. Another leap and a giant heave toward the next wooden slat. I grunted with the strain, barely noticing the splinters cutting into my palms. It was no worse than a coil of old line.

Hurry. If someone walked by and gave a shout...

I finally made it to the top floor, level with the upper window of the room where I hoped Aden was imprisoned. Now I had to figure out how to get there. The scaffolding ended fifteen feet before the hoist pole.

Fifteen feet. Had I really done that so many times on the *Majesty*? I'd felt invincible with a moving ship beneath me. This time the ground seemed an eternity away.

I took a deep breath to calm my mind. I was on the *Majesty*, standing in the nest high above the world. My target lay slightly above me and a little to the right. Just another secure line, nothing difficult. And my father wasn't watching.

I took a few steps back and sprinted toward the edge. Then I was airborne. I threw my arms forward, fingers separated, eyes wide and focused.

Contact. One hand grabbed hold...and slipped off.

My heart nearly stopped.

The other hand caught.

I clung to the pole, trembling, letting my body swing high above the ground. I'd done it. But this wasn't finished yet. The window lay a single unforgiving step downward. One mistake and I'd end up a bloody corpse on the street below.

I lowered one cautious foot to the windowsill, then the other. I expected a musket blast from inside, but there was no sound. Either Aden was alone or I'd guessed the wrong room. I gathered my wits and gave the glass a sharp kick. It sounded like a pistol shot. The glass shattered.

I ducked inside, avoiding the few shards still clinging to the window frame, and squinted in the low light.

Aden stood next to a chair, his hands gripping its sides awkwardly as if he was preparing to throw it. He blinked, looking positively dumbfounded. *"Lane?"*

If I hadn't heard him speak, I doubt I would have recognized him. Both eyes were swollen almost beyond recognition, and a new bruise formed at his cheek. He stared at me as if from a dream.

"You're alive," he said. "You're *here*."

Footsteps sounded in the hallway. I rushed to close the door, but two guards entered before I could reach it. They gaped at me like Aden had.

"Now, what is this?" the first muttered, his blade ready.

"It's a lass," the other said. "Must've come through the window."

I snorted. Never mind the axes in my hands or my low soldier's stance. It was my gender that mattered.

Fine. At least they hadn't recognized me from the *Majesty*. Lane was invisible—a boy beneath men's notice, scrawny and quiet. But Laney? She had possibilities. Men noticed her, but they also made assumptions they shouldn't. Assumptions I could use to my advantage.

The first pirate took a step forward. "This building's occupied, lass. You'd best leave before Belza finds you. Unless you're here for a little company." He grinned.

The other followed him. He aimed a pistol at my forehead, gaze darting between my axes. This one was smarter.

I examined the still-open door. There was something odd about it. It looked to have been reinforced with an extra layer of timber. The edge of a bolt extended near the top. This was Aden's cell, but they'd obviously prepared for an attack from the outside as well. I smiled.

The first pirate frowned when I didn't reply to his not-so-tempting offer. "You have five seconds to take your pretty weapons and walk out that door. One."

Pretty weapons? It took all my willpower not to bash the man in the face. But I managed to give him a nod as I moved toward the door. If I'd been a boy, there was no doubt I'd have been dead by now.

"Two."

Aden still gripped his chair, frowning. The second sailor cocked his pistol.

Now.

I whirled and heaved an axe into the second man's back. I hadn't intended to hit spine, but he went down immediately, his pistol clattering to the floor. The first man lunged, swinging his cutlass at my head. I blocked it with one axe and sent a strike toward his face with the other. He ducked and scooped up the fallen pistol. Then he shouted toward the doorway. "Ren, armed intruder!" Someone returned the yell from below.

I cursed. So much for our quiet escape.

"Should have run, lass," the man said, looking me up and down. "If you're an assassin, you're too late. The admiral already left."

Belza had probably stormed off as I'd slipped out the kitchen window. I cursed again, though unsure what I would have done had the man appeared in front of me. Could I kill him as carelessly as he'd killed Father? Would having his blood on my hands heal my ragged heart, or would it harden me into something unrecognizable? Perhaps it was best I hadn't come across him yet.

Boots pounded on the stairs. They'd be here in seconds.

Aden threw his bound arms over the pirate's head and pulled him backward. I was already moving. As the pirate brought his pistol upward, I swung my axe at his arm, making contact just above the wrist. The pistol flew from his hand and hit the floor. It discharged. The wall exploded, sending a burst of plaster at our legs.

The pirate howled, gaping at his arm. My stomach turned over. His hand was a bloody mass of ruined flesh. I glanced at the other man on the floor. He hadn't moved.

Men in the hall.

I sprinted to the door and shoved it closed. My fingers fumbled with the bolt. The men arrived on the other side just as the bolt slid into place. They slammed into it and shook the handle. The door held.

There was a *thump* behind me. I turned to find Aden standing over the fallen pirate, chair in hand. He'd knocked the injured man unconscious. He tossed the chair aside and glanced at the door. The pirates on the other side had begun to pound on the wood.

"This isn't good," he said. "I don't know how you climbed up here, but I'll never make it."

Even if I climbed back out to the pole, I couldn't get the running start I needed to make that leap again. Aden was right. The chances of us both making it were slim.

I wiped my bloody axe clean on the fallen man's shirt, then sheathed it and approached Aden. I took his hands and began sawing gently at his bonds with the other blade. I tried not to think about how warm his hands felt and how he smelled of wind and leather even after days of captivity.

The rope split apart. He rubbed his wrists and sighed, looking back at the door. "You shouldn't have done this, Lane. You could have run away."

"Plenty of time for running later." I hurried to the shared wall and examined the shot hole. It went several inches deep. I placed my fingers inside, moving carefully so I wouldn't burn them on a spent pistol ball. I couldn't find it. It had gone straight through.

This was our only chance.

"Stand back," I said, rising to my feet. Then I swung the axe at the wall. It caught.

"I'll help." Aden took my other axe and positioned himself next to me. A heavy *thud* sounded from the other side of the door. We didn't have long.

Swing-*strike*. Swing-*strike*. We fell into a rhythm, timing our blows with the other. As I'd suspected, the wooden wall gave way easily at first. Then I reached a layer of hardened mud.

Now it was Aden who cursed. "Backup plan?"

"We push through," I muttered. The men at the door had gone quiet. A bad sign. "I think—"

Something exploded behind us.

Splinters peppered the room, and I turned away to cover my face. When I looked back, there was a smoking hole in the door just above the handle. An arm shoved its way through and fumbled with the handle on our side.

"You idiot," another man said. "The bolt's higher than that."

I threw myself at the wall in a frenzy, sending blow after jarring blow. My arms and shoulders screamed for relief. Aden turned back to the door, axe at the ready.

A crack formed in the wall, then widened. I slammed into it with all my strength.

Another blast from the door. A cheer from the other side.

The plaster in front of me crumbled, leaving a gap about two feet square. A burst of stale air blew in. It would have to be enough.

I sheathed my weapon and pulled Aden toward the hole. He held fast. "No, you first."

There wasn't time to argue. I dove at the opening leading to the neighboring building, ignoring the pain in my knees upon impact. Then I half scrambled, half slithered through. Aden followed just behind me. His breath was ragged and loud, echoing in the small space. A shout rose behind us as I climbed out into an empty room.

The fit was tighter for Aden, but he managed to grab hold of the hole's edge and pull himself through, emerging on his hands and knees. Then he stood, handed over my other axe, and brushed plaster off his face. There was movement visible through the hole. If Aden fit, the pirates could too.

I pulled him toward the stairs. "Hurry."

We stumbled for the steps and leaped together, skipping the broken ones. Then we tore through a back door to the alley and sprinted away. The pirates' yells faded behind us.

39

Several minutes later, we pulled into an alley near the harbor. My lungs screamed for relief. Aden placed his hand on a building to steady himself, gasping for air. He moved a mite more slowly than he should have. Whether from weakness or pain, I couldn't tell.

His injuries were clearer in daylight. Beneath the gray of old plaster and dirt lay a patchwork of colorful bruises. Belza had obviously beaten him at every opportunity. A combination of hatred for Belza and sorrow for Aden brewed inside me. We'd both suffered the unthinkable at the pirate's hand, just in different ways.

Aden's gaze met mine. We stood there for a long moment. The ground felt like a ship, plummeting under my feet and sending my stomach tumbling. There was a new pain in his eyes that hadn't been there before. My hand lifted to his face before I could stop it, brushing away a spot of plaster from his cheek. If only removing pain were so easy.

"You are a marvel, Lane Garrow." He leaned forward and brushed his lips against my forehead.

Something inside me cracked into a thousand painful, nerve-slicing pieces at his touch. "Call me Laney."

"Laney."

His whisper sent that surge of warmth through me again. I took a step back, breaking the contact. This was just too much. I couldn't contain the emotions his tenderness brought. Especially when both of us knew this had to end eventually.

"The pirates will be looking for you," I managed. "I have a hiding place near the bay."

"They're long behind us. Surely we can take a second to catch our breath."

It would take a lifetime to catch my breath when he looked at me like that. I strode past him, hoping my pink cheeks weren't obvious to everyone around us. Aden paused before jogging to catch up. His clenched jaw was the only indication that anything had occurred. Minutes later, we reached the end of cobblestone and the beginning of gravel marking the edge of town.

"Your hiding place is close to the ocean." He stroked the dark stubble on his chin, keeping his tone light. "Why am I not surprised?"

"The ocean always provides." It took too, but I didn't want to dwell on that. I plunged into the woods, using the off-road trail I'd found on the way here. Aden fell into step behind me.

"I have no right to ask anything else of you," he said. "Especially after today. But I need to know what happened."

Simply thinking upon the events of that day made my insides feel like they were being scraped clean by a butcher's knife. Voicing the words aloud would be impossible. How could I explain something I didn't yet believe myself?

"They're . . . gone." It was all I could manage.

"Oh, Laney." His voice was heavy as an anchor. He placed his hand on my shoulder as if to pull me into an embrace, then seemed to think better of it and withdrew his hand again. "I'm so sorry. Really."

I nodded, keeping my gaze fixed on the ground. I refused to stop, to let Aden's pity catch up to me. We had to reach the shelter, had to escape the pirates, had to keep moving.

"Your father fascinated me," Aden said. "He arranged his life around you, you know. Paval told me Garrow had other investment opportunities, but he insisted on staying with you on the *Majesty*. Said he was a father first and captain second." He snorted quietly. "With my father, it's backward. A king at all times and a father when he feels like it."

An irrational frustration swept through me at his words. It wasn't fair that my father should die and a murderous king should live. My father had made mistakes in his life, surely, but he'd been trying to overcome them. He'd been remaking himself into a better man and died struggling to protect a daughter he loved.

Aden didn't even know the truth about my father. I hadn't told him, and he'd missed Belza's declaration to the crew. *My father was a pirate.* Aden had been right all along, but it wasn't foolish pride that kept me from saying the words. Few people living knew Father's secret, and I knew he'd want it to remain that way. Besides, his secret was my secret now—and Aden remained a prince of Hughen.

Even if a girl sailor could be forgiven, perhaps a pirate's daughter could not.

There was, however, something Aden needed to know immediately. "I overheard a conversation in there," I said slowly. Then I told him about King LeZar's betrayal.

His pace slowed as I finished. I turned to face him, sensing a new chill in the air, and instantly regretted it. The devastation on his face nearly broke me all over again.

"I—I don't understand," he finally said, his voice heavy with emotion. "Are you certain it was LeZar? I mean, he's like an uncle to me. He and my father have spent countless nights discussing policy and playing cards. He—they've come to each other's aid since the very beginning."

I nodded. "He seemed afraid of Khral Rasmus. Maybe he owes a debt. Or he's being blackmailed." There was no excuse for the man's behavior, but I couldn't bear the pain in Aden's eyes.

"The latter seems more likely. LeZar would never beg money off a Messaun. Any ruler with sense knows better than that." He groaned. "I'm such a fool. I really thought my father was right, and King LeZar would solve all our problems. I was so desperate to find him, yet he was on his way here to betray us all along."

I said nothing. No words could make this right for Aden—just as nothing could ever bring back what I'd lost.

His gaze softened. "Look at me, going on about politics at a time like this. Forgive me for being an idiot." He reached for my hand, but I pulled it back. His mouth set in a firm line.

"Aden," I began, steeling my heart. "I'm here to help you, but don't read more into this than there is. We can't—"

Footsteps sounded nearby, accompanied by a shout. Aden looked down and groaned. The ground was muddy this far into the forest, and we'd left a perfect trail of footprints.

"Time to run for it," I told him, stepping off the trail. "Follow me."

We reached the shelter less than an hour later. It had begun to rain, drenching my hair and clothing yet again, but I only felt relief. We'd lost our pursuers a couple of miles back, and the rain would finish off what was left of our footprints. It would buy us an hour or two of rest at the very least.

I strode inside and swiped the blanket, suppressing another shiver as I sat against the wall where I'd spent the night. Aden just stood in what remained of the doorway, looking about. "Nice place."

"Thanks."

He sighed and began to unclasp his shirt.

My eyes widened, but I didn't stop him. He'd dry much faster without it. But I had a very different problem. I no longer wore bindings beneath my own shirt, which meant removing it would mean a kind of exposure I wasn't ready for. I pulled the blanket up until it reached my chin.

He slipped his shirt off and hung it over a chair. Then he sat beside me. I opened the blanket, allowing him to slide over until we were smashed together underneath, side by side.

I sat stiff as a corpse, suddenly aware of the endless inches of bare skin pressed against me.

He looked down. "You seem uncomfortable. Maybe you should take the blanket."

"Um." I gripped the blanket tighter. "I mean, it's nothing I haven't—I saw plenty of shirtless men on the ship. But I've never... touched one."

His eyes grew round. "Of course. I'll put my shirt back on." He removed the blanket and began to stand.

"Nay," I said, grabbing his arm. "Let it dry. It's just something I'm not used to."

He sat back, leaving a few inches between us this time. "You never did let your disguise fall. Not even to steal moonlight kisses with a handsome young sailor?"

The heat in my face was a raging flame. "No kiss is worth risking your life for."

Our gazes met in the darkness, and the shirt was forgotten. My words felt wrong in the cold space between us. Our futures were more intertwined than ever. If Aden was discovered, I'd be executed along with him.

"You were so angry that night after the duel," he said softly. "I thought you'd never speak to me again. The fact that you came all this way for me . . . I'll admit, it gives me the tiniest spark of hope."

I didn't dare move. I wanted to cover his mouth and smother the words while longing for them at the same time.

"Suppose you hadn't found that missive," he said. "Suppose the duels never happened and the pirates never came. Suppose we were still on your father's ship, alone in the nest with the entire world before us." Aden paused, uncertain, his face so close I felt his breath on my face. "Would you have made an exception for me?"

My heart pounded as if determined to leave my chest and soar to the night sky. I was cold and warm and tired yet more alive than I'd ever been. He was just inches away, his lips parted. We breathed the very same air, inhaling and exhaling in perfect unison, like sailors rowing the same boat.

Aden had fought Kemp with an intensity that burned my insides, right down to my feet. It was that same fire I felt in him now, barely restrained, tense. Waiting. *Wanting*.

Aden wanted me. Me, Laney Garrow, a girl who dressed in men's clothing and longed to become a sea captain. A girl with a dangerous heritage, who ignored the risks and plunged headlong into danger.

He waited.

Aden wasn't his father. He was polite, patient. Nobility was in his blood. A prince like him wouldn't simply take what he wanted.

But I was no royal, and my blood demanded differently.

I grabbed his head and pulled it down, pressing my lips to his.

He tensed only a moment, his mouth curving into a grin, and then

I felt something within him snap. He held my face in his hands and took our kiss to a new level, his lips firm and demanding. He pulled me toward him until we'd closed every inch of distance between us, wet against dry, my shirt against his bare chest. His fingers threaded in my hair, holding me tight against him, protecting me from the world.

I'd been wrong about the politeness and patience in his blood. This was a man who knew what he wanted, and I was it.

His kisses—one upon the other, until I was desperate for air— sent heat racing through my body. I trembled in his arms. And then his kisses slowed, growing more tender and soft. His lips were a brush on mine, a quiet promise.

He pulled away and I moved to follow, a drunken sigh escaping me, but he placed his forehead against mine instead. His breaths came in quiet gasps.

"I've thought about doing that a hundred times," he said, his voice raspy. "I can't believe you're really here."

"Then don't question it. Let it just be."

"I want nothing more." He paused, then raised an eyebrow. "Well, I do want more, but first we'll have to win my kingdom back."

I gave him a wry grin. Aden's little problem of being royal wasn't our biggest issue right now. We had to discover the state of his government. Then he had a rebellion to organize. Then, somehow, we had to sneak into the palace and rescue Aden's family. Failure during any of those steps would mean death for us both.

It felt utterly impossible. Of course, Aden and I had just experienced a moment I would have deemed impossible too. Perhaps impossible just involved taking desperate risks that turned wonderful in the end.

"We can't do anything till we're dry," I reminded Aden, reaching for him again. He chuckled and leaned in once more.

40

The night passed quickly. By sunrise, the only sign of the pirates' chase was a few muddy footprints near town. I imagined Belza's enraged tantrum when they'd told him Aden was gone. That image, along with Aden's fingers intertwined with mine, made me grin as we walked. It didn't stop me from scouring the forest around us, though. I kept my free hand on one axe just in case.

The morning was a crisp one, the murky air cleared by last night's rain. The cobblestones beneath my boots were still damp as we reached the outskirts of town, rivulets of water slanting downward toward the canals. The water level had risen even higher since I'd been here last. It had been three weeks since I'd met Aden and embarked on my very last voyage on the *Majesty*. Three weeks since I'd first suspected my father was a pirate. It had seemed like the worst thing imaginable.

It felt like a lifetime ago. Or perhaps a different lifetime altogether.

"I still think I should have come alone," I told Aden. "Even if the pirates aren't looking, the Messaun soldiers might be. Someone is sure to recognize you."

He stroked his stubbled chin. "Not with this, they won't. I doubt they would recognize me anyway, considering my family only travels in covered carriages. Besides, you've been through enough. I'm not sending you anywhere I don't dare go myself." He gave my hand a squeeze. "Even this princeling has a little pride."

My cheeks warmed under his gaze. I finally ducked and let my hand drop, failing to hide a smile. "Let's get this over with, then. You wanted to gauge the military presence in the square, right?"

"The palace gates actually, if we can get close enough. I need to know what I'm up against." His stomach rumbled, echoing the hollowness of my own. "I don't suppose you have any coins left?"

"Nay, but I have a baker friend who might be able to help us. The market should be open on our way back." Assuming life had resumed as normal and the soldiers didn't immediately spot Aden and chase us down. I wasn't all that certain of either. I was accustomed to sneaking about in this city, staying beneath the guards' notice. Yet beard or not, Aden was far from inconspicuous. His face looked better, but the bruising was impossible to hide, and his clothing was in shambles. It was hard to see any of that when he strode with such confidence. He walked more quickly every minute, the light in his gray eyes increasing with each step closer to home and family.

Meanwhile, my own uneasiness increased as we approached the palace and the city began to awaken. The embargo and the soldiers on the beach were enough of an indication that something wasn't right. But even now, as the sun chased away the night's shadows, I could tell the town had changed since my visit yesterday. No children darted about the walks on their way to school. No carts rolled by, laden with goods to be sold in shops or at the market. The usual contingents of soldiers were absent. Very few people walked the streets, and they hurried past with their gazes fixed on the ground. It was as if Hughen itself cowered, holding its breath. Waiting for something.

It reminded me of Messau.

"Aden," I whispered.

"I know." He increased his stride even more, almost running now.

Less than five minutes later, we reached the park leading to the palace gates. The cobblestone here was older but clean, the trees neatly trimmed and rustling gently in the morning breeze. Any other day, the silence would have felt peaceful. Today it was positively eerie. My skin crawled as if covered in a thousand wood beetles. My instincts screamed for me to grab Aden's hand and run. The sour stench in the air didn't help.

Footsteps approached. I pulled Aden behind a cluster of trees just as a group of Messaun soldiers walked by, green uniforms and all. They scanned the park with hands on their weapons. I eyed their path and did some quick calculating. If they followed the palace wall around, we had five minutes, maybe ten.

We waited a full minute after they were out of sight before stepping toward the gate once more. Then Aden's ragged breathing hitched.

I followed his gaze. The palace gate was tall and regal, a structure built to last thousands of years. The pillars were carved from stone and the metal bars forged by expert blacksmiths. The gate itself was closed, of course. But Aden stared at the wall to its right, his face draining of color. A series of long shadows hung from the bars. Suddenly the stench made more sense, and my stomach nearly turned over.

Bodies.

Eighteen of them, still as death. Two were ladies. Their colorful gowns fluttered quietly in the wind. What kind of a sick, twisted mind displayed his victims in such a manner?

Ever so slowly, Aden crept toward the nearest body. He crouched to see the victim's face, then crumpled to his knees. "No."

It was Aden's father, the king.

This was the man who'd taken Elena's head with her own axe. This man was the reason I'd grown up in fear, hunted for who I was, hoping against impossible odds for a life that could never exist. My imagination had made him out to be some kind of legend—yet here he hung, as human as anyone who'd ever lived.

He hated sailor women, but one had saved his own son's life. If he'd lived to see it, would that realization have softened his heart?

Warmth welled up in my eyes. This time, I let it stay for Aden's sake. "I—I don't know what to say."

"They couldn't even allow him a dignified death." His voice sounded small, strangled.

By the dried blood staining the king's chest, it had been a violent death indeed. I was sad for the man, I realized. For the memories he would never get to make with his family, for his inability to see the potential of women sailors. For the peaceful, full life he could have enjoyed with his subjects.

Hanging the king's body here was the ultimate insult. Worse than an insult. Rasmus had meant it as a message. Displaying the corpse in the square would have curbed any uprising in town, but Rasmus didn't seem concerned about that. He'd hung it here, where anyone threatening his newfound power would be sure to see it. No wonder the khral had aligned himself with pirates. He had far more in common with them than with any aristocrat.

"We'll give him a proper, respectful burial as soon as we can." I glanced over my shoulder. That group of soldiers would return any minute now, assuming there weren't others. It wouldn't take long to connect the boy kneeling at the king's feet with the missing prince. "Are the rest of your family...here?"

It seemed an eternity before he slowly lifted his head to scan the others. Finally, he let his shoulders sag. "No."

"Good. That means they're alive, Aden. We can still save them."
I placed a gentle hand on his shoulder. "But we have to go now."

A deep shudder racked his body. "I'm sorry," he gasped. "I'm so,
so sorry, Father. I never should have left."

"If you hadn't, you could be hanging right there next to him. You
may yet." A chill gripped my spine as I realized it was true. My axes
were the only weapons we had, and we stood completely exposed.
I scanned the park again, fighting a rising sense of panic. Every
shadow looked like a soldier ready to pounce. This was a bad idea.

I crouched beside Aden, placed his arm around my shoulders,
and stood with a grunt. It worked. He looked almost surprised to
find himself standing, eye level with the downcast face of the man
he'd once admired.

He tore his gaze away. "It doesn't matter now," he said softly.

I stepped between the two men, forcing him to look at me. "It
does. It matters more than ever. Your family waits for you. There's
nobody else to save them, Aden. Just you."

His expression was haunted, broken. "Just me."

I paused, then placed a hand on his cheek. "But you can't do
anything for them if you're caught. Let's go back to the house now
and sort everything out. Aye?"

He nodded. It was far from convincing, but it was something.

I took his hand and pulled him away.

I sat on the blanket in the abandoned watch house, knees pulled to
my chest, listening to the rain. It was different, the sound of rain
on land. I'd seen hundreds of storms on the *Majesty*, all unique in
their intensity. The rain was our cradle—it caressed the ship like a

mother stroking her sleeping child. I'd fallen asleep to the sound of water pelting the deck and collecting in puddles that would later be swept away by the crew. Rain wasn't our enemy. It was our neighbor.

But here, it felt completely different. Raindrops hit the metal roof like swords striking, sharp and loud, and the wind shook the shelter so hard I heard rattling from the tresses above. I stared at the puddle collecting by my soggy bare feet. I'd turned my boots over to let them dry. It didn't look like that would happen anytime soon.

It wasn't just the rain I listened for now. Aden was out there somewhere, lost in his grief. When we'd arrived, he'd asked to be alone. I knew better than to argue. His world had collapsed on top of him, and I knew too well how that felt. Except he also had an entire kingdom at stake and few options that allowed him to save it.

He'd been out there for hours. There was only so long a grieving person should be alone.

I stood and made my way outside, leaving my wet boots behind. Aden was a light figure against a grove of distant trees. The forest floor was soft underfoot as I made my way toward him, placing my feet carefully to avoid puddles. A faint smoke traveled in the late-afternoon breeze, more memory than substance. Probably nothing more than what remained of a beach patrol's fire, but I scanned the trees carefully as I walked anyway.

Aden stared blankly into the forest as I arrived, his eyes red and slightly puffy. His hair was plastered to his forehead and his shirt clung to him, unclasped and wet. He didn't seem to notice my presence.

I slipped my hand into his and gave it a squeeze. "I wanted things to end differently for you. I'm sorry."

"Master Nomad's Law," Aden muttered. "*Your word is your power.* Messau and Hughen had a peace treaty."

"A treaty Rasmus's father signed, not him," I said. "I'm not saying it's right, because it wasn't. But it's clear now we can't trust anyone."

A long silence fell. A bird shrieked high overhead, followed by rustling somewhere in the brush.

"I can't do this." He sounded strangled. "I have no army, no allies. Not even a weapon." His expression was so full of pain, so raw, that my heart broke open all over again. "This wasn't supposed to happen. It doesn't feel real."

"The believing part will take a while," I said softly.

"I didn't want to go at first," Aden whispered. "I told him I wouldn't."

"Your father?"

He nodded. "I thought he was overreacting. Even told him that. Then he warned me about Varnen and what he was capable of. I told my father to assassinate him instead and leave me be."

His hand was cold. I gripped it in my other hand and began to rub some warmth into it. "He convinced you eventually."

"He did." Aden tore his gaze away, staring at the forest floor. He looked positively shattered. "He made it sound noble, like this was a bold mission that he trusted me to fulfill. I thought he was trying to manipulate me. It wasn't until I was in the brig of a pirate ship that I realized his mission was doomed from the start. There was never enough time to get help, even if things had gone smoothly. He never expected me to succeed. He just wanted me to be safe." His voice cracked on the last word. "I was too angry to tell him goodbye."

"You feel guilty for surviving when he didn't. You feel guilty for every time you disobeyed, every lie you told, every roll of the eyes. Every time you yelled that you never wanted to be like him." I swallowed back the lump in my throat. "Because you know that was a lie too."

"Laney," he said softly, and pulled me against his chest. His arms closed around my waist in an embrace, and he placed his chin on my head as if to hold me there. I clung to him with the same ferocity.

Neither of us needed to speak. We understood each other more deeply than anyone else in the world, and neither wanted that connection to end.

"The sea nearly beat me," I said after a while, my voice muffled against his shirt. I looked upward to find him watching me. "Not because I almost drowned, but because I almost considered letting it win. It was after my father died and the ship started going under. The sea took him and the *Majesty* and everyone I cared about. It would have been so easy to let the water take me too."

"But you chose to fight instead. Why?"

"I found a purpose, something bigger than me. Something impossible enough to distract me from the pain for a while."

"My dramatic rescue."

I felt a tiny grin escape. "It was rather dramatic, wasn't it?"

"And now that you've succeeded?" His voice was flat as he pulled slightly away. "This morning, you said I was all my family had. You avoided using the word *us*."

My grin faded and I stared at the ground. "I told you once that I was never the type to save kingdoms. Once you were safe, I planned to hunt down Belza the way he hunted my father. I wanted him to feel my axe in his belly and know it was me who killed him. I still want that." The truth of the words chilled my heart. I meant every single one.

Aden waited a moment, then prodded. "But?"

I shrugged. "I'm not done with the first task yet."

"I should send you away. This is no mutiny of a few dozen men. It's me against an entire army."

I placed a finger to his lips, rendering him utterly and completely still. "Us. It's us against an army. And a mutiny is exactly what this is. Just, you know, on a larger scale. The same rules apply."

"I thought there were no rules in battle."

"See? You're finally learning."

He sighed, sounding defeated. "I suppose we should go inside and make some kind of plan."

"First we'll get you dry. When this rain lets up, I'll go into town and find some food. *Then* we can discuss how to make our own dramatic rescue."

He hung back for a moment before following me to the shelter.

We'd just rounded the corner when a figure stepped inside the door ahead of us.

Aden went rigid. "Pirates."

I squinted at the open doorway. "That was an awfully small pirate."

"Whoever it was, they've found us. It's time to go." He turned away.

I grabbed his arm. "Not yet. I left my boots in there. And I'm not leaving without my axes."

"I'll find you another pair. Come on."

I jerked free of his arm and crept toward the door, stepping carefully with my bare feet to avoid where the wood creaked. Aden muttered something under his breath and followed. I peered inside.

Pain slammed into my head and everything went dark.

41

I lay sprawled on the floor. The partially intact ceiling made the cloudy sky above look broken. I stared at it for several seconds before my wits returned. *Someone is here.*

Flinching at the ache at the base of my skull, I turned my head to find Aden locked in combat with a dark figure in the shadows in front of me. He shoved my attacker to the ground and advanced with fists raised.

I finally realized what was happening. "Aden, stop!"

He stepped back to look at me, relief in his expression. Then he turned to the figure on the floor, and his eyes widened.

Aden's opponent pushed herself to her feet and stepped into the fragmented light, glowering at us. By the girl's stature, she had to be around thirteen, maybe fourteen. Her hair was fashioned in a messy braid. But the strangest part was the gown. It fell past her waist in elegant folds that rustled like expensive satin, the hem at least a foot too long.

I rose as well, if a little shakily, and pressed a hand to the back of my head. A piece of rotted wood sat on the floor by the doorway. I gave it a good kick, sending it across the room.

"You all right?" Aden asked me, still eyeing the stranger.

I groaned. "Just lovely."

"You tore my dress," the girl snapped at him, and began to brush dirt off the fabric.

Aden went still. "Elyss?"

The girl paused. "You know me?"

"You're Lili's maid," he said. Then he leaped over to grab her shoulders. "Where is she? Is she alive?"

The girl's eyes went round in horror. "Sire?"

"Yes, it's me. You need to tell me what happened to my family."

Elyss looked as dazed as I felt. She glanced at me helplessly, then back at Aden. "Beg pardon, Prince Cedrick. I—I couldn't tell it was you, what with the bruises and the...beard. We all thought you were dead."

"Elyss," he said firmly. "Where is Lili?"

"I don't know. As soon as the palace was attacked, I ran. She told me to." Elyss looked down. "She wouldn't come with me."

"The palace?" Aden dropped his hands and took a step back. "But she wasn't at the palace. My father hid them with relatives."

"Aye, in Nathaniel," Elyss said. "I went along. Your mother got a missive from the palace and said we were to return immediately. We arrived just before the feast. But then soldiers came running in, and there were people screaming, and—I tried, Highness, I swear it. Lili kept saying she wouldn't leave without her mum."

A missive from the palace. Orders forged by Varnen himself, no doubt.

Aden looked devastated. "Lili is only eight year-days old. You shouldn't have given her a choice."

"They searched the servants as we left, Highness. They were looking for members of the royal family. She wouldn't have made it out anyway."

"But have you heard anything about them? Have they been taken away, or are they still in the palace?"

She swallowed. "All I know is what I've heard in town. Nobody has seen them leave, so they must still be there."

I thought of the wall of bodies and flinched. That didn't mean they were *alive*.

"All right," Aden said, wringing some of the water from his shirt. "I can work with that. It's not ideal, but at least they're all in one place."

The girl tensed, pulling at the folds in her dress. I examined her for a long moment, noting the elegant lines of the cloth in her hands. The hem was covered in mud, and dirty fingerprints dotted several areas.

"Elyss," I said gently. "That dress isn't yours, is it?"

She went rigid. "Course it is."

Aden turned, his gaze locking on mine as understanding dawned. "I've seen that before. Did you steal that from my mother's wardrobe?"

"No, Your Highness. I would never do such a thing." She'd backed up against the wall, dirtying the dress's skirt even worse.

"You're lying."

"It's mine, I swear it." Her voice was a squeak now.

Aden opened his mouth to retort, but I placed a hand on his arm. "Elyss, you've suffered a lot, and you don't have much to show for it. Maybe you thought the dress adequate payment for your trouble. The fact is, if you were able to return to the palace to...borrow it, maybe you can help us sneak in."

A furious blush had taken hold of her cheeks. "'Twasn't safe to wear my maid's uniform in town. They were looking, you see. And there's someone there who said he'd take me in when the danger was over. He likes me dressed up nice."

"Someone in town," Aden repeated. "A lord?"

"Of course not. But he does drive the lord's wagon. Most of the nobility were killed at the feast, but this lord was ill and didn't attend, so his household survived. They're helping gather support in the city. If you have a message for them, I'll deliver it."

"What of sneaking us into the palace?" I asked.

A second's hesitation, then her voice grew stronger. "Fact is, Highness, what you're asking is risky. If you win, I don't want to be a maid anymore. I want my own maids."

I gaped at the girl.

Aden hid a smile. "Done. You help us free my family, and I'll make sure the crown prince rewards you well."

Elyss winced at the words. Not a good sign.

"You aren't telling us everything," I said.

"Course I am." Her voice had gone shrill.

"What aren't you saying?" Aden asked.

She took a deep breath. The words came in a desperate rush. "Your brother, Mael, disappeared the night the king died. Nobody knows what happened to him except for the rumors."

Aden paused. "What rumors?"

"Some say he was killed and dumped into the bay with the servants. Others say he leaped from the cliffs to avoid your father's fate. None of the accounts line up exactly, but in all of them…" She shrugged.

Aden simply stared at Elyss, his face turning a pasty white. My expression likely looked much the same.

"That makes you the crown prince," I whispered.

"Wrong, miss. That makes him king."

Aden flinched at the word *king*. He dropped my hand and stepped away, placing his back to us. Even Elyss looked a little pale now.

An image of Aden's body hanging next to his father's slammed into my thoughts, all too real. If Mael was truly dead and Aden the rightful king, our presence here had just become even more dangerous.

"Your allies will be relieved to know you're alive," I told him gently. "Put your support behind them, meet with them. Lead them. You can strengthen one another."

"Allies?" he asked incredulously. "My allies just murdered my father, burned our agreement, and did a little dance on top. What you're talking about are townspeople with torches and cooking knives. Even if I wanted to risk their lives, which I don't, we would never beat Rasmus's army."

I raised an eyebrow. "Never underestimate a determined person with a knife."

Some of the life returned to his eyes. "True. I keep making that mistake, don't I?"

"So will Rasmus, which means we have a chance," I said. "We need a plan, then. We'll send Elyss back to the palace to find out where they're keeping your family. Then we'll meet with the lord and his followers to plan the attack."

Aden shook his head firmly. "Too long. We'll have to assume my mother and sisters are in the dungeons. Elyss, how quickly can your friends be ready to attack the palace?"

She cocked her head. "I'm not certain, Sire. Why?"

"Because I've seen enough. I refuse to leave my family in the hands of that man another day." He leveled his gaze on Elyss, then me. "We're getting them out of there tonight."

42

It rained as if the spirits themselves were determined to hinder our progress as we made our way toward town. The wind blew sideways, putting out the street lanterns and forcing us to make our way more by feel than sight. At least that strange smoke in the air had left for now.

We took a shortcut, winding through the city's slums. Aden grew increasingly quiet as we drew closer to the palace. His gray eyes swept the muddy streets, taking in the run-down conditions of the poorer neighborhoods. They hadn't bothered to lay cobblestone here, nor would they ever, by the looks of things. Elyss, on the other hand, simply appeared worried. I lengthened my stride to catch up with her.

"How long have you worked at the palace?" I asked.

She frowned. "Three years."

"Are your parents worried about you?"

"Dead ten years past. My grandmother got me the position and left. I haven't seen her since."

Elyss was as street worthy as I was. It made me like her the tiniest bit. "I'm glad you found a place to belong. That's more than most of us can say."

"The royals are decent enough people once you get to know them." She nodded toward Aden, who walked slightly ahead. "He's going to be all right, isn't he?"

"Not for a long time."

It was another half an hour and several mud-ridden streets before the palace came into view, a dark shadow against a black sky. It towered over the coastline. I tried to follow my own advice and stay fixed on the plan, but all I could think about was that day weeks ago when, in the shadows of this very palace, Father had given another of his lectures about staying safe. I would have given anything for yet another lecture right now.

Aden must have seen my expression, because he slowed to let me catch up, then quietly slid his hand over mine.

The wind whipped my damp shirt again, and for the fiftieth time, I wished for my coat. By this time tomorrow, we'd be warm and dry. Or dead.

Elyss took her place in front like a page announcing her master, a basket of fabric in hand. We reached a corner with a great stone column. Earlier, Aden and I had cut straight through the park. Tonight, we turned right at the massive gate and followed it around the coastal side to the service entrance. We kept to the shadows but held our heads high, as if entitled to be here. A group of soldiers walked by, barely giving us a glance. Either our disguises were better than I'd assumed, or they'd grown overconfident. I thought of those bodies at the gate and decided it was the latter.

A few minutes later, Elyss halted at what looked like a wall. "The servants' entrance is behind there. I'll check it out. Wait here." She disappeared into the shadows.

Aden leaned over to speak after a moment, but flinched at the sound of a yell. It was unmistakably Elyss's voice. She seemed to be arguing with someone.

I plunged after her.

"Laney!" Aden hissed from the shadows, but I ignored him and raced toward the open doorway I hadn't seen earlier.

The maid's voice grew louder as I approached. "...needed it so bad she sent me out in the rain. If you don't let me back in, she'll just send others out looking. She's not a woman who likes waiting."

"I've received no orders about a servant girl fetching a basket for the cloth master," a deep voice said. "Now run along before I toss you into the dungeon."

Elyss gave an exasperated sigh. "And lose my job because the door guard wasn't listening when he got his orders? Let me in now, or I'll tell them about the bottle you're hiding behind your back. Stealing wine from the king's kitchens? When he finds out, you'll lose both your hands—"

"Fine!" the guard barked impatiently. "Stop yer shouting." The door creaked.

Elyss caught a glimpse of me approaching, but she didn't let on. "Remember me next time. Have fun standing in the rain *all by yourself.*"

I slowed, confused. Then I realized what the maid meant. She was signaling me, telling me the guard was alone.

The man held the door open just long enough for her to slip through, then began pulling it closed.

I yanked out my axes and leaped.

He turned before I got to him. With a startled grunt, he reached for his sword. Too late. I performed a quick X-block and twisted the sword from his hands, tossing it aside. Then I slammed the side of the axe at his head.

He slumped silently to the ground.

Aden emerged as Elyss whispered, "Come on," and held the door wide.

I grabbed the guard's boot, motioning to Aden to take the other. We pulled the man into the narrow entrance. There was a loud *thud* as Elyss secured the door. He'd come to by morning, but our task would have succeeded or failed by then.

"The servants' quarters are this way," Elyss said.

The air was thick with dirt as we ducked inside. I'd expected the long hallway leading upward, but not the slickness of its walls and floor after a hundred years of use. This entrance had been carved into the mountain itself. It looked like a tunnel dug by a child and reinforced with rotting wooden beams. Thankfully, someone had laid loose wooden planks down for footing. Three gaslight lanterns hung from the wall, though only one was lit.

Elyss pulled the lantern down from its hook. "You bring it with you to navigate the tunnels, then return it when you leave."

"I didn't realize it was in such poor condition," Aden said with a frown, taking in the rudimentary walls and flooring.

"It's always looked like this." Elyss motioned for us to follow. As if we'd do anything else.

"Do the Messaun soldiers ever come through here?" I whispered as we walked.

She shrugged. "I haven't been back in days. I'd be wary just in case."

The tunnel rose slightly, then ended at a flight of slippery stairs. I stepped carefully, clinging to the rail so I wouldn't fall on Aden. Forty steps. Those stairs had to be a nightmare for the poor kitchen and laundry servants carrying burdens. By the deepening frown on Aden's face, he thought the same thing.

A turn later, the tunnel branched off in two directions. Elyss chose the right. "The men's quarters are to the left. Although you'll come with us, Your Highness."

"Delightful," Aden muttered, his shoulders squared.

We reached a door. Elyss knocked twice, paused, then twice more. A lock slid on the other side, and the door swung open. A large cavern met us. It held an assortment of unmatched beds. Some were little more than woven straw mats on the rocky ground. Ropes had been strung across the room to hang clothing, and a partition separated the far end for privacy. A single cracked mirror hung near the door.

Despite the four lanterns lighting the room, only one servant occupied the space. It was a stern-looking woman with a plump fig-ure. Wisps of curly dark hair slipped from her once-tidy bun. The rumpled uniform contrasted with the sharpness in her eyes. Lands only knew what this woman had been through.

"Halt," she snapped, blocking the door and glaring at each of us in turn. "Who are you?"

Elyss lifted the lantern closer to Aden's face.

The woman gasped. "Your Majesty." She dropped into a shaky curtsy. "Your face! I didn't recognize—I mean, the bruises...Pardon my poor manners." She glowered at Elyss. "What are you thinking, bringing him here? That madman would give anything to get his hands on the boy." She turned back to Aden. "Er, man. Excuse me, Highness."

Aden held up his hand. "I'm aware of the risk. What is your posi-tion, and where are the others?"

"Magie Ker, Highness. I serve your mother. Or did, before the Messauns imprisoned her." She paused. "Most of the servants ran, like Elyss here. The rest of us swore fealty to the khral. A few fought in the name of the king, may their souls rest."

The servants' bodies wouldn't be displayed on the wall, I knew.

They'd probably been dumped over the cliff and now lay at the bottom of the sea, just like my father. I swallowed hard.

"My presence must remain a secret," Aden said. "Even from the loyal Hughen servants, at least for now. Tell me where my mother is being held."

"In her chambers. They moved her from the dungeon yesterday when she said she'd marry that awful khral."

Aden choked. "She said what?"

"He threatened your sisters if she didn't agree. What was she supposed to say? Poor dear." Magie shook her head.

He muttered a curse. "Do you know what happened to Mael?"

Magie shook her head. "We haven't found his body yet, but I'm afraid he's gone, Highness. We're all very sorry for your loss." She ducked her head. "Unfortunately, I have more bad news. The succession law says the crown falls to the next male heir. If one can't be produced, it goes to the queen's husband. If this wedding takes place tomorrow, the khral will officially rule both countries."

I frowned. Yet another unfair law. How horrible for the queen, being refused any real power of her own.

"He can't do that!" Aden burst out. "He can't just kill the king and...and force the queen to marry him."

"Who's to stop him, Highness?" Magie asked. "He could take the crown upon himself at any moment if he wished. But he knows the country won't be his till he has the people's support. They love their queen. This way he wins their allegiance *and* their loyalty."

"He doesn't care about their loyalty," I spat. "He'll destroy Hughen. I've seen what Rasmus has done in his own country."

"I'll have his head before my father's crown touches it," Aden said. "But first, we get my mother and sisters to safety. The girls are still in the dungeon, you say?"

"Delivered their dinner myself, poor things."

"How many guards are stationed at my mother's chambers?"

"Two. But Rasmus ordered an increase in security today, so there could be more. His men are everywhere in preparation for tomorrow."

Aden pursed his lips. "Elyss, we can take it from here. I have a message for you to deliver to your friends in town. Magie, I don't suppose you have anything we can use as a disguise?"

A few minutes later, I stood in front of the broken mirror wearing a kitchen maid's uniform. It had been white once, though now it was splattered with grease stains. It hung loose to my ankles. Although I wore more fabric than usual, I felt completely exposed without my comfortable trousers. Worse, the waist didn't allow for a belt and pair of axe scabbards. I'd hidden my weapons in a pile of bedding. The comb remained safe in my pocket.

"This is the only uniform that would fit those thick shoulders of yours," Magie explained, pinning my hair into a tight bun. "I hope that holds. Your hair needs a good washing."

Aden stepped out from behind the divider, fastening his shirt clasps. The outfit had completely transformed him. He'd managed to look regal even in a sailor's tattered clothing, but with his mussed hair and scruffy beard, he almost passed for a Hughen servant.

"You'll have to hunch a bit, Highness," Magie said. "You'll fit right in with those bruises. Some of the other servants were beaten as well. But try not to look directly at faces. No servant does that."

"Bad posture and stare at the ground," Aden repeated. "Anything else?"

"Don't let them discover you, or we're all done for." Magie opened the door and tapped her foot impatiently.

Aden looked me up and down, grinning at the skirt. "Thank you, Laney."

I rose to my toes and gave him a peck on the cheek. "Let's go save your family."

43

I'd gazed many times at the Hughen palace high above the city, wondering what it looked like on the inside. I'd imagined an array of elegant, colorful art and woven rugs, all framed by regal stone walls. But the reality of it all had me staring in wonder. Intricate wood carvings were everywhere—the ceiling patterns, the wall moldings. Every inch of it was an incredible work of art, and servants walked right past it all like it was nothing. The cost of the ornate carpets themselves could have fed a city.

We passed through the kitchen, which boasted a massive window and no less than six stoves. The divine smell of baked goods permeated the air around a dozen cooks hurrying about in heavy aprons. Exhaustion was written on their faces. With tomorrow's festivities, I doubted they could rest anytime soon. They didn't even seem to notice the four brilliant chandeliers over their heads.

Magie set a furious pace, marching us through the palace like she was the queen herself. She looked back often to issue a sharp command to keep my eyes down or stop walking like a man. Aden chuckled at the latter.

We soon passed a giant set of gilded doors, one of which had been propped open. I peeked through and stopped with a gasp. It was the largest room I'd ever seen and the most luxurious by far. Nearly every inch of the walls were windows, each lined in drapes long enough to catch a sea wind. The floor was inset with dark and light woods mirroring each other in an intricate floral pattern. It made the *Majesty*'s architecture look like toddler's play. Great golden chandeliers shaped like gulls lined the edges of the ceiling, all leading toward the pillars centered at the back wall, where a massive blue tapestry covered the wall above a tall throne.

"Don't gawk," Magie hissed. "You're supposed to be a servant, remember?"

I couldn't speak. That room could fit the *Majesty* within its walls. The extravagance of it all, the attention to detail—I'd just experienced an entire side of life I never knew existed.

Aden leaned over. "I could spend a full day explaining the symbolism of everything in that room."

His breath warmed my ear. I grinned at the pleasant tingle. "Sounds like the perfect day."

Servants scuttled past despite the late hour, carrying decorations and flowers hurriedly gathered for the ceremony. Few looked in our direction. It wasn't until we turned a corner to the main hall that we ran into soldiers.

There were eleven of them, all with varying shades of white-blond hair, standing around and teasing the Hughens as they worked. Their laughter died as we approached. Aden lowered his head. I focused on their pale faces, watching for any sign of recognition. But there was only amusement.

"A bearded Hughen servant?" The shortest one chuckled. He wore a set of impressively curly eyebrows to match his mustache. "Does your king know of your disobedience? Oh, right. He's dead."

His companions laughed. Color had risen to Aden's cheeks, but to his credit, he kept his head down and continued to walk past.

"The hair itches as it grows in, but the ladies love it," the guard called after Aden. "Who's that lovely little maid you've got there? Haven't seen her before."

Aden increased his pace, and I trotted to keep up. We were nearly to the corner.

"Hey, girl," his companion called out. "He'll never please a pretty thing like you. Come back later and I'll show you how it's done."

We turned the corner. Aden's jaw tightened.

"I'll show him an axe to the face," I muttered. As if Aden needed another reminder that his father was dead.

We climbed the servant staircase, which was still fancier than anything I'd seen before, and turned into the royal living wing. Aden grew increasingly quiet with each step. Magie's frown deepened.

Finally, she turned to face us. "Rasmus ordered the family's wing sectioned off. No Hughens are allowed. If the guards don't believe our story, we'll be thrown into the dungeon and beaten." She didn't say what we were all thinking. It would be far worse for Aden if he were discovered.

"You don't have to do this, Magie," Aden said. "You may return to your quarters if you've changed your mind."

She huffed. "And leave the rightful king to deal with the guards alone? I should say not." The woman whirled about and stalked down the hallway, looking almost insulted. We hurried to follow.

I knew instantly which door belonged to the queen. It was gilded like the ballroom doors, except the design was different. The carving was heavier near the bottom and boasted a haphazard pattern of swirls, like an ocean with foaming waves. It had been meticulously painted in green and blue. A bird coasted above it all with wings spread.

Four guards stood outside the doors. They straightened at our approach, gripping the pistols at their belts.

Magie didn't slow. She marched right up to them and stood there expectantly. "Well? You'd best have an explanation for this."

The guards frowned down at her. The tallest of them wore a yellow beard that ended in actual ringlets. He pushed the others aside and stared her down. "Ye looking to get yerself shot?"

Magie pointed at Aden and me. "They roused me in my sleep and dragged me here to style the queen's hair for the wedding. At *this* time of night. Just how long does the khral think it'll take me to curl a woman's hair, I ask you?"

The guards looked at one another. Pretty Guard scowled. "We've received no orders—"

Magie slapped her hands together. "Well, that's just wonderful. You can style the queen's hair yourselves, then. I'm sure you'll do it to the khral's satisfaction. I'm returning to my warm, soft bed, and if you dare rouse me again, I'll stab you in the eye with a hairpin. And you'd deserve it, scaring an old woman half to death in her sleep." She spun on her heel and shoved past us.

"You will not defy the khral's wishes," I called out, following her cue and running to block her way. "You've sworn the oath. You may not return to your bed until Her Highness is ready for the ceremony."

Aden, finally understanding, grabbed her arm and practically dragged her toward the door. Magie thrashed in his arms, looking very much the grumpy maid. Three bewildered guards scurried to open the door while the fourth looked on.

We were nearly through the doors when the largest thrust his broadsword in front of us. "Wait. Is that really the queen's maid?"

"Yes, sir," one of the other guards said. "She's tended the wench every day since my post here."

He gave a sharp nod. "Search them first."

His companions began patting us down, digging through pockets and feeling at our hair. I was glad I hadn't tried to bring my axes. Then they stepped back. "No weapons, sir."

The guard grunted and opened the door. Then he motioned us quickly inside.

44

The doors closed behind us.

Magie gave a relieved sigh, but my eyes were locked on Aden. He hurried toward a door at the other end of the room, barely giving his surroundings a glance. His face was drawn and somber as he threw it open and pushed inside. I hung back. This moment was between him and his mother. I forced myself to examine my surroundings instead.

No less than six gaslight lanterns lit the sitting room, which was decorated in a series of familiar blues and foamy greens. A large white shell gleamed prominently on a side table. I wasn't the only one here who loved the sea.

Magie stood by the door Aden had just entered, looking as hesitant as I felt. A moment later, she motioned to me. "Come. Her Majesty has summoned us."

The second room looked similar to the first except for the tables along the wall, displaying pair after pair of elaborate, feminine footwear. A heavy wardrobe stood open next to the window. A woman with long, wavy brown hair sat in a chair opposite the wardrobe, her face covered by a dark veil. She wore a black dress, though the beautiful satin was torn in two places. With her regal manner, she was precisely what I'd imagined the queen of Hughen to be.

Aden knelt at her side, grief heavy in his eyes. Then he began to motion quickly. "Mother, this is Laney, Captain Garrow's daughter."

His *daughter*. I'd never heard that introduction from my father's own lips, but it felt exactly right.

The woman watched me, then lifted her hand to return the gesturing motion. Her fingers moved in a rapid, deliberate manner.

Lands. The Hughen queen was deaf. Why hadn't I known that particular detail?

She signed for a long moment. Aden shook his head and began again before she'd finished.

"She says he's in danger here," Magie said, moving to stand beside me. "That they'll kill him too and he should have stayed away. He says he will always come."

"She hates veils," Aden muttered, more to himself than anyone. He hesitated, then reached up and yanked the veil off his mother's face even as her fingers moved to stop him.

We stared. I'd heard that the queen was a beautiful woman, with soft, gentle features and perfect skin. But it was hard to see all that now. Colorful bruises covered her cheeks as if a painter had used her as a violent canvas. The only recognizable feature was her eyes, a fierce and intelligent gray. Aden's eyes.

Aden growled and tossed the veil aside. "What man beats a widow and calls himself a king?"

Magie signed his words, then interpreted the queen's furious reply. "I'd share my bed with the devil himself if it meant safety for my children. Any mother would."

"Rasmus will feel every blow he inflicted upon you." Aden raised his head stubbornly, his hands a storm of motion. "No, more than that. He'll suffer every drop of blood he tore from Father and every tear he's caused this kingdom. And then he'll feel it all over again."

"He only has a few hundred guards in the palace," Magie broke in, speaking for herself now, though slowly so she could sign her words. "But Rasmus sent for more troops just hours after the king's assassination. They'll be arriving soon, not to mention the guests for the ceremony. I've heard rumors that Rasmus also sent for men to occupy the noble houses. They'll be bringing their own servants and slaves. To say we're outnumbered is a monumental understatement."

"What of our military force?" Aden asked, his voice rising as his hands moved. "Surely Varnen didn't convince them all to turn. Some of them must be loyal."

Aden's mother began signing again, and Magie spoke the words. "Varnen kept detailed records of who was loyal to the crown and who could be persuaded to his own ends. He sent the most loyal abroad. Any who remained were burned in their beds the night of the feast. We lost sixteen bunkers in a massive fire. If there were survivors, they fled."

A chill gripped my spine. That explained the smoke earlier.

Aden gritted his teeth. "Mother, do you know what happened to Mael? Could he possibly be alive?"

There was pity in her eyes. "I wish for that as well, my boy. But we mustn't cling to false hope. If he were alive, Rasmus would have used him against me too. We need to accept that he's dead and move on."

"I fear Her Majesty is correct," Magie said, looking pained as she continued her signing. "There is nothing to be done. The wedding is in just a few hours, and then the union of our two nations will be announced. Hughen will soon become a province of Messau once again."

Aden's jaw clenched. "Not as long as I draw breath."

The room fell silent.

I stepped in. "Your Majesty, how long does Rasmus intend to keep your daughters in the dungeons?"

Aden frowned and signed my question. The queen's hands moved vigorously.

"The girls will be released after the wedding." He paused as her hands grew still. "But if I free them, Rasmus won't have any leverage over you. You won't have to marry him."

The queen stared at him, her expression dark. Then she began to motion again.

"You'll never get to the dungeons unseen tonight, let alone free them," Magie interpreted. "But the ceremony could serve as a distraction. With so many important guests coming, Rasmus will wish to put on a show of power. He'll draw guards from below."

"Leaving the girls under minimal security," Aden mused. "But that wouldn't save you from marrying that monster, so it isn't an option."

They fell silent. The open wardrobe caught my eye. In the center was an ornate red dress. A heavy white veil hung beside it.

"Is that the wedding gown?" I asked, walking over to it.

Aden signed my question, and the queen nodded.

"Red," Aden muttered. "Seems fitting."

I fingered the cloth. It was fine, far nicer than any I'd seen. This dress had to cost more than a ship. I wondered what it would be like, wearing soft material like this all the time.

I picked up the veil and held it toward the light. The folds were too thick to see through very well, although it made sense now that I'd seen the queen. Rasmus wouldn't want his distinguished guests to be shocked by his bride's beaten face.

"Who will be attending the ceremony?" I asked.

"I don't rightly know," Magie said, speaking for herself now. "At least one foreign vessel arrived yesterday, and I saw two others the day before."

That didn't make sense. It would have taken the invitations weeks to travel to their respective targets, then several weeks more for the guests to arrive. Had Rasmus planned this takeover so far in advance? What if something had gone wrong?

Then it hit me. Aden had raced across the ocean to deliver his message to LeZar in Ellegran, but the man had been traveling to Hughen. Were there other important guests standing by as well, waiting for the grand scheme to take its course?

Had the entire world known about this plot except for the Hughen royal family?

"I want the girls released as much as you do, my Aden," Magie interpreted, watching the queen's hands, "but it's too dangerous for you to stay. If they capture you, the kingdom is truly lost. Gather troops to help free your sisters, then we'll worry about taking back the crown."

"Rasmus is too incompetent to rule his own country," Aden said. "He won't get his filthy hands on ours, not even for a day. And I'll die before I let that man touch you again." His voice softened. "Father sent me away to survive so I could make things right. I'm not leaving until the kingdom is ours."

The queen frowned, her expression pleading. Her hands moved more gently this time.

"What your father wanted doesn't matter anymore," Magie interpreted. "Oh, dear."

I touched the dress fabric again, deep in thought. There had to be a way to defeat a man like Rasmus. The Elena way required an army we didn't have, and defensible as the palace was, we'd likely fail even then. Was there a smarter strategy? Something that struck deeper than a weapon?

Rasmus had crafted this takeover down to the very last wedding guest. Once the world's highest rulers acknowledged him as Hughen's leader, the conquered people would be forced to fall into line. Rather than defeating the nation city by city as his father had done, Rasmus had simply slaughtered its king and invited his friends to a fancy celebration party—with bodies on the gate as badges of honor.

Appearances were very important to Rasmus. *A show of power*, the queen had called it.

"We don't have to kill Rasmus," I said. "We just have to humiliate him in front of the right people."

I lifted the veil to my face and turned toward the mirror. My features were completely indistinguishable through the fabric. Then I grabbed the dress from its perch and held it up, examining the image in the glass.

"Be careful with that gown," Magie said, frowning. "I've no time to scrub it."

Understanding dawned in Aden's expression, and his eyes went round in horror. "No. Absolutely not."

"What?" Magie's gaze was still fixed on the dress as if worried I would drop it.

Aden strode over and yanked the dress from my hands. "Laney, I know what you're thinking, but it's beyond dangerous. It's *insane*."

"He won't know it's me until the end," I said. "It'll give you and your family plenty of time to escape. I'll wait until the last minute to reveal myself, and when I do, his guests will see him for the fool he is."

Aden was shaking his head. "Laney, Rasmus wouldn't stand by and watch you tarnish his reputation. He'd run you through in a blink and execute every Hughen in the room out of anger."

"I won't give him the chance."

"You *won't have a choice!*"

The room went quiet as everyone stiffened at Aden's shout. Magie froze her hands in the act of interpreting our argument for the queen, looking panicked. Aden closed his eyes to gather his composure.

There was no sound from the sitting room door. Either the guards hadn't heard, or they weren't suspicious about a screaming servant.

"They will kill you," Aden finally said, his voice lower this time. He handed the dress to Magie, then grasped my shoulders, looking deep into my eyes. "Laney, you are the bravest, most incredible woman I've ever known. But I just got you back, and I'm not letting you go again. We'll find another way."

"Aden." I placed my palm on his cheek. "There is no other way. And you aren't *letting* me do anything. I'm a sailor. I come and go as I please, and I'm doing this because I want to. What choice do we have? Let your mother marry him and hand over your country?"

"Laney—"

I motioned toward his mother, who watched us from her chair, expressionless. "You see those bruises? Those are just the beginning, if he lets her live at all. She'll be a prisoner the rest of her life."

"And you'd be dead," Aden snapped. "We'll send a servant instead."

"Elyss is too thin, assuming we could even sneak her inside, and there isn't exactly an abundance of Hughen maids about tonight. Even if you found someone else who was willing, would you hinge your family's safety on her? You need a girl who isn't afraid to stand up to Rasmus."

He pulled away. "I refuse to discuss this."

"I have a plan. I'll need someone to give Elyss a message, and we'll have to smuggle in a knife, but I'm sure it will work."

"There's a knife hidden in the queen's chambers," Magie said, still signing for the queen's sake. She shrugged when Aden shot her a dark look.

"Rasmus's reputation is more important to him than you think," I told Aden. "You have to trust me."

"I can't," Aden said, running a hand angrily through his hair. "I won't subject either of you to this. There has to be a way to get everyone out before the ceremony."

Magie shook her head slowly. "There isn't. Not unless we jump out the window to our deaths. But even that wouldn't stop Rasmus from taking over."

The queen smacked her hand on the armrest, emitting a sharp crack. Aden jumped, then walked back to her with a frown. His mother signed faster than ever.

"She wants to speak with him alone," Magie said, pulling me toward the door. "Come. We'll wait in the sitting room."

As the minutes passed, my nerves were too ragged to let me sit long. I kept glancing at the closed door, wondering what Aden and his mother's conversation would decide. Finally, I made my way to the window, clasping my hands to keep them from shaking. Moonlight fell on the waves far below. I could see why Magie had joked about making the leap. A fall from this height would kill a person surely as tumbling down any cliff.

I frowned at my reflection in the glass. Just weeks ago, I'd been reluctant to help Aden at all. Now I was volunteering to face a mad dictator alone and unarmed. Was it my feelings for Aden, or did I have something to prove to myself?

Twenty minutes later, Aden emerged. His jaw was set in anger, yet his eyes looked haunted. His hands clasped into fists and then opened again. He paced back and forth for a few seconds before he stalked through a second door and closed it firmly behind him.

"He's retreated to Her Highness's bedchamber," Magie explained. "I think that means you've won." She rose and returned to the queen.

I hesitated at Aden's door, wishing I could comfort him. He'd already suffered so much. It hurt to think that a portion of the pain he suffered now was for me.

I felt as though a stone were lodged in my throat. I swallowed and entered the dressing room.

The queen stood now, holding the red gown, tall and regal, a commander more than a prisoner. This was a woman who had suffered much but refused defeat. Her eyes bored past my unkempt appearance and into my soul. Then her hands began to move.

"Aden sees the wisdom in your plan, though it hurts him to admit it," Magie interpreted. "Thank you for reuniting us and arranging our escape. We will not forget your sacrifice, regardless of the outcome."

The full meaning of her words wasn't lost on me. There were only two outcomes here, life and death. Neither meant I could have Aden. I'd come intending to help him save his family, and I would. But there were no promises for after that. If Aden uttered such a thing, it'd be a lie, as would my acceptance of it. We both knew I could never stay.

I glanced toward the door. Still closed.

"He has withdrawn to give us privacy," Magie said with a sad smile. "That gown will need a few alterations. Her Highness wishes to teach you protocol and a few basic signs, and you'll practice training your movements to match a queen's grace."

I remembered Magie's continual reminders about my stride and grimaced.

She wrinkled her nose. "But first, a long soak in the bath. With a *lot* of soap."

45

Several hours later, as the first rays of sunlight entered the room, I stood in front of the mirror once again. Only this time, the image in the glass was unrecognizable.

The red dress, hastily taken in to fit my smaller bust, accentuated all the parts I was used to hiding. The neckline was too low and the waist clung to my hips before flaring out and falling softly to the floor. The sleeves didn't have tassels, thankfully, but the cut was distinctly Messaun. I adjusted the neckline for a third time.

"I'll bet Khral Rasmus chose it himself," Magie muttered, frowning. "Must have thought displaying Eurion's widow as a half-naked trophy would reflect well on him."

"At least nobody will be looking too closely at the veil," I said, forcing a chuckle. Inside, my body had decided to rearrange itself. My stomach had crept to my feet and my heart pounded in my ears.

I'd had the brilliant idea to use makeup to imitate the queen's bruises. Now dark spots were barely evident through the thin cloth veil. Once removed, the differences would be obvious, but hopefully it would ensure Rasmus left it on until after the ceremony.

Then my plan would begin. Magie had agreed to fetch Elyss to help. She'd even retreated to the sitting room to explain it to Aden in her most reassuring manner. It was the only comfort I could give him. Aden's mother was asleep in her bedchamber now, gaining strength for her journey.

I gave my hair a pat. Magie had styled it in a pile of curls atop my head, fastened into place with the comb she'd found in my discarded clothes. Captain Dayorn's warning had made me hold my breath as Magie placed the comb, but thankfully, the woman didn't react to it at all. She likely assumed I'd stolen it. The veil covered how short my hair was, although I was pleased to see that it shone like the queen's now, a warm auburn color. I'd never given it a good look before. It was almost...pretty.

"Enough staring," Magie said, turning back to the dressing room. "Now, let's practice your walk again. Can't have you stumbling around and falling on your face while we're smuggling the royal family out."

Since my shoes wouldn't be seen, I'd chosen the most practical from the queen's collection, a sturdy pair of boots with a low heel. That hadn't stopped me from walking like a man, apparently.

"We've been at this for hours. I need a break." I'd absorbed as much of the woman's lessons as possible under the circumstances, but it all felt so unnatural and awkward. It was like teaching a rock to dance.

The maid clapped her hands. "One last turn about the room first."

I sighed and began to walk, focusing on setting my feet down softly.

"Hips," Magie instructed.

I blinked and started to sway with an exaggerated motion.

"You seem drunk," Aden said from the doorway. "A sailor girl told me that once."

Magie laughed, though there was a nervous tinge to it. It seemed I couldn't pass as the queen from sheer determination alone.

"I'll take it from here," he told Magie.

"You?" She looked skeptical before seeming to remember who she addressed. "Yes, Sire." Magie stepped out quickly and gave us one last worried look before closing the door.

Aden came over to me, examining the dress with little expression. My cheeks were ablaze now. I turned away, feeling humiliated and exposed.

Aden leaned forward. "There's never been a woman more beautiful than you, Laney." His voice was a whisper. He lifted his fingers and let them trace down my arm. It left a trail of heat behind.

A shiver shot through me. "It's a costume. A disguise." Different from the one I'd worn most of my life, but a disguise all the same. A lie.

"The dress itself is dreadful, I'll give you that. But you are radiant. I've never seen your eyes shine like they are now."

I looked up at him, startled. I'd expected him to object, to threaten, to stop this plan from going forward. But instead of seeing anger in his gaze, I saw admiration. Respect. And a tiny glint of that same determination I'd seen in his mother. Magie must have given him a remarkable talking-to.

"Magie's overwhelming you, isn't she?" Aden asked.

"Maybe a little," I admitted.

"You were my teacher once. Now it's my turn." He gave me a sideways look. "She means well, but that crowd gathering down there are mostly men. You don't want them watching your hips while you walk. You want them to see *you*. Your confidence, your regal bearing. Show them you deserve more than they're giving you." He swept a piece of my wayward hair aside and let his hand linger against my face.

"I thought I was supposed to look like your mother," I said with a weak smile.

"That's exactly what she would do—hold her head high and show Rasmus what he's dealing with. Now show me the signs you learned."

I reviewed them, stumbling over the motions. Aden positioned himself behind me, my back solidly against his chest, and took my hands in his. His breath against the back of my neck sent sparks jumping along my skin.

"When the officiator asks for your name," he said softly, "you'll do this. Sweep your heart with your left hand, then tap your three fingers together in a line across your body."

"What does it mean?" I asked, ignoring how my heart pounded through my back, as if trying to reach him.

"Marina. *Lover of the sea.*"

Another reason to like the woman. I nodded, grateful he couldn't see my cheeks flush at being in such an intimate position. And me in a *dress*. "What else?"

"He'll ask whether you agree to the terms of marriage. You'll make a fist and nudge it forward."

I smirked. "Maybe you should show me that too."

I felt his laugh more than heard it, a deep rumble in his chest near my ear. But instead of taking my hand again, he wrapped his arms around my waist and kissed my head.

I leaned into his touch, letting my head fall back against his chest. His kisses moved downward to my temple, then my cheek, then my jawline. He spent a long moment there, sending my heart fluttering until I was sure it would stop altogether.

"This wasn't how I saw our grand rescue going," Aden whispered. His voice was rough, almost shaky. "I knew I'd never deserve you, but I'd hoped for more time to try."

Him deserve *me*? I hadn't heard correctly. My head was too light to get a grasp on any of this.

"I said I'd never send you where I didn't dare go, yet here we are." A wry chuckle. "I know it makes you uncomfortable, but I can't let you enter that room without telling you how I feel. You've changed me, Laney Garrow. You opened my eyes long before those pirates came. And then they made me a prisoner, and I thought I was alone in the world, but you jumped through that window...well, it made me decide something. If we do survive this, my first act as king will be to rescind my father's Edict. I don't know much about ruling a country, but I do refuse to become a monster. Women like you deserve as much freedom in this world as any man. I won't be the one to take it away."

The thrill at his words ignited into something much warmer as he moved his hands on my stomach, turning me around to face him. Then he began again, leaving a trail of hot kisses down my neck. Just when I couldn't bear it any longer, he placed a gentle hand behind my neck and tilted my head upward.

His lips were a soft whisper against mine. His arms encircled my back, cradling me like I was some infinitely precious treasure. I sank into him, feeling my heart yield until I wondered if it had always been his. And then his hand tightened and his chin was rough against my face and he wanted more, demanded more. The very air was aflame, singeing through me with every desperate, shuddering breath I managed to steal.

This kiss contained the thousands of moments we should have had, if only the world would let us be. I clung to him, the only solid part of a wavering, uncertain reality. I'd been wrong about one very important thing.

Some kisses were worth risking your life for.

I barely heard the distant knock. It came once, then again. *The outside door.* I pulled away with a start.

Magie ran in, eyes round. "They're here! Quick, the veil."

Aden stepped back while I dashed over to the veil and slid it on. Magie secured it in place, giving it a few more pins than necessary. Then she peeked into the queen's bedchamber to ensure Aden's mother was hidden. The knocking gave way to pounding.

Aden took my hand as I headed for the door. "Show them," he whispered, his eyes so intense I nearly fell right into them. Then he disappeared into the bedchamber.

I felt as if he'd taken a part of me with him. I followed Magie to the door as she brushed invisible dirt off the dress and checked my hair one last time.

Show them. Rasmus wanted a beaten, defeated bride. Well, he was in for a surprise. I had everything in the world to fight for.

The door opened before Magie turned the handle, and she had to leap backward against the wall to avoid the man striding inside. His hair was patched with gray and he had the squarest jaw I'd ever seen. His vulgar gaze fell on me. I had an overwhelming urge to cover myself.

I straightened. Aden was right. Yesterday I had been a sailor girl, but today I had to be a queen.

"It's time." His words were clipped.

I dipped my head in acceptance, grateful I didn't have to speak today. I couldn't have done it convincingly, not after Aden's devastating kiss. I could still taste him on my lips.

I swept past the man and into the corridor, holding my head

high. An entire contingent of guards waited outside. Their gazes swept down my body as the door closed behind me. Someone cleared his throat. Many of them smirked.

I halted and leveled my gaze at them, almost daring them to speak. The guards' smiles faded and they looked away.

"Follow me," the gruff man said.

46

Paval once said my mother wore green to her wedding.

A small, intimate ceremony with a few family members and friends, he'd called it. My parents spent the next few days at an inn owned by a friend, less than a mile from the docks. Father bought her a home in the poorer section of town and furnished it with a few secondhand pieces before setting sail for the islands. He returned seven months later to find his wife ill and living at her parents' house, heavy with child.

The thought of Mum suffering alone all those months should have made me sad for her, but it didn't. At least she had her family. My father had no one. By law, he couldn't bring his wife onto his own ship. They both would have been executed, child or not.

Had any of that occurred to Mum as she walked down an aisle much like this one in her fancy green dress? Had she felt a little thrill at seeing him in his best suit? Had she known what would be required of her?

Why was it my mum who drew my thoughts now, while guards escorted me to a murderer's side? I didn't know where I'd be next year. *Lands*, I didn't know where I'd be tomorrow. But one thing was certain—I wouldn't be visiting that woman. She'd chosen to face her troubles alone.

Yet I couldn't help but wonder. Would Mum be disappointed to know her daughter sailed on ships she wasn't allowed to board, surviving battles she wasn't supposed to survive, and loving men she wasn't allowed to marry? And now that girl would stand in the place of a queen.

The throne room I'd admired earlier was no longer empty. Chairs extended all the way back despite the fact that only half were full, and a wide aisle had been created in the center. Guards lined every wall, standing at attention with dull eyes. I recognized the man nearest the door. He'd been the one to make that disgusting proposition last night.

The front was even more heavily guarded. Two entire rows stood behind the figures at the front. The officiator was easy to identify. He wore only black and looked nervous. That meant the other man was Rasmus. His white-blond hair was braided back, and he wore a sickly red suit with an elaborate golden cape. He watched with a practiced smile as I walked. It looked more like a smirk.

It swept the nervousness from me in an instant. He was just a man, and I could fool men. I'd been doing it my entire life.

I slowed my steps, pretending to be overwhelmed by the intensity of the moment. I was a proud, mourning widow. A queen who wouldn't hurry to take another husband. The seconds passed slowly. Aden would be on his way to the dungeon by now. He needed every moment I could give him.

The officiator stood directly in front of the throne. A crown rested on the throne's cushion. This was more than a wedding, then. It was also a coronation.

"Move faster, woman," the escort growled behind me.

"She can't hear you," the other guard said.

The audience lowered their heads as I passed each row. There were a few Hughen traitors in the crowd, but they kept their eyes trained on the ground. I recognized King LeZar near the front. High Advisor Varnen stared at the wall, looking bored. I fought back the urge to strangle both men.

Perhaps it would be best if I didn't look too closely at the audience.

I kept my pace slow and careful but reached the front too soon. The officiator nodded to the audience, who sat. Rustling and whispers filled the giant room like a long sigh. Then the man dressed in black began to speak, slowly and deliberately, as his hands signed the words. At least *he* was respectful.

I settled in to listen, keeping my posture straight. The eyes of hundreds bore down upon my back. My part was simple now. *Watch me carefully, guests. Don't think about the dungeon. Don't—*

My gaze fell upon a guest in the front row beside me, and my heart leaped into a furious rhythm. A man with long white-blond hair pulled into one long braid. He wore an intense expression as he watched the officiator, hands resting in his lap. He wore a deep gray gentleman's suit that barely fit.

Captain Belza.

Familiar faces dotted the row around him. Their clothing was more ragged and obviously thrown together at the last moment, but they'd all made an attempt at smoothing their appearances. They looked as bored as Varnen. I took a deep breath to slow my pounding heart and tried to calm the panic gripping my mind.

Of course they would be here. Belza had likely been ordered to attend by Khral Rasmus himself, and Aden's rescue obviously hadn't deterred them. The pirate captain's eyes flicked to me. I pulled my gaze away, breathing hard, feeling more exposed than ever before. My knees actually shook. Why hadn't I prepared for this possibility?

"Please state your name, Your Highness," the officiator said to Rasmus.

"Khral Jerald Rasmus the Third, monarch of the powerful brother nation of Messau."

"And you, my lady?" the man asked, his fingers moving quickly.

Whispers peppered the crowd. They hadn't missed the lack of title in my address. Aden's mother had been demoted to lady. It wasn't the queen bestowing power upon a foreign king—it was Rasmus giving her a title. What a revolting man.

I signed the name as Aden had taught me, remembering how it had felt with his hands guiding mine. It calmed my shaking fingers.

"Thank you. Now will the groom please take the bride's hands?"

My hands.

Shock raced through my system. Even if my signing had fooled Rasmus, my hands never would. They were rough, dry, and calloused. Far from the queen's dainty, tailored fingers.

Rasmus held out his hand. I pulled away and took a step back, shaking my head. Rasmus's smile froze.

The room erupted in laughter. It seemed to remind Rasmus who was watching, because he let his shoulders fall and pasted on a fake smile. "I always did like the coy ones."

The audience laughed again. The guards behind the khral grinned, their eyes fixed on the neckline of my dress.

"She will submit to my touch soon enough," he told the officiator. "Continue."

My cheeks warmed behind the veil as I flexed my fingers, wishing I had my axes. I would carve that smug smile right out of Rasmus's face.

I kept my hands clasped behind me as the officiator continued, which seemed to amuse Rasmus and his guests. It was a simple ceremony, probably shortened, and I had to force myself not to stare at the pirates. If they were armed, their weapons were well hidden.

I forced my attention back to the officiator's droning. He was saying something about tradition, honor, and love. His voice faltered at the word *love*, and his eyes fixed on me. Could he see through the veil over my face? Too many questions, too many unknowns.

When the time came for me to agree to the terms, I waited four heartbeats before unlocking my hands to sign *Yes*.

"The couple may now seal their matrimony with a kiss, upon which time they will be legally wed." The officiator paused, looking pained. "Then we will proceed with the crowning ceremony for His Honorable Khral and King Jerald Rasmus the Third."

The moment had arrived.

I sank to the floor as if overcome and felt around at my ankle. The queen's knife was concealed in my boot, and I closed my fingers around the handle. It wasn't the long, familiar handle of my axe, but it would do until Elyss brought my weapons from the servants' quarters.

"May we have a long and happy life together, my sweet," Rasmus called out, his fingers closing around my arm. He yanked me back onto my feet and pulled me close. There was brandy and rosewood on his breath. He obviously preferred strong liquor to light Hughen wine.

As he reached for my veil, I thrust the knife toward his throat.

He caught my arm just in time. The blade hovered there, an inch from his skin, and I grunted with the strain. His hand closed around my wrist. With a deep growl, he threw me backward. There was a collective gasp from the audience.

I stumbled on the gown and landed on the floor. Blasted skirts.

The khral looked down on me with his mouth twisted in disgust. "I intended to let you live, but if you refuse to cooperate..." Then he looked over his shoulder. "McCullough! Bring me my sword."

The steward with graying hair who had escorted me here approached the khral with a sword resting on his palms.

If I had my axes, I wouldn't have missed. I rose to my feet and faced the audience. Aden and his family needed more time. If I meant to humiliate the Messaun khral, it would have to be now.

I yanked off my veil.

The crowd went absolutely still. Then the whispers began again. Advisor Varnen leaned forward in his chair, squinting at me. Rasmus stood rooted at my side, his mouth agape in horror.

"I'm sorry for the disappointment," I called out, "but this man is not king of Hughen. He just married a common sailor. We thank you for attending our wedding anyway." I gave a low bow.

The audience responded slowly. A few hid smiles behind their hands, and a young woman finally giggled. The sound yanked the crowd from their stupor. The laughter began in earnest.

Rasmus went purple. He wrenched his sword from the guard and lifted it to strike.

I was ready. I dodged a guard's hands and hiked the dress above my ankles before turning to run. Soldiers had begun to fill the aisle, cutting off my exit, but the main doors weren't my goal. I sprinted toward a side door. Elyss waited there, a nervous stiffness in her stance. My axes were barely visible behind her back. With axes in hand, I would publicly challenge Rasmus and cover her escape.

I stumbled on my skirts once again. Just a few more feet.

Captain Belza stepped in front of me, forcing me to pull to an abrupt halt or barrel right into him. His blond braid trailed down one shoulder. He studied me with a frown, massive cutlass in hand.

How he'd managed to smuggle that past the guards was a mystery. Or perhaps the guards hadn't dared stop him. His men hurried to his side, blocking my path completely.

"Pirates!" someone shouted.

The entire room erupted in commotion. Men and women stood and drew shield wards across their chests, stumbling over one another in their haste to reach the door. A few Hughens took up a shout and pulled out knives they'd hidden from the guards. Someone screamed.

Belza simply looked at me with a dark expression. "The sailor from the *Majesty*, with the axes."

"She's the one who freed the prince, Captain," one of the pirates said. It was the man we'd knocked unconscious during Aden's rescue. A sleeve covered his ruined hand.

I muttered a curse, reaching for my knife before remembering Rasmus had knocked it away. I couldn't get to my axes surrounded like this. A dozen swords slid from their hidden scabbards and lowered toward me. If I so much as breathed too deeply, I'd feel the tip of a blade.

Rasmus pulled up beside me. He eyed Belza's cutlass with a dark look. Had he truly thought he could ban the pirates from their weapons? "Secure the girl if you've got any use at all. Pirate fools."

The men stood in silence, obviously waiting for Belza to confirm the order. They wore various expressions of disgust and loathing as they watched the khral. The pirate captain just stared Rasmus down. *Lands.* His eyes were so clear that I could almost see through them. He looked ready to strike the ruler, crown or not. Whatever agreement they had was a tentative one.

Rasmus didn't cringe under the pirate's vicious gaze. "Admiral Belza, have your men secure the girl or step aside so my men can."

"I will question her first," Belza said, then nodded to his men. They lowered their blades and wrenched my arms behind my back. I heard a rip from the fabric at my shoulder. This dress was the least practical form of clothing ever.

Rasmus's mouth snapped shut, his face reddening. "To what purpose? She's obviously a maid. I've already sent men to find the real queen."

"I'm a sailor," I snapped. "I told you that already. You wouldn't have these issues with women if you'd just listen."

Rasmus growled again and whipped out his sword, but Belza blocked it with his own. The clang of metal was a strange one—a long, thick cutlass against a thin dueling blade. Several guards trotted up behind Rasmus, their weapons half-raised at the sight of their surrounded khral. It seemed nobody knew whose side the pirates were on.

I knew. I'd heard it from the pirate's own mouth. Rasmus ruled a nation, maybe two. But Belza wanted to rule the sea. If he succeeded, he'd hold more power than all the countries put together. We relied too heavily on trade. No country had an economy strong enough to produce what they needed alone. Belza would isolate us all before uniting us under his own rule.

He wouldn't serve Rasmus. He intended for the man to kneel at his own feet.

The pirate captain glowered at the khral until he withdrew his weapon and took a step backward. I could feel a tenseness in the air, their stances, their words. Elyss's frightened eyes locked on me from the door. She hadn't run at the pirates' approach. *So close.*

Finally, Belza turned back to me and narrowed his eyes. "Tell me how you came to be here."

I had no axes, but sometimes words made the strongest weapons, and I had plenty of those. "You've failed, Captain Belza. You failed to sell Prince Cedrick to King LeZar. You failed to deliver him to Rasmus because he escaped. You even failed in your oath to extinguish Captain Garrow's crew, because *I* survived. Now you want to steal Elena's legacy and rule land and sea." I smiled. "I'm here to make sure you fail there too."

The pirate captain stiffened. For the first time, his eyes wore a glint of uncertainty. Whatever he'd expected me to say, it wasn't that. He looked past me at Rasmus's guards, who stood with weapons raised.

Khral Rasmus stared at me, then at Captain Belza and back again. "You told me Prince Cedrick was *dead*."

"The girl lies. She'll say anything to save her miserable life." Belza glared at his men. "Bring her to me."

They shoved me forward, their hold on my arms threatening to separate my shoulders from their sockets. I gritted my teeth against the pain and scrambled for my next accusation. "He even promised King LeZar power over you if he joined him."

Rasmus stalked over to us, pushing pirates aside to reach me. To my surprise, he shoved me aside as well, forcing my captors to loosen their holds. Then he was face-to-face with the pirate captain. "You lying piece of horseflesh. I will not be betrayed, and certainly not by bloody filth such as you."

My right arm was loose. I took a tiny step backward to put distance between me and Rasmus, who seemed to have forgotten me entirely. I glanced toward the doorway. Elyss was nowhere to be seen.

Rasmus's voice rose higher in pitch. "I freed you from prison. These men who serve you—I chose them myself. It's my signature on that commission writ. I made you what you are!"

"And I handed you a kingdom. Look how you've fouled it up. I should have taken it myself."

The khral sank backward into dueling stance. "Try it, and I'll take your head like my father should have done. Guards!"

His men came running. The pirates straightened, raising their weapons again to meet them. The two sides were equal in number and skill, but the pirates were considerably nastier looking. They smiled while examining their opponents, their yellow teeth bared. Rasmus's guards looked unsettled as they gripped their weapons.

That had gone even more perfectly than planned. Now I just had to keep them focused on one another instead of Aden's family. I had just opened my mouth to make another accusation when a guard ran in.

"Your Majesty!" he shrieked. "The queen is gone. We've searched everywhere."

A thrill shot through me. They'd made it.

Rasmus shook with anger now. "Men, watch this filthy pirate. Make sure he doesn't leave." Then he turned to me. "The boy and his mother must be together. Tell me where they are."

I lifted my chin. "I wouldn't know."

The blow came, snapping my head sideways. Lights danced in front of my eyes as he got right in my face. "Tell me *now*."

"I will not."

"Tell me now and I'll spare your life."

"Liar."

He growled. The strike was harder this time, nearly throwing me off my feet. Hands clasped my shoulders from behind. They smelled of tar and mint. Belza just stood by, thick fingers drumming on his weapon. Waiting.

Rasmus plunged into the crowd of pirates behind me. He

emerged a moment later, yanking a girl by the hair. He threw her to the floor at my feet. My insides lurched. *Elyss.*

"A new deal, then," he spat. He placed his sword to Elyss's throat. "Tell me where the boy is, and I'll spare *her* life."

I hesitated. Her eyes were wide in terror, and her shoulders shook as her body was racked with silent tears. There was pleading in her gaze.

She wasn't holding my axes. She'd left them by the doors. I couldn't even break free to help her escape.

It was a monumental effort to swallow. "I—"

His blade swept across her neck in one swift movement.

Elyss dropped to the floor, convulsing, blood pooling beneath her throat. It filled the dress's ornate bust with sickly red. I shoved forward, but the guards yanked me backward and held my head in place, forcing me to watch.

One last shudder. Then she sank into the floor and went still.

It took all my strength to hold back the sob that followed. *Elyss, I'm so sorry.*

"There are plenty of Hughens," Rasmus said, bursting through the haze of my thoughts. "I'll kill them one by one, each more brutally than the last. And when they're dead, I'll start on the children. Now, we'll try this again." He backhanded me across the face once more, snapping my head to the side. "Where." *Slap.* "Is." *Slap.* "The boy?" He lifted his hand.

"Right here," a voice rang out from the main doors.

Rasmus's head snapped to the side. His guards turned to look. Belza went rigid, and those in the audience who'd stayed to watch began their whispering all over again.

The true king had returned.

Aden stood in the doorway, sword raised to the sky. The hallway behind him was filled with townspeople clutching shovels and makeshift weapons, even a Gallen whip. Several were women.

I stared at Aden. He had gotten his mother to safety. Then he had *come back*.

"There's only one person standing between you and that crown, Rasmus," Aden shouted. "Me, the rightful king of Hughen."

My emotions ranged from delight and relief to anger. I'd made this sacrifice so he could escape. This was the absolute worst place for him to be right now. My mind cried out at the absurdity of it. But I couldn't hold back the stupid grin crossing my face. Aden had come back. He'd probably planned to all along.

The wedding guests pressed themselves against the wall as Aden and the group strode in. He scanned the crowd and spotted me. The relief on his face was unmistakable.

Rasmus pursed his lips. "Dispose of the commoners and bring me the boy."

With a yell, the guards rushed at the townspeople, who met their attackers with a swell of sound. It was too familiar—shouting, metal on metal, shots being fired. The guests screamed and sprinted for the side door where Elyss had stood. *Elyss.* Her body still lay where it had fallen.

Aden strode past all of it to the enraged khral. "Jerald Rasmus, I challenge you."

The khral snorted. "I've already taken your kingdom, boy. The wedding was a formality."

"You've yet to secure the palace, let alone the kingdom. But kill me in front of these witnesses, and it's yours. You'll rule both nations."

Rasmus looked around. Nearly all his guards were engaged in the battle. Aden's small army fought bravely, though there were already several commoner bodies on the ground. They had answered Aden's call, feeling the same pull to him that I had. They also sensed that aura of royalty. Except *royalty* wasn't the right word. *Majesty.*

"Do you accept my challenge, sir?" Aden pointed his blade to the ground. Duel protocol. Aden was royal to the last. It was adorable and frustrating at the same time.

Rasmus glowered at him. "I'll just order my guards to run you through."

"Your reputation demands a greater show than that, does it not? Messaun monarchs don't defeat their enemies by proxy. Free the girl and face me like a king."

Rasmus's expression closed, but I detected a hint of a smile. "Belza, you may do with the girl as you wish." Then he lowered his sword and assumed dueling stance.

Aden's eyes flicked to me. I just nodded. *Win this. I can handle myself.*

"Hold the girl," Belza said, watching the two with a dark expression. That glint in his eyes was too familiar. Both Aden and Rasmus had underestimated the pirate. He would kill whoever won that duel and take the crown for himself. That meant I had to kill Captain Belza before Aden's duel ended. I eased my shoulder away from the pirate on my right, but he held even tighter. His breath smelled of rotting meat.

Aden and Rasmus stood still for a moment, swords pointed downward, sizing each other up. The Messaun was a good six inches taller and far more muscular than Aden. He also moved with a grace that said he'd spent a lifetime practicing swordplay. But I'd seen Aden beat a larger man with the wrong hand on a bucking merchant ship. The match wasn't as uneven as the khral assumed.

Rasmus was the first to strike. Aden knocked it away easily. Rasmus redirected for a quick side blow, which Aden blocked. Then the fight truly began.

The swords clashed, again and again, so quickly I could barely see the blades. Aden was light on his feet. He seemed to anticipate each strike before the blade reached him, his brows lowered in concentration. It was a dance of royals, a performance of perfect skill. Awe surged through me. Aden was incredible. The Right of Steel duel had truly been nothing to him.

Rasmus's mouth twisted into a crooked smile as he parried, thrust, and thrust again. The whipping blades were a blur of motion. Rasmus's face grew more intense, his smile tighter, and Aden's face broke out in a sheen of sweat. Rasmus had a slight edge now. Aden reacted somewhat slower than he had before, and the khral was pushing him backward toward the windows and their impossibly long curtains.

The hand on my right shoulder had gone slack again. I slipped my foot slowly behind the pirate's. The man felt my shift and gripped more tightly, but I was positioned now. I threw my elbow backward as my foot swept forward, sending him stumbling to keep his footing. A quick kick to the other pirate in his manly parts and my shoulders were free. I bolted for the side door.

"Bring her back alive, you idiots," Belza snapped at his men.

I swallowed at the memory of Elyss waiting in the doorway just a few minutes before, then skimmed the ground for any sign of my weapons. The axes were tucked in a pile behind the open door, hidden from sight. Blessed girl. I grabbed them just as four pirates barreled down on me.

I slid behind the door and yanked it partially closed. The heavily gilded wooden door cracked and flung toward me with the force of the strikes, but I held the handle firm. Then I shoved it *hard*. It caught two pirates in the face. They threw their hands around now-bleeding noses and stumbled backward as I whirled to face the other two. I had to adjust my stance, but thankfully my sleeves had both torn, allowing for the movement I needed.

"Watch those axes, Carn," a pirate called out from across the room, one of Aden's former guards. The man in front of me stepped back, placing distance between us with sword raised.

Shouts sounded from where Aden and Rasmus fought, pulling my attention away. Rasmus wore a fresh cut on his cheek. The khral's guards stood by, waiting for orders to engage, not caring that interference would invalidate the duel's results. There were no townspeople waiting around to help Aden.

The battle still raged near the doors, but there were far more bodies than before. Many children would be orphaned today.

Then the pirates were upon me. I managed to block one set of hands but missed the second. The closest curved his fingers around my throat and slammed my head against the heavy door. Pain exploded in my skull.

I was being lifted off my feet. Something tugged at the axe in my right hand. I tightened my grip.

A cry from Aden sent a surge of alertness through me. The second pirate ripped the axe from my left hand. I swung the weapon in my right, throwing my entire body into it.

The pirate's eyes widened as the blade made contact with his head.

I hit the floor, scooped up my other weapon, and sprinted past the collapsing man as his partner stared in horror. Belza was where we'd left him, still watching the fight. His shoulders were even more square from behind, bulky and thick from every angle. This man had torn nearly everything I loved from me. Now he threatened what remained.

I swung my axe.

Clang. Something hard met my strike, sending a jolt of pain up to my elbows. One of the guards I'd left at the doors had caught up just in time and thrown his sword up in defense of the captain. Another pirate wrapped his arms around me, holding my own arms in place as my axes were ripped away. This time, I felt something cold against my temple. A pistol.

Belza turned around at the commotion. He wore no surprise at the sight of his men wrestling me into submission. He stalked toward us like a giant cat, still gripping his long cutlass. Then he stopped to look down upon me. So tall.

"Intriguing, this one," he said. "My men say you're also the lass who stole the young prince."

"I'm Captain Garrow's daughter," I hissed. "I survived your attack, and I'm going to avenge his death."

"His daughter?" He outright laughed now. The crew joined in, then cut off abruptly when he stopped. "Ah. That's why you look familiar. Interesting that the man who claimed honesty and morals turned out to be the biggest liar of us all."

I'd once thought the same thing, but hearing it from this man's filthy lips made me wish I'd swung my axe a little faster. "He left piracy to protect the woman he loved. I'd say that's a moral thing to do."

He laughed again, louder this time. "Who, his wife? She's more pirate than he ever was."

My breath hitched. *What?* He was wrong. He had to be. "My mum is a lady."

"Nara is pirate and lady both. Served me for years before leaving with that fool Garrow. She soon learned what a coward he was and came running back. I took her in out of kindness."

I gaped at him. The man was bloody mad. "You lie."

"Do I? Saw yer mum last a few months back, just before she returned to that dull house of hers in Ellegran."

He knew where she lived. Could it be true? Had Mum left my father and me for... Captain Belza?

I wasn't meant for this life, she'd said. *My dreams lie elsewhere.*

I'd assumed she'd run off to marry some rich lord worthy of her station. It had never, ever occurred to me that the life she resented was the safe, quiet one my father offered. He *had* said Belza fancied her once, hadn't he?

Nay. I refused to believe such a thing of her, no matter how I despised the woman. "Surely you think of someone else. My mum wouldn't be foolish enough to join a crew full of impostors."

The crew chuckled again. Another cry came from across the room. Aden had been injured. The fighting resumed immediately, but it couldn't last long. I *had* to kill Belza before that duel ended.

"Impostor? I'm as real as they come." The captain's grin widened.

"I was there for all of it—Elena's victories, losses, her doubts. I was the son who stayed, the one who refused to abandon her. When she died, I was the one who carried her legend. My brother deserved the coward's death he received. You were there for that part, as I recall."

My lungs strained for air, but there was none to be had.

The room spun about me, and a distant nausea swelled inside. I'd heard wrong. My father and Belza were old friends, not brothers. Absolute madness. Because if that were true, it meant...

Captain Garrow of the *Majesty* was *Elena's son*.

Belza hadn't simply taken Elena's cause as his own. He'd inherited it from his mother. My father and Belza's quarrel had never been about the *Majesty*. Father's fate was sealed the moment he rejected his brother's plan of revenge.

I was Elena the Conqueror's granddaughter.

I had her legacy, her very blood running through my veins. The revelation should have excited me. All I felt was a numb deadness inside.

"But...but Father is Hughen, and you're from Messau."

"A simple stretch of the truth, girl. Naamon was born in Hughen waters and I off the coast of Messau. It wasn't the first lie our mother concocted to protect us, nor the last." Belza chuckled, running his hand across my half-styled hair. Then I realized he was pulling out the comb. Trusses of unbound hair fell into my eyes, and I blinked them free.

"Only three of these exist," he continued. "All gifts from Elena to her children. I demanded that Naamon return his, but he said it was lost."

I didn't have time to ask who had the third. Belza only examined the comb for a moment, then dropped it to the ground and crushed it under his massive boot.

My breath stilled. I couldn't tear my eyes away from the twisted metal and its shattered jewels. *The comb.* Of course. It had never been a gift for Mum. He'd kept it for *me*.

Now it, along with everything else, was gone.

"Garrow wasn't always a coward," Belza continued. "He fought in a few battles before Nara muddled his head and he stole my ship. He always knew he'd pay for that someday. Don't tell me he didn't."

You hide our daughter away, but I would present her to the world, Mum's missive had read. *She deserves to walk with her head high, to take pride in who she is.*

"But enough of the past," Belza declared. "Our victory is nearly here. My men say you've a hand for combat, girl. This—fighting for kingdoms and thrones—is below someone of your bloodline. Serve me and take your father's place. This is the life you were meant to live." He looked past me to the duel. "Or I suppose you can join the boy in death."

I glanced at Aden. He was tiring, his movements growing slower. He held his own, but he'd switched to the defensive. Rasmus, however, looked exhilarated. He was within moments of his goal.

Captain Belza wanted me to be a pirate. He had *offered me a place on his crew.* I was too stunned to laugh.

"Royals are all the same," Belza said, gesturing to the dueling men. "Children. Even your precious little prince, fighting over land and resources and who gets what. One moment he's begging for your protection, the next he's ordering your execution."

I bared my teeth, fighting against the arms that held me. "You dare talk to me about executions? You *murdered* my father."

"An end he chose for himself, not the one I wanted for him. You, though—you have potential. We will conquer those who hate you. Your name will be feared across the Four Lands. Join us and take up your grandmother's cause or die with a weak king who never intended to keep you anyway."

I refused to accept his words, however true they felt. Captain Belza was pure evil, the cause of so much terror and pain. He would have slaughtered me by now were it not for my bloodline. I was an opportunity and little more.

What are you to Aden? a tiny voice whispered. It awakened my earlier doubts all over again.

Movement behind the captain caught my eye. Magie? She breathed hard as if she'd been running. Or fighting, by the blood on her blouse. She extended her hands, making the motion of something tall and narrow. An axe? Then she raised a finger and crept away.

"The oath," Belza snapped. "Or death. I'll have your choice now."

The pistol at my head tightened. I detected the faint smell of gunpowder. My mind raced, scrambling for more time. "You're wrong if you think employing me would give your cause credibility. Elena wanted to save the world, not defeat it."

"She knew precisely what her goal would cost. Your grandmother was the most brutal woman who ever lived, girl. *That's* the blood in your veins. That's your legacy. Now speak the oath or feel my blade as your father did." He raised his sword and placed the tip to the skin of my chest. It was cold.

"Laney!" Aden cried out.

My body felt suspended in midair. Fighting blurs moved around me, screams of pain slicing the air and bodies slamming to the floor. Was this how my father had felt, moments before his death? Had he also been torn between the many pieces of himself?

Nay. He'd been at peace, his decision made long ago. He'd chosen me. My own choice was made as well, though I hadn't realized it until now.

I chose Aden. No matter the cost.

"I do carry the blood of a pirate," I finally said. "But I'll never join you. Laney Garrow serves under no one. If the Four Lands speak my name, it will be to praise how I defeated you—and every other man who threatens those I care about."

Belza growled. He didn't notice the axe handle sliding between his companion's legs.

It wrenched upward, surprising the poor soul above it. He sank to the ground in pain and shock as Magie shoved the axes, sending them sliding along the intricate floor toward me. She scrambled away.

I was already moving. The man's cry had surprised the one holding the pistol to my head, and I yanked an arm free to elbow him in the face. Before the pirates realized what had happened, I stood glaring at them in my torn and bloody dress, an axe gripped tightly in each hand, the windows overlooking the ocean at my back.

For the first time, Belza looked taken aback. He let his blade drop a few inches as he stared at me.

"She looks just like Elena," a watching pirate muttered.

A yell turned me back to Aden. He grasped his arm, red blossoming and staining his shirt. It wasn't a mortal wound, but it would cost him strength. Rasmus didn't give him time to recover. He swung his blade down in a very Kempton-like maneuver, which Aden blocked with his sword just in time. Then another round of strikes began. It was all Aden could do to stop them. We were out of time.

Belza pushed through his men and halted a few feet away, his cutlass—the one he'd used to murder my father—held loosely in one hand. "If the girl wants a duel of her own, she'll have it." His men shuffled backward to give us space.

I set my feet in spear stance, both axes at the ready. Anger pulsed through my limbs. My father had defeated this man once. I had to find a way to do the same.

We struck simultaneously.

His blade hit my axe as we aimed for each other's throats. He shoved my other blade aside with the hilt, cracking the handle and sending my left axe across the room. It crashed to the ground in two pieces. Then he threw another blow at my head.

Stunned to be left with a single axe so quickly, I blocked and redirected my axe toward his chest. He swept the handle aside with one massive arm and lifted the cutlass over his head, intending to slice me in half.

It was a pirate move, dramatic and definitive. I only had one axe and a small one at that. If we continued fighting like men, he would defeat me without question. I had to fight like a woman.

I spun just in time, feeling a burst of air from the blade as it swept past. Knowing he expected me to arc my axe downward in response, I lifted it over his head as I completed my spin, positioning myself behind him. A second later, my axe handle sat tight against his throat.

He coughed in surprise, letting his blade drop. Then he reached around to tear me off his back. I gripped the handle for my life, digging my elbows into his thick shoulders.

He stumbled toward the wall between the huge windows. Then he turned and smacked me against the wall. This loosened my grip, and I scrambled to regain my hold. Too late. He'd shaken me free, and a pirate had just tossed him his cutlass.

Something soft brushed my hand. Drapery?

I gave it a soft tug. The fabric was linen, not the canvas I was accustomed to, but it seemed sturdy enough. I wrapped it around my axe handle and waited for the strike.

The cutlass swung through the air sideways, straight for my throat. He intended to take my head.

Now.

I spun the opposite direction, barely dodging his strike, and circled around him again. This time it was the curtain I swept around his neck. I gave my wrapped axe a twist, tightening the fabric around his throat like a fancy blue scarf. A startled grunt escaped his mouth, but it was too late. I twisted my body toward the windows, pulling the pirate off balance.

"Captain, look out!" a voice shouted.

I hit the wall hard, but my aim was true. The captain's momentum followed mine, sending him stumbling into the window.

It shattered.

Glass flew in slow motion as the captain hovered in midair, his eyes bulging in shock. His boots struck the bottom of the window as he grabbed at the fabric around his neck. His braid followed him out the window like a leash. There was a snap as the curtain ended and broke free, sending both axe and pirate plunging toward the ocean.

Then the scream came.

It sounded as inhuman as its master, a deep, wrenching cry. It faded into a distant sound. Then there was nothing except familiar waves far below.

The crew stood there, bewildered and stunned.

"Captain," one man whispered. He reached the window and peered down the cliff toward the water. His companions followed him, staring downward in horror.

My feet were tarred to the floor. My body wasn't my own, and it refused to respond to commands. All I could see were those shards of glass clinging to the windowpane where Belza had just stood. Small pieces littered the ground.

Shock held me captive, overwhelmed by sounds that shook my very soul. That inhuman scream, the pained cry of his men. Pistol blasts and metal against metal. It felt as if I lived two moments in one, two battles, two opposite endings. Both felt utterly unreal.

Captain Belza was dead. My father's murderer, my uncle. A man who had mercilessly slaughtered an entire crew of men. His blade had sent hundreds of corpses into the sea, and thousands had suffered and died at his order. Now they had finally found justice. I had brought it to them.

But no pride swelled in my chest. Only a dull ache that said nothing had changed, not really. Belza's death hadn't restored a thing.

Fighting yielded a victor and a loser. I would always be both.

A grunt from across the room brought me back to the moment. *Aden.*

Still breathing hard, I sprinted toward Aden, leaping over bodies and dodging the soldiers fighting off the townspeople. A horn sounded from somewhere outside, long and low.

"Laney," Aden breathed with relief as he blocked another strike. He managed to beat Rasmus back for a second of reprieve. He was soaked in sweat, and his upper sleeve was wet with blood. Then he turned to me. "Are you all—"

Rasmus ran him through.

48

Aden sucked in a gut-wrenching gasp and fell to his knees, eyes wide in horror. His face was ashen.

"Aden!" I shrieked.

Rasmus jerked at the sound of my voice, narrowing his eyes at me and gripping his bloody sword. Aden's blood. It looked just like my father's, dark and thick.

A body lying still on the deck.

Aden sucked in a painful breath as he struggled to remain upright on his knees. "I was distracted, Rasmus," he managed through gritted teeth. "You disregard the rules of combat."

"What rules?" Rasmus barked a laugh. "It's against international trade laws to tax sea routes, yet that did not stop your father. It's also illegal to mine ore in a neighboring country and smuggle it out, is it not? Or to send spies to my palace as your father did. He even sold me orphans stolen from your streets, defying his own slavery laws."

His terrible accusations barely registered. Aden was *down*.

There was only one living person my battered heart felt connected to. I was about to lose him as well.

"My father didn't deserve to die," Aden gasped. Blood seeped from the wound in his side. His face was growing paler by the second. He would collapse any moment.

Rasmus circled Aden, swinging his sword in the air playfully. "Your father made a terrible king. Hughen hasn't been a military power in decades. He only managed to win your freedom through trickery. Now that Hughen is back in Messaun hands, I'll return it to the glory it should have boasted all along."

Aden gritted his teeth. He swayed where he knelt, looking like he would pass out, but he drew in a long breath and raised his weapon with his good arm, clutching his wound with the other. "I'm not dead yet."

Rasmus smiled. Then he lifted his sword.

"You can't win, Rasmus," I said quickly. "Captain Belza is dead and your men defeated. The townspeople have been mobilized. They'll fight you, town by town, until you're driven out of their land."

The khral stared at me in confusion, then scanned the room. Only a few dozen guards and commoners remained, swinging their weapons and shouting. Most of the survivors had fled. The pirates had all gone, probably to search for their captain's body in the bay. That or scouring the palace for valuables.

That's right. Focus on me, the room, your men. Anyone but Aden.

"Your backup forces will arrive too late," I told him. "You planned this carefully, but you neglected the commoners. Some people have loyalties that can't be bought. We Hughens aren't perfect, but we are loyal to our king."

Rasmus's face turned scarlet. He moved so quickly, there was no time to react. He raised his sword and slashed me on the cheek.

I gasped, stumbling backward. My face burned like he'd taken a hot branding iron to it. I clasped my face in one hand, then pulled my palm away. It was bloody.

Rasmus smirked again. "Not such a pretty little thing anymore, are you?"

A blade burst through his chest.

Rasmus stiffened, his eyes round with shock. He looked down, staring at the blade in wonder, then slid to his knees. A second later, he toppled sideways to the floor.

Aden pulled the blade free as he stood above Rasmus's writhing body, sword aimed at the downed man's neck.

Rasmus struggled for breath. "Stabbed me...in the back...the rules."

Aden's jaw clenched. "What rules?"

The khral sucked in a breath, which rattled around for a moment, and then his lungs released the air one final time. He went still, his eyes staring sightlessly at the war-torn room before him.

A yell went up from one of the remaining townspeople. "King Cedrick has conquered!"

The room filled with cheers. The Messaun soldiers stared at their khral's body. A few approached cautiously, but at the sight of Aden standing above their liege with a bloody sword, they stumbled for the doors.

The townspeople, looking exhilarated at their victory, shouted at one another to follow. As a wave of men charged after the green uniforms fleeing the room, it went strangely quiet.

It was then that Aden collapsed.

49

I sat in a hard chair next to Aden's bedside, legs tucked beneath me. I wore a clean shirt and new trousers, though both felt odd without axes at my waist. My cheek still ached. The surgeon, or physician as they called him here, had stitched it together before placing a bandage on my cheek. It felt heavy and annoying. I couldn't wait to tear it off.

Aden wasn't as fortunate. He lay in his bed on a mountain of pillows, eyes closed. His chest moved slowly up and down under the sheet. I stared at him, memorizing the lines of his face.

He hadn't gained consciousness since the events of this morning. The physician insisted the blade had missed his lung, if barely. Movement would be painful for months, and his skill with the sword would never be the same. But he would live a normal life. If being the young king of a battered nation could mean normal.

Like the queen's chamber, Aden's rooms had a sitting area. Its colors were darker and more sophisticated, and it had only one window, but it felt exactly right. It even smelled like him. I imagined Aden playing in here as a boy, irritating his tutors with ill-timed jokes and constantly messing up his hair. It brought a smile to my face, pulling the bandage on my cheek tighter.

A rustling sound approached at the door. I looked up to find Aden's mother and Magie entering. As Magie stationed herself by the door, the queen came around the bed to stand beside me and pointed to Aden in a questioning manner.

I shrugged. "His color is better than before."

She nodded, seeming to understand. Magie had brought the queen and her daughters back from the watch house shortly after the battle's end. I couldn't imagine the regal woman hiding in such a dark, tattered place. She seemed like the type to be born in a lace-trimmed gown.

My smile faded at the thought of dresses. Elyss's body had been taken for burial in town with the others. I hadn't left Aden's side for the service, but Magie said it was an honorable one, well attended and respectful for those who had sacrificed all. Elyss had been laid to rest in the same blue gown she'd chosen for her escape.

At least the pirates were gone. They'd fled within the hour, taking their ships with them. A few of the foreign nobles still remained, though most had left nearly as fast as the pirates. Any Messauns who lingered had been arrested. The dungeon was overflowing.

Aden's mother caught sight of the broken comb in my hands and raised an eyebrow. I shoved the pieces into my pocket, feeling my cheeks warm.

"Her Majesty recognized the comb right away," Magie said, signing again. "Don't fret. She trusted you then and she trusts you now."

If I'd been blushing before, now my face burned. "I didn't know what it meant."

"And if you had?"

I wasn't sure whose question it was, but it gave me pause. Would knowing my family's legacy have changed my path? Father hadn't trusted me to know, though I suspected it was the last secret he'd meant to share that day in the brig. Belza sided with Rasmus because he promised power and glory. Did a tiny part of myself long for that as well? Had Father been right to worry?

"Everything would have played out the same," I said, still unsure whether it was true.

As Magie finished interpreting, the queen nodded again. She reached up and brushed my face, her eyes deep in thought. Then her finger traced the bandage on my cheek.

I pulled away, suddenly self-conscious. Rasmus's words echoed in my mind. *Not such a pretty little thing anymore, are you?* Surely Aden's mother was thinking the same thing.

Aden was a king, and I—what was I? Not a sailor, not without a ship. Not a captain's boy, yet not a lady. There were so many parts to me that felt fragmented, broken like the glass being swept up in the ballroom right now.

"Laney Garrow," Magie said hesitantly. She glanced at the queen and swallowed. "There's been news."

I sat a little straighter. By their solemn expressions, this couldn't be good.

Magie pointedly avoided looking at Aden. "Don't worry, it isn't bad. That is to say, it's very good news. Prince Mael has returned."

I nearly choked. "What?"

"He apparently faked his death. For his own protection, I'm sure." Her face soured at that. "When Aden awakes, he'll be very glad to hear his brother is alive."

And shocked to hear that the crown he'd defended—nearly with his life—wouldn't be his after all. An anger I couldn't articulate began to boil inside. "Let me make sure I understand. Mael ran away and hid until Aden won his kingdom back for him. Now he's returned to take control."

Magie's hands went still a moment, her expression uncertain. "As second son, Aden was never meant for the throne. His purpose was to defend the crown, and he did that. I'm certain he'll be pleased that he can return to his regular duties."

I was far from certain. A surge of disappointment rushed to mind as I remembered Aden's promise. He no longer had the power to take back his father's Edict. Would Mael do it instead?

The queen, examining my face, began to sign.

"I see your anger," Magie said for her. "While I'm sad that my Aden will not take the throne, I'm relieved that he's now free to choose the course of his life. Wherever that may take him."

I stared at her, not daring to hope. Surely she didn't refer to Aden and me. We were more doomed even than my father's marriage. The queen, of all people, had to know that.

"Take my seat, Your Highness," I said. "He needs to see you when he wakes."

She didn't turn to Magie for a translation. Instead, she placed a finger on my mouth to silence me and shook her head slightly. Then she gently brushed her fingers around her face.

"Beautiful," Magie interpreted softly.

I looked at them in disbelief.

The queen patted my chest now, just above my heart. Then she began to sign again.

Magie's voice wobbled with emotion. "She says your pirate's blood lent you strength, but your woman's heart chose your direction. She sees why her son favors you."

I had once loathed everything about women like Marina. Yet amid the softness, I saw that hard glint in her eyes, that determination from earlier. I marveled at the queen who had captured the heart of a mourning king and raised four children. Her face boasted a collection of deep purple and blue bruises. She certainly didn't look like a spoiled woman.

Beautiful.

I'd spent my life believing that my femininity was something to hide, to bury deep inside with shame. It made me different and vulnerable. But Aden's mother was both soft and strong, loving and fierce. Her womanhood gave her a unique kind of power. I felt a longing deep within me, hoping I could accept who I was like this woman had. It didn't matter whether Aden would become king or not. I had work to do, and do it I would.

Suddenly overwhelmed, I blinked back tears. "Thank you."

She took my hand and gripped it tightly. Her hands were soft and manicured against my rough calluses, but she didn't flinch. Then she turned to her son. I saw the fondness in her eyes.

We sat there for a long moment, the two women who loved Aden most. And there, for the first time, I understood what home meant.

50

The palace's massive hallway was quiet as I crept barefoot along its elaborately woven carpets. I carried a bag slung over one shoulder and my boots in one hand, moving silently. My bag contained everything I owned in the world—a new shirt, my repaired and wrapped axes, and what remained of my father's comb. Even now, two weeks after the Messauns' panicked withdrawal, I gazed at the grandness around me in silent awe. For a girl accustomed to the low ceilings and swaying floor of a ship, it felt as if the very universe and its stars could fit inside this place.

I was grateful for that feeling of discomfort, because I couldn't let myself grow used to this. It wasn't my world. Nor could it ever be.

Early morning sunlight filtered through the tall stained-glass windows as I exited from a side entrance and put my boots on. A group of servants walked past, whispering among themselves. I nodded to them and they inclined their heads, but no more. Nobody knew quite how to address Prince Cedrick's…whatever I was. I shouldn't have been allowed to enter the palace, let alone stay there as a guest of honor. The royal family had defended my trousers and the pair of axes I wore everywhere, but I saw a familiar wariness in the servants' eyes. A man who killed pirates would have been respected as the warrior he was. But a girl with pirate weapons and a scar on her face, especially one the prince favored? I didn't belong. Laney Garrow was neither foe nor friend, and the entire palace knew it. That was one reason I'd chosen the early morning hours for my departure.

Another was that I'd said enough goodbyes. I couldn't bear another, this one in particular.

The town felt like an old friend as I wound slowly through its muddy streets. Nearly everything was as it should have been now. The sharp sound of hooves on cobblestone meant carts delivered their wares as normal. Children played about in the streets, dodging irritated adults who shouted after them. The air no longer felt strangled, the people frightened into silence. King Eurion and his lords had received an honorable burial. And then last night, Prince Aden had been declared healthy enough to leave his bed and walk freely about the palace.

The only thing out of place was me.

King Mael now wore the crown on his cowardly head. He hadn't lifted his father's Edict about women sailors, instead granting me immunity at Aden's insistence. Apparently their argument had lasted hours. It seemed King Mael was a slightly younger version of King Eurion.

The trip to the docks took longer than I remembered. When I arrived, everything looked exactly as it had when the *Majesty* had docked weeks before. I half expected my father to clasp me on the shoulder and hand me a few coppers for dinner. The sense of loss felt like a sword through the gut, sharp and permanent. I doubted it would fade anytime soon.

But even deeper, I knew he would be proud. I'd brought Aden home and defeated my father's murderer. Most of all, I was Laney

Garrow, confident and skilled. Not the lady's daughter he'd hoped for, perhaps, but still the sailor he'd raised me to be.

The ship I waited for was a dot in the distance, but I recognized its sails. I patted the bulge in my pocket. The queen had offered a reward without my asking. I'd refused my portion, but the bag of gold I carried rightfully belonged to Captain Dayorn. She approached for a larger purpose now, however. One far more important to us both.

In two hours' time, Captain Dayorn and I would depart for KaBann and its Council meeting. There Elena "Laney" Garrow would begin her destiny.

Fighting a surge of nervousness, I found a seat next to the fish exchange to await the ship's arrival. The smell was overpowering, but it was the perfect spot to watch the activity on the docks. An unfamiliar vessel to my right made lazy preparations to embark, a stunning new man-of-war. She was larger than the *Majesty*, with three masts and more than two dozen guns. A military vessel. Too bad she hadn't been ready to sail when the Messauns had attacked. Or perhaps it was a good thing—it meant she had come out of the war unscathed. The wood was crisp, untouched by sun and storm, and the lines looked like they'd been raised just days before. It was about to leave on its maiden voyage.

Lane would have asked to sign on. It was work, after all, and I was now immune to the horrid Edict that would take my life. But Laney would do no such thing. Joining the Hughen navy said I meant to serve the king, and I couldn't do that. Not when the Edict remained in force. Not when Hughen itself disagreed with who I was about to become. Not even Aden would understand.

I imagined life on a new ship, learning the names of a new crew and visiting the same ports as always. That dream felt empty now. Who would I argue with about politics? Who else would I sneak to the nest with and tease about his crisp accent? No other man in the world could compare to Aden. But he had his family back now.

And princes didn't marry pirates.

"Pardon me," a deep voice called.

I turned to find a sailor in a navy uniform approaching from the direction of the ship. He had to be just a few years older than me.

"They told me who you are," he said, ducking his head shyly, "but I wanted to see for myself. Is it true you killed Captain Belza?"

It was then that I noticed work on the navy vessel had essentially stopped. Dozens of sailors gawked at me from the deck, whispering to one another. A few waved.

"Aye" was all I could say. Had word truly flown so fast?

He took my hand in his and plastered a wet kiss right on top. "Belza killed my pap at sea. I've been looking forward to his death for a long time. Thank you."

"Pleasure." The odd thing was, it hadn't been much of a pleasure at all. Having Belza gone hadn't changed my life that much. If anything, I felt a little emptier.

"Laney!"

Aden trotted up on horseback, breathless, and dismounted before the horse had fully stopped. The sailor's eyes went round, then he bowed and darted back toward his ship as Aden handed the reins to the guards who'd come with him. They glared disapprovingly at their prince for trying to ride through the city by himself.

I rose to my feet. "You shouldn't be riding yet."

"And you shouldn't run off like that," Aden said, breathing a little too hard. He hid the pain well, though. "I thought you'd left me for good."

I pressed my lips together and looked away. Now I'd have to say goodbye, and I wasn't sure my heart could take it.

Aden's shoulders sagged as he took in the bag slung over my shoulder and realization sank in. "It's the KaBann captain, isn't it? She's coming to take you away."

I said nothing.

He sighed, squinting out at the bay. "Can we walk? This won't take long."

"Here on the docks? Everyone will see us."

He took my hand in answer, his fingers threading through mine like they had a hundred times before. I tried to memorize how it felt, enjoying his warmth one last time. Somehow, the thought of this ending left a physical ache in my gut, like a permanent hunger.

"My mother wanted to give you a position in court and your own room in the palace." He grasped my shoulders and stroked them with his thumbs. "But I know you. You tolerate it here, but you're restless. The sea isn't something I dare compete with."

He didn't understand. I did love the sea, but I also loved him. I wanted both.

Aden plunged on, looking nervous. "I talked to Mael's new general, and he agreed to give you a position in the navy, if you want it. You would return here every three months, so we could still be together often." He dropped his voice to almost a whisper. "You told Rasmus something interesting that day. 'We Hughens are loyal to our king.' You already see Hughen as your home. I'm just offering you a little part of it."

He made a persuasive argument, but there was one thing missing. I didn't want a little part of his country. I wanted him, and all of him. It was precisely why I had to leave.

"It wouldn't be fair to pretend any longer," I said. "Your kingdom is shaky enough. The longer I stay, the more questionable my presence will become. I may technically be an exception, but in the eyes of the entire world, I shouldn't exist."

"You don't understand. That's exactly what I want to change. We can all build a better kingdom together, men and women sailors alike. When they see how capable and honorable you are, the court will support changing the law. If we apply enough pressure—"

"That's not what I meant. I'm not who you think I am, Aden. Captain Belza was my uncle. My father was Elena's son. I'm her granddaughter. Even my mother was a pirate."

To my surprise, he chuckled. "I know. I suspected when I saw your father fight Kemp, but there was no question when I spotted that ugly comb in your hair."

I stared at him dumbly. He'd known. Of course he had.

"That never mattered to me," he said gently. "Your ancestors did terrible things, but so did mine. Most people walking this planet can say the same thing."

I looked away. He didn't see it. It wasn't just the ocean that pulled me. Elena had chosen a brutal, bloody path, true, but that path still had a destination that nobody had reached yet. And at the end of it lay a world far less broken than this one. A world where nations were truly brothers and children were truly free. Where women on the high seas worked as capable partners, not enemies. The dream gripped my mind even now, a chest of treasure just waiting to be won.

Aden turned back to the bay. Captain Dayorn's ship was clearly visible now against the morning horizon. "I hoped to convince you to stay, but I'm doing a terrible job. It seems there's just one thing to be done."

"Which is?"

"Pack. I won't bring much, but I'm determined to have more to my name than I did last time. It was uncomfortable, wearing the same clothes every day." He gave a wry grin.

It took a second for the full meaning of his words to register. "You aren't serious."

"I'm very serious."

"But…your country, your family. You're supposed to protect them."

"No, the navy is supposed to protect them. The generals. The new advisor. I have more important work to do. I think it involves changing the world, aye?"

I smiled. It did indeed. "You'd best be hurrying back to the palace to say your goodbyes, then, Your Highness. In an hour, I intend to kidnap you."

"Sounds much more pleasant than the last time I was kidnapped."

"And after that, perhaps we'll make a thorough inspection of the crow's nest."

He chuckled and kissed me. "There's nothing I would like more."

Sometime later, the *Bram's Uncle* left the Hughen harbor. There was no fanfare, no party to see us off. Just heavy flapping of canvas around us as we clung to the sides of a wooden box aloft.

As the docks grew smaller behind us and the palace loomed high on the cliffs above, this felt precisely right. Nothing was how I had planned. But as Aden took my face in his hands and lowered his lips to mine, I knew exactly who I was.

And soon, the world would know it too.

ACKNOWLEDGMENTS

My name may be on the cover, but don't think for a second that *Tides of Mutiny* is the product of one person. The truth is that Lane's story was shaped by dozens of talented individuals who believed in me, gently (and sometimes not so gently) guided me in the right direction, and kicked me in the pants when I felt overwhelmed with the possibility of yet another rewrite. Every single one of them deserves to share that cover space.

Without my Pitch Wars mentor, critique partner, and friend Abigail Johnson, this book would still be a jumbled mess on my laptop. She plucked it out of the Pitch Wars pile and took us both on a ride that would change my life forever. Thanks, Abigail! I'm so happy that we get to cheer each other on through this wild ride of a career.

I'm so grateful that my incredible agent, Kelly Peterson, decided to take a chance on this over-the-top perfectionist of an author. (Kelly, I added more horses just for you.)

I'm over-the-moon happy that JIMMY Patterson editor Caitlyn Averett saw the potential in Lane's story and kept pushing me until I saw it too. (Caitlyn—kitties!) And I'm thankful that we found an enthusiastic champion in Regan Winter at Little, Brown Books for Young Readers. Loads of gratitude to the JIMMY and LBYR teams who made *Tides* polished and beautiful. Copyediting, formatting, cover design, and marketing are tough jobs, and I will love you forever for your tireless dedication.

Special thanks to my author friend Jennifer Moore, who combed through *Tides* to make sure my ship details weren't too far off (which they were, but she helped with that too). I also appreciate that sweet library research assistant who helped me find some of my favorite historical details way back in 2017, whose name I stupidly forgot to write down, as well as my deaf sensitivity reader (who wished to remain unnamed) for ensuring I represented the queen accurately and well. Heidi Brockbank and Sabine Berlin, thanks for your editorial notes on a very early and extremely rough draft and especially for begging to know more about Lane's world.

I'm the luckiest writer in the world to work with amazing critique group members Adrienne Monson, Karen Pellett, Roxy Haynie, Angela Brimhall, Karyn Patterson, Mary King, Ruth Craddock, Lindzee Armstrong, Darren Hansen, LaChelle Hansen, Nichole Eck, and David Powers King. They somehow managed to avoid grumbling each time I submitted a new first chapter of this book. (And there were a lot of those. Sorry, guys.)

Big thanks to my father-in-law, Hugh Rode, who read an early version and became its first fan. Much love to my parents, Brad and Lisa, who planted the seeds of creative hunger inside me and have become my loudest cheerleaders. Thanks to my stepmom, Gayle, for buying copies of my books for every room in the house "just in case." A gentle hug to my sister, Kalimba, for whom the past two years have been extra hard but who managed to read and encourage anyway. Love you, sis. You should totally write that book.

To Mike & Ike candies—you sustained me through the publishing roller coaster, but my waistline says it's time for a break. I'm sure I'll return to the comfort of your sugary perfection very soon.

To my girl—you are brilliant and fierce. Your dreams matter. Keep fighting for them.

To my boys—embrace adventure, never stop reading, and listen to those big, wonderful hearts of yours. They're usually right.

To my husband—this book exists because of you and we both know it. May every girl be lucky enough to find a prince like you.

REBECCA RODE

is an award-winning author of YA fantasy and science fiction that stars fierce girls crushing societal barriers. Her work has appeared on the *USA Today* and *Wall Street Journal* bestseller lists. She lives in the Rocky Mountains with her family, two cats, overflowing bookshelves, and nerdy sock collection. Learn more about her books at AuthorRebeccaRode.com.